Raves for

LAST PUZ

"Cora is emerging as a lovable and unique sleuth. [She's] no sweet-natured Jessica Fletcher or wise-as-an-owl Miss Marple. . . . This series is a joy for lovers of both crosswords and frothy crime detection."
—*Chicago Sun-Times*

"[*Last Puzzle & Testament*] has its merry way with the cozy concept of the small-town spinster-sleuth."
—*Los Angeles Times*

"Fun from the first page . . . This cozy mystery has a slightly different point of view and pair of detectives."
—*The Dallas Morning News*

"Takes a sweet-faced grandmother on the gumshoe spree of a lifetime."
—*The Washington Post Book World*

"Cora's heart-of-gold personality gives *Last Puzzle & Testament* a special feel that turns this novel into a keeper that will be read many times over in the years to come."
—*The Midwest Book Review*

"The author proves himself very adept at constructing the puzzles that are at the core of his mystery. The reader gets a chance to solve the puzzles before the protagonists do, which adds to the fun."
—*Pittsburgh Post-Gazette*

"A de   *reative Logic*

Raves for Cora Felton's debut in

A CLUE FOR THE PUZZLE LADY

ALSO BY PARNELL HALL

A Clue for the Puzzle Lady
Puzzled to Death
A Puzzle in a Pear Tree
With This Puzzle, I Thee Kill
And a Puzzle to Die On
Stalking the Puzzle Lady

LAST PUZZLE & TESTAMENT

Parnell Hall

BANTAM BOOKS

New York Toronto London Sydney Auckland

This edition contains the complete text
of the original hardcover edition.
NOT ONE WORD HAS BEEN OMITTED.

LAST PUZZLE & TESTAMENT

A Bantam Book

PUBLISHING HISTORY
Bantam hardcover edition published September 2000
Bantam mass market edition / September 2001

ISBN-13: 978-0-553-58143-0
ISBN-10: 0-553-58143-0

Published simultaneously in the United States and Canada

Bantam Books are published by Bantam Books, a division of Random House, Inc.
Its trademark, consisting of the words "Bantam Books" and the portrayal of a
rooster, is Registered in U.S. Patent and Trademark Office and in other countries.
Marca Registrada. Random House, Inc., New York, New York.

PRINTED IN THE UNITED STATES OF AMERICA

OPM   10 9 8 7 6 5 4

33614059702554

For Alice, who might have been a writer.

A GRID FROM THE PUZZLE LADY

The following crossword puzzle grid will be used in the course of the book. This copy is supplied for your enjoyment. If you would care to use it to attempt to solve the puzzle ahead of the characters in the story, feel free. The clues will be along shortly.

Prologue

IT ALL BEGAN WITH A BREAK-IN.

A botched break-in.

It might have gone differently if the intruder had been sober, but Jeff Beasley, in addition to a penchant for illegal entry, also had a weakness for alcohol, and when confronted with the daunting prospect of the Hurley house, had fortified himself with a drink or three before heading out. Jeff had also seen fit to slip a half-pint of rye in his hip pocket, on the off chance his courage should happen to wane along the way. Whether it would have or not was a moot point, as Beasley managed to finish off the bottle before he even got there. Were it not for that, he might have been more careful. He might at least have broken a side window, instead of the one right next to the front door. But by then Beasley had lost grasp of some of the finer points of his trade. He staggered up onto the front porch of the huge, sprawling, gothic mansion, smashed the pane of glass with a rock, reached in, undid the lock, flung up the window, and fell right through, landing on the floor of the foyer in an ungainly heap.

Treating his clumpy entrance as a matter of course, Beasley sat up and took stock. The first thing he checked was his hip pocket. The bottle of rye wasn't broken, but it wasn't full, either. That surprised him. Somehow, he had expected to find it replenished. Refusing to abandon that hope, he jammed the empty bottle back in his pocket and staggered to his feet.

It was hard to keep his balance in the dark. Realizing that reminded Beasley of the flashlight he had slipped in his jacket pocket back in more rational times. He groped for it, pulled it out, switched it on. Winced to discover it was pointed directly at his face. It was several seconds before his eyes could focus. He stood there, swearing, blinking, with the light wandering aimlessly around the room. While Beasley got his bearings, the beam traveled over the red-velvet draperies, the mahogany-paneled walls, the silver candlestick holders, the marble-topped end tables.

The knight with the battle-ax!

Beasley staggered back in horror.

No, just an old suit of armor. Beasley gawked at it in amazement, his brain slowly processing what it was. For a fleeting second it occurred to Beasley to wonder if he really wanted to be doing this.

His flashlight lit up the circular front stairs with the carved wooden banister. Beasley reacted first with delight, then with increasing misgivings. On the one hand the stairs would lead to the master bedroom. On the other, they looked formidable.

Beasley's trip up the stairs was perilous at best. While he did not actually crawl, he did not actually walk, either. He stopped once to catch his breath, once to sit, and once to recall whether he was going down or up.

Eventually he reached the top, shone the light around, and recoiled involuntarily from the grim visage of Evan Hurley in the huge oil painting that dominated the upstairs landing. The cold gray eyes of the venerable, bulldog-jowled former patriarch of the Hurley family seemed to look right through him, as if challenging his right to be there, and Beasley quickly averted the light.

Off the landing was a hallway with several doors. Beasley first tried a bathroom, a linen closet, and a knob that proved to be a brass wall ornament.

The next door was the jackpot. Even Beasley could tell. From the marble fireplace, Queen Anne chairs, vanity table crammed with cosmetics, and four-poster canopied bed, this had to be old lady Hurley's room. Jeff Beasley shone the light around with a sense of satisfaction.

And confusion and doubt.

So much furniture.

So many places to look.

A rolltop writing desk in one corner of the room, with numerous drawers and cubbyholes, a veritable treasure chest, attracted his attention.

It did not hold it.

Beasley found himself drawn to the four-poster bed. He walked over to it, shone the light, touched the soft, puffy comforter, ran his hand over the smooth, polished, ma-hogany wood.

Jeff Beasley blinked, frowned.

Tried to remember why he was there.

It was nearly three hours later when Bakerhaven Police Chief Dale Harper, cruising North Elm Street on a routine patrol, stopped to check out an open window on the Hurley house. Old Mrs. Hurley had died the week before, the mansion had been locked up, and that window had no right to be open. So, on inspection, Chief Harper was not surprised to find there had been a break-in.

He was surprised to find the perpetrator sound asleep in Mrs. Hurley's bed.

SHERRY CARTER WAS HAPPY. SHE RAN HER HAND through her hair, pushed the bangs off her forehead, tugged at her earlobe, and smiled across the table at Aaron Grant.

The young reporter was wearing a sports jacket with his shirt collar unbuttoned and the knot of his tie pulled down. His brown hair was wavy and slightly mussed. And he was clean shaven—it occurred to Sherry he was *always* clean shaven, *very* clean shaven, almost as if he was too young to shave.

"How's your soup?" Aaron asked.

Sherry barely heard him. "Huh?"

"How's your gazpacho?"

"Oh. It's okay."

"I could have warned you," Aaron said. He gestured with his spoon. "Chicken soup you can't go wrong. Anything else you take a chance."

"I said it was okay."

Aaron smiled. "Yes, you did. But *okay* is not a word of praise. It is an equivocation, indicating a reluctance to make a value judgment. And implying a less than favorable assessment."

Sherry tried to scowl, but made a poor job of it. Her eyes twinkled. "Does everything with you have to be wordplay?"

"Not at all," Aaron replied. "Just look me in the eye and tell me the truth—your gazpacho is barely adequate, and you could make much better yourself—which I am quite sure is a fact—and I would do nothing but agree."

"Oh, you like women who brag about their accomplishments?"

"Who said anything about women? I like *people* who are straightforward. Sex doesn't enter into it."

"That's for sure."

"I beg your pardon?"

"Does that happen to you often?"

"What?"

"That sex doesn't enter into it?"

"Now who's indulging in wordplay?"

"I wasn't," Sherry replied. "I was just looking you in the eye and telling you the truth."

Aaron Grant laughed. Sherry laughed back. They found themselves leaning on their elbows, smiling at each other.

Aaron and Sherry were having lunch at the Wicker Basket, a small family restaurant on Drury Lane, just off Main Street in Bakerhaven, Connecticut. The restaurant was a step up from the local diner, featuring tables, not booths, with red-and-white-checkered tablecloths and linen napkins. It was a quiet, homey place, and while the food was nothing special, on this occasion the atmosphere was more important.

It was their first date.

And by Aaron and Sherry's standards, it was going

well. Even if they had taken refuge in the safety of word-play. Both were linguists. Aaron was a writer, Sherry was a crossword-puzzle constructor, and as such they were highly competitive. Sherry loved sparring with Aaron, loved having an intellectual equal who was capable of giving it back as good as he got it. Bantering with Aaron Grant was a treat.

It was also safe.

It kept Sherry from exposing herself, from opening up, from talking about the things that really mattered. Like their relationship, for instance, and where it was going.

There were lots of things unsaid.

Sherry was older than Aaron. Just a few years, but with an unsuccessful marriage to her credit. Aaron was only a year out of college and still lived with his parents, which made him seem young on the one hand, and precluded him inviting her up to his room on the other. Or so Sherry imagined. Their relationship hadn't gotten to that point yet.

For her part, Sherry lived with her aunt. And while the much-married Cora Felton couldn't have cared less if Sherry had invited Aaron over—on the contrary, from the start Cora had been the one pushing the relationship—Sherry still would have felt inhibited by her presence.

So they really had nowhere to go.

As if that weren't enough impediment to the relationship, Sherry had one more stumbling block.

Sherry's aunt, Cora Felton, was famous. She was known as the Puzzle Lady, both for her national TV ads and for her syndicated crossword-puzzle column. Two hundred and fifty-six newspapers carried that column, including Aaron's paper, the *Bakerhaven Gazette*. Cora Felton's beaming face appeared in the *Gazette* every morning.

That in itself would not have been a problem, but Cora Felton didn't write the crossword-puzzle column.

Sherry did.

Cora Felton merely provided the image. Her face was Sherry's conception of what the Puzzle Lady should be. Which apparently was everybody else's, for the Puzzle Lady puzzles were wildly popular.

At the moment, this too was complicating Sherry Carter and Aaron Grant's relationship.

Aaron knew Sherry was the Puzzle Lady.

Sherry didn't know he knew it.

Aaron had found out while covering the Graveyard Killings, as the Bakerhaven murders had come to be known, figured it out himself and then finessed a confirmation out of Cora Felton, who couldn't stand up to his cross-examination. Cora had left the task of telling Sherry up to him. So far he hadn't gotten around to it.

Though, Aaron realized, that wasn't quite the case. In fact, it wasn't the case at all. It wasn't that he hadn't gotten around to it. Aaron wanted to tell Sherry more than anything. It was one of the reasons he'd invited her to lunch. And yet, he still hadn't told her.

Because, more than anything, he wanted *her* to tell *him*.

It really bothered him that she hadn't. That after all they'd been through together, she didn't trust him enough to let him know. Not that Aaron couldn't make allowances. He knew Sherry had suffered at the hands of her alcoholic ex-husband. But he knew that from Cora, not from Sherry. And he wanted to hear the truth from Sherry badly, so badly he was holding off telling her just to give her the opportunity.

But he could not hold out long. Aaron had made up his mind. If Sherry hadn't told him by the end of lunch, that was it. He'd give in and speak first. Not that he thought he'd have to. From her manner, he had a feeling she was about to tell him.

And she was.

As Sherry Carter sat in the Wicker Basket, smiling across the table at Aaron Grant, she felt at peace with the world. Because she knew she could tell him, and it would be all right. She could tell him about being the real Puzzle Lady. And she could tell him about her abusive ex-husband. And Aaron would understand. In spite of his jovial manner, in spite of his never taking anything seriously, Aaron was basically a good guy, and he would take it the right way. He might joke, sure, but it would be a friendly joke, a supportive joke, an accepting joke. He would put her at her ease.

Sherry was sure of it.

So why was she hesitating?

She wasn't.

She would tell him now.

Sherry put her hands on the table, opened her mouth to speak, and—

Stopped.

Aaron Grant wasn't looking at her. He was looking past her. The expression on his face was hard to read. Surprise, yes, but beyond that. Was it a pleasant surprise? It was hard to tell. But he appeared to be blushing. What was he looking at?

A figure appeared in Sherry's peripheral vision and bore down on their table. Sherry looked up, frowned.

It was a young woman in a purple pants suit. Her blond hair was sculpted, curling down the side of her head in a casual, careless swoop that Sherry knew took patience to perfect. She was in her mid-twenties, but looked older, without looking old. She also looked sophisticated without looking sharp, stylish without looking styled. She looked intelligent, competent, totally self-assured. A woman who knows precisely what she wants. And knows exactly how to get it. That was Sherry's first impression.

Stunning.

Totally stunning.

Aaron seemed stunned. He gawked at the woman, apparently incapable of speech.

She smiled. "Hi, Aaron."

"Becky," he murmured.

Then he was smiling and on his feet, totally recovered and performing introductions. "Sherry, this is Becky Baldwin. Becky, this is Sherry Carter. She's the woman who helped solve the murder case."

Becky Baldwin smiled and arched an eyebrow. "Really? I don't recall reading that in the paper."

"No," Sherry said, matching her smile. "Aaron was nice enough to keep me out of it."

"Oh, really? You didn't want the credit? How modest of you. And how fascinating. You mean you actually solved these crimes?"

"No, I did not," Sherry said. "And if you don't mind, I would appreciate your not giving everyone in the restaurant the impression that I did."

"Oh, was I talking too loud?" Becky Baldwin said, innocently. "I'm sorry. Occupational hazard."

"Don't tell me. You're a cheerleader."

Becky laughed. "I'm a lawyer."

"You passed the bar?" Aaron said. "Congratulations."

"A lawyer," Sherry said. "So, you're here to start a private practice?"

"Hardly," Becky answered. "Bakerhaven's not big enough to support another lawyer. I'm interviewing with some firms in Boston."

"So you're just passing through?" Sherry said. It bothered her how relieved she was to hear it.

"Yes, this is a hit-and-run," Becky said. "Check in with my folks. Pack up some of my stuff." She smiled at Aaron. "Look up old friends. Oh, and what do you do?" she asked Sherry.

It was clearly an afterthought. Never had Sherry's impulse been so strong to tell someone she wrote a nationally syndicated crossword-puzzle column. She restrained it. "I teach school."

"Oh, a schoolteacher. So you're off for the summer?"

"Actually, I'm off most of the time. I'm a substitute teacher. I only go in when they call me."

"Oh, a substitute. That must be stressful." Becky smiled at Aaron. "I remember the trouble we used to give substitutes."

"At age three?" Sherry said.

"I beg your pardon?"

"I teach nursery school. Three-year-olds are not so rebellious."

"Oh," Becky Baldwin said.

The conversation ground to a halt.

Sherry wanted to ask, "When are you leaving?" but knew it would sound catty. She was relieved when Aaron asked it for her.

Until she heard Becky's answer.

"I don't know. I have a case to handle first."

"A case?" Aaron said. "You're kidding. How could you have a case?"

"I dropped by Arthur Kincaid's law office to tell him I passed the bar, and he asked me if I'd handle something for him."

"How come?"

"I don't know. Some sort of conflict of interest where technically he's retained on the other side." Becky Baldwin pointed to a paper bag a waitress had just placed beside the cash register. "Anyway, I'm picking up salad to go, and having lunch with Arthur. He's gonna brief me for the pre-arraignment, then I gotta get over to the courthouse and bail out my client."

"What's the case?" Aaron Grant asked.

Becky waved the question away. "Oh, it's nothing. Town drunk broke into a house, was found passed out in bed. Hardly the crime of the century. Shouldn't take long. Well, enjoy your lunch."

Becky Baldwin paid for her salad, smiled, waved, and went out the door.

"Nice woman," Sherry said.

"Uh huh," Aaron said.

That was their entire conversation regarding Becky Baldwin. Still, her presence seemed to linger. The atmosphere certainly wasn't the same as before she'd appeared.

Good intentions vanished.

Sherry didn't confess to Aaron she was the Puzzle Lady, and Aaron didn't confess to Sherry he knew.

They finished their lunch.

It was perfectly amiable.

And wholly unsatisfying.

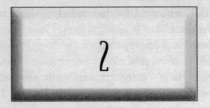

2

SHERRY CARTER DROVE UP THE DRIVEWAY TO FIND CORA Felton on her hands and knees with a trowel, planting flowers next to the front steps. Sherry was surprised on several counts. It was a hot, hazy July afternoon, not conducive to outside work; it was late in the season to be planting anything; and, despite its pleasant, one-acre country lot, her aunt had never shown any interest in their prefab rental house before, let alone in its gardens.

"Aunt Cora," Sherry said. "What in the world are you doing?"

Cora Felton looked up from the hole she'd been digging. She had a red kerchief tied around her curly white hair, and there was a smudge of dirt on her nose. She smiled brightly, the trademark smile that stood her in such good stead in her TV advertisements.

"Hi, Sherry. I thought the house could use some brightening up. What do you think?"

"Come again?"

Cora gestured at the cardboard box of flowers she'd

been transplanting. "I was thinking of a geranium on each side of the steps. How does that sound?"

"Aunt Cora. Why are you doing this?"

"Well, the place looked so drab."

"Uh huh." Sherry sat down on the front steps next to her aunt. "Aunt Cora. It's me. Sherry. I know you. You're a city girl. Your idea of flowers is something someone brings on a date. But here you are wearing overalls and a work shirt—very color coordinated, by the way—and rooting in the dirt as if you liked it. So, what's up?"

Cora Felton stuck the trowel in the ground. *"People,"* she replied.

"People?" Sherry echoed.

"The magazine," Cora said. "They called, want to do a feature on the Puzzle Lady. An interview plus a photo spread. They want to send a photographer out, take some candid shots, show the public what the Puzzle Lady's really like. You know, like what I do in my spare time."

"Such as?"

Cora Felton made a face. "Well, there you are." Cora jerked a pack of cigarettes out of her overalls, took one out and lit it. She took a deep drag and exhaled. "Unfortunately, my main leisure activities are drinking and gambling. I didn't think you'd want them to photograph that."

"You're planting flowers for *People* magazine?"

"Well, why not? Isn't that the whole point? Don't we want people to see us as we really aren't?" Cora took a drag, flicked the cigarette. "So, how do you like geraniums by the stairs?"

"When is *People* magazine coming?"

"Oh, not till next week. But I thought I should practice. I'd hate it if they set up the camera and then it turned out I couldn't plant the damn things."

There was a half-full glass of Bloody Mary on the front steps. Cora Felton picked it up, took a noisy slurp.

"Perfect," Sherry said. "Is that how you're going to have *People* magazine photograph you? Smoking and drinking?"

"Of course not," Cora said. "Don't be such a grouch. I'm just trying to chase a hangover."

"I'm sure *People* will love that."

"They're not going to see that," Cora said. "I'll be on my best behavior." She puffed out her chest. "What do you think of the outfit?"

"I think you bought it just for the article."

"Well, of course I did. You think I have gardening clothes in my wardrobe?"

"Yes, but I had the car this morning. How did you get out?"

"Out?"

"Yes. How did you get to the store to buy the clothes?"

"Did I say I bought them this morning?"

"No, you didn't. You bought them yesterday. Or maybe the day before. Just when did *People* magazine call?"

"Sherry."

"You didn't want to tell me because you knew I'd be upset. Instead, you went out and bought the clothes to show me what a fine, upstanding image you're going to produce for the magazine. The same reason you bought the flowers. Not to impress the magazine. Just to impress me. Which might have worked better without the cigarette and the drink."

Cora Felton took another sip of the Bloody Mary, studied Sherry's face. "You're in a fine mood," she commented. "How was your date?"

"Oh."

Cora raised her eyebrows. "Oh? There's an *oh*?"

"It was all right."

Cora struggled to her feet. "All right is not good. All right is not what I want to hear. Why was it just all right?"

"Well, we didn't talk about anything."

"Like the fact you write the column?"

"Yeah, we never got around to that."

"What did I tell you?" Cora said.

"I know what you told me."

"You can't start a relationship off on a lie."

"It's not a relationship."

"That's not the point. The point is, you've gotta tell him."

"I was about to. Something came up."

"What was that?"

Sherry told her about Becky Baldwin interrupting their lunch.

Cora Felton's cornflower blue eyes narrowed. "A girl from high school? What did she look like?"

"A lawyer."

"She looked like a lawyer?"

"She *is* a lawyer. She *looked* like a high-fashion model."

"You look good."

"You should have seen *her*."

"Was she nice?"

"Perfectly nice. Friendly. Pleasant."

"I hate her. Did she stay for lunch?"

"No. She had to meet with some lawyer. She's appearing in court this afternoon."

Cigarette ash dribbled on the front of Cora's new shirt. "I thought you said she was leaving town."

"She is. She's just passing through."

"But she took on a case?"

"So she said."

"Uh huh," Cora said. It was an eloquent statement, conveying mountains of skepticism and doubt. "So, anyway, *she* didn't stop you from talking to Aaron Grant."

"What do you mean?"

"About the column. Telling him you write the cross-word-puzzle column."

"It's not important."

"It is to me. As long as I'm getting credit for it."

"I'll get around to it, Cora. It just wasn't the right time."

"Uh huh," Cora said. "So, what did you talk about? After this Becky what's-her-name left?"

"Baldwin. I don't remember. I think Aaron said something about his job. He needed to find something to write about for the paper."

"But nothing personal?"

"Aunt Cora," Sherry protested. "You're really making too much out of this. Everything is fine."

Sherry smiled reassuringly and went in the front door.

Cora smiled back, but she was not at all happy. Sherry might think everything was fine, but Sherry was still young. Cora Felton, with age, experience, and several husbands to her credit, was more cynical. Nothing was ever fine.

Not when men were involved.

Men were capricious and unpredictable on the one hand, and totally predictable on the other. If Sherry didn't learn that, she was in for a lot of trouble.

Cora Felton took a long sip of Bloody Mary, then frowned at the wickedness of the world in general, and men in particular.

Sherry Carter was a very bright woman, except when it came to men. Here her judgment was not always sound. Her ex-husband was a case in point. The man had been an absolute disaster, a conceited, self-indulgent, obsessive, abusive jerk. Sherry had learned from the experience, would not make that mistake again.

But she might make others.

Like being too trusting, for instance.

But not if Cora could help it.

So, Becky Baldwin was just passing through?

Passing through, hell.

Cora Felton tossed off the rest of her Bloody Mary, stubbed out her cigarette in the empty glass, turned in her trowel, and headed for the shower.

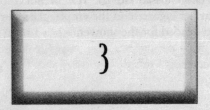

3

CORA FELTON, CLEANED AND POLISHED AND LOOKING HER conservative best in a discreet gray sunbonnet, white blouse, black skirt, and black and white linen vest, parked her car in the lot between the town hall and the Congregational church, and ambled across the Village Green. As usual, she saluted the statue of the horse and rider as she went by, and wondered who they were. She had stopped once to find out, but the metal plaque was too worn to read. And the wrought iron rider's clothes were too nondescript to offer a clue. The statue could have honored a Revolutionary War hero, Pony Express rider, or Kentucky Derby winner.

Cora crossed the green and headed for the county court. She was on her way up the steps when Chief Harper came out the door.

"Miss Felton," he said. "This is a pleasant surprise. What brings you by the courthouse this afternoon?"

Cora Felton thought fast. The amiable Bakerhaven police chief was in many respects a friend. But there was no way she was ever admitting why she was really there. Fortunately, Chief Harper didn't know her secret. He still deferred to her as the Puzzle Lady.

Which would work.

"Just doing a little research," Cora said.

"Research?"

"For my column. Thought I might work in a little legal anecdote. And the truth is, I've never really seen a courtroom proceeding. Outside of movies and TV. And how accurate is that?"

"Probably accurate enough for what you need," Chief Harper replied. "You're certainly welcome to watch, but I've got to warn you, real courtroom proceedings are pretty dull."

"I'll take my chances," Cora Felton said. She smiled at Chief Harper and made her way into the courtroom.

Henry Firth presided over the prosecution table. A little man with a thin mustache, a twitchy nose, and an insinuating manner, the Bakerhaven prosecutor always reminded Cora Felton of a rat. Cora had never dealt with Firth directly, and hoped she never would. Watching him from a distance was quite enough.

At the defense table sat an elderly man in a three-piece suit. He was tall, thin, and distinguished-looking, with an angular face and a very pointed nose, the tip of which supported a pair of half-glasses.

Next to him perched a scruffy man who seemed to be having a hard time staying awake. His head kept bobbing forward, and it seemed as if he had to keep catching himself to avoid curling up like a cat right there on the table. He was unshaven, and his hair was a matted mess. His clothes looked like they'd been slept in for several days. The man was of indeterminate age—he could have turned out to be anywhere from twenty to sixty without surprising Cora in the least.

Especially since she wasn't really paying that much attention to him.

Her eyes were glued on the young woman behind the defense table who was leaning over the spectators' railing, her long blond hair cascading in careless curls that jiggled while she talked, her purple pants suit gaping fashionably at the neck, her makeup understated, brilliantly accentuating her near-perfect features.

Cora Felton took this all in at a glance, scowled, and almost wished she hadn't come.

The man who was sitting in the front row of the press section just behind the defense table, the man the young woman had leaned over to talk to, was none other than Aaron Grant.

Cora Felton watched a few minutes while Becky Baldwin flirted with Aaron Grant. Even from the back row, Cora Felton could see that Becky Baldwin's eyes were bright, her smile wide, her cheeks flushed, her face animated.

And Aaron Grant seemed to be eating it up. Although, Cora conceded, that was hardly a fair assessment, considering she could only see the back of his head.

The door behind the judge's bench opened, the court officer intoned, "Please rise," and a white-haired man in a black robe came in and sat at the bench. Cora Felton did not know the judge, but realized she'd seen him around town, most likely at Cushman's Bake Shop, where she often had coffee.

The court officer droned, "Court is now in session, the Honorable Judge Winston Hobbs presiding."

Judge Hobbs put on reading glasses, fumbled with some papers, and said, "What have we today?"

Prosecutor Henry Firth was on his feet. "Your Honor, first on the docket we have a citation for speeding issued to one Ira Greenspan, for doing seventy-two miles per hour in a fifty-five-mile-per-hour zone. The amount of the citation is eighty-five dollars, at five dollars a mile for every mile over the speed limit."

"I see that it is," Judge Hobbs said. "And why has this routine matter crossed my desk?"

"Mr. Greenspan doesn't want to pay it, Your Honor."

"Oh?"

A plump, middle-aged man sitting near the front of the court got up and pushed his way through the gate. "That's right, Your Honor," he said, sounding aggrieved. "I'm Ira Greenspan, and I'm pleading innocent."

"On what grounds?"

Ira Greenspan seemed startled by the question. "I wasn't speeding."

"I see." Judge Hobbs nodded. "Very well. Is the arresting officer here?"

"He is." Henry Firth turned, gestured. "Officer Finley."

An officer with sandy hair and freckles got to his feet and pushed his way through the gate. Cora Felton smiled. Dan Finley was a Puzzle Lady fan, young and impressionable enough to be flustered in her presence. But in the courtroom the youthful police officer seemed right at home. He stepped smartly up to the judge's bench, said, "Yes, Your Honor?"

"Officer, there is a dispute as to the citation you issued to this gentleman. He claims he was not speeding. Mr. Greenspan, how fast were you going at the time?"

"Fifty-five, Your Honor."

"Officer Finley, how fast do you claim he was going?"

"I clocked him at seventy-two."

"I see," Judge Hobbs said. "Mr. Greenspan, this is a very simple case. We have conflicting testimony. It's just a question of whom you believe. I choose to believe the officer. I find you guilty as charged. Pay the bailiff a hundred and eighty-five dollars and you're free to go."

Ira Greenspan was incensed. "*A hundred* and eighty-five dollars? The ticket's eighty-five."

"Yes, but you didn't want to pay that, and now you owe the court costs. I would suggest next time you don't try to argue with the radar gun. Next case."

While the court officer ushered out a sputtering Ira Greenspan, Henry Firth checked his notes. "That would be Jeff Beasley, Your Honor."

"Ah, yes." Judge Hobbs glanced at the defense table where the defendant had curled up with his head in his hands, the very picture of misery. "And what has Mr. Beasley done now?"

"He was apprehended last night breaking into the Hurley mansion."

Becky Baldwin shot to her feet. "One moment, Your Honor. I object to the prosecutor summarizing the charges in this manner. My client was not arrested breaking into the Hurley mansion."

Henry Firth appeared amused. "That's right, Your Honor. He was found passed out in an upstairs bedroom."

"I object to the term *passed out*," Becky Baldwin said.

Judge Hobbs frowned and put up his hand. "Pardon me, young lady, but just who are you?"

"I'm Rebecca Baldwin. I'm Mr. Beasley's attorney."

"Oh? I thought Arthur Kincaid was attorney of record."

"I was, Your Honor." The distinguished silver-haired man sitting next to the defendant stood and adjusted the glasses on his nose. "As you know, I have represented Mr. Beasley in the past, and when this matter arose he consulted me again. However, when I learned the facts of the case, it turned out it involved the Hurley estate. As I am the Hurleys' attorney, it was clear there would be a conflict of interest. So I asked Ms. Baldwin if she would represent the defendant in this action."

"I see." Judge Hobbs nodded. "And just what is the defendant charged with?"

"Breaking and entering, breaking and entering with intent to steal, burglary, larceny, trespassing, drunk and disorderly," Henry Firth said.

"Oh, for goodness sakes," Becky Baldwin said. "What about jaywalking? How did you ever miss that one?"

"One moment," Judge Hobbs said. He frowned. "Mr. Kincaid, this arrangement may not be entirely felicitous. Young lady, there is no reason to take an attitude with the Court."

"Maybe not, Your Honor. But so many charges certainly seems like overkill. I mean, this is not the crime of the century here."

"I would agree, Your Honor," Arthur Kincaid interposed. "It is my understanding that Mr. Beasley was found asleep on the premises. Since he did not attempt to leave the premises, and since there is no evidence that he attempted to steal anything, as the attorney for the estate I have no real wish to press charges."

"Uh huh," Judge Hobbs said. "And do the heirs share your feelings in this matter?"

Arthur Kincaid shrugged. "It's a moot point, Your Honor. The will is to be read at ten o'clock tomorrow morning. Until such time, the heirs have no rights in the estate. Indeed, until then, it is not clear just who the heirs are."

Judge Hobbs scowled. "Surely *you* know."

"I don't, Your Honor." Arthur Kincaid smiled. "As you know, Emma Hurley was rather . . . eccentric. Her last will and testament is sealed. Her final instructions to me were to gather the heirs, or potential heirs, and then, and only then, to break the seal and read her will."

"Is that so?" Judge Hobbs cocked his head. "Well, in that case, I see no reason why we can't come to some understanding."

Henry Firth cleared his throat. "Your Honor, I must point out these charges are not Mr. Kincaid's to drop."

"Of course not," Judge Hobbs agreed. "However, in light of the situation, I see no reason why this case can't reach a speedy resolution. Attorneys, if I could see you in my chambers."

Judge Hobbs left the bench and went out the back door, followed by the three attorneys. That left Jeff Beasley sitting alone at the defense table. It occurred to Cora Felton that if Beasley wanted to he could just get up and walk out of court. That must have occurred to the court officer too, because he went over and sat beside him. Mr. Beasley hardly seemed a flight risk, however: he was snoring.

In the front row of the courtroom, Aaron Grant stretched, looked around, and spotted Cora Felton. He smiled and waved, but it occurred to Cora he looked suddenly sheepish. She sat in the back row, waited for him to come and join her.

He walked up, smiling, and said, "What brings you here?"

"Just getting material for my column," Cora answered.

"But you don't write a column," Aaron objected.

"Exactly," Cora said. She cocked her head. "You think you might mention that to Sherry?"

"Oh."

"Yeah. Oh. You know how awkward it is for me pretending you don't know?"

"I can imagine."

"And it's not like I told you. You figured it out on your own. If you hadn't decided to burden me with the information, there would be no problem."

"I'll tell her."

"When?"

Aaron was saved from having to reply by the return of the judge. He crept back to the press row while the lawyers resumed their places at the tables. The court officer left the prisoner in the care of his attorneys, who managed to shake him awake.

"So," Judge Hobbs said, when everyone was once again in position. "Let me state for the record that the charges against the defendant, Jeff Beasley, have been amended as follows: all charges of breaking and entering and attempted burglary and larceny shall be dropped; the defendant shall plead guilty to criminal trespass and drunk and disorderly, in return for a sentence of three days in jail and a twenty-five-dollar fine."

Jeff Beasley spoke for the first time. "No jail!"

Judge Hobbs frowned. "I beg your pardon?"

"I ain't goin' to jail! If I have to go to jail, it's no deal."

"Mr. Beasley," Judge Hobbs said. "Let me try to explain. You are a repeat offender. This is not the first time you've stood before me. This will not be your first drunk and disorderly charge, nor your first criminal trespass. But that's beside the point. Three days is nothing. Are you aware of the penalties for breaking and entering with intent to steal if those charges are allowed to stand?"

"No, but they ain't." For a man who had been unconscious moments before, Beasley was remarkably sharp. "Those charges are dropped."

"Those charges are *provisionally* dropped," Judge Hobbs corrected, "on the stipulation that you would plead guilty to lesser charges."

"Well, I never agreed to that."

"Your attorney did."

"My attorney?" Beasley said. "My attorney's Arthur Kincaid. Then I come to court and some schoolgirl I never seen before agrees I should go to jail? Now, tell me, Judge: What's fair about that?"

Judge Hobbs frowned. "If the defendant does not wish the matter disposed of in this manner, he certainly has that right. Therefore, the original charges are reinstated. I hereby arraign him on breaking and entering, and bind him over for trial."

"Trial!" Beasley bellowed. He turned on Arthur Kincaid. "You said I wouldn't go to jail!"

"Oh, Your Honor—" Becky Baldwin protested.

"Not my doing," Judge Hobbs cut in. "Talk to your client. When you do, Ms. Baldwin, you might point out he'll probably serve more than three days just waiting for the case to come to trial. Defendant is remanded to custody."

"Without bail, Your Honor?"

"Bail is set at five hundred dollars."

"Arthur, you'll help me on this?" Becky said. At the lawyer's nod, she turned to the judge. "We can make that, Your Honor."

"Very well," Judge Hobbs said. "I'll recess for fifteen minutes to allow you to pay bail. Then we're back here with—let me see—the theft of a hubcap and a domestic disturbance." He banged the gavel. "Court is in recess."

As the court officer moved in again to escort Jeff Beasley away, Aaron Grant approached Arthur Kincaid. "Excuse me, Arthur. With regard to the Hurley inheritance. I'm wondering if you could give me an interview."

The elderly lawyer smiled. "There's nothing to tell."

"Yes, but there's a story in that," Aaron replied. "Usually, a lawyer would know all the facts."

"Well, thank you very much."

"You know what I mean. I'm a column short for tomorrow. Whaddaya say?"

"At the moment I have to help Becky arrange bail." Arthur Kincaid nodded in the direction of a teenage boy sitting in the second row. "I'm also the attorney for the alleged perpetrator in the theft of the hubcap. After that, I have a meeting with a client and I'll be lucky if I'm not late.

I'm not sure I could give you an interview anyway, but I'll tell you what, Aaron. I'm having drinks tonight at the Country Kitchen with some of the Hurley heirs. If you were to show up, I don't know what I could do about it . . ."

"Around when?"

"I would imagine around seven."

"Interesting," Aaron said. "I just might stop by."

Cora Felton, who had crept forward when court broke up, was close enough to hear Aaron Grant say that.

And to see that Becky Baldwin had heard him say it too.

4

SHERRY CARTER, SITTING SIDEWAYS IN THE PASSENGER seat, leaned her arm out the window and watched Cora Felton pilot the red Toyota around the curves in the winding country road. "Tell me again."

"Tell you what?"

"Why we're going out to dinner."

"You need to get out more. You never get out."

"I was just out to lunch."

"That's not the same thing."

"Why not?"

"It just isn't."

The wind was blowing her hair in her eyes. Sherry pushed it off her forehead, said, "Then why the Country Kitchen? You play bridge there. You drink there. You're there all the time. What's so special about that?"

"You don't go there."

"That's right. I don't. That's your life. I don't interfere. If you'll recall, you're very *particular* that I don't interfere."

"Sherry. It's just dinner."

"Uh huh. So, where'd you go this afternoon?"

"Out."

"I *assumed* you went out. You go out, you don't say where, you come back, you're all hot to go to dinner."

"You should have been a detective."

"Oh? What am I detecting?"

"You know, Sherry. You should have your own car."

"What?"

"I go out, you're stuck in the house. It's not like New York City. There's no public transportation here. Without a car, you can't get around."

"It's not a problem."

"Well, it should be. Young girl like you. You wanna be stuck in the house with your crosswords and computers? By the way, could you work something into the column about a trial?"

"A trial? Why?"

"Chief Harper wanted to know why I was at the county courthouse. I told him I was doing research for my column."

Sherry's eyes widened. "You went to the courthouse?"

"I dropped by."

"You went to spy on Becky Baldwin?"

"*Spy.* What a nasty word." Cora Felton spun the wheel, swerved into the parking lot.

"It's from the Greek *slceptesthai*," Sherry said automatically. "*To watch.* Is that what we're doing at the Country Kitchen?"

"We're here to have dinner." Cora stopped the car, rolled up the windows, and got out.

"Aunt Cora—"

But Cora Felton was already padding across the parking lot. Sherry sighed, then headed after her.

Inside, a waitress with an armful of menus stood at the door to the dining room. "Two for dinner?" she asked.

"We'll be having a drink at the bar first," Cora answered, guiding Sherry firmly in that direction.

It was late enough that most people had moved on into dinner, and the bar was not that full. Half the stools were empty and most of the booths. Cora Felton headed for a stool in the middle of the bar.

"Wouldn't you prefer a booth?" Sherry asked.

"What, and wait for service? Hey, the bartender's right here." Cora beamed at him. "I'll have a martini on the rocks with a twist, young man. And go easy on the vermouth. Just kind of wave the bottle over it once while you stir it around. You don't even have to take off the cap."

The bartender grinned. "And you, young lady?"

"I'll have a Diet Coke."

Cora Felton shuddered. "Sherry. Honey. You're out on the town. Live a little."

"Okay," Sherry said. "Make it a regular Coke."

The bartender moved off down the bar to make their drinks.

Cora Felton rolled her eyes. "You're an impossible date. It's a good thing you're good-looking, or men wouldn't bother with you at all."

"Uh huh," Sherry said. "Now, you wanna tell me what you were doing at the courthouse today?"

"I will if you'll keep your voice down," Cora Felton said. "You see the man sitting down the bar? Tall, white hair, three-piece suit?"

"Yeah. So?"

"That's the local lawyer. Only game in town till what's-her-name showed up."

"Becky Baldwin. So what?"

"He's handling the Hurley estate. That's old Mrs. Hurley, croaked last week. Very wealthy eccentric recluse. Lived alone, died alone, left a ton of money. Mansion boarded up since her death. Heirs in town tomorrow for the reading of the will. A will even her lawyer hasn't seen."

"So?"

"Interesting story, don't you think?"

"What's it got to do with us?"

"Don't you find it interesting?"

"No, I don't, Cora. It's none of my business. Or yours. It doesn't interest me at all."

"Maybe not, but it might interest other people. It's a story. People love a story. And—" Cora Felton broke off and her eyes widened.

Sherry saw this, turned and looked.

Aaron Grant and Becky Baldwin had just come through the door.

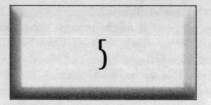

5

"SHERRY, YOU DON'T UNDERSTAND."

"Oh?" Sherry said. "What is it I don't understand?"

Aaron Grant jerked his thumb in the direction of Becky Baldwin, Arthur Kincaid, and Cora Felton. He had piloted Sherry away from them after perfunctory introductions. "I'm here to interview Arthur Kincaid for the newspaper."

"You must have a low opinion of my intelligence. I understand that perfectly well."

"I'm sure that you do. The point is, I didn't come here with Becky Baldwin."

"Yes. I saw you not come here with her. You did it well. In fact, I just saw the two of you, not coming in the door."

"I didn't come here with her. She met me in the parking lot."

"Is that where you meet most of your women?"

"I can't believe we're having this conversation."

"I can't either. If I'd stayed home, as usual, it never would have happened. You can blame Cora. She insisted I go out."

"You're here for dinner?"

"Yes. Would you and Becky care to join us?"

Aaron grimaced. "This is unbelievable. Suddenly, I'm back in high school."

"Yes. That is where you know her from, isn't it?"

"That's not what I meant."

"I'm sure it isn't. Shouldn't you be conducting an interview?"

Aaron Grant glanced down the length of the bar and smiled. "I believe the man has his hands full at the moment."

He certainly did, in the form of Jeff Beasley, showered and shaved, and sporting a fresh change of clothes. As Aaron and Sherry watched, the little housebreaker stuck his finger in Arthur Kincaid's face and demanded, "Buy me a drink. Least you could do, after cutting me loose. It's a fine thing, hang a man out to dry, say, Sorry, I'm not your attorney anymore."

"There's a conflict of interest," Becky Baldwin explained.

Jeff Beasley looked at her as if she were some barfly butting in on the conversation. "Conflict of interest? A lot you know. Hell, there ain't no conflict of interest. It's in everyone's interest to get me off on that charge."

"I'm working on it," Becky Baldwin said.

"Working on it? Did you hear that, Arthur?" Beasley demanded, his voice dripping with irony. "The little lady's working on it. And I bet she just finished law school. Well, I guess my worries are over."

"Now, now." Arthur Kincaid stepped between them. "Becky, Jeff doesn't mean it, he just likes to complain, you have to get used to him. Jeff, stop your grousing and I'll buy you a drink. Then you go home and get to bed before you do something else we have to bail you out for."

Jeff Beasley snorted contemptuously, but allowed Arthur Kincaid to summon the bartender.

From her perch on a barstool, Cora Felton watched with great interest. As she did, the loudest sports jacket she had ever seen came in the door. It was worn by a man with dazzling white teeth and jet black hair. The teeth were way too bright for a man his age, just as the hair was way too dark and full. The teeth and hair adorned a round, jowled face, which somehow still managed to appear angular. The man looked as if he were about to sell someone aluminum siding against their will.

He strode up to the lawyer and said, "Arthur Kincaid?"

"Yes?"

"Philip Hurley. We spoke on the phone. We've met before, though it's been years. And this is my wife, Ethel," Philip said, thrusting forward a diminutive blonde with a face-lift, much in the manner of one presenting a bargaining chip in a deal one was conducting.

Ethel, clearly uncomfortable in a red sheath dress that was way too young for her, glared back at her husband before taking the lawyer's hand. "Pleased to meet you," she said. Her nasal whine could have cut glass. "We're here for the reading of the will."

Philip Hurley rolled his eyes. "He knows that, *honey,*" he said, managing to convey with the one-word endearment what a lesser man could not have accomplished with the phrase *stupid, pusillanimous ignoramus.* "He *knows* we're the heirs. He's the one who called us."

Jeff Beasley had been studying the new arrivals. The burglar's face brightened. "You're the heirs? Then you owe me a drink." He thrust out his glass. "I'm drinking bourbon."

Philip Hurley's lip curled. "And you would be?"

"Jeff Beasley. Pleased to meetcha."

"The pleasure is yours," Philip Hurley informed him. "And what earthly reason do you have for thinking I owe you a drink?"

"Jeff Beasley was my client," Arthur Kincaid explained. "I had to let him go due to a conflict of interest over your aunt's estate. He feels you cost him a lawyer, so you owe him a drink."

"Is he nuts?" Philip Hurley sputtered. "That's the stupidest thing I ever heard."

"Spoilsport," Beasley grunted. "Come on, just one drink."

"I just bought you a drink," Arthur Kincaid pointed out.

"And I drank it." Jeff Beasley held up the empty glass. "And now I need another." He thrust his chin out at Philip Hurley. "You putting up or not?"

"He's not," Arthur Kincaid said firmly. "Jeff, I can't have you harassing the heirs. I'll buy you one more drink, but then you're on your own." He signaled to the bartender, pointed to Beasley's glass. "One more on my tab."

"Now see here," Philip said. "That better not come out of the estate." He jerked his thumb at his chest. "Because that money is coming to me."

"That's right." Ethel Hurley's piercing whine cut through the squabble. "What about the inheritance? How much is it?"

"*Honey,*" Philip Hurley snapped. "You can't ask *that.* It's an improper question. It's *vulgar.*" He rolled his eyes and shook his head, inviting the lawyer to share in his contempt for his moron of a wife. "*You're* not the heir, *I* am." He narrowed his eyes. "So, how much is it?"

"Mr. Hurley—"

"I heard fifteen million. Is that right?"

"Where did you hear that?"

"What's the difference? The point is, is it true?"

"It's a large fortune. Fifteen million is an approximation. But probably not an unfair one."

Philip Hurley smiled like he'd just sold four hundred

acres of Florida swampland. "And that money is mine," he declared. "I'm entitled to it. I don't care what that old biddy says in the will, the money belongs to me."

Arthur Kincaid raised his eyebrows. "You plan to contest the will?"

"Of course not," Philip Hurley said. "I plan to inherit under it. I'm just saying, if I don't, be ready for trouble."

"I'm not looking for any trouble," Arthur Kincaid said.

"Oh?" Ethel Hurley exclaimed. "Are you trying to tell us something? That sounds like you're trying to tell us something."

"There's nothing to tell," Arthur Kincaid replied with dignity. "As I said on the phone, my instructions are to read the will after I've assembled the heirs. And not before. So you see, there's nothing I can tell you."

"Yes, there is," Philip said. "Who *are* the heirs?"

"I beg your pardon?"

"Who have you been instructed to assemble?" Philip said. "Just who did Emma want present at the reading of this will?"

"All of her relatives."

"*All* of her relatives?"

"That's right."

Philip Hurley frowned. "Surely not Jason."

Arthur Kincaid said nothing.

Philip Hurley set his bulldog jaw. "Are you telling me my brother's included?"

"No one is excluded, Mr. Hurley," Arthur Kincaid answered.

"But that's absurd. Surely Emma wouldn't think of leaving anything to him."

"She must if she asked for him," Ethel interjected. "Isn't that right? If a person is summoned, it's to share in the money?"

"Shut up, Ethel. Don't talk stupid." Philip Hurley

wheeled on the lawyer. "Is that how it works, Mr. Kincaid? If he's invited, he inherits?"

"Not necessarily. A person could be mentioned in the will for the specific purpose of disinheriting that person."

"That's more like it." Philip nodded. "That's what old Emma would do. Get Jason here just to disinherit him. Tell me, Mr. Kincaid, did you specifically invite Jason?"

"I left messages at his last known address. Whether he got them, I couldn't say."

"And what *was* his last known address?"

"Denver, Colorado."

"Ah." Philip Hurley's look was knowing and eloquent, dismissing anyone who chose to live in the Rockies as having far too frivolous a nature to be taken seriously.

Cora Felton, at the bar, lit a cigarette, and watched with interest. No one had thought to introduce her, and she was glad, preferring to sit back and watch the scene unfold. Arthur Kincaid hadn't introduced Becky Baldwin either, and Cora was pleased to note the young woman was looking somewhat put out. Becky kept hovering near the lawyer's shoulder, looking to edge her way in.

Cora smiled, took a drag on her cigarette.

"The Puzzle Lady smokes?"

Cora Felton frowned.

Not here.

Not now.

Not in front of Sherry.

A nebbishy-looking man, with a bald head, black-framed glasses, prominent nose, and receding chin was smiling all over his face and regarding Cora with a look that was at once admiring and disapproving.

Cora sighed in relief. Not a muckraking journalist. Just a fan.

Cora Felton smiled. "I not only smoke, I can blow perfect rings."

She proceeded to do so.

"I'm impressed, but I still disapprove," the nebbishy man said. "You're shattering my image."

"Oh, you'll get over it," Cora told him. She picked up her martini glass from the bar. "If your heart can take it, I also drink."

"Oh, so do I." The man held up a glass of what appeared to be sherry. "To puzzle making."

"I'll drink to *that*!" Cora Felton announced heartily, pointing her finger in a theatrical manner.

He raised his eyebrows inquiringly.

Cora grinned. "Lee Marvin, as the drunken gunfighter in *Cat Ballou*."

"Yes, of course." The nebbishy man nodded approvingly. "He won the Oscar for it. In fact, that's how I'd clue the word *Marvin. Best actor of 1965*."

Uh oh.

Alarm bells jangled in Cora Felton's head. This was worse than a journalist. Worse than a TV reporter. Worse, even, than an obsessed fan.

This was a peer.

A colleague.

A *constructor.*

"How *you'd* clue it?" Cora Felton said, with mounting misgivings.

The man's smile stretched from ear to ear. He paused portentously, then announced, "I'm Harvey Beerbaum."

Cora Felton's cornflower blue eyes widened. "Is that right?" she said. She grabbed his hand, pumped it up and down. "I'm so pleased to meet you." She patted him on the shoulder. "Now, if you would just be an angel and order me a drink, I will be right back."

Cora Felton flashed Harvey Beerbaum her most winning smile, slipped off her stool, and hurried down the bar to where Sherry Carter was talking with Aaron Grant.

As she went by Cora Felton leaned close, hissed in Sherry's ear, "Mayday!" and kept on going.

"What was that all about?" Aaron asked as Cora Felton hurried off.

Sherry frowned. "Aunt Cora's in trouble. I gotta go help."

"In trouble?"

"Someone's probably hitting on her. I'll be right back."

Sherry slid off her stool and headed for the ladies' room. She pushed open the door, found her aunt standing there waiting for her.

"Okay, what's the problem?" Sherry asked.

"You see the man standing next to me at the bar?"

"No."

"Nerdy little guy, just came in."

"I didn't see him. What about him?"

"He's a constructor."

"Oh?"

"At least I think he is. He announced his name like he expected me to swoon."

"What is it?"

"Harvey Beerbaum."

Now it was Sherry's eyes that widened. "Uh oh."

"Who is he?" Cora demanded.

"He's not just a constructor. He's a *famous* constructor. Almost as famous as Will Shortz. He contributes regularly to *The New York Times*. What in the world is he doing here?"

"I have no idea. The minute he announced his name I had to get out of there before he realized I didn't know it."

"Okay, you know it now. Go back out there and bluff it through."

"Sherry."

"Cora, you can do it. You know you can. You've done it before. You give him the I-don't-talk-shop routine, and get him to buy you a drink."

"I don't know . . ."

"I do. I happen to know you. You're devious on the one hand, and utterly charming on the other. I wouldn't be surprised if he offers to marry you."

"Sherry, I'm not in the mood."

"Don't tell me, tell him. Cora, most likely this guy's just passing through. You hand him a line, you make him feel good, that's the end of it."

Sherry pushed open the ladies' room door and went back to the bar. A quick glance showed her the tableau had changed. Jeff Beasley had somehow managed to corral *two* drinks, and had moved to a booth where he sat, hunched over, with his arms protectively around them. Becky Baldwin sat opposite, and appeared to be trying to reason with him.

So, the man standing alone in the space left by Cora Felton and Becky Baldwin had to be Harvey Beerbaum, legendary crossword-puzzle constructor and expert, whose work was discussed regularly on CRUCIVERB-L, a daily digest Sherry subscribed to on the Internet. Under other circumstances, Sherry would have relished talking to him. Not tonight. Instead, Sherry joined Aaron at the end of the bar.

"So?" Aaron said.

Sherry shrugged. "Just as I thought. Cora's being bothered by a crossword-puzzle expert. She doesn't want to offend him, but she doesn't want to encourage him either. It happens all the time."

"Then she should know how to handle it," Aaron pointed out.

Sherry glanced at him sharply, but Aaron didn't seem to mean anything by the remark. "Well, will you look at that," he said.

Sherry followed his gaze down the bar to where Philip Hurley stood looking at . . .

Philip Hurley!

It wasn't, of course.

It was his twin. His double. His doppelgänger. A man who looked exactly like him. With dark black hair and flashing teeth and the same bulldog chin. Though somewhat more conservatively dressed in a blue leisure suit.

Sherry blinked.

Not a blue leisure suit.

A blue *pants* suit.

Despite all outward appearances, Philip Hurley's mirror image was undoubtedly a woman.

While Sherry watched, the unmistakably female voice pierced the air. Ethel Hurley's voice was bad, but this put Ethel's to shame. "Philip!" shrilled the dragon-lady voice. "You old crook, how are you? Still under investigation for mail fraud?"

Philip's lips curled into a sneer. "Well, well, sister Phyllis as I live and breathe." He pointed to the wimpy-looking man in the gabardine suit standing slightly behind her. "Is this the current Mr. Phyllis Hurley? Hasn't anyone pointed out to him how your husbands have a habit of dying after making out insurance policies in your favor?" He said to the wimpy man, "You wouldn't be carrying life insurance, by any chance?"

Without looking, Phyllis put her hand in her husband's face, in the manner of one instructing a dog to stay. "Don't bother, Morty. My honor doesn't need defending from *dear* brother Philip. So, where's the lawyer?" She glanced around, spotted Arthur Kincaid. "You look like the lawyer. Are you? Sure you are. Same face, but older. I remember now. I'm Phyllis Hurley Applegate. This is my husband, Morty Applegate." She spread her arms. "And he is here to watch me as I inherit the Hurley fortune."

"You inherit? That's a laugh." Philip sniggered.

"As oldest surviving niece, I think not."

"Then you think wrong. I inherit, as oldest surviving nephew."

"Nonsense. As the oldest sibling, I take precedence."

Philip and Phyllis instantly squared off, jaw to jaw. It was quite a sight. Whether Philip had chosen his hairpiece to mock his sister, or she had cut and dyed her hair to mock him, the effect was mind-boggling. They looked exactly the same.

"You're not older," Philip snapped.

"Yes, I am."

"We're the same age."

"I'm still older."

"By half an hour."

"There you are!" Phyllis said triumphantly. "You heard him. He admits it. I'm the eldest. And I will be inheriting under Aunt Emma's will."

"Oh, I don't think there's much chance of that."

The voice came from the doorway.

Philip and Phyllis Hurley turned to look.

Their identical bulldog jaws dropped in unison.

"Jason," Philip Hurley murmured in a voice loud enough to carry to the end of the bar.

But the newcomer clearly wasn't Philip's brother. The young man was no more than twenty-five years old. He wore boots, blue jeans, and a black leather jacket. His dark hair was long and stringy, and hung down the sides of his face. His beard was scraggly and untrimmed. But his eyes were blue and bright, even in the dim light of the bar. His eyes twinkled as he looked at the battling Hurleys. He strode across the room.

"Is it possible? Could it be? Uncle Philip and Auntie Phyllis? And just look at you. Good lord, Philip, where'd you get that hair? Don't tell me, you sell used cars. Did I get it right?"

Philip Hurley's eyes widened. "My God, you look just like him."

The young man laughed. "Well, not quite, I think. Dad never wore a beard. Among other things."

Phyllis Applegate gawked at him. "You're *little* Danny?"

"Not quite so little anymore, but I'm Danny, all right." He grinned. "Didn't realize you were so old, did you, Aunt Phyllis? But here I am, Auntie's principal heir."

"Is that true?" Philip Hurley demanded of Arthur Kincaid. "Does he share in the dough?" As the lawyer opened his mouth to speak, he added, "I know you don't know. I mean, did you ask him here?"

"Indirectly. I invited his father and all of *his* heirs. Which includes any offspring. Just as it includes any children of yours."

"I have no children."

"That's not the point. The fact is, if you did they'd be included."

The young man spread his arms. "And Jason did. And here I am. What do you wanna bet I wind up with the whole shooting match?"

"And where's Jason?" Philip Hurley demanded.

The young man shook his head. "We're not the tightest-knit family in the world, are we? Dad's dead. Nearly two years now. Mom nearly four. Amazing you don't know that, but there you are. I am an orphan, an only child, a sole surviving son. A direct descendant of the Hurley millions, which will doubtless bypass you and come straight to me. Sorry about that, but I think you'll find Auntie always favored Dad. Had a soft spot for the renegade. Chip off the old block. Eccentric, like her. When the dust clears, you can line up for a handout. You and all the rest. Apply to my solicitor. For funds to cover your shortfall. Which I have no doubt you have."

The young man stood, hands on hips, head thrown back arrogantly, taunting them. Then he turned and surveyed the room in quest of fresh game. As his eyes traveled down the bar the sardonic smile froze on his face, was replaced a moment later by a look of genuine bafflement. He blinked twice, and said:

"Sherry?"

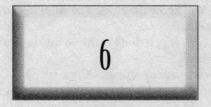

6

IT WAS ALL CORA FELTON COULD DO TO KEEP FROM FALL-ing into her French toast. She propped her elbows on the table, rested her chin in her hands. "Sherry, sweetheart, be an angel, make me a drink."

"Drink your coffee."

"I can't *find* my coffee."

"By your elbow."

"Which elbow?"

"Aunt Cora."

"You never should have woken me up," Cora Felton whined. "I'm not ready to get up."

"Aunt Cora. You're the one who woke up."

"Oh. Well, I had a dream. A bad dream. A nightmare. I was having drinks with a walking thesaurus who kept gabbling about *words*."

"That wasn't a dream. That was a puzzle expert. And you handled him just fine."

"I did?"

"You must have or we'd have heard about it by now. Eat your French toast."

"Is that what this is?"

"Aunt Cora."

"One Bloody Mary, Sherry. I'd make it myself if I could stand up."

"Sorry. You know the rules. You want it, you get it."

"Stupid rule."

"Great rule. If you don't drink so much, you'll be sober enough to drink."

"That even *sounds* stupid," Cora snapped. "I'd better have a cigarette. If I don't have a cigarette, things could get nasty."

Cora Felton was wearing her Wicked Witch of the West dress, the tattered black smock decorated with liquor stains and cigarette burns. She reached in the pocket, came out with a crumpled pack of cigarettes, extracted one, lit it, and took a greedy drag.

"There, that's better. So what happened last night? Last I remember the Hell's Angels had just arrived and one of them said he knew you."

"Daniel Hurley."

"Oh?"

"I went to school with him. At Dartmouth." Sherry grimaced. "He knows Dennis."

"Uh oh."

Sherry shook her head. "No, I don't mean now. He knew him then. A friend of his, not mine. But I knew him. Though back then he didn't have a motorcycle. Or a beard."

Cora's head bobbed as she tried to follow all that. She gave up, exhaled. "All right," she declared resolutely, "I *can* make a Bloody Mary."

Cora staggered to her feet and careened around the kitchen, fetching glass, ice, vodka, tomato juice, and whatever spices she could find. Her accuracy was not one hundred percent. Her celery salt, for instance, was actually cinnamon.

When Cora was finished, she dropped the spoon down the garbage disposal, brought the glass to the table, and slumped in her chair. She took a huge sip, sighed happily, then frowned at the aftertaste. "Not quite right." She squinted up at Sherry. "You were saying?"

"I wasn't saying anything."

Cora nodded. "No wonder I was confused. It's better when you say something. So, what happened to what's-her-name?"

"Who?"

"Becky-wecky. You leave her with Aaron?"

"No. But she must have wound up with him."

"Why do you say that?"

Sherry pointed to the morning paper on the breakfast table. "It's on page six. NEW ATTORNEY IS BAKERHAVEN HIGH GRAD."

"He wrote about her?"

"It's his job."

"Writing is his job. Writing about her is not. I knew this would happen. You should have stayed."

"Yeah, but you had to go. Before you told Harvey Beerbaum your life story."

"That's his name?"

"Yes, it is. Try to recognize it the next time it comes up." Sherry cocked her head. "Do you think you'll recognize *him*?"

"Are you kidding? I'll see *him* in my dreams."

The front doorbell rang.

"That's probably him now. Wanting to know why I ran out."

"It better not be," Sherry said darkly.

Sherry padded into the living room and looked out the

window. There was a car parked behind the Toyota, but she couldn't see it well enough to tell whose it was. She opened the door.

Aaron Grant was standing there. "Hi," he said. "Are you busy?"

"What?"

"Are you doing anything this morning?"

"Just feeding my aunt breakfast."

"Oh. Are you almost done?" Aaron pushed past her, heading for the kitchen.

"Aaron Grant," Sherry said.

He stopped. "What?"

"You ever hear of the words *come in*? That's how someone invites you into their home. What if my aunt weren't dressed?"

"Your aunt's naked?"

Cora Felton appeared in the door to the kitchen. "I beg your pardon?"

Aaron turned, saw her. "She looks dressed to me."

"I most certainly am," Cora Felton said. She waved her Bloody Mary in Aaron's direction. "And it's nice of you to notice." She smiled, then winced, raised the glass, and pressed it against her forehead, her eyes shut. "Sherry, do the two of you have to talk so loud?"

Sherry took a moment to compose herself. Then, in an exaggeratedly quiet voice she said, "Not at all. Why don't we go into the kitchen, sit down, have some coffee, and read the morning paper."

"That's what I wanted to talk to you about," Aaron said, as he followed Sherry and Cora into the kitchen.

"Oh?" Sherry said. "Coffee?"

"No thanks. I've had breakfast," Aaron said. "I wanted to explain about the article in the paper."

"Oh?" Sherry said. "What article?"

Cora Felton, who had sat at the table, found herself between Aaron and Sherry, who were standing on either side. After looking back and forth from one to the other like a spectator at a tennis match, she said, "Uh oh," heaved herself to her feet, and lurched over to the kitchen counter.

"I meant my article," Aaron Grant said. "The one I wrote about Becky. I wanted to explain that."

"Whatever is there to explain?"

"Why I wrote it. I was supposed to interview the other lawyer, Arthur Kincaid. But he had his hands full with the heirs. It was getting too late, I had a deadline, and I had to come up with something fast."

"So you interviewed Becky Baldwin instead?"

"I didn't even interview her. I rushed back to the paper, banged it out, and got it in."

"Why didn't you interview her?"

"I was waiting to interview him. By the time I realized I wasn't going to, it was too late."

At the kitchen counter, Cora Felton poured a generous shot of vodka into her glass. For a heavy drinker, Cora had a strict rule of only one drink before dinner. Cora never violated this sacred rule.

Except when she did.

There was usually a reason.

"Anyway," Aaron said, "I had a story to write, and this seemed like a natural. A lawyer passing through town stops and takes a case. Put together she's a Bakerhaven High grad, and it's her *first* case, and the story's too good to pass up."

Sherry put her hands on her hips, cocked her head. "Why are you telling me this?"

"Actually, it's a tangent," Aaron Grant said. "The point is, I never got to interview Arthur Kincaid. So I called him this morning, he hemmed and hawed, and we kicked it around a bit, and the long and the short of it is he wound up inviting me to the reading of the will."

"Oh?"

"Yes. I'm on my way now, it's going to be an absolute hoot, and I thought you might like to go."

"Me?" Sherry said.

"Why not?"

"You can't crash someone's will."

"You can if the lawyer invites you. The way I understand it, none of the prospective heirs have enough clout to say boo. Because no one knows who inherits Emma Hurley's fortune until the will is read. Anyway, that's the story. I came here to explain the article in the paper and take you to something special. So, whaddaya say?"

"Are you inviting Cora too?"

"Sure, if she wants to go."

Cora Felton waved her hand. "Stuffy old lawyers. Boring old wills. But don't let me spoil your fun. You kids run along, have a good time."

"Are you sure?" Aaron Grant said.

"Go, go, go." Cora shooed him out.

Aaron looked at Sherry. "Come on. Whaddaya say?"

Sherry gave in with a smile. "Okay," she said, and the two of them went out the door.

Cora Felton made sure they were gone, then brought out the Bloody Mary she'd been holding behind her back. She'd wanted Sherry to go, was afraid her niece wouldn't leave her if Sherry'd realized she was mixing another drink.

Cora Felton took a sip of Bloody Mary, shook her head thoughtfully.

That was a bit of a fib, pretending she wasn't interested in the will. The Hurley will was absolutely fascinating, and it killed Cora not to go to the reading, but she didn't want to tag along. She didn't want to cramp Aaron's style.

Cora Felton took another slurp of Bloody Mary, frowned. For some reason she couldn't taste the vodka. Perhaps she hadn't put enough in. She'd poured without looking, so Sherry wouldn't notice.

Cora smiled.

Sherry. Out with Aaron Grant. On a date. An early morning date. In a lawyer's office. Listening to a will. Even for a modern young couple, that was not your average outing.

Cora chuckled at the thought, and absently reached for the vodka bottle.

7

BECKY BALDWIN WAS THERE. THAT WAS THE FIRST THING Sherry noticed, and it bothered her. Why should she care if Becky Baldwin was there? Why should she even notice?

Particularly in a room so crowded.

Arthur Kincaid's law office was on Cedar Street a block off Main, on the second floor above an antiques shop. The conference room was unusually large for a lawyer with a one-man practice, and it occurred to Sherry that in a town this size it would be rare that Kincaid actually needed it. However, today was certainly one of those occasions. The conference table seated eight. Every single seat was taken.

At the head was Arthur Kincaid, whose briefcase was closed on the table in front of him. To his left sat Philip and Ethel Hurley, dressed as game-show hosts, and fidgety as game-show contestants. Today, Philip's sports jacket was wildly yellow, perhaps out of deference to Ethel's puce dress. Taken together, they reminded Sherry of a salamander.

Across from Philip sat Phyllis Hurley Applegate. Severe, in a prim gray dress, she could have passed for the warden of a women's prison. Though not smiling, she still managed to appear smug and gloating.

Her husband, Morty, sitting next to her, was doing a remarkable job of appearing insignificant.

Next to Philip and Ethel Hurley sat an elderly man with bad teeth. He had other features—a bald head, big ears, and a hook nose chief among them—but the teeth were the first thing Sherry noticed. They were remarkably bad—black, broken, twisted, or simply missing. One of his front teeth was gone. The other looked as if the dentist had filed it down for a cap, and then neglected to put the cap on. The end result was wholly unattractive.

The ugly man was dressed like a lumberjack. In spite of the heat, he wore a flannel shirt and overalls, the type with a bib and shoulder straps. The pockets in the bib bulged with assorted junk—Sherry noted a paint-smeared screwdriver handle, a twisted pipe cleaner, a gnarled pencil, and a broken straw.

Across from the old man sat a woman who looked like she'd been kicked in the face by a horse. Her nose was flat, not the way a boxer's broken nose might be flattened, but simply in that it did not protrude from her face. It was not broad, either, just a flat little nose that sat above thin lips, and a bulldog jaw. The woman looked as if she'd just sucked a lemon.

At the end of the table, opposite the lawyer's chair, slumped Daniel Hurley, who had obviously not cleaned himself up for the occasion. The young man was still dressed in boots, jeans, and leather jacket.

In addition to those seated at the table there were several people standing, including Aaron Grant, who was at Sherry's side; Becky Baldwin, who was standing behind the Hurleys; a teenage boy who didn't seem connected to anyone at the table and who looked exquisitely unhappy to be there; and a gaunt woman, inexpensively yet impeccably dressed, whom Sherry immediately pegged as a spinster, then chided herself for doing so.

Arthur Kincaid looked at his watch, rose, and cleared his throat. The room fell instantly silent.

"Ladies and gentlemen," Arthur Kincaid said. "The time has come for the reading of the will. It is my responsibility—"

Before the heirs could learn what the lawyer's responsibility was, however, footsteps pounded up the stairs and Chief Harper walked into the room.

"Excuse me, ladies and gentlemen. Sorry to interrupt. Police business. I'll try to be brief. Arthur, if I could have a moment . . ."

Chief Harper pushed to the front of the room and led the lawyer off into a corner, where the two men proceeded to converse in low tones. Neither looked happy.

Neither did the heirs. All watched Chief Harper and Arthur Kincaid with deepening distrust and suspicion.

Arthur Kincaid returned to the head of the table, stood with his hands resting on the back of his chair. He cleared his throat again. "Excuse me, ladies and gentlemen. Before we get to the reading of the will, Chief Harper has another matter he needs to address. He has promised to be brief. I ask you all to give him your cooperation so we can get the matter out of the way as quickly as possible."

All eyes were glued to Chief Harper.

"Thank you," the Chief said. "Some of you are aware there was a break-in at the Hurley mansion the night before last. A man by the name of Jeff Beasley was apprehended on the premises—"

"Is that the man last night said I owed him a drink?" Philip Hurley interrupted.

"That's him," Arthur Kincaid said. "If you would let the Chief finish."

"Thank you," Chief Harper said. "But, actually, you're getting right to the point I want. Jeff Beasley was drinking last night at the Country Kitchen. I'm wondering how many of you happened to see him there."

"Why?" Becky Baldwin demanded.

"Can I assume you saw him there?"

"Of course I saw him there. He's my client. Why?"

"Were you there when he left?"

Becky Baldwin smiled. "You're talking to a lawyer, Chief. I let you sidestep the question once as a courtesy, now I'd like to know. Why are you asking?"

"Early this morning Jeff Beasley was found dead in a drainage ditch."

There were gasps around the conference room.

Becky Baldwin's perfect face fell, and Sherry suddenly felt sorry for her. Becky was not some high-powered attorney. She was a fledgling lawyer, a vulnerable young girl, who had just been cruelly deprived of her only client. There was even a tear in her eye. As Sherry watched, Becky reached up, wiped it away. But when she spoke, her voice scarcely trembled. "How did it happen?"

"That's what I have to determine," Chief Harper replied. "It's an accidental death, and that's probably all it is, but I have to make sure. So it becomes necessary that I trace his movements. So, is there anyone who recalls when Jeff Beasley left the Country Kitchen last night?"

"Absolutely not," Philip Hurley said. "The man wasn't important, there was no reason to notice him at all."

"I thought you said he hit you up for a drink," Phyllis Hurley Applegate put in.

Chief Harper looked from one to the other. "You would be the Hurley twins? Remind me of your names."

"I'm Philip. My snide, insinuating sister is Phyllis."

"Snide? Insinuating?" Phyllis snorted. "Did you or did you not say that sot pestered you for a drink?"

"That was before you got there. I didn't see him after that. I can't say the same for you."

"Did you see Jeff Beasley leave the Country Kitchen last night?" Chief Harper asked Phyllis.

"Well, I like that." Phyllis stuck her nose in the air. "Are you going to let him put ideas in your head?"

"No, but I intend to get the answers to some questions. Right now I want to know if anyone saw Beasley leave the Country Kitchen last night."

"I saw him leave."

Heads swiveled to the end of the table, where Daniel Hurley sat sprawled in his chair, feet out, head back, lounging in a youthful, insolent manner.

"You saw him leave?" Chief Harper said.

"Absolutely. I saw him stagger out the door."

"You left then too?"

"Yes, I did. I didn't offer him a ride. If I had, I probably would have saved his life."

"Why didn't you?"

"He's not the sort of person you'd want on the back of your motorcycle."

"Ah, yes." Chief Harper nodded. "So you drove off and left Beasley there? In the parking lot?"

"That's right."

"You see anyone else in the lot?"

"Matter of fact, I did. Nerdy chap, was talking to Sherry's friend. The old lady."

"Sherry?"

Daniel Hurley gestured. "Sherry Carter. Who happens to be here. For no good reason that I can think of, although I am personally pleased."

"Uh huh," Chief Harper said. "And this nerdy man was talking to the Puzzle Lady?"

"Who?"

"Cora Felton. Sherry's aunt."

"Yes, that's who." Daniel Hurley cocked his head at Sherry. "She's the Puzzle Lady? Just what is that?"

Chief Harper put up his hand. "If you don't mind, we'll socialize later. For the moment, I'm interested in who else noticed when these three left. By that I mean, Jeff Beasley, you, young man—and your name is?"

"Daniel Hurley." He smiled. "Hurley relative and profit participant."

Philip Hurley stiffened. "Now, look here, young man—"

"Please," Chief Harper interjected. "If we could move this along. And the third person in the parking lot was a man known to your aunt, Miss Carter? And would you know who might that be?"

"Harvey Beerbaum," Sherry replied. "He's a cruciverbalist. A crossword-puzzle expert. He was boring Cora with his expertise."

"And did you see Mr. Beerbaum leave?"

"No. Cora and I left first."

"Uh huh. How about the rest of you? Did any of you see this man leave? Or Daniel Hurley or Jeff Beasley, for that matter?"

"I wasn't in the Country Kitchen last night," the flat-faced woman next to the Applegates declared.

"Yes, Annabel, I quite understand," Chief Harper said. He took out a notebook, flipped it open, and wrote. "Annabel Hurley, no. And is there anyone else who was *not* in the Country Kitchen last night?"

"I wasn't." The elderly man sitting next to the Hurleys had a surprisingly clear voice for one with such bad teeth.

Chief Harper smiled. "Yes, Chester, I'm sure you weren't." He jotted on his notepad. "Chester Hurley, no. And you, Mildred," he said to the woman Sherry had categorized as a spinster, "weren't there either. Mildred Sims, no. And Kevin Holbrook," he said to the teenage boy, "who I would not have expected to be drinking at the Country Kitchen." Kevin Holbrook tugged at his shirt collar, looked embarrassed. "Fine. That's who I *don't* have to deal with, that leaves the ones I do. How about it? Aside from Daniel Hurley, did anyone actually see Jeff Beasley or the puzzle maker in the parking lot?"

No one said anything.

"Okay, I guess that's it. I'm sorry to hold you all up. I have just one more thing to ask. Would anyone mind if I stuck around to hear the will?"

Arthur Kincaid frowned. "For what purpose?"

"Probably none," Chief Harper answered. "But Jeff Beasley broke into the Hurley mansion, spent last night harassing the Hurley heirs, and wound up dead. I know it's a long shot, but I have to ask myself, is there any possibility that there's anything in the Hurley will that could shed some light on that. So would anyone object if I heard the will?"

"I insist on it," Daniel Hurley said.

All eyes turned to him.

"What?" Phyllis Hurley Applegate demanded.

"Absolutely," Daniel Hurley said. "And you should insist on it too. I have nothing to hide. I know that there is absolutely nothing in that will that could possibly implicate me in this man's death in any way. And I would think that would be true of all of you. But I must say, I would be utterly fascinated to see which of you might possibly object." He looked around the room, smiling broadly. "Are there any of you who feel threatened at hearing the contents of Auntie's will? If so, please speak up. If not, then let's let the nice policeman stay. Let's let them *all* stay. Sherry, wouldn't you like to hear the will? You can stay. And the reporter and the lawyer. You can stay too, if you weren't already invited. Does anyone object to these people staying?"

There was a very sullen silence.

"Fine," Daniel Hurley continued. "Mr. Kincaid, is it? I think you may proceed."

Daniel Hurley tilted his chair back, cocked his head. "Let's hear the will."

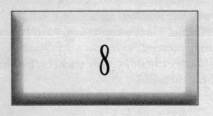

8

ARTHUR KINCAID SNAPPED OPEN HIS BRIEFCASE, TOOK out a sealed envelope, and held it up. "This is Emma Prentice Hurley's will, executed entirely in her own hand, sealed in this envelope, and not to be opened until we were all assembled here."

"If you didn't open it, how do you know that?" Phyllis Hurley Applegate demanded.

Arthur Kincaid took a second envelope from his briefcase. "From this," he replied. "Emma Hurley's instructions to me. Which I have read, and which I shall read to you now."

The second envelope was unsealed. Arthur Kincaid took a letter from it, unfolded it. Again, he cleared his throat.

"To my solicitor, Arthur Kincaid. Since you are reading this," Arthur Kincaid read, *"it means that I am dead. I must say, rather than depressing, I find the concept quite liberating. Since I am dead, there is nothing anyone can do to me. And yet there are still things that can be*

done, things that I can do, actions that I can take, through you, as my solicitor. My wishes can be carried out in death, perhaps even more so than they ever were in life. I find it, by and large, quite a satisfactory arrangement.

"I hope that you will pardon my whimsy. If you won't, too bad. Be that as it may, please think of me as smiling with glee as you carry out my instructions.

"But, to be serious: I have given a good deal of thought as to who should inherit my estate. None of my relatives are what you would call close, unless you count false flattery and sycophantic toadying as forms of endearment. Indeed, I have few good feelings for the most solicitous of my kin, knowing from what rapacious motivation their attentions sprang."

"Aha!" Philip Hurley said, grinning wickedly and pointing his finger at Phyllis Hurley Applegate.

"Aha yourself!" Phyllis shot back. "You're the one she's talking about."

"Yes, Philip, I'm talking about you," Arthur Kincaid read. *"You and your get-rich-quick schemes. Which you were always ready to embrace as long as they didn't involve any actual good old-fashioned work."*

"See?" Phyllis gloated.

"And I'm talking about you, Phyllis," Arthur went on, *"and your never-ending quest to marry for money. Did either of you ever succeed? Somehow I doubt it. I must admit, I long ago lost touch with my family through the simple expedient of burning all correspondence unread. So I have no idea if any of you ever amounted to anything, indeed, if you are even still alive. If you are, it pleases me no end that your very greed shall force you to*

*stay and hear my insults. So hold your snippy little
tongues, and prick up your avaricious little ears."*

Daniel Hurley's grin grew enormous.

*"Are you enjoying this, Jason? You probably are. You
always loathed your brother and sister, didn't you? At
least you pretended you did, knowing I loathed them. Just
as you pretended not to like me. Or was that really pre-
tense? You certainly acted as if it were. Tried to give
everyone the impression you were a romantic renegade,
turning your back on the family fortune. Why did you do
that, Jason? Did you see some movie where the dying patriarch turned out to be secretly fond of the renegade son?
Well, guess what? Bad news. I am no more enamored of
those who despise me openly than I am of those who love
me only for my wealth."*

"Aha!" Philip and Phyllis said it in unison, gloating gleefully at Daniel. The effect was disconcerting, to say the least.

*"None come in favor, all come in sufferance, any
could I cut off with nary a qualm.*

"So, whom shall I call? Why, all of them, of course.

*"I charge you to summon my heirs. All of my siblings,
and all of their descendants. Specifically, my sister, Alicia
Hurley, deceased, and her daughter, Annabel Hurley; my
brother Randolph Hurley, deceased, and his daughter,
Phyllis Hurley, and sons, Philip and Jason Hurley. I bid
you summon them and their offspring to the reading of
my will.*

*"To this number add the following: my trusted com-
panion, Mildred Sims, whose loyalty and service were un-
equaled, would my relatives only have been so nice; my
yard boy, Kevin Holbrook, who kept the view from my*

bedroom window pleasing to the end; and last, but not least, my brother Chester, who will resent being mentioned, and will not want to come. Drag him, kicking and screaming, for I hereby charge you that my will shall not be read outside his presence, be he still alive. I am sorry, Chester. You may have avoided me in life, but you will not in death. So close that gap-toothed mouth of yours, sit quiet, and give ear. After this, you'll be free to do as you like.

"*I charge you, Arthur Kincaid, to assemble the aforementioned people, and then—and only then—in their presence, to break the seal and read my will.*

"*Should you fail to do so, should this letter in some way disappear, should the provisions of my last will and testament not be carried out in full to every last detail and specification, I assure you I have set the wheels in motion that this act shall be discovered and exposed.*

"Signed, *Emma Prentice Hurley.*"

Arthur Kincaid set down the letter, surveyed those around the table. "You can see why I was unable to give any of you information. Emma Hurley's last wishes were, to put it mildly, somewhat . . . eccentric. I have carried them out to the best of my ability. It is my belief that I have summoned and caused to be present all of the persons specified in this letter. Having done so, I may now read the will."

Arthur Kincaid picked up the second envelope. "This envelope is inscribed as follows: *Last Will and Testament of Emma Prentice Hurley. To be unsealed, opened, and read, only in the presence of my heirs.*"

Arthur Kincaid turned the envelope over, held it up, and pointed. "You will note that this envelope has been sealed in the old-fashioned way, with sealing wax. I shall break the seal now."

He took a silver letter opener from his briefcase, inserted it in the flap, and slid it down, breaking the wax seal. He pulled back the flap of the envelope, took out some folded sheets of paper. He unfolded them, adjusted his glasses, cleared his throat.

"Last Will and Testament of Emma Prentice Hurley. I, Emma Prentice Hurley, being of sound mind and body, though perhaps not as sound a body as I would like, do hereby make my last will and testament. I hereby revoke all prior wills, stating that this will, and only this will, reflects my true last wishes.

"Before disposing of my property, I would like time to reflect. I know this will not please you. You are a greedy lot. Indeed, there is probably not one among you who is not delighted to see me dead. Be that as it may, I forgive you all your prejudices. But that is not enough to excuse you from hearing me out one last time.

"Lately, I have become mindful of the wickedness of the world. This has been brought forcefully to my attention by the recent killings in Bakerhaven. I have followed with great interest both the problem presented by these murders, and the ultimate solution. Doing so has given me a new perspective on life.

"And death.

"In the meantime, I have tried to determine to whom I should leave my money. Believe me, it has not been easy. As I have indicated, I have little love for my nieces and nephews, who have little love for me. Still, the money must go to someone. Who should that be?

"Pause here, Arthur, dramatically, before continuing. Keep them in suspense. Keep yourself in suspense. Try to figure out what I am about to do."

Arthur Kincaid did pause at this juncture, coughed apologetically, looked around the room. All eyes were on him, expectant, waiting, impatient. Greedy.

"But before I tell you," he read, and the groans were audible, *"I would like to reflect again on what I learned from the Bakerhaven murders. I think the first thing I learned is that crime does not pay. Eventually, the chickens come home to roost. I always wondered what that meant. I don't know what it means now. Perhaps what I mean is the postman always rings twice. Be all your sins remembered, be all your deeds exposed. Both good and bad. Be all crimes cleared.*

"I was fascinated by the solution to the Bakerhaven murders. Probably not unusual for an old lady confined to her room to find a vicarious thrill.

"It also gave me an idea.

"An idea to solve all my problems regarding my estate.

"An idea that pleases me no end.

"With that in mind, I hereby make the following bequests."

Everyone leaned forward, in anticipation.

"To my yard boy, Kevin Holbrook, the sum of five hundred dollars, in the hope it will compensate him for the loss of his job, for there is no guarantee he will be asked to stay on by my heir."

Kevin Holbrook perked up considerably. "Five hundred bucks?" the teenager said. "I just got five hundred bucks?"

He was immediately shushed by both the Hurleys and the Applegates.

Arthur Kincaid held up his hands. "If I may continue. *To my faithful companion, Mildred Sims, for years of devoted service, I leave the sum of ten thousand dollars."*

Mildred Sims didn't bat an eye. From her expression, it was impossible to tell if the thin woman was disappointed or pleased.

"All the rest, remainder, and residue of my estate—"

This was met by squeals of astonishment and protest.

"What!" Philip Hurley shouted.

"Ridiculous!" cried Phyllis Applegate.

Even Daniel Hurley seemed shocked into sincerity. He tipped his chair back on the floor, sat up straight.

Arthur Kincaid spread his hands. "Please," he said.

"That's absurd," Phyllis Applegate snarled. "There's a lot of us here. Why did she cut us all out and give the property away?"

"I don't know," Arthur Kincaid said evenly. He held up the will. "Would you like to find out? Or would you like to speculate among yourselves?"

In spite of this pointed comment, there was considerable grumbling before they calmed down and he had their attention.

"All right," Arthur Kincaid said. "To resume. *All the rest, remainder, and residue of my estate, I leave to whichever of the following heirs shall prove him- or herself worthy.*"

There were no shouts this time, just open mouths and incredulous looks.

"Inspired by the puzzle of the Bakerhaven murders, I have constructed a puzzle of my own. It pleases me greatly to have done so. It is an old puzzle, over forty years old, but nonetheless valid. Indeed, it is perfect for the occasion. I hereby charge my heirs with the solving

of this puzzle. Specifically, the following and any off-spring: my nephew Philip Hurley, my niece Phyllis Hurley, my nephew Jason Hurley, and my niece Annabel Hurley.

"Included is my brother Chester Hurley. You may play the game, Chester. You may not wish to, but you have the right. You are every bit as much a contestant as any of the others. Should you solve the puzzle, the money would be yours. I know you are old, and would gain little by such a feat, but the Hurley property would be yours to dispose of as you pleased. And perhaps there is some justice in that.

"At any rate, to the victor belongs the spoils, including my property, and all the rest, remainder, and residue of my estate, excluding the following behests:

"To each and every losing relative, excluding spouses, either married or divorced, and including all offspring and brother Chester, should he lose, I leave the sum of ten thousand dollars, some lovely parting gifts, and a copy of our home game.

"For the benefit of the nitpicking lawyers of the afore-mentioned heirs, the parting gifts and home game were a harmless pleasantry not to be taken seriously, and the ten thousand dollars a genuine bequest to all those who fail to solve the puzzle."

"WHAT puzzle?" Phyllis Hurley Applegate bellowed "What are you talking about? Where's the puzzle? Do you have it?"

"I'm reading this for the first time," Arthur Kincaid reminded her. "Let me finish and we'll know."

"Yes, shut up and let him finish," Philip Hurley scolded.

"Don't take that tone with my wife . . ." wimpy Morton Applegate ventured diffidently. He blushed violently.

"Or what?" Philip Hurley snarled. "Didn't you hear the will? Spouses don't count. You're out of it."

"Only if we lose." Morton Applegate held up one finger and lectured his brother-in-law pedantically. "If we lose, my wife gets ten thousand dollars. If we win, the two of us inherit the estate."

"The two of you?"

Arthur Kincaid folded the will, slipped it back in its envelope, and sat down. This was met with cries of protest from around the table. He merely sat silently and waited for all voices to subside.

"Thank you," he said. "If I may continue."

He stood, took the will from the envelope.

"All the rest, remainder, and residue of my estate shall go absolutely, irrevocably, and without question to whichever of my heirs shall be the first to correctly solve the puzzle. I know you are all probably shouting 'What puzzle?' and giving Arthur a hard time. Please do not do so. The poor man has no more idea than you do. He did not draw this will. He does not know the contents. He has no idea what I have planned.

"I will tell you now.

"To begin with, the puzzle is not your ordinary kind. To solve it will take more than intelligence. It will take ingenuity, intuition, persistence, and perhaps a trace of luck. Solving it will indeed be an interesting challenge. I wish I were around to see it.

"As to determining the winner. I would find it inappropriate, Arthur, to leave you sole arbiter and judge. Wouldn't you agree? At any rate, I am taking you out of the loop. Your function shall not be as judge, but merely as observer and facilitator. For instance, the first clue can be found in the rolltop desk in my master bedroom. I charge you with granting access to the heirs. The keys to

the estate are in the possession of my banker, Marcus Gelman. His instructions are to open the doors for no one but you, Arthur. It shall be your responsibility to make sure this clue is available. As you shall make available any subsequent clues.

"But as for judging the solution, I leave that in other hands.

"Why?

"Don't worry, Arthur. I'm not going to point out your shortcomings. But this is a puzzle for which I have not supplied the solution. It will be up to the judge to solve it first, ahead of the field, and then determine if any of their solutions are correct. It is an awesome responsibility. Few would be up to the task. Fortunately, we have such a person in our midst. If she could solve the riddle of the Bakerhaven murders, she should have no problem with my simple game. I have not asked her, but I am sure my proposition will appeal to her. And she shall be superbly compensated for her service.

"I therefore leave the sum of fifty thousand dollars, contingent on her solving my puzzle, validating the solution, and determining the winner, to the Puzzle Lady, Miss Cora Felton."

9

CORA FELTON BATTED SHERRY'S HANDS AWAY. "STOP IT!" she muttered.

"Aunt Cora."

"Leave me alone."

"Aunt Cora. Wake up."

"No."

Sherry Carter had found Cora Felton passed out on the kitchen table. Shaking her wasn't working. So far Cora hadn't even opened her eyes.

"Come on, Cora," Sherry said. "You have to wake up."

"Go away."

"Okay," Sherry said. She hurried to the sink, filled a glass, came back, poured it over Cora's head.

Cora Felton's arms flailed the air. "Hey!" she shouted. "What're you doing?"

Sherry set down the glass, grabbed her by the shoulders, shook her. "Aunt Cora. Listen to me. A man is dead."

"Dead?"

"Yes."

"You killed Aaron? Oh, poor Aaron . . ."

"Aunt Cora!"

Cora Felton's left eye opened, peered up at Sherry. Her glasses had fallen off on the table, so all she saw was a blur. "Who are you?"

"Cora, it's me, Sherry. I need you to concentrate. Jeff Beasley is dead."

"Beasley?"

"The drunk."

"Who's drunk?"

"Jeff Beasley. The town drunk. He was found dead. Chief Harper's investigating."

Cora Felton's other eye opened. "Murder investigation?" she murmured. At least that's what she tried to say. It sounded more like *marmalade*.

But Sherry got it. "That's right, Cora. A murder investigation. And they need your help."

"My . . . ?"

"Right. Chief Harper needs your help. So you gotta pull together, you gotta sober up, and you gotta come with me. Right now."

"Right now?"

"Yes. Because everyone's waiting for you."

"Everyone?"

"They're out there now. I figure we've got five minutes tops before they break down our door."

"What?"

"That's how long we've got to pull this off."

"Pull what off?"

"Come here."

Sherry yanked Cora out of the chair, dragged her through the living room to the front window, propped her against the wall, and pushed the curtain aside. "Look," Sherry said. She jammed Cora Felton's eyeglasses on her nose, pointed her in the right direction.

Outside in the driveway were Chief Harper's police

cruiser, Daniel Hurley's motorcycle, Chester Hurley's pickup truck, and half a dozen cars filled with Aaron Grant, Becky Baldwin, bank president Marcus Gelman, and the rest of the Hurley heirs.

"There." Sherry yanked Cora away from the window. "They're all waiting for you. And we're going in the bedroom, and I'm pulling the first available dress over your head, and slipping a pair of shoes on your feet, and you're going to walk with me out to your car as if you hadn't a worry in the world."

"Uh huh," Cora mumbled, as they entered the bedroom. She was beginning to wake up a little. "And then they're going to ask me about the murder?"

"Well, not right away."

"No?" Cora said, as Sherry pulled the Wicked Witch of the West dress off over her head. "Why won't they ask me?" She scowled as her mind slowly began to work. "And why are there so many people here?"

Sherry grimaced.

"Well, that's the other thing . . ."

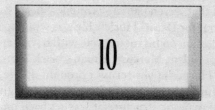

10

THE PROCESSION WOUND ITS WAY AROUND LILAC LANE and up the hill to the Hurley mansion. Arthur Kincaid led the way in a vintage Mercedes that still ran smoothly but had seen better decades. He was followed closely by the Applegates and the Hurleys, who kept vying for position as though the order of arrival at the house might in some way affect the outcome of the will. Phyllis Hurley Applegate was hanging right on his bumper in a Ford Fairlane with Pennsylvania plates, so as not to be edged out by Philip Hurley, tailgating her in a Chevy rental. The maneuvering involved considerable shouting and honking, and an occasional rude gesture.

Behind them came Chester Hurley, who had given a ride to the woman with the flat face. Chester's battered Ford pickup was more rust than metal, and clearly had no shocks. The woman jounced stoically along on the front seat, her head nearly hitting the ceiling on every bump.

Next came Cora and Sherry's red Toyota. Sherry was driving with one hand, and propping her aunt up with the other. Cora was wearing a seat belt, but her head and shoulders kept lolling forward in an unlikely position for anyone even remotely conscious, and Sherry was acutely aware of the fact that Aaron Grant's Honda Accord and Becky Baldwin's compact rental were following close behind. As if that weren't enough trouble, Sherry had to keep watching out for Daniel Hurley. He was weaving in and out of the procession on his motorcycle with boyish enthusiasm.

Bank president Marcus Gelman's black Mercury sedan and Chief Harper's police cruiser brought up the rear.

The Hurley house was impressive in daylight. An imposing and majestic structure, it was set back on the top of the hill in front of a circular drive. The sprawling three-story mansion featured garrets and cupolas and eaves and balconies. Recently painted blue with white trim, it resembled an elaborate wedding cake of Victorian design. The sheet of plywood over the window to the right of the front door was like an ugly scar.

Chief Harper took a look at the people piling out of the cars and shook his head. "I don't like this," he said. "This is a crime scene."

Cora Felton, who had been slumped on Sherry's shoulder, perked right up. "Crime scene? Where's the crime scene?"

Cora lurched toward the front porch, and nearly went head over heels off the first step, before Sherry managed to grab her and unobtrusively pull her back.

Fortunately, Arthur Kincaid had everyone's attention. "This may be a crime scene. But at this point the breaking and entering would seem somewhat moot."

"That's not what I mean," Chief Harper said. "The man is dead."

"Yes, but he didn't die here."

"Come on, come on," Phyllis Hurley Applegate said impatiently. "Open up. Let us in."

"Let who in?" Philip Hurley said. He pushed in front

of his sister. "Don't let yourself be rushed, Mr. Kincaid. We're all going in, but we can certainly take our time."

"I'm not so sure we're all going in," Chief Harper said. There were immediate cries of protest.

Marcus Gelman pushed forward. A balding, chubby man in a three-piece suit, he clearly would have been more at ease in his air-conditioned bank. He tugged a handkerchief out of his pocket, wiped the perspiration off his brow.

"Hold on now," he said. "I would like to make my position clear. I am here to carry out the instructions of the late Emma Hurley, who was one of my bank's largest investors. If you intend to stop me from doing so, Chief Harper, then you better do so legally and officially, so as to relieve me of my responsibility. Aside from that, I am charged with following the instructions of Arthur Kincaid. And if he tells me to open the door, that is what I am going to do."

This declaration was met with rumblings of approval from the heirs.

"All right, all right," Chief Harper said. "Let's calm down. I didn't bring you out here just to bar the door. I may not like this, but I didn't say I wouldn't go along. The only question is, Who's going in? Mr. Kincaid, as the solicitor, who do you want in there?"

"It's who Emma Hurley wants in there," Kincaid pointed out mildly. "That's all of the heirs with the exception of Kevin Holbrook and Mildred Sims, who have been given specific bequests and are not playing the game. But all the rest. And of course Miss Cora Felton, who is judging the event."

Cora Felton was standing next to the front porch with an owlish expression on her face. It was an expression Sherry knew well, Cora's I-am-sober expression, an expression, that to Sherry, indicated anything but. Sherry was standing with her arm unobtrusively around Cora's waist, keeping her from listing in any direction.

"And I will be accompanying my aunt," Sherry said.

"Why?" Phyllis Applegate demanded. "There's nothing in the will about *you*."

"I'm her assistant. I help edit her puzzles. If she's going to be the judge, she needs me to keep score."

"That's not fair," Phyllis objected shrilly. "We're not bound by your judgment."

Philip Hurley laughed. "Good move, Sis. Real bright. Pick a fight with the judge."

Arthur Kincaid put up his hands. "Please, let's not bicker. We're all here, we're all going in. Including all interested parties. Aaron Grant is not an heir, but he's covering this for the paper. And Becky Baldwin is my associate, and the attorney for the deceased Mr. Beasley. Aaron and Becky technically have no right to be here, but I would rather let them in than exclude them and have them ask why. Is that clear to everyone? Then let's go."

Marcus Gelman took a key from his pocket. He unlocked the front door. The Hurleys and Applegates nearly shoved him over in their haste to enter.

Chief Harper frowned. "All right now. We will have none of that. No crowding, no pushing. Arthur and I are going to go on ahead. You will all follow behind, giving us room. If you don't, we will stop. If you want to see this through, then behave."

In spite of this admonition, the Applegates and the Hurleys almost trampled themselves on their way up the front stairs. The rest of the entourage followed at a slightly more decorous pace.

Sherry and Cora brought up the rear, Sherry guiding her aunt with one hand on her shoulder and the other in the small of her back. Fortunately, no one was looking, for Cora resembled nothing so much as the heroine in a horror movie. Like Jeff Beasley, she recoiled from the knight with the ax in the foyer, and gaped at the hideous painting of old Evan Hurley at the top of the stairs.

"Where *are* we?" she muttered, utterly baffled.

"Shh," Sherry whispered. She led Cora into Emma Hurley's bedroom, where the heirs were already crowded around the rolltop desk.

"All right," Arthur Kincaid said. "This is the desk described in the will. Emma said the first clue was in the rolltop desk. You will note that the top is down, that it locks with a key, that the key is in the lock."

Arthur Kincaid put his hands on the bottom of the rolltop, pushed up. "It appears to be unlocked."

The top slid up and back, disclosing the interior of the antique desk. On the desktop was a large blue blotter, a jar of black ink, and a pen. Above it were two small wooden drawers, and a series of cubbyholes.

"The drawers, look in the drawers," Phyllis Applegate urged.

The first drawer contained several small stationery store items, such as pencils, erasers, and paper clips. The second drawer held scissors, tape, and a box of name tags that had clearly been used for wrapping gifts.

"Try the blotter," Daniel Hurley said.

"Huh?"

"The blotter." Daniel pointed. "It's in a frame. Pull the frame off."

Arthur Kincaid picked up the blotter. But he didn't have to pull off the frame.

"Look!" the heirs cried.

Under the blotter was a manila envelope. Arthur Kincaid took it, undid the clasp, and pulled out a stack of papers. He held the papers against the envelope, so that it shielded them from the heirs. He took one look; then he held the envelope and papers against his chest.

"Chief Harper, I think I'd like you to witness this," Arthur Kincaid said. "You too, Mr. Gelman. And you too, Ms. Baldwin. Due to the unusual nature of the circumstances, I would like another lawyer present."

"What circumstances? What are you talking about?" Phyllis Applegate was bewildered.

"Why don't you be quiet, Sis," Philip Hurley snarled, "and you'll find out."

"That would be good," Arthur Kincaid agreed. "And if you'd all stand back and give us a little room, I'll be able to hold this up so we can all see." He lifted the manila envelope and turned it around to show the paper on the other side.

It was a crossword-puzzle grid, similar to those that appeared in the daily paper.

This sight was accompanied by *oohs* and *ahs,* and intakes of breath.

"Is that what I think it is?" Daniel Hurley said.

"I should think so," Arthur Kincaid replied. "But I'm going to have our expert check it out. Miss Felton, what do you make of this? Is this Emma Hurley's puzzle?"

Sherry nudged Cora in the ribs. Cora's head jerked up. "Emma Hurley?" she mumbled.

"Yes," Arthur Kincaid said. "In your expert opinion, is this the puzzle mentioned in her will?"

"Dunno," Cora said. She crinkled up her nose, peered at the lawyer. "Is *she* the one?"

Arthur Kincaid frowned. "The one? What do you mean, the one?"

Cora Felton drew herself up, poked her glasses back on her nose, and elevated her chin.

"Well, she was murdered, wasn't she?" Cora declared.

There was stunned silence.

The heirs gawked at each other, too astonished to speak.

Sherry jumped in. "Aunt Cora. Don't be silly. Emma Hurley wasn't murdered."

"Oh?" Cora pouted. "I thought you said she was murdered. Didn't you say murdered?"

"No, no," Sherry said, trying to save the situation. "I said *Jeff Beasley*. The drunk. That's who was murdered."

"Oh." Cora's manner indicated this *clearly* wasn't as good.

"Now, just a minute," Arthur Kincaid objected. "That was an accident. Jeff Beasley wasn't murdered."

"So it *was* the old lady." Cora nodded complacently. "I thought so." With the prospect of a murder investigation she began to pick up steam. "And you want me to find out whodunit? Okay, let's check motives. Who profits if she's bumped off?"

Philip Hurley's mouth dropped open. "My God, the woman's plastered. Are you telling me *this* is our judge?"

Cora Felton fixed him with an evil eye. "Now, you see here, young man—" She broke off as she noticed Phyllis Applegate standing next to him. She blinked in amazement. "Why are there two of you?"

Before Phyllis could protest, Sherry jumped in. "Aunt Cora. This is not the murder. This is the other thing. The puzzle that you have to judge. They want you to take a look at the puzzle."

"She's in no shape to look at anything," Phyllis Applegate said.

"Oh, yeah?" Cora said. She thrust out her chin. "That's what you think. Let me see." She wheeled around, grabbed the paper out of Arthur Kincaid's hand. "Well, what do we have here? Ah, yes. Stupid puzzle." Cora looked at it. Her eyes crossed, then refocused. "*Very* stupid puzzle. No clues."

Philip Hurley, who'd been about to make an abusive comment, stopped himself. "Hey, that's right. Where's the clues? Aren't there any clues?"

Arthur Kincaid shuffled through the papers. "It would appear there are. Yes, here's a sheet of clues. And another which appears identical. Here, take a look."

He held up one of the pages.

Cora snatched it out of his hand.

On it was written:

ACROSS	DOWN
1. Italian village	1. Ricardo
6. _____ fall	2. Woodwind
13. WWII vessel	3. Entre _____ (fr)
14. Sharpen	4. Tibetan town
16. Place to woo?	5. Swear
19. Affirmative	6. Call
20. Ages	7. Deckhand
23. Useful quality	8. R.S.V.P.
	9. Youth
	17. Stockings

"It's the clues, all right," Cora declared.

Sherry Carter coughed discreetly.

Cora peered at the page again. "At least, they look like the clues. There's the *across*. The *down*." She stared at them. Frowned. "There aren't very many of them, are there?"

"There certainly aren't," Sherry said. "Good point, Cora. It would appear that a large number of these clues are missing."

"What?" Phyllis Applegate said. "What kind of flim-flam is this?"

Cora Felton's eyebrows launched into orbit. "Flim-flam?" she waved her arm, nearly lost her balance. "Are you accusing me of a flimflam?"

But Phyllis Applegate ignored her completely. "Where's the other clues?" she snarled at Emma's lawyer. "Are they there?"

Arthur Kincaid shuffled through the papers. "They are not. The rest of the papers are the same as the ones we have here."

"What about instructions?" Philip Hurley asked.

His sister turned on him. "Instructions? You need instructions? You don't know how to solve a crossword puzzle?"

"I don't know how to solve one without all the clues. And I don't mean instructions for solving the puzzle. I mean instructions on winning the game. If the clues aren't all here, how do you win?"

"Yeah, how do you win?" Cora Felton muttered, obviously intrigued.

"Well, there you are." Philip Hurley rolled his eyes at Arthur Kincaid. "Your 'expert' is no help, so *you* tell me. How do I win this game?"

"I don't know," Arthur Kincaid replied. "But I can make a suggestion. You have one piece of the puzzle here. I suggest you take it, go away, and work on it. Perhaps solving it will tell you what to do next. Perhaps it won't. But in the meantime, Cora Felton will solve it. So, if you're not clear what to do, you call her and ask her."

"As if *she'd* know," Philip Hurley snorted.

"Philip, don't be rude," his wife, Ethel, said.

"Rude, hell," Philip shot back. "Fifteen million smackeroos at stake, she's drunk, and nobody knows what to do. And *I'm* rude?"

In a lifetime of hard drinking, there was nothing that sobered Cora Felton up faster than someone calling her drunk.

"I know what to do," Cora said. "I don't know about you, but *I'm* solving this puzzle."

Her declaration might have sounded more convincing if she hadn't slurred her words; still it was enough to spur the heirs into action.

Philip and Phyllis Hurley looked at each other, and turned to the lawyer.

"Give me one," Philip said.

"Hey, I was first," Phyllis said.

"Were *not,*" Philip said.

"Now, now, don't push. There's enough for everyone," Arthur Kincaid said, handing them grids and clues. "And here's a set for you, Daniel. And one for Annabel." He handed sets to the bearded youth and the flat-faced woman. "And one for you, Chester." He held a set out to the old man with bad teeth.

Chester Hurley made no move to take the pages. He stood with his hands folded over the bib of his overalls, and snorted contemptuously. "Stupid game."

"You don't have to play if you don't want to," Arthur Kincaid told him.

"Damn right, I don't," Chester Hurley said. "I don't have to do anything. I'll take this because Emma wanted me to. Why, I don't know, but she did, so I will. But that don't mean I'm gonna play."

Chester Hurley stomped across the beautiful old bedroom in his work boots, snatched the grid and clues from the lawyer. "Come on, Annabel," he said to the woman with the flat face. "You want a ride, let's go. I'm gettin' out of here."

But he stopped in the doorway. "Stupid game," he repeated, and ushered Annabel out the door.

The remaining heirs all looked at each other for a moment, then turned and bolted for the door.

Only Daniel Hurley lagged behind. "I gotta go along with the old man," he said. He chuckled, shook his head. "Stupid, stupid game."

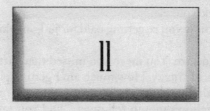

11

"OH, MY HEAD," CORA GROANED, AS THEY DROVE AWAY from the Hurley mansion.

"Could you look a little less like you're dying?" Sherry asked. "There's cars behind us."

"Who?"

"The banker, for one."

"Banker? What banker?"

"Aunt Cora, how much of what just happened actually registered?"

"Don't be disrespectful." Cora Felton jerked her thumb at herself. "I'm the judge!" She smiled, then frowned and looked puzzled. "What am I judging?"

"Aunt Cora."

"No, no, I remember. Some whacko puzzle." She frowned again. "Why am I judging a puzzle? I thought there was a murder."

"There may be a murder. It could be accidental."

"What could be accidental?"

"The drunk died in a drainage ditch."

"The dr— That's a tongue twister. You mean it's not a murder?" Cora sounded disappointed.

"We don't know. But right now we need to concentrate on the puzzle."

"Whacko puzzle."

"You know you're getting paid for judging this puzzle?"

"I am?"

"Yes, you are. You mean you missed that part too?"

"It's a trifle fuzzy. How much am I getting paid?"

"Fifty thousand dollars."

Cora Felton's mouth fell open. "Did you say fifty dollars?"

"Fifty *thousand* dollars."

"Fifty thousand? Sherry, can you solve the puzzle?"

"I don't know. I don't have all the clues."

"You don't have all the clues?"

"Cora, don't you remember anything?"

"It's a little vague. What about the clues you've got?"

"I haven't had time to look at them."

"Look at them now."

"I'm driving the car."

"I'll drive, you look."

"Not on your life."

Sherry drove on, ignoring Cora's protests.

At the gas station on the edge of town Sherry saw a motorcycle parked by one of the pumps. Daniel Hurley stood next to it talking to Becky Baldwin, who had pulled up alongside.

Sherry frowned. By rights, Daniel should be working on his great-aunt's puzzle, not talking to a lawyer. And why was Becky talking to him? Wasn't she leaving town? After all, her client was dead now. Sherry had to tell herself it was none of her business.

Sherry drove home, parked the car in the drive, shook Cora Felton awake, and wrestled her inside.

"Sherry," Cora said. "Thank goodness it's you. You gotta help me. Someone's dead, and there's a puzzle."

"There certainly is," Sherry muttered. She dragged Cora into the office, flopped her in a chair, and sat down at the computer.

"What are you doing?" Cora said. "You've gotta work on the puzzle."

"I am working on the puzzle."

Sherry moved the mouse and clicked on the Crossword Compiler icon. "This is how I work."

A blank crossword-puzzle grid filled the screen. A fifteen-by-fifteen grid of all-white squares. Sherry began to re-create the grid from Emma Hurley's puzzle on her screen. When she was finished, she had a grid exactly like the one on the piece of paper Cora had received from Arthur Kincaid.

She propped the clues up below it.

ACROSS

1. Italian village
6. _____ fall
13. WWII vessel
14. Sharpen
16. Place to woo?
19. Affirmative
20. Ages
23. Useful quality

DOWN

1. Ricardo
2. Woodwind
3. Entre _____ (fr)
4. Tibetan town
5. Swear
6. Call
7. Deckhand
8. R.S.V.P.
9. Youth
17. Stockings

Cora Felton peered over her shoulder. "Can you solve it?"

"I should think so," Sherry said. "In the first place, it's a quadrant."

"A what?"

"It's a quarter of the puzzle. All of the clues are from the upper-left quadrant. There are no clues from the other three quarters of the grid."

"Huh?"

"Tell you later," Sherry said. "Anyway, it's only a quarter of Emma Hurley's puzzle. I assume I can solve it. But what good will that do?"

"You got anything yet?"

"Sure. Six across. Blank *fall* has to be *prat*."

"Great. You're practically done." Cora put her arm around Sherry's shoulders, leaned on her heavily. The odor of stale Bloody Mary was overpowering. "What else have you got?"

"It's hard to concentrate with you bugging me."

"Hey. Let's remember who's the judge."

"Okay, Judge. Let's make a deal. Division of labor. I'll solve the puzzle. You get sober enough to tell people you solved it."

"Well, I like that," Cora said. She hiccuped, clapped her hand to her mouth. "Oops. On second thought, maybe I could make some coffee." She peered over Sherry's shoulder at the grid and chuckled.

Sherry looked at her in annoyance. "What's so funny?"

"I was just wondering."

"What?"

"How our heirs are doing."

12

"COME ON, COME ON, READ ME THE CLUES," PHYLLIS HURley Applegate snarled as she sped along the narrow country road.

"Slow down!" her husband squeaked. "What good will it do to solve the puzzle if you kill us all?"

"I'm not going to kill us all. I just got a little excited and drove in the wrong direction. It could have happened to anyone."

"Of course it could. Now slow down."

"And let Philip get ahead? No way. Read me the clues."

"You have to concentrate on your driving."

"I can concentrate."

"Phyllis."

"Read me the clues or I'll grab that darn paper and read 'em myself."

"Okay, okay. Give me a minute."

"Are there blanks?"

"Huh?"

"I thought I saw clues with blanks. If there's any clues with blanks, start with them. They're easier."

"Yes, there's two blanks. Six across. Blank *fall*."

"Waterfall."

"No, it's four letters."

"Why didn't you say so?"

"I'm saying so. Blank *fall*. Four letters."

"I don't know. Any others?"

"Yeah. Three down. *Entre* blank. Four letters. And it's French."

"French?"

"It says *fr*. Doesn't that mean French?"

"How should I know. You think I do crossword puzzles?"

"Well, that's the clue. *Entre* blank. You know what that is?"

"You have any damn clues in English?"

"One across. Italian village."

"*Italian* village?"

"That's what it says."

"I said in English."

"The clue's in English."

"The answer isn't. What else have you got?"

"Thirteen across. *World War II vessel*. Five letters."

"World War II, for cryin' out loud!"

"Phyllis, I didn't write these clues. I'm just reading them."

"Well, you're not making me happy."

"I know. And, Phyllis . . ."

"Yes?"

"There's some other clues aren't going to please you much."

"Such as?"

"Four down. *Tibetan town*. Three letters."

"Oh, for goodness sakes."

They were hurtling down the main street in town. Phyllis Applegate slammed on the brakes, skidded to a stop in front of the police station, waved the car behind her around, made a U-turn, and pulled up in front of the Bakerhaven library.

"Phyllis!" Morty shrieked. "You just made a U-turn in front of the cops."

"Big deal. There's no one there." Phyllis Applegate jerked the door open and got out of the car, cutting short her husband's protests. "Come on, you want Philip to beat us?"

"What are we doing here?"

"You know a three-letter word for Tibetan town?"

"No."

"Neither do I. Let's go."

Edith Potter the librarian looked up expectantly when the front door opened, but Phyllis Applegate ignored her, glanced around, and declared, "Oh, there's the reading room," in a voice loud enough to make Edith wince. Phyllis pushed by the front desk, stalked to the table, took out the puzzle and clues, and announced, "Let's get organized. First off, let's make a list of anything we need to look up."

An old man with a newspaper cast an evil eye in her direction and said, "Shhh!"

Phyllis Applegate took no notice. "Start in on the Italian village. If we get that, it will help with the Tibetan town."

Edith Potter appeared in the doorway. "I will have to ask you to keep the noise down. People are trying to read."

"Sure, sure, lady." Phyllis did not lower her voice one decibel. "Listen, where do you look stuff up?"

"Stuff?"

"Stuff you need to know. Like a town in Tibet. Stuff like that. Where would you find it?"

"If you keep your voice down, I can help you. If you're going to be loud, you'll have to leave."

"We'll be quiet as mice," Phyllis Applegate vowed, raising her voice for emphasis.

Edith Potter rolled her eyes and went and flushed her son, Jimmy, from the stacks, where he was at work shelving books. A tall, gawky boy of college age, Jimmy Potter had always been a little slow, but was a diligent worker, and loved to have a task.

"They want me to look stuff up?" Jimmy said.

"Yes," Edith Potter said. "Help them look stuff up, but try to keep them quiet. Make sure they don't disturb the other people in the reading room."

"Okay, Mom," Jimmy Potter said. And he certainly had the best of intentions. But when he saw they were working on a crossword puzzle, he completely forgot, and spoke right out loud. "Crossword," he exclaimed, and grinned a big grin. "You're working on a puzzle? Wow. Just like the lady on TV."

"Who?" Phyllis Applegate scowled.

"The Puzzle Lady on TV. Didn't you ever see her? She's right here in town, you know."

Phyllis Applegate nodded grimly. "Yeah, kid. We know."

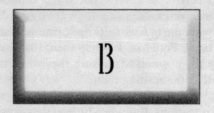

13

DANIEL HURLEY DUMPED CREAM IN HIS COFFEE AND pushed the pitcher across the table. Becky Baldwin added cream to her coffee, regarded him with interest.

Becky Baldwin was not used to men like Daniel Hurley. She was used to men who would defer to her sex, would make a point of offering her the pitcher first. The fact that he hadn't intrigued her.

It seemed absolutely casual. Just two people having coffee. He takes some cream, and offers her some. Treating her as an equal with no ulterior motive.

Or he takes cream first deliberately, as a calculated display of flouting the conventions.

Or he is merely young, stupid, boorish, and doesn't know any better.

Becky Baldwin peered at the man behind the beard, tried to determine which.

"You asked me for coffee," Becky Baldwin reminded him.

"Yes, I did," Daniel Hurley said. He raised his cup. "Cheers."

Becky Baldwin took a sip of the coffee, which was rather bad, evoking memories of the diner from her high school years. "Thank you. I just wonder how you can take the time."

"You mean when there's a puzzle to be solved?"

"Exactly. The other relatives took off like there was no tomorrow. I'm sure they're all working on it now. And here you sit, having coffee."

"And rather bad coffee at that," Daniel Hurley said. "You might have warned me. Or haven't you eaten here before?"

"Not in years. I would have thought by now they'd washed the pot."

"That's even worse," Daniel said, "if this place is so bad you haven't been here in years."

"It's not like I've been avoiding it. I've been away at law school."

"Oh, that's right. You're a lawyer." He frowned. "So, what brings you back to town?"

"Actually, I'm on my way to Boston. I just stopped off to see my folks."

"Oh? So you're staying with them?"

"Yeah. They have a house on Chestnut, just off Glen."

Daniel shrugged. "Wherever that is. I'm in a bed-and-breakfast up the street."

"Stone Mill Inn?"

"That's the place."

"What did the Walanders think of the motorcycle?"

"That's their name? I don't think they saw my bike until after I signed the register."

"They saw you, didn't they?"

"Yes, they did," Daniel Hurley agreed. "But they couldn't think of a reason not to rent to me. I bet they would have loved to be able to say the place was full."

"Uh huh," Becky Baldwin said. "So what do you do when you're not inheriting millions?"

"Well put," Daniel Hurley said. "You're right, I'm a bum, guilty as charged. I have no money. I drift from job to job."

"You've got a pretty neat motorcycle."

"Dad had some insurance. Don't ask me why. No car, no house, no possessions to speak of. And yet, a life insurance policy. Not large, but welcome. I immediately invested the money in a tangible expression of Father's accomplishments."

"Uh huh," Becky Baldwin said again. She took a sip of coffee, grimaced. "All right, you've waited me out. I can't take it any longer. You gonna look at the puzzle or not?"

"Is that why you agreed to have coffee with me?"

"Come on, give me a break," Becky said. "I don't know if I'm supposed to find this intriguing or what, but, frankly, your calculated indifference is getting on my nerves. Yes, I want to see the puzzle. I can't imagine why you *don't* want to see the puzzle."

"Okay," Daniel said. He fished two folded sheets of paper from the back pocket of his jeans. "Here you go."

Becky Baldwin smoothed the pages out on the table in front of her, and studied them eagerly.

Daniel Hurley watched her with some amusement. "So," he said, "you get anything?"

"Lucy."

"Huh?"

"One down is *Lucy*."

"Are you sure?"

She pointed. "The clue is *Ricardo*. So it's *Lucy*. From *I Love Lucy*. Lucy Ricardo."

"Why does it have to be Lucy? It could be Desi."

"No, it couldn't."

"Why not?"

"Because it's not Desi Ricardo. It's Desi Arnaz. It's *Ricky* Ricardo. And Lucy Ricardo. And Lucille Ball. If the clue was Arnaz, it could be Desi. And if it had five letters, it could be Ricky. But a four-letter *Ricardo* has got to be *Lucy*. See?"

Daniel shrugged. "Puzzles were never my thing."

"Really? Then how do you expect to win?"

"I don't know," Daniel Hurley replied pleasantly. "But I do know this. What I have here is only the first piece of the puzzle. So solving this, big deal. When someone solves this we'll find out the next piece of the puzzle."

"*They'll* find out the next piece of the puzzle."

"Maybe, maybe not," Daniel Hurley said. "I would say there's a good chance someone solving the first piece would result in a general announcement. In which case, I'll learn the same thing they do. Without lifting a finger."

"You don't know that."

"No, I don't. But I do know I'm no good at puzzle solving."

"You want help?"

"I thought you were just passing through."

"I was. But I got roped into taking a case, and now my client's dead. I guess I gotta stick around till that gets straightened out."

Daniel grinned. "And in the meantime, you'd like to help me solve the puzzle?"

"Not really. I was thinking of something else."

"Like what?"

"The whole setup. I'm not sure it's legally binding."

"What do you mean?"

"An elderly woman writes a holographic will without benefit of legal advice, and bequeaths an enormous fortune to the winner of a foolish game. If one wanted to, there would seem to be lots of grounds to contest such a will. Would that interest you?"

Daniel Hurley pushed his coffee cup aside, put his elbows on the table, leaned his chin in his hand.

"Tell me more," he said.

14

CORA FELTON NEARLY SLOSHED HER CUP OF COFFEE. "You solved it already?"

"Sure, I did. It wasn't hard. It's a simple, straightforward crossword puzzle. There are no tricks. It can be solved by anyone who's used to doing daily puzzles."

"By one of the heirs?"

"I don't know," Sherry said. "Frankly, none of them strike me as the type. But that doesn't mean they couldn't do it. Anyway, take a look at the puzzle."

"Sherry, I have a headache."

"I can't help that."

"And I'm no good at puzzles."

"That's why I'm going to explain it to you."

"I'm not great at explanations, either. This puzzle stuff leaves me cold."

"I know that. But you've got to know enough to fake it. You're the one who has to explain it to the heirs."

"Yes, I know. But—"

"Fifty. Thousand. Dollars."

Cora sighed. "Keep reminding me of that, will you?"

"Never fear," Sherry said. "Okay, take a look at this."

Cora Felton leaned in and looked at the computer. Sherry had typed in the answers to the clues in the grid.

LONGA
PRAT
UBOAT
HONE
COURTHOUSE
YES
EONS
N
ASSET
A
TE
E
G
R
E
R

ACROSS

1. Italian village
6. ______ fall
13. WWII vessel
14. Sharpen
16. Place to woo?
19. Affirmative
20. Ages
23. Useful quality

DOWN

1. Ricardo
2. Woodwind
3. Entre ______ (fr)
4. Tibetan town
5. Swear
6. Call
7. Deckhand
8. R.S.V.P.
9. Youth
17. Stockings

"Okay," Sherry told Cora. "Here's the solution to the first quarter of the puzzle. Or, what we have been referring to as the first quarter of the puzzle. Actually, it's somewhat less."

"How is that?" Cora said.

"Well, take a look. To begin with, let me explain something about the grid. There are four long clues in the puzzle, ten letters each. There's sixteen across, ten down, twenty-seven down, and fifty-eight across."

"And you got one. *Courthouse*."

"Right." Sherry nodded. "Sixteen across is *courthouse*. It's a pun. A rather bad pun, by the way. I mean, come on, *Place to woo* means *courthouse*? Really. Anyway, it starts in the upper-left-hand corner of the grid. Ten down starts in the upper-*right*-hand corner of the grid. Twenty-seven down *ends* in the *lower*-left-hand corner of the grid. Fifty-eight across *ends* in the lower-right-hand corner of the grid. While they're not exactly quadrants, the four long clues occupy four separate sections of the grid.

"Which is the point. All of the clues that we were given were for words that affect the long clue, sixteen across. Note that we are given clues seventeen down and twenty-three across. Note that we are *not* given clue twenty-five across, even though it is in the upper-left-hand quadrant. Why? Because the third letter of twenty-five across is also the first letter of twenty-seven down, which is the long answer for the lower-left-hand quadrant. See what I mean?"

"You lost me after *courthouse*."

"Aunt Cora. Try to concentrate."

"It's all Greek to me."

"Fifty thousand dollars."

Cora Felton grimaced. Sighed. "Run it by me again."

Fifteen minutes later, after Sherry Carter had delivered an impromptu lecture on crossword puzzles in general and this puzzle in particular, and Cora Felton had drunk three and a half cups of coffee, Cora said, "Okay, I call up the lawyer, I tell him I solved the puzzle and the solution is *courthouse,* the long solution for the quarter of the clues we have."

Cora pushed her glasses down on her nose, peered over them at Sherry. "It is my belief, world-famous cruci-whatchamacallit expert that I am, that the next set of clues will all relate to one of the other long answers. As to what it all means, I have no clue, but the word *courthouse* is certainly suggestive." Cora pushed her glasses back up again. "How'm I doin' so far?"

"Excellent," Sherry replied. "As long as you don't try to pronounce *cruciverbalist,* he'll never suspect you don't know what you're talking about."

"Thank you so much," Cora said happily. "And since the clue is *courthouse,* I suggest he meet us at the courthouse, so we can put our heads together and try to come up with the other clues."

"Fine, but lay off the *us,*" Sherry said.

"You're not going?"

"I'll go, but stop referring to me. You're the big-deal Puzzle Lady. I'm just the helpful, secretarial person. It's not *we* did this, *we* think that. It's *I* solved the puzzle. *I* have a theory. Look at *my* solution."

"I can't play humble?"

"Humble is tough when you have so much to be humble about."

"Hey, don't get nasty," Cora said.

"And don't you be silly," Sherry said. "Your credibility is not high at the moment. I don't know how much you remember about our trip to the Hurley house, but you happened to accuse the heirs of murdering their aunt. That and the fact you almost did a header into the four-poster bed puts you on rather shaky grounds."

"Murdering their aunt?"

"Instead of looking at the crossword puzzle, you announced to the world in general that Emma Hurley had been killed. Not the brightest move you could have made."

Cora Felton pursed her lips. "But not that off-the-wall either, with fifteen million dollars involved."

Sherry snorted in exasperation. "Aunt Cora. Please. Emma Hurley was a very old lady who died of natural causes. So get murder out of your head and concentrate on the crossword puzzle."

"But I *like* murders," Cora grumbled. "I don't *like* crossword puzzles."

"Do you like money?" Sherry asked.

"Yes, I do." Cora nodded. "Point well taken. I like *this* crossword puzzle. Come on. Let's go call the shyster."

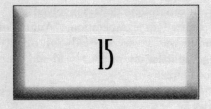

15

HARVEY BEERBAUM SEEMED NERVOUS. CHIEF HARPER
sensed it immediately. Not that he'd had that many murder
investigations—he certainly hadn't—but Chief Harper had
been a policeman for years. He had investigated robberies,
assaults, traffic accidents, enough to know when witnesses
were cooperating fully, and when they were holding something back.

Not that there was anything to withhold. Still it *was* a
homicide. Medical examiner Barney Nathan had con-
firmed that fact. Jeff Beasley had been struck from behind
with a blunt object. So *someone* had killed him. *Someone*
was guilty.

Could that someone possibly be Harvey Beerbaum?

Chief Harper didn't think so. Harvey Beerbaum looked
more like a computer nerd than a killer. True, some killers
were that way. Quiet, loners, kept to themselves. In Harvey
Beerbaum's case, however, Chief Harper just couldn't see
it. Sneaking up behind someone, bashing him on the
head ... The image of a weapon in the hands of Harvey
Beerbaum was laughable.

And yet there was something.

"You saw him in the parking lot?" Chief Harper asked.

"Oh, yes," Harvey Beerbaum answered. "Quite drunk, and quite obnoxious. I'm sorry Mr. Beasley's dead, but that's a fact."

"What did he do?"

"Hassled the kid on the motorcycle."

"Daniel Hurley?"

"If that's his name. The boy with the beard and long hair."

"Why did he hassle him?"

"I don't know. Is it really important? I mean, I'd like to help, but I am quite busy, and—"

"Just a few more questions," Chief Harper said, and once again sensed something wasn't right. He'd really just begun, and as for busy, how busy could Beerbaum be? The man was at home in the middle of a workday, so he didn't have a nine-to-five job. And while he'd just moved into Bakerhaven, his house was in no way unsettled. In fact, the living room in which they now sat was immaculately furnished, down to the least little knickknacks adorning the bookshelves and the walls. It was so well put together, Chief Harper would have suspected Harvey Beerbaum had rented it furnished, had it not been for such personal touches as a framed crossword puzzle over the bookcase, and a trophy on the mantelpiece on which Chief Harper could see the name *Beerbaum* inscribed.

"Where are you employed, Mr. Beerbaum?"

Harvey Beerbaum blinked. "That's your question?"

"No, I'm just curious. You mentioned you were busy."

"Well, I am. Perhaps not in a way you recognize. I'm self-employed. I'm a writer and a constructor."

"Constructor?"

"I construct crossword puzzles. And write books about them."

"You do this for a living?"

"I do not," Harvey Beerbaum said. "I do it for fun. It provides me a living, but that's a bonus. I happen to relish my work."

"I'm glad to hear it," Chief Harper said. *Relish*. "And that's what you're so busy at?"

"Did you ever attempt to construct a crossword puzzle, Chief?"

"No, I did not."

"Well, trust me, it's hard work. Enjoyable, but hard. One gets a train of thought going. And when it's interrupted . . ."

"It's hard to get back to," Chief Harper finished pleasantly. "But since I've already interrupted, you might as well just go with the flow. You'll get back to your puzzle soon enough."

Harvey Beerbaum took a breath, exhaled in exasperation. "So what do you want to know?"

"When Jeff Beasley accosted Daniel Hurley in the parking lot, what went on?"

"I don't know. I couldn't hear. I saw him stagger over, toward the boy. I saw him put his hand on the motorcycle."

"Jeff Beasley put his hand on the motorcycle?"

"He grabbed the handlebar, yes. Possibly to keep from falling, but he did grab it."

"What did the boy do?"

"Pushed him away."

"*Pushed* him?"

Harvey Beerbaum held up his hands. "Oh, now, look. Don't put words in my mouth."

"They're your words," Chief Harper pointed out. "You said, *pushed him.*"

"Maybe *shooed him* would be better. Or *brushed him off.* I wouldn't want to give the impression the boy did anything violent."

"But he did push Beasley away?"

"In a manner of speaking."

"I see. What did Beasley do then?"

"He went back to him. Which shows it wasn't a violent encounter. If it had been violent, he would have gone away. Or fallen to the ground. A man that drunk would have trouble keeping his feet."

"Okay," Chief Harper said. "Jeff Beasley grabbed the handlebars, Daniel Hurley pushed him away, Jeff Beasley came back. What happened then?"

"Beasley said something to him—I don't know what— and then stood there, gesturing. *Not* grabbing the motorcycle. At least he'd learned that lesson. And the boy didn't push him again."

"Did he drive off?"

"Who? The boy?"

"Yes. Daniel Hurley. Did he drive off on the motorcycle?"

"Not while I was watching."

"So you drove off and left the two of them in the parking lot?"

"I drove off. Whether that left the two of them in the parking lot, I can't say. I didn't pay the slightest attention to either of them once I started my car."

"And earlier in the bar, did you overhear Jeff Beasley talking to anyone?"

Harvey Beerbaum hesitated.

"Yes?" the Chief prompted.

Harvey Beerbaum waved his hand. "No, no, it's nothing. It's just I don't want you getting the wrong idea."

"About what?"

"Well, it's the boy again."

"Daniel Hurley?"

"Yes, but it was nothing."

"What was nothing?"

"What he said."

"Which was?"

"Beasley was amused by him. He thought it was funny the boy was there."

"Yes, but what did Beasley say?"

"Prodigal son."

"Huh?"

"That's what he said. Prodigal son."

"I see," Chief Harper said. Actually, he didn't. He had no idea what *prodigal son* meant, but he was damned if he was going to let Harvey Beerbaum know that. "And what do you think he meant?"

"He was drunk and rambling, and reacting to the boy's appearance. I would attach no importance to it whatsoever."

"Uh huh," Chief Harper said. He tried a few more questions, which got him absolutely nothing, and left him fairly dissatisfied with the interview. For the life of him, he couldn't figure out what it was Harvey Beerbaum was hiding.

Chief Harper got in his car and drove off.

Harvey Beerbaum watched the patrol car leave from his dining room window. He waited until Chief Harper reached the end of the block, turned left on Main, and drove out of sight. Beerbaum let the blinds fall back into place, went to the study, opened the door, and let the Hurleys out.

"It's about time," Philip Hurley complained.

"Yes," Ethel Hurley whined. "I thought he'd never leave."

"Did you hear?" Harvey Beerbaum asked.

"Every word," Philip said. "What's this about him and Daniel had a fight?"

"Not a fight. A discussion."

"Hey," Philip said. "Let's not mince words. A discussion

could be an argument could be a fight. The fact is, those two were mixing it up. And if this drunk is dead and there's anything suspicious about it, it's Daniel the police should be suspicious of."

"Maybe so, but that's not what I said."

"I never said it was," Philip snapped. "Ethel and I are certainly not suggesting that you say anything that isn't true. But what you did say is dead right. The only one the drunk really talked to was Daniel."

"Enough about Daniel." Ethel was getting impatient. "Come on, come on. I've gotta know. Can you solve this thing or not?"

"Before the policeman arrived," Harvey Beerbaum reminded her, "I was explaining my position."

"And I was explaining mine," Philip Hurley countered. "I stand to inherit a bunch of money. You stand to be cut in on it. Now, all the will says is whichever of us heirs solves the puzzle first gets the money. It doesn't say anything about how we solve it, it doesn't care anything about that. And *I* think the smartest way to solve a puzzle is to hire an expert. It occurs to me that's what the smartest heir would do, and the smartest heir ought to inherit. And, since there's nothing in the will that precludes that possibility, it seems to me the smartest heir, the one who ought to inherit, should be *me*."

Philip Hurley smiled at Harvey Beerbaum. "Now, can you point out any flaw in that logic?"

16

Arthur Kincaid stood waiting on the courthouse steps. Sherry Carter pulled by, parked in the lot, and she and Cora walked back to meet him.

"You solved it already?" Arthur asked Cora, skeptically. His manner implied he was surprised to find she was even upright, let alone lucid.

Cora Felton bristled. "Yes, I did," she snapped.

"The solution is *courthouse?*"

"Yes, it is." Cora took a breath, plunged ahead. "And it's either a dead-end solution, or it happens to be the next clue. If the next clue is *courthouse,* now what could that mean?"

"I have no idea," Arthur Kincaid said. "But this is the only courthouse in the district."

"That's what I thought," Cora said. "Tell me, did Emma Hurley have any dealings in the courthouse in the later part of her life? Anything at all that would have brought her in this vicinity?"

"The answer is no. For the last six months Emma Hurley was confined to her home. Trust me, she went nowhere. Certainly not near the courthouse. As to the last time she was here, I really couldn't say. She might have had jury duty, but that would have been years ago."

"That doesn't sound promising," Cora said. "All right, let's try the courtroom."

"Court might be in session," Arthur Kincaid pointed out.

It wasn't. The courtroom was empty. They entered from the back, made their way down the aisle to the rail.

In spite of her best intentions, Cora Felton was not entirely sober, and at the sight of the empty courtroom she just couldn't help herself. "I've always wanted to do this," she said. She came through the rail, walked up to the judge's bench, and smiled. "Your Honor. Ladies and gentlemen of the jury. This witness has told a very interesting story, but he happens to have testified to several things that are not true. I intend to cross-examine him on them now." She turned to Arthur Kincaid. "How is that?"

"Actually," he said, "you're not supposed to make a speech before you cross-examine a witness."

Cora Felton waved this away. "But you lawyers always do, don't you? Though you're awfully good at pretending that's not what you're doing. Look at Perry Mason."

Before Arthur Kincaid could protest, Cora Felton had hopped up to the bench, sat in the judge's chair, and picked up the gavel. "Overruled," she growled. "And let me warn you, another outburst like that, and I will clear the courtroom."

"Miss Felton—"

Cora banged the gavel. "Silence! Order in the court!"

"Cora . . ." Sherry warned, pointing over her shoulder.

Cora banged the gavel again. "What's the matter, didn't you hear me?"

"*I* heard you," Judge Hobbs said dryly from behind the bench.

Cora Felton turned with a start. "Oh, Your Honor, I

didn't realize you were there." She got up from the chair. "I hope I'm not in contempt of court. No, that's silly. Court's not in session. Oh, you know what I mean. Don't you? Sure you do."

Judge Hobbs countered Cora Felton's babbling with an impassive stare. "Arthur, what's going on here?"

Arthur Kincaid shrugged helplessly. "It's the Hurley will. Old Emma Hurley's got the heirs on some weird treasure hunt, and one of the clues appears to lead here."

"Here? To the courthouse?"

"Yes. And Miss Felton's been appointed judge of the contest. I'm afraid she took her role too seriously."

"Well, no harm done," Judge Hobbs said. "But what do you mean the clue leads here? I don't really want the heirs swarming over my bench."

"I assure you that won't happen. We'll keep them out of here. It's just, if there is a clue, we have to find it. So the others won't have to look."

"Now, wait a minute," Cora interjected. "Suppose the heirs *have* to come in here? Suppose the next clue is painted on the ceiling? And the only way they can find it is if they come in here, sit down in the chairs, and look up?"

"Nonsense," Judge Hobbs said. "I assure you there is nothing painted on the ceiling."

"Of course not," Arthur Kincaid agreed.

In spite of these assurances everyone looked at the ceiling. There was nothing there.

"Let's check out the witness stand," Cora Felton said. "Is there any chance Emma Hurley would have been on the witness stand?"

"Not as a *juror*," Arthur Kincaid said.

"Too bad," Cora Felton said, undaunted. "There's something attractive about the witness stand. Let me see. If I were to sit here . . ." Cora Felton sat on the witness stand, looked out over the courtroom. "And if I had something to hide . . ." She looked around. "I would be hard pressed to do so." She peered under the chair. "And it doesn't look like anyone has."

"Of course not," Judge Hobbs told her. "That's utterly ridiculous. You expect to find something scrawled in lipstick on the bottom of my witness stand?"

"We don't know what we expect to find," Cora said. "We only know we need to look. Let's try the jury box. There should be twelve chairs, right? For the twelve jurors."

"Sixteen," Judge Hobbs said.

"I beg your pardon?"

"There's sixteen chairs, for the twelve jurors and four alternates."

"Yes, I see," Cora said. She batted her eyes at the judge. "Thank you for pointing that out."

Sherry Carter suppressed a smile. Her aunt had been married several times, and Judge Hobbs was not all that elderly.

Sherry Carter began inspecting the bottom of the wooden chairs in the jury box. They were attached together and bolted to the floor. The seats flipped up, which made them easy to inspect. Sherry Carter started at one end of the first row, and Cora Felton started at the other. They met in the middle.

"Nothing here," Sherry reported.

They moved to the second row.

It was under the third chair.

Sherry flipped the seat up, and there it was.

"Got it," she said.

Cora Felton, Arthur Kincaid, and Judge Hobbs crowded around to look.

A manila envelope was taped to the bottom of the seat. There were strips of masking tape across all four corners. One corner had pulled free and was hanging down. The other three still held in place.

"Okay, this is obviously it," Cora said. "So what do we do? Leave it in place, or remove it from the seat?"

"We've already settled that," Arthur Kincaid said. "Judge Hobbs is not going to allow his courtroom to be used for any scavenger hunt. If this is what I think it is, we are going to take it outside."

"Great," Cora said. "Sherry, take it off the seat."

Sherry pulled the masking tape off the bottom of the seat, and held up the envelope. It wasn't sealed, it was fastened with a metal clip. Sherry straightened the clip, opened the flap, reached in, and pulled out the sheets of paper.

"More puzzle clues?" Cora asked.

"Take a look," Sherry said. She passed the pages over.

It was indeed another set of puzzle clues.

ACROSS	DOWN
10. Pod dweller	10. Place to go after
15. Going, going, gone	leaving skating rink?
18. Norway capital	11. They (fr)
21. Idle talk	12. Love
24. "I shot _____"	15. Desert succulent
("Standup Comic")	22. Entertain
28. Swallow up	29. Bites
31. Side order	33. Secondhand
32. Enjoyment	34. Loch _____ monster
38. Exact	39. Hansoms
43. High pair	
46. Sticks in	

"It's another set of clues, all right," Cora said. "Apparently for the next quadrant of the puzzle."

"What about these new clues?" Arthur Kincaid asked. "How long will it take you to decipher them?"

"I won't know till I try."

"Can you do it now?"

Cora shook her head. "I can't work with people looking over my shoulder."

"If we leave you alone—"

"No!" Cora said sharply.

Arthur Kincaid frowned.

Cora Felton smiled contritely. "I'm sorry," she said. She lowered her voice confidentially. "I'm just a little embarrassed. I forgot to bring the grid. So I really *can't* work on these clues till I get home."

"But you can solve it, can't you?" Arthur Kincaid asked.

Cora Felton smiled, the trademark smile from her crossword-puzzle column photo, and patted him on the cheek.

"Piece of cake."

17

THE ANSWERING MACHINE WAS BLINKING WHEN THEY got home. Sherry Carter walked over to the shelf next to the kitchen wall phone and pressed the button.

Beep.

"Hello? Cora Felton? Is that you? It's not your voice. Is that the other one? The woman who came with you? Is this the right number? If it is, this is Philip Hurley. And I solved the puzzle. It's three-seventeen P.M., please make a note of that: Philip Hurley is done at three-seventeen. Give me a callback and let me know what I'm supposed to do next."

Philip Hurley repeated his phone number twice just to be sure. "Please call me right away. I'll be standing by. And if for some reason this is *not* Cora Felton's phone, please call and tell me that too, so I can get the right number."

"Uh oh," Cora Felton said.

"Yeah," Sherry said. "Wanna bet right now the man is driving Information crazy trying to verify the number?"

"It's in my name," Cora pointed out.

"Even that may not satisfy him. The guy sounds frantic. Wanna give him a call?"

"No, I wanna solve the puzzle."

"Be my guest."

Sherry handed Cora the manila envelope.

Cora looked betrayed. "Sherry. Don't be silly. I mean, I want *you* to solve the puzzle."

"Thought it was a piece of cake," Sherry teased.

"Well, if you're going to quote every little thing I say. But if you wanna start solving the puzzle, I'll be happy to look it over while you work."

"It's a deal," Sherry said.

The phone rang.

Cora Felton's face fell.

Sherry walked over to the wall phone, scooped up the receiver. "Hello."

"Hi, Sherry. It's Aaron."

"Oh, hi."

"Listen, I just heard from Chief Harper. It's official. The Jeff Beasley case is a homicide."

"You're kidding."

"Nope. He finally got the medical report. Which confirms it couldn't have been an accidental death."

"Does he have any leads?"

"If so, he didn't say. The fact it's a murder is all he's giving out."

"I see."

"You getting anywhere with the puzzle?"

Sherry waited a beat. "Cora's working on it."

"Then I guess I should be asking her. But you must know. What's the deal? You got anything for publication?"

"What's the matter? Isn't a homicide enough?"

"It would be if I had any facts. I got Chief Harper saying it's a homicide. I got Barney Nathan saying that's his finding. And I got Henry Firth saying something should be done about it. All of which is mighty thin, even if the victim had been someone of importance. The fact he was the town drunk doesn't help."

"You're saying all citizens don't have equal rights under the law?"

"Give me a break. Who's talking equal rights? Celebrities sell papers. As it is, it's a toss-up whether my managing editor picks the Beasley murder or the Hurley will for page one. So, if you had something to tip the scale . . ."

"You must know we can't."

"Does that mean you do?"

"Aaron."

"Sorry. It's the reporter in me."

"Sherry," Cora said. "Stop flirting and get off the phone." Sherry quickly covered the mouthpiece. "Aunt Cora!"

"Any other time, dear. Right now, you're busy."

"Aaron, I gotta go. Call you later."

"Okay. Bye."

Sherry Carter hung up the phone, turned around to glare at her aunt.

Cora Felton put up her hands. "I'm sorry. Any other time. Right now we've got work to do. We got the puzzle, plus we got this doofus on the answering machine I gotta call back."

"Right. What are you going to tell Philip Hurley?"

"I don't know. By rights, I should give him the next part of the puzzle. But I don't want to give it out when you haven't even solved it yet."

"But as soon as I do, you will?"

Cora Felton frowned. "Not quite. This is why I get the big bucks. What's that lawyer's number? Let's give him a call. Before someone else calls us and ties up the phone."

Cora Felton looked up Arthur Kincaid's number, punched it in.

The lawyer was surprised to hear from her so soon. "You mean you solved it already?"

"No, I haven't, thank you very much. But I've had a phone call from Philip Hurley, claiming he's solved the first part. Which is all well and good, but I don't intend to have these people traipsing over to my house at all hours of the day and night. So here's the deal: Would you kindly inform the heirs that I will meet them all in your office at ten o'clock tomorrow morning? At that time, any of them who present me with the correct solution to the first set of clues will receive the next part of the puzzle."

"Philip Hurley is not going to like that," Arthur Kincaid said.

"No, I don't imagine he will," Cora Felton retorted. "Which is why I thought I'd let *you* be the one to tell him."

"Thanks a lot," Arthur Kincaid said. "Any reason for this decision?"

"None that I'd like you to give out. But if the rest of the puzzle is the same, that is, if the solution keeps telling us where the clues are hidden, I don't want any chance of anyone solving it first and beating us to them."

"Good point."

"*You* wouldn't happen to know where the next clue was hidden, would you, Mr. Kincaid?" Cora asked sweetly.

"Of course not. How could I?"

"It's rather obvious Emma Hurley didn't tape that envelope to the bottom of the seat in the jury box. Someone must have done it for her. I'm wondering if that was you."

"Then let me set your mind at rest, Miss Felton. Emma Hurley did not entrust me with any such mission. The puzzle came as much a surprise to me as it did to anyone. As soon as you solve it, I'm dying to know the answer. So don't wait till ten o'clock tomorrow, give me a call."

"And you'll contact the heirs?"

"I'll call them," Kincaid promised. "Which doesn't

mean they won't call you. They're not going to be happy. You might let your answering machine pick up."

"Thanks for the advice," Cora said, and hung up the phone. "You get the gist of that?" she asked Sherry.

"Kincaid didn't plant the clues?"

"So he says. Whether I believe him or not is another story. Anyway, we stall on giving out these clues until tomorrow morning. Which gives us time to solve the puzzle and find the next set of clues before anybody else does. Arthur Kincaid suggests we let the answering machine pick up from now on, and I think that's a pretty good plan."

The phone rang.

Sherry and Cora looked at each other.

"Fine," Sherry said. "We'll let it pick up."

The machine answered on the second ring. Sherry Carter's voice said, "You have reached 555-4827. We're not in right now, but please leave a message after the beep."

Beep.

"This is Chief Harper. Please call me right away. I got the autopsy report on Jeff Beasley, and—"

Sherry Carter snatched up the phone. "Hi, Chief. We're here. We're just screening calls. I hear Jeff Beasley's a homicide."

"You hear right. How'd you hear so fast?"

"Aaron Grant called."

"It's a wonder the boy has time to write. Is your aunt there?"

"Yes, she is."

"Put her on, willya? I gotta ask her something."

Sherry handed the phone to Cora.

"Hi, Chief," Cora said. "We got us another murder?"

"*I* have another murder," Chief Harper corrected. "But I could use your help."

"Sure thing, Chief. You need me out at the crime scene?"

"No, but I want your help with one of the witness statements."

"You got it, Chief. Who we gonna grill?"

"You're not gonna grill anybody. The questioning's already been done. I need your help with something someone said."

"What's that?"

"Prodigal son."

"Huh?"

"Prodigal son. That's what the witness said. Jeff Beasley used the term *prodigal son,* so I need to know what it means."

Cora Felton waved her hand, and her eyes flashed distress signals to Sherry Carter. "You want me to define the term *prodigal son?*"

"That's right."

Sherry mouthed a word, but Cora couldn't catch it.

"I thought you wanted me to interrogate a witness," Cora said, stalling for time.

Sherry Carter grabbed a piece of paper, wrote *wasteful, extravagant* on it, and handed it to Cora.

Cora squinted at the scrap of paper. Frowned. "*Prodigal* means *wasteful* or *extravagant,* Chief."

"Wasteful or extravagant?"

"That's right."

"So a prodigal son . . . ?"

"Is a wasteful, extravagant son."

"That's less than helpful."

Sherry drew a halo around the top of her head with her finger, then pantomimed opening a book.

Cora gawked at her.

Sherry grabbed the paper, scribbled *Bible.*

"Excuse me, I think I hear the doorbell," Cora said.

"What?" Chief Harper said.

Sherry scrawled *parable* under *Bible*.

Cora squinted at the paper. "Yeah, could you hold on. I think there's someone at the door." She buried the receiver in her stomach, glowered at Sherry. "I can't *read* that."

"It's a parable from the Bible," Sherry hissed. "The prodigal son loses all his money, then returns home, and his father takes him in and kills the fatted calf."

"What?"

"And his brother's jealous," Sherry added.

Cora looked at Sherry, then at the phone, then back at Sherry. Cora's mouth was open and her eyes were wide. She blinked, then reached up on the wall and pushed the button on the phone, breaking the connection.

"Oops," Cora said. "Oh, what a shame. The Chief got disconnected." She glared at Sherry. "Don't ever get a job as a mime."

"Don't ever get a job as a linguist," Sherry countered.

"Never fear," Cora vowed. She released the button, was rewarded by a dial tone. "Now, before the Chief has a coronary, fill me in on *prodigal son* so I can call him back."

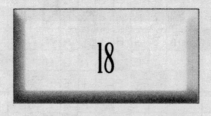

18

"OKAY, I GOT IT," SHERRY ANNOUNCED.

"Have you really?" Cora was nursing a tall gin and tonic. "I was close to it myself. As a matter of fact, I had narrowed ten across, *pod dweller*, to either *pea* or *man*."

"*Man?*"

"You know, like in a space capsule."

"It's *pea*."

"So, what's ten down? *Place to go after leaving skating rink?*"

"*Post office.*"

"*Post office?*"

"Sure. It's another terrible pun. *Post* is *after*, and *leaving skating rink* is getting *off ice*."

"*Post office.* Of course. So that's where the next clue is. Of course it's probably closed by now."

"I would imagine," Sherry said. "It's nearly seven."

"No wonder I'm hungry. Pity I never learned to cook. Do you suppose that's why I could never hold a husband?"

Cora kicked her feet off the couch. "Come on, let's see the grid."

ACROSS

10. Pod dweller
15. Going, going, gone
18. Norway capital
21. Idle talk
24. "I shot _____"
    ("Standup Comic")
28. Swallow up
31. Side order
32. Enjoyment
38. Exact
43. High pair
46. Sticks in

DOWN

10. Place to go after
    leaving skating rink?
11. They (fr)
12. Love
15. Desert succulent
22. Entertain
29. Bites
33. Secondhand
34. Loch _____ monster
39. Hansoms

Together, they peered at the screen.

"Nice job," Cora said, approvingly. "You seem to have filled in all the clues. I would be inclined to let you move on."

"You mean if the post office weren't closed?"

"Exactly." Cora smiled. "At least, we've accomplished one thing. By not giving out these clues, we can be assured no one will be breaking into the post office tonight to try to get the next set."

"Unless we do?" Sherry said.

Cora Felton looked at her. "You wanna?"

"I was joking."

"Where's your sense of adventure?"

"I know where *yours* is," Sherry said, indicating the gin and tonic.

"Don't snipe. I hate it when you snipe. It only makes things worse."

"Sorry. I just wanted to make this very clear. I am *not* breaking into the post office."

"Fine. You wanna break into the Hurley house?"

Sherry's eyes widened. "Aunt Cora!"

"Just a thought. Anyway, it would probably be easier than the post office."

"And just why would you want to break into the Hurley house?" Sherry asked suspiciously.

"I thought we might find a clue."

"A clue to what?"

"Sherry, just because everyone says Emma Hurley wasn't murdered doesn't mean it isn't true."

"Oh, for goodness sakes. Emma Hurley was dying. Everybody knows that."

"Is a dying woman immune to poison? I read this Agatha Christie where—"

"I can't believe we're having this discussion. You're getting paid fifty thousand dollars to referee a crossword-puzzle treasure hunt. But that's not exciting enough for you. You have to invent a murder."

"Invent? What do you mean, invent? Jeff Beasley was killed, wasn't he? If someone killed him, why not her?"

"Cora—"

"After all, Beasley was found in her bed."

"Exactly," Sherry said. "And that's what put the idea in your head in the first place."

"That doesn't mean it's wrong."

"No, Cora. *Common sense* means it's wrong. Anyway, I'm not breaking into the Hurley house."

"Oh, all right," Cora pouted. "Point well taken. Now, if we could return to *my* point. About food. Since you've been cracking puzzles instead of cooking, we don't have any. Food that is. You wanna go out and eat?"

"Where? To the Country Kitchen?"

"I was thinking of something more downtown. You know. Near the post office."

"Aunt Cora."

"It doesn't hurt to go *by* the post office. It's not like I was going *in* the post office. But it doesn't hurt to look."

"The only place I know downtown is the Wicker Basket."

"So?"

"I was there yesterday for lunch. If I show up again, people will think I can't cook."

"There's nothing wrong with people who can't cook."

"I didn't say there was. I just don't happen to be one of them."

"So, you wanna go eat, or not?"

"I guess I am hungry," Sherry admitted. "You wanna call Arthur Kincaid, tell him you solved the puzzle?"

"Nope, let him sweat," Cora replied. "We're gonna see him tomorrow morning, ten o'clock, that's soon enough."

"Fine," Sherry said. "Whaddaya say let's go?"

"You wanna change?" Cora said.

Sherry was wearing jeans and a cotton shirt. She grinned. "To go out with you? I think not. Of course, if you'd like to change, in case you should run into that judge . . ."

"Why, Sherry Carter. The very idea." Cora considered the dress she was wearing, frowned, shrugged, then headed for the bedroom. "I'll only be a minute."

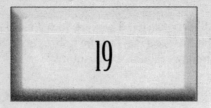

19

CORA FELTON LOOKED QUITE FETCHING INDEED IN A LIT-
tle red number that had been one of her former husbands'
favorites, and while she'd been embarrassed to discover she
could no longer remember which former husband had
been partial to the dress, she had been pleased enough at
how she looked in it not to mind Sherry's ribbing about
how it would appeal to Judge Hobbs.

Or that it was about as unobtrusive as a fire engine.

As Cora Felton walked around the post office, she had
to admit she certainly stood out.

"It's all right," she told Sherry. "It's not like I was going in."

"I never thought you were," Sherry said.

"Well, I'm not." Cora frowned. "Do you suppose there's
a back door?"

There was a back door to the post office. It was locked.
Nor was there any suitable back window. Cora Felton reluctantly completed another circuit of the building, returning to the sidewalk in front.

Cora shrugged her shoulders. "Well, when you're right, you're right," she said. "Whaddaya say we go eat?"

"I favor it over breaking and entering," Sherry said pleasantly. She gestured to the front door, where a sign proclaimed the post office hours. "It opens at eight o'clock. We'll be here first thing in the morning."

"I hate getting up," Cora said.

"I can always come without you."

"Over my dead body. Okay, where's the restaurant?"

"Right around the corner," Sherry said. "Come on. I'm starved."

They walked around the corner to the Wicker Basket. The dining room was half full. Cora Felton, cynical after her many marriages, half expected to find Becky Baldwin dining with Aaron Grant, but the only one she recognized in the restaurant was Daniel Hurley, who was dining alone at a table in the corner.

A young waitress, most likely home from college for the summer, guided them to a table on the other side of the room.

Cora Felton sat down opposite Sherry, picked up the menu. "What do you recommend?"

"Avoid the gazpacho. Aside from that, you're on your own."

The young waitress returned with her notepad. "Do you need a moment?"

"We could order drinks," Cora Felton said decisively. "Do you have a liquor license?"

"We have wine by the glass."

"What's good?"

"The house cabernet's quite popular."

"Let me try a glass."

"And for you?" the waitress asked Sherry.

"I'll have a Diet Coke."

"Have you always been a teetotaler?" Cora Felton said as the waitress left. "Or is it just since we've been living together?"

"Aunt Cora. I was married to an abusive drunk."

"I know."

"I know you know." Sherry picked up her menu. "So what you gonna order to go with that wine?"

"Oh, I'm no good at this. That's the trouble. A martini goes with everything."

"What a charming philosophy."

"So help me out. What's the cuisine?"

"It's American eclectic."

"What the heck does that mean?"

"Basically, don't expect much." Sherry giggled, glanced around to make sure she hadn't been overheard. "Will you listen to that, I'm a snobby New Yorker."

"The salmon filet sounds good," Cora said, "with green salad and rice pilaf. Or do I have to have white wine with fish?"

"Oh, absolutely," Sherry said. "Otherwise you'll wind up on the front page of the *Bakerhaven Gazette*. PUZZLE LADY FLOUTS CONVENTIONS, CHOOSES WRONG WINE."

"Well, excuse me for asking," Cora said, "but you're so finicky about my image."

"It's the quantity, not the etiquette."

"Ever the wordsmith," Cora said, ironically.

Sherry raised her eyebrows. "Uh oh. Look who's here."

Daniel Hurley walked up to their table. In his boots and motorcycle jacket, he looked extremely out of place in the Wicker Basket, as if he were not there to eat dinner, but had merely stopped to ask directions. Although asking directions would have seemed uncharacteristic also.

"Hi there," Daniel Hurley said.

"Good evening," Sherry replied. "How's your dinner?"

"I've had better."

Sherry noticed he didn't bother to lower his voice or look around to see whether anyone overheard. "Oh? What did you have?"

"Veal piccata. I should have realized it was risky." Daniel smiled at Cora Felton. "Well, you seem to have sobered up."

Cora Felton bristled. "I *beg* your pardon?"

Daniel Hurley took no notice, went on as if perfectly sure of his welcome. "Listen, can I ask you something?"

"Not if it has to do with the puzzle," Cora said curtly. "I'm off duty till tomorrow morning."

"Yeah, I got your message," Daniel said. "The lawyer called my bed-and-breakfast. Funny. The woman who runs the place—she's been treating me like I crawled out from under a rock—and then the lawyer calls, suddenly she realizes I'm a Hurley heir, and now butter wouldn't melt in her mouth."

"I take it you didn't disillusion her," Cora said.

"What's to disillusion? I *am* a Hurley heir."

Cora Felton waggled a finger. "Technically, you're a *potential* Hurley heir. The outcome of the will is yet to be determined."

Daniel waved this away. "Yes, of course. That wasn't what I wanted to talk to you about."

"Oh? And what was?" Cora wondered when her wine would come.

Without asking permission, Daniel pulled up a chair and sat down at their table. He leaned in conspiratorially. "All right, look. You know this cop. You've worked with him before."

"Chief Harper?" Cora Felton asked innocently.

"Yeah, him. Harper. What's his story?"

Cora shrugged. "No story. Just a small-town cop doing his job."

"Does he know his job?"

"Why do you ask?"

"He hassled me this afternoon. Came to see me at the bed-and-breakfast, asked me a whole bunch of questions about this guy who croaked."

"Jeff Beasley?"

"Right. And we went through all that this morning. As I pointed out. But now Harper's got all these new questions, like did I see him in the parking lot—which I already told him, yes, I did—but here he is asking again like it's a new idea. He's basically asking me for an alibi, and how can I have one when I live in a bed-and-breakfast and no one sees me come in?"

"What happened in the parking lot?" Cora asked innocently.

Daniel Hurley turned to her. "You too? You're asking that too?"

Cora Felton smiled. "It's a relevant question. You're the last person to see the victim alive. Of course I'm curious. What did he want?"

Daniel Hurley held his hands apart, gestured with them. "That's the whole thing. I don't know. Here's this incoherent drunk latching on to me as I'm trying to leave. If I had a car, I'd climb in, lock the doors, and that would be the end of it. But, wouldn't you know it, the bike doesn't start the first time and hangs me out to dry."

"And what did Beasley do then?"

"He laughed. He said, 'You're never gonna get the money, are you?' "

Cora blinked. "You mean the inheritance?"

Daniel shrugged. "Your guess is as good as mine. All I know is that's what he said."

"Fascinating."

"Yeah, the cop seemed to think so too. As if I'm responsible for what some old drunk says. Anyway, he goes on and on about where I live, what I do—the cop, not the drunk—as if that had anything to do with it."

"I wouldn't let it worry you," Sherry said. "Cops ask everything. It's what they do. And if they don't know what they're after, their questions can be way off the point."

"I'll say," Daniel said. "But I have to tell you, it doesn't feel good when it's a murder they're asking about. Which I understand this now is. And, guess what? The cop doesn't tell me that straight off. He asks all his questions. *Then* he springs it on me. *And, by the way, this is a homicide.* Which, the way I understand, would make anything I told him inadmissible in court."

"You spoke to a lawyer?" Sherry said.

Daniel Hurley grimaced. "Actually, I did. That Baldwin chick. I asked her the score. Granted, she's new at it, she's not going to know everything. But she's pretty sharp. I'd be inclined to believe what she says."

Sherry Carter looked at him narrowly. "Chief Harper upset you enough that you consulted a lawyer?"

Daniel Hurley grinned. "You're pretty sharp too. No, of course not. I was talking to Becky about the other thing. You know, Auntie's will. No offense meant, but, frankly, puzzles aren't my bag. It occurred to me there might be some way around this whole competition."

"You asked Becky Baldwin to break the will?" Sherry said.

"I asked her to look into it. Which certainly couldn't hurt. In the meantime, nobody's running away with it. Not with only part of the puzzle given out. So why not take my shot?"

Sherry frowned. "I thought Becky Baldwin was just passing through town."

"She is. But she's gotta stick around until the Beasley thing gets straightened out. Why shouldn't she pick up some cash on the side?"

"Why, indeed?" Cora Felton said sweetly. "So how come you're not dining with her?"

"She's out working on my case."

"Oh?"

"She went to pump that newspaper reporter, see if she can dig up any dirt."

Cora Felton carefully refrained from looking at Sherry. "How very interesting. You mean about the will contest?"

"No. About the murder. I called Becky after the cop left the bed-and-breakfast, said he's treating me like suspect numero uno. Becky said she'd dig around, see what she could get."

"I'll bet she did," Cora Felton muttered.

Daniel Hurley scowled. "You think I'm in trouble?"

"How could you be?" Cora Felton said pleasantly. "You didn't do anything wrong."

"Well," Daniel Hurley said. "I guess I read too many murder mysteries. The cops always seem to pick the wrong man."

The waitress arrived with Cora's wine and Sherry's Diet Coke. "Will there be something else?" she asked Daniel Hurley.

"No, I'm just on my way out," Daniel told her.

He got up from their table, went over to the cashier, paid his check. Then he went back to his table and left the tip. He flashed the waitress a dazzling smile as he went out the door.

"Wanna order?" Cora asked Sherry. "Or have you lost your appetite?"

"Of course I wanna order," Sherry snapped.

"I thought maybe we should pop by the paper, get the latest dope."

"Becky Baldwin's doing that."

"Yes. You think she'll share the info with us?"

"Aaron will."

"Then we're going over there?"

"Not at all. When I talk to him, he'll tell me."

"You're just going to ignore the fact Becky Baldwin's over there right now?"

"Yes, I am. It's none of my business where Becky Baldwin is right now."

Sherry called the waitress over and ordered dinner. She ordered the penne with dried tomatoes and mushrooms; Cora ordered the salmon filet.

"There," Sherry said, as the waitress scurried off to the kitchen. "I'm going to put it out of my head, sit here and enjoy my dinner."

"I wouldn't be too sure of that," Cora Felton said darkly.

Sherry frowned. "What?"

Cora Felton raised her eyebrows, gestured with a look over Sherry's left shoulder.

Sherry turned and looked.

Bearing down on the table was one of the heirs.

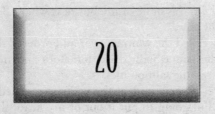

20

"I'M SORRY TO BOTHER YOU AT DINNER," THE FLAT-FACED woman said, "but I was walking by the restaurant and I saw you in the window."

Cora Felton's smile matched the one in her TV ad. "Is that so? And just what is it that you want?"

"May I sit down? I don't want to impose, but I find I get so tired these days." Without waiting to be invited, the woman slumped into the chair Daniel Hurley had just vacated. "Oh, that's better. Have you eaten yet? I don't want to interrupt."

Cora Felton started to say they'd just ordered, but was pretty certain the woman would take that as an invitation to join them for dinner. Instead, she repeated, "What is it that you want?"

"It's about the will."

"I'm not discussing the will," Cora told her. "I'm not discussing the puzzle. I can't give you any help. I can't answer any questions or make any rulings. Anything you wanna know, ask me ten A.M. tomorrow in the lawyer's office."

The woman seemed flustered. "No, no, you misunderstand. I don't mean about the puzzle."

"What do you mean, then?"

"Do you know who I am? You're new in town, the two of you, so maybe you don't know who I am. Or who Emma Hurley was, for that matter."

Both Cora and Sherry looked perplexed.

"I'm Annabel Hurley. Alicia Hurley was my mother. Emma Hurley's sister." After a pause, she added, "Emma Hurley's *older* sister."

Cora Felton frowned. "So?"

Annabel Hurley paused. "Do you know any of the background?"

"Assume I don't," Cora Felton told her. "Spit it out."

"I'm talking about the will. The old will. Evan Hurley's will."

"*Evan* Hurley?"

"Then you *don't* know. I figured you didn't, being new in Bakerhaven, and all that. Evan Hurley was my grandfather. I was a girl when he died, but I remember him. Tight-fisted, miserly, strict. Puritanical. It's his will I'm talking about. The one that left the family fortune to Emma. The one that cut my mother out."

"Why?" Cora Felton said.

"Why, indeed? My mother was the eldest. Evan's money should have gone to her. Or to Chester, as the eldest son. Or even to Randy's children. Instead, it went to *her*."

"Why?" Cora repeated, less patiently.

Frown lines wrinkled Annabel's flat face. "Goody Two Shoes. That's what Emma was. Little Miss Goody Two Shoes." Her lips compressed in a grim line. "And Mamma wasn't."

"What do you mean?"

"Mamma was wild. By Grandpa Evan's standards. She and Daddy weren't married. That's why I'm a Hurley.

Why I have her name." Annabel Hurley sighed. "Daddy died when I was two. Mamma never married. She mourned his death with alcohol and men. Grandpa didn't like that. He tried to control Mamma the best he could, was always butting into our business.

"Right up until he got sick. Cancer. Treatment wasn't so good then. Doctors gave him six months. Evan lasted ten. Long enough to write a new will."

"And that's the will you wanna talk about?"

"That's the one. That's what did my mother out of her rightful inheritance. That's the reason Emma Hurley had any money to give."

"And your point is?" Cora Felton asked.

Annabel Hurley sniffed. "I'm getting to it. You have to understand the background."

Cora Felton was sorely tempted to tell Annabel Hurley she didn't have to understand anything, she hadn't asked for this conversation, and if Annabel didn't want to say squat, that was okay with her.

Except Cora wanted to know.

"A week before he died, Grandpa called Mamma in and told her the facts of life. I was young but I understood, at least the gist of it. Grandpa didn't approve of Mamma, Grandpa wanted Mamma to straighten herself out, Grandpa was revising his will to make sure she did.

"Mamma thought she knew what he meant. A trust fund of some type. A provision stating she couldn't touch the principal until she was forty or fifty or so. That she was prepared for. But not the other."

"He cut her off?"

"Not entirely. He left her ten thousand dollars. Just like Emma's doing now. Just to rub it in. He left ten thousand to her, ten thousand to Chester. Ten thousand to each of Randy's kids—Philip, Phyllis, and Jason. Randy was dead by then—killed in a car crash. His widow, Jean, might have expected better, what with three little kids to raise. But Grandpa set no store by spouses. Or grandchildren, for that matter. He cut them off with only ten thousand each.

"Same as Mamma." Annabel Hurley sniffed again. "He left the rest to Emma. Free and clear. To do with as she liked."

"It was his money," Cora pointed out. "I guess he had a right to do so."

"A team of lawyers studied the language in that will. They couldn't break it."

The waitress slid salads in front of Sherry and Cora, and looked inquiringly at Annabel, who shook her head.

"I still have no idea why you're telling me this," Cora said as the waitress moved off.

"I just want you to have the background, that's all. And the background is a monumental injustice. Because Emma Hurley was not what she seemed. Goody Two Shoes, that's what Grandpa saw. But Emma was sharp, Emma was crafty, Emma was *sly*."

"How do you know this?"

"A lot is what my mother told me, and, granted, she'd be prejudiced. But I've also seen for myself. I knew Emma many years. In the humiliating capacity of a poor relation. And Emma wasn't the saint Grandpa thought she was. The real Goody Two Shoes was Chester. He was the real chip off the old block. A grim, prim, straitlaced Hurley. Only Grandpa had a blind spot. And Emma poisoned his mind against Chester. I don't know how she did it, but she did. Or he never would have cut him off."

Cora Felton picked up her fork, poked at her salad. "What's this got to do with the present will?"

"It's all wrong. In the same way Grandpa's will was wrong. It's arbitrary and unfair. Which makes sense to me, if Emma wrote it. I would expect her will to be arbitrary and unfair, compounding the sins of her father."

"Suppose it is," Cora Felton said. "What do you expect me to do about it?"

"I expect you to figure it out. That's what you're good at, isn't it, figuring things out? And not just the puzzle. That's not important—no disrespect meant—I know puzzles are important to you. I mean the *reason* behind the puzzle. What Emma was getting at. What she meant in the will."

"Uh huh," Cora said. "And just what was that?"

"Well, that's the thing. She said that the puzzle was forty years old, that it was out of the ordinary, that it was complex, and that it would take cunning and ingenuity to solve it. Which makes no sense. In the first place, Emma didn't do crossword puzzles."

"How do you know?"

"I know Emma. And she didn't do them."

"Maybe not normally. But she was confined to her bed. She might have gotten bored, wanted something to do."

Annabel Hurley looked at Cora Felton skeptically. "You mean this was a new preoccupation? Which is why I didn't know about it?"

"Isn't that possible?"

"In that case, where did a *forty-year-old* puzzle come from?"

Cora Felton frowned.

"But that's beside the point," Annabel Hurley continued. "Emma talks about the puzzle being special and challenging. Yet here you hand me a perfectly ordinary crossword puzzle that could have come out of the daily paper. What's so special about that?"

"It didn't have all the clues," Cora pointed out.

"But I have to assume eventually we'll get all the clues. Otherwise, what would be the point? And, once we do, what have we got? What if it turns out we have a perfectly ordinary crossword puzzle? My question to you is, what does it mean? Never mind who solves it first. I know that's your primary concern. You determine who solves it first, and that person gets all the money. But what does the puzzle itself *mean*? That's what you need to determine."

"That's what *I* need to determine?" Cora Felton said.

"Exactly. Emma Hurley named you. She entrusted you with the job of finding the solution to her puzzle. And your responsibility goes beyond solving some crossword puzzle. It goes to interpreting what these things mean."

Sherry Carter had been studying Annabel Hurley's face during this long exchange. "Let me ask you something," Sherry put in. "Have *you* tried to solve the puzzle?"

"No, I haven't."

"Why not?"

Annabel Hurley rubbed her chin. "That's a complicated question. I guess the answer is money doesn't matter to me. Maybe at one time it did, but not now. I get ten thousand just for losing. That's more than I need. And, as for the rest . . . I wouldn't want to win it to have it. Only to keep the others from getting it. And that's no way to go through life. You have to let go."

Cora Felton frowned. "I'm not sure I understand."

"You really don't have to understand," Annabel Hurley told her. "As long as you're willing to figure it out. And not give the money to the first person who claims it."

"I think you can trust me on that score," Cora Felton said. "Was there anything else?"

Annabel Hurley hesitated. "What you said this morning—at the house—about Emma being murdered—you weren't serious, were you?"

Cora looked at her sharply. "Why?"

"You seemed a bit . . . confused." Annabel Hurley said it delicately. "So I don't know if you mean it. But I have to tell you. I don't think it's true. But I wouldn't put it past them."

"Them?"

"Any of them. But Philip and Phyllis in particular. They had it in for Emma ever since she kicked them out. But you don't know that either. Emma took the kids in after their mother died. Or, perhaps, took them in is the wrong choice of words. Moved in on her is what they did. After all, they were grown by then. They certainly could have set out on their own, if they hadn't happened to have a rich relative."

"You said she threw them out," Cora Felton prompted, but Sherry could see she was interested.

"Yes, she did, and who could blame her? After her money, every last one of them. Well, maybe not Jason. But certainly the twins."

"*Why* did she throw them out?" Cora persisted, sounding a little impatient.

"Philip was a schemer, was always trying to get Emma to invest in his shady deals. Of course, she never would. But he used her name without her knowledge—something about collateral—so that when his deal fell through, the investors came back at her."

"I see," Cora said. And she did. Her fourth husband, Henry, had a weakness for business deals. "And that was when she threw Philip out?"

"Yes. And Phyllis too. That's why she hates him so much. Phyllis, I mean. Why she hates her brother. Not that it wasn't always a fierce rivalry, but she blames him for that."

"What about Jason?"

"Oh, he was long gone by then. Off on some romantic lark or other. The house was empty after Emma threw out the twins. Just as it's been ever since."

"So, when you say you think they're capable of murdering your aunt, it's Philip and Phyllis you're talking about?"

"Don't get me wrong." Annabel Hurley looked Cora Felton right in the eye. "I don't for a minute think they killed her. I'm just saying they *could* have. So you must make sure they didn't."

Annabel Hurley got up from the table, started for the door. She turned back. "The boy. Jason's son. Do you know where he's staying?"

"A bed-and-breakfast. I don't know which one, but it must be near here."

"How do you know?"

"Because he was in here for dinner, and I didn't hear his motorcycle."

Annabel Hurley smiled. "Ah, you *are* good at figuring things out. I just know you'll be able to solve Emma's puzzle." She smiled again, and went out the door.

"Did you hear *that*?" Cora Felton asked Sherry. "*She* thinks her aunt was murdered."

"She thinks nothing of the kind," Sherry scoffed. "She ridiculed the suggestion."

"She said Philip and Phyllis had a motive."

"Yes, but she doesn't think they did it."

"She said she thought they were capable of it, and asked me to look into it."

"She asked you to *eliminate it as a possibility*," Sherry said.

"Right," Cora said. "And that's *exactly* what I intend to do."

Sherry didn't like the gleam in her aunt's eyes. "Aunt Cora."

"You don't want to break into the Hurley mansion?"

"No, I do *not*."

"Okay. Compromise. How about the post office?"

"Aunt *Cora*. We are not breaking in *anywhere*."

"No, of course not," Cora said. She pushed her salad

around with her fork. Considered. "Still, it is a small town."

"So?" Sherry said suspiciously.

Cora Felton shrugged.

"I wonder where the postmistress lives."

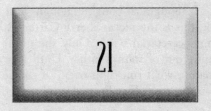

21

SHERRY CARTER MANAGED TO DISSUADE CORA FELTON from rousting the postmistress from her bed to let them in, but could not prevent her aunt from dragging her to the post office at seven-thirty the next morning.

"In case she opens early," Cora said, steamrolling over arguments to the contrary.

It was all Sherry could do to grab a cup of coffee before her aunt whisked her out the door. Cora Felton was bright-eyed, bushy-tailed, and sober. It was not lost on Sherry that having a mystery to unravel was helping her aunt tread the straight and narrow.

"I bet that's her," Cora Felton said at five minutes to eight when a front door opened three houses down the block.

Sure enough, the woman bustling down the front steps was the one Cora had bought stamps from just the week before.

The postmistress came walking up. She was an exceptionally plump woman with red hair and bright rosy cheeks. She smiled when she recognized Cora Felton. "It's you. I thought it was you. What brings you here so bright and early?"

Cora Felton smiled back. "No stamps. I have deadlines, and no stamps. I feel like such a fool. I was in here in just last week. I thought I bought enough. But I thought wrong. Oh, this is my niece, Sherry Carter. A big help to me with my secretarial work. Only she didn't notice we were running out of stamps either. Until this morning. I said, no matter, we'll run right over. Of course, we didn't know when the post office opened until we looked on the door."

The postmistress said, "Aha." Her tone had become slightly less cordial. "Well, I certainly hope you won't make an issue of it. There are those who think I should open at seven-thirty. I have to tell you, that is just too early. There is not enough demand." She slipped back into bubbly mode, smiled at Sherry Carter. "Hi, I'm Betty Roston. And I don't mean to complain. It's just some people like to tell other people how to do their jobs."

Betty Roston pulled out her keys, unlocked the front door. She ushered them in, flicked on the light switches on the wall.

The Bakerhaven post office was an L-shaped affair, at least the part for the public was. The L was formed by the rectangular room where Betty Roston worked. On the short, front wall of the room was a door and a postal window. On the long side wall were the individual mailboxes.

Betty Roston unlocked the door to the inner room and slipped inside. Lights went on, and moments later the frosted postal window slid up.

Betty Roston leaned out, smiled at Cora Felton. "Now, what kind of stamps would you be wanting?"

Sherry Carter left the two of them negotiating and looked around.

On the long wall of the post office were two counters

with various postal labels—insured mail, return receipt requested, change of address forms—as well as several Express Mail and Priority Mail envelopes approximately the same size as the manila envelope that held the first set of clues. It occurred to Sherry if the clues were hidden in one of those they would be very hard to find.

Sherry walked over to the counters. Glancing back to make sure she wasn't seen, she bent down, looked under the first counter. There was nothing there, but there certainly could have been. There was a lip around the countertop that would have hidden anything taped underneath.

Sherry moved to the second counter, bent down, looked up.

And there it was.

An envelope, just like the one in the jury box, taped in the same way.

Sherry glanced swiftly over her shoulder to make certain no one was looking, then reached up and pulled the envelope off.

The post office door opened.

A man came walking in. He was looking right at Sherry. He saw her hastily straighten up. If this interested him, he didn't show it. He had an envelope in his hand. He walked right in, headed for the postal window.

Sherry heaved a sigh, put the envelope down on the counter.

And here he came again. He'd evidently dropped his letter in the slot, and now he was headed straight for her.

Sherry had a moment of incredible panic, which was totally irrational, because, of course, she wasn't doing anything wrong. So what if the man saw her take the envelope? At worst she'd have to call Chief Harper and straighten things out. Sherry's heart was beating very fast.

The man paid no attention to her. He moved over and unlocked one of the little mailboxes.

Sherry turned her attention to the envelope. She unobtrusively tore off the masking tape from each of the four corners, wadded it up, and threw it in the wastebasket under the counter. The manila envelope was now no different than any other piece of mail. Sherry flipped it over, checked the seal. Like the one in the jury box, the envelope was fastened only by the metal clip. Sherry pulled the prongs back, opened the flap, looked inside.

Sure enough, it was another set of puzzle clues. Sherry didn't bother reading them. She closed the flap, bent the metal clips back in place, folded the envelope in half, and walked over to her aunt.

"Got your stamps, Cora?"

Cora Felton smiled, and indicated the postmistress, who was leaning on the counter to talk to her. "Actually, Betty and I were chatting about the puzzle. The whole town's talking about it, of course. Everybody knew Emma Hurley, isn't that right? So everyone wants to know where her money's going."

Betty Roston's plump face registered amused indignation. "Well, now, that's not how I put it. But everyone's certainly interested in those heirs. Been a long time since most of them been around."

"And some of them never," Cora said meaningfully. "Like this Daniel Hurley."

"I haven't seen him yet," Betty Roston said. "Though I heard the motorbike going by."

"There aren't any other motorcycles in town?" Sherry said.

"Oh, I'm sure there are. And some do go by. But not at two in the morning. That's when I heard his. Loud enough to wake the dead. Granted, didn't wake my husband, but certainly the dead."

"That's funny," Cora said. "You seen any of the other heirs? Any of them come by here?"

"Not the out-of-towners. Philip and Phyllis I remember, of course. I haven't seen them since they've been back. They haven't been around. Of course, you wouldn't expect them to. Them that lives here's another story."

"Emma Hurley used to come here?"

"All the time. Up until the poor old thing took sick. After that, of course, no. She still bought stamps and mailed letters, but it was the housekeeper that always did it. Mildred Sims. You know her? She's sort of an heir, isn't she? Came into some money."

"How do you know that?" Cora Felton asked. "Was she in here yesterday?"

"No, I heard it from someone."

"One of the heirs?"

"Right. Not one of the out-of-towners. One of the locals who's in all the time."

"And who would that be?"

"Annabel Hurley. Told me about the will. Just yesterday afternoon."

"Annabel Hurley was in here?"

"Large as life. Told me about Mildred Sims. I was glad to hear it. Fine woman, Mildred. Hardworking. Long-suffering. Deserves every penny she got."

"I'm sure she does," Cora Felton said. "What did Annabel Hurley come in for?"

"First-class stamps, same as you. Why do you ask?"

"Oh, no reason," Cora said. "It's just, well, so many things happened yesterday. The heirs heard the will, and found out about the puzzle, and got the set of clues. I don't know, you'd think an heir would be too busy to be buying stamps."

"I know what you mean." Betty Roston nodded. "But Annabel said she's not playing."

"Oh?"

"She said she doesn't do crossword puzzles. They bore

her to tears. And she's not after Emma's money, she's just interested to see how it all comes out."

"That's quite a way to feel about it."

"Isn't it? Though, in her case, I suppose it's true."

"Uh huh," Cora said. "I don't suppose any other heirs were around here yesterday?"

"Not that I noticed," Betty Roston replied. "Of course, you wouldn't expect them to be."

Cora Felton nodded. "I certainly wouldn't."

22

"WHAT WAS THAT ALL ABOUT?" SHERRY SAID AS THEY drove away from the post office.

"Is that the envelope?"

"Sure is."

"Clues in it?"

"Sure are."

"You look at 'em yet?"

"Just enough to make sure that's what they were."

"What's twenty-seven down?"

Sherry smiled. "Why, Cora, I'm impressed. You've actually paid enough attention to know twenty-seven down is the next long clue."

"So what is it?"

"Close recycling place, so to speak?"

"So to speak? What the hell does that mean?"

"I won't know till I solve it."

"And what about *close*. Is that *close* as in *shut down*?"

"Right."

"Really? Wouldn't that be a verb?"

"Aunt Cora, you're getting better and better. I bet you could solve this whole thing yourself."

"Oh, stop it. Puzzles aren't my thing. Mysteries are. And look what's happened here."

"What's happened here?"

"Annabel Hurley was in the post office yesterday afternoon. Where she had no right to be."

"But if she's not playing the puzzle . . ."

"Do you buy that? I don't. I *hate* puzzles, and I can't help trying to solve this one. And I don't stand to inherit umpty million dollars for doing it. No, the only way this makes sense to me is if Annabel Hurley isn't working on the puzzle because she already knows all about it."

"And how would she know that?"

"Because Emma Hurley took her into her confidence."

"Oh, come on."

"What's wrong with that? It had to be someone. Emma Hurley's laid up; she can't move. She has this elaborate plan to set up. She needs someone to do her legwork. Why not a close relative living in town?"

"But if they were estranged . . ."

"What makes you think they were?"

"The way Annabel Hurley talked about her. How Emma pretended to be this paragon of virtue but she really wasn't, she was scheming and cunning."

"Right," Cora said. "But that was all in the past."

"Huh?"

"That was forty years ago. When Emma Hurley came into the money. By tricking her father into thinking she was something she wasn't. That doesn't mean Annabel feels the same way now."

Sherry sighed. Sometimes life seemed more complicated than puzzles.

Cora Felton reached over, tapped the manila envelope.

"When Annabel Hurley was in the post office yesterday afternoon, I bet you a nickel she was planting these clues."

"I thought your theory was the lawyer planted the clues."

"Yeah, but I could be wrong."

"No kidding."

Cora Felton turned into the service station on the outskirts of town.

"We need gas?" Sherry asked.

"No, I'm just stopping a second."

"Why?"

"Because I'm having a thought."

"You don't wanna get home and work on these clues?"

"I think this might be more important. If Annabel Hurley planted these clues, it kind of all fits."

"No, it doesn't," Sherry said.

"Why not? It explains why she's not working on the puzzle."

"But not what she said about it. Which was, that she doesn't understand it because Emma Hurley didn't do crossword puzzles."

"Right," Cora said. "That's one of the things that makes me know she and Emma Hurley were close."

"Yeah, but it's not just that," Sherry argued. "Didn't she also tell you to scrutinize the crossword puzzle very carefully because she can't believe there can't be more to it than just a simple solution? If Annabel was in league with Emma Hurley, wouldn't she know *all* about the puzzle?"

"Not necessarily. Emma Hurley may have given her instructions on planting the clues without telling her what the puzzle meant." Cora sounded quite certain of her theory: her eyes were bright with satisfaction.

"Then why isn't she playing the game?"

"That was part of the deal. She's Emma Hurley's secret accomplice, so she has to stay out of it."

"But why would she do that? Screw herself out of all that money? By *not* playing she doesn't get any more than anybody else."

"She doesn't get any more now," Cora Felton said.

"What do you mean?"

"What was to stop Emma Hurley from giving her something *before* she died? For all we know, the woman already got a million bucks and is walking around laughing at everyone."

"Then what was last night all about?"

"Exactly what I said. Annabel was taken into Emma's confidence, but only to an extent. She may or may not know the solution to the puzzle, but even if she does, she doesn't know squat about what it means. And she's desperate to know. Not for any material gain. Just to know."

"Fine," Sherry said. "Maybe you're right. Now, would you mind telling me what we're doing in this gas station?"

Cora put the car in gear, drove past the pumps to the phone booth on the far side of the lot.

"I wonder if there's a phone book," Cora said.

There was. It had a listing for an Annabel Hurley at 14 Green Street.

"Where's Green Street?" Sherry asked.

"Back near the post office."

"You know Green Street?"

"No, but it figures. Annabel said she saw us in the window when she walked by the restaurant. She probably lives real near."

She did. Green Street was two blocks from the post office, and ran parallel to Main Street. Fourteen Green Street was three blocks down.

It was an insurance company.

The two-story frame house had doubtless at one time been a private home, but a wooden sign by the front door read BECKER & TAYLOR INSURANCE.

"Are you sure this is the right address?" Sherry said.

"No, I'm not. But it's the one in the phone book. Maybe there's a side entrance."

There wasn't, but there was one in the back. A wooden door with glass windowpanes. Through them Sherry and Cora could see a narrow stair leading up to the second floor.

To the right of the door was a metal mailbox with the name A. HURLEY. Underneath the mailbox was a bell. Cora Felton pressed the button decisively. They heard the chime ring upstairs.

"You suppose it's like New York and they buzz you in?" Cora said.

"I would tend to doubt it."

"Then she'll have to come downstairs. It's barely eight A.M. If she's still in bed, she won't be happy."

"She won't be happy anyway," Sherry said. "We could have called first."

"I didn't want to give her time to make up a story." Cora pushed the button again. "Miffed, I can handle. I prefer not to be lied to."

They waited several seconds. There was no response. Cora pushed the bell again.

"Maybe she went out to breakfast," Sherry said.

"It's pretty early."

"*We're* up."

"Yes, but we had a reason."

"Maybe she did too."

Cora rang the bell one more time. She pressed her ear to the door, listened, reached out, and tried the doorknob.

"What are you doing?" Sherry said, her heart sinking.

The door clicked open.

"I can't get used to country living," Cora said. "The woman doesn't even lock her door."

"Yeah, because no one barges in on her," Sherry said. "And we're not about to."

"No, we're not," Cora agreed sweetly. "I'll go in alone. You stay here, warn me if someone comes."

"That's not what I meant—" Sherry began, but Cora was already pushing the door open. Ahead of her was the narrow stairs.

Cora turned back to Sherry. "If someone comes, push the bell. If it's her, ring twice."

Cora closed the door and went up the stairs.

At the top was a tiny kitchen with a pantry alcove and a breakfast nook. It was immaculately clean. There were no dishes in the sink, or even on the drain board. Everything from the last meal had been put away.

Cora Felton moved from the kitchen into the living room, or what Annabel Hurley undoubtedly referred to as the parlor. The couches were period pieces, as was the coffee table. The entertainment unit consisted of an ancient wooden radio console. It stood on the floor to the right of the Victorian love seat, which was upholstered in red velvet. There were lace doilies on the arms of the couches and chairs. There was no sign of a magazine, book, newspaper, or any personal object in the room.

Except for two sheets of paper on the coffee table. Cora Felton picked these up. One was the first set of clues. The other was the crossword-puzzle grid. It was empty.

Cora Felton put the papers back on the coffee table, and continued her search of the apartment.

The bedroom was a marked contrast from the parlor. Though not large, it was a hodgepodge of styles. Bureaus, bookshelves, end tables, a wardrobe, all strewn with clothes, books, papers, reading glasses, jewelry boxes, a sewing kit, an umbrella stand, hatboxes, shoe boxes, cardboard cartons, a metal trunk.

The clutter, though extensive, was not enough to obscure the body of Annabel Hurley lying in the middle of the floor.

23

CHIEF HARPER PUT HIS HANDS ON HIS HIPS AND SCOWLED at Cora Felton and Sherry Carter, who were standing in front of Becker & Taylor Insurance. "You want to tell me how you came to find the corpse?"

"I told you on the phone," Cora said.

"All you said was you went to see the woman and she was dead."

"Well, that's what happened."

Chief Harper's scowl deepened. "Don't try my patience. I got a woman up there with her throat cut. I don't need Quincy to tell me it's a homicide. I got a crime scene to cover that I'm ill-staffed to do. Dan Finley's up there taking pictures with his Polaroid till he runs out of film. After that, we'll have to wait until the drugstore opens before he can take any more. But when he's finally done, I gotta process the place for fingerprints. Right now I am wondering how many of them will be yours."

Cora Felton looked pained. "Give me a break, Chief. It's not as if I *knew* the woman was dead."

"No, of course not. You just walked in on her uninvited expecting to find her alive."

"That's not what happened."

"Oh? You expected to find her dead?"

"I didn't expect anything."

"Then what, may I ask, were you doing in that woman's home?"

Before Cora could answer, Sherry Carter jumped in. "Excuse me, Chief, but I think my aunt's a little shaken at finding a dead body. I think maybe I could explain."

"I think maybe you better. But let me warn you, this one's gonna take a hell of an explanation."

Sherry Carter told Chief Harper about Annabel Hurley crashing in on their dinner, and then turning out to have been in the post office the same afternoon.

Chief Harper was skeptical. "That's it? That's all you had to go on?"

"Actually, it's quite a lot," Sherry said. "The woman's turned her back on the money and isn't playing the game. But she wants to know the answer. And she comes and asks Cora to be careful to get it right. She seems to have inside information the other heirs don't have. Which makes it likely she was in league with Emma Hurley. We know *someone* was in league with Emma Hurley because Emma Hurley wasn't healthy enough to have personally planted the clues. If Annabel planted the clues, then everything fits."

"So why is she dead?"

"She was on to something. Something that had to do with the inheritance. How, exactly, I don't know. I'm not saying that's why she's dead. I'm just saying that's a fact."

"She talk to anyone else last night besides you?"

"Obviously, since she's dead. But I don't know *who* she talked to."

"She mention talking to anybody else?"

Sherry hesitated.

Chief Harper pounced. "What is it?"

"Well, now, to be perfectly fair, she didn't mention talking to anyone."

"But?"

"She asked where Daniel Hurley was staying."

"Did you tell her?"

"We didn't know."

A Volvo drove up and the trim figure of Barney Nathan stepped out. The coroner cocked his head at Chief Harper. "All right. Where is it?"

Chief Harper pointed. "Down the alley, up the back stairs. If you could keep your hands in your pockets, we still have to process for fingerprints."

"Oh, gee, thanks," Barney Nathan said witheringly. "I've never seen a crime scene before."

He took his black bag out of the car and stomped on down the alley.

A police car pulled up and Sam Brogan got out. The cranky Bakerhaven officer was chewing a fat wad of gum. As usual, he looked unhappy. He stepped up on the sidewalk, said, "What's this I hear Annabel Hurley's dead?"

"You hear right," Chief Harper said. "Get a crime scene ribbon, string it across the mouth of this alley before people start getting curious."

"She lives there?"

"You didn't know that?"

"Never dated her." Sam Brogan stroked his mustache, popped his gum. "Am I on the clock?"

"It's a homicide, Sam."

"This is not my shift."

"You're on the clock. Go string that ribbon."

Chief Harper turned back to Sherry and Cora. "Okay, you've had time to think. What were you doing in that apartment?"

"I told you what I was doing," Cora said.

"Yeah, and you made my day. I need something I can tell the press. Aaron Grant's gonna be here any minute, and I don't like your story at all."

"It's not a story. It's what happened."

"That may be, but it's not good. You were basically breaking and entering."

"The door was unlocked."

"That's irrelevant. You had no right whatsoever to go in there."

"Maybe not, but you're lucky I did. If I hadn't you wouldn't know she's dead. No one would have known till she failed to show up at the lawyer's office this morning. Even then it would have been a while before anyone bothered to look. As it is, the doctor's up there now, you got a good chance to nail the time of death, and you're getting the clues while they're fresh."

"Second only to you," Chief Harper pointed out. "Speaking of clues, these puzzle clues you're talking about. The ones you think Annabel Hurley might have planted. If they're as important as you say, they're evidence."

"Of what?"

"I don't know, but if her death had anything to do with 'em, they're evidence."

"Fine, Chief," Cora Felton said nonchalantly. "You take 'em, you solve it. Save me the trouble."

Chief Harper opened his mouth, closed it again. "All right, you win. I want to know what this puzzle is all about. I want to know where the next set of clues are planted."

"I thought you might."

"Well, do you know? Have you worked it out yet?"

"I told you. I just got it."

"But you think you know the clue for the location. Because the one clue was *post office,* the other clue was *court-house.* And the long clue this time is what?"

"I don't recall."

"Refresh your memory," Chief Harper said sarcastically.

Cora Felton opened her car, took out the manila envelope. She unclasped it, slid out one of the clue sheets.

"Close recycling place, so to speak?"

"I beg your pardon?"

"Take a look." She held the clue sheet up, pointed out the clue.

"Recycling place?" Chief Harper said. "What's a recycling place? And what would it mean to close one?"

"I have no idea," Cora said. "I'd have to get some of the other words going across."

"Can you do that now?"

"Not on your life. I just saw a bloody corpse. That may be routine to you, Mister Police Officer, but I am somewhat shook up. And all you want to do is gripe about the fact I found it."

"All right. But you're gonna solve the puzzle this morning."

"Not the whole puzzle. I still don't have all the clues."

"I mean the part you have. In particular the one about the recycling place. You'll be solving that today."

"Thanks for your vote of confidence, Chief." Cora Felton looked at her watch. "By the time we're done here I think we'll be due at the lawyer's."

"The meeting's ten o'clock?"

"That's right."

"And the heirs will be there?"

Cora Felton jerked her thumb over her shoulder in the direction of Annabel Hurley's apartment.

"All but her."

24

PHYLLIS APPLEGATE WAS FIT TO BE TIED. *"AGAIN?"* SHE sputtered. "You're doing this *again*?"

"I beg your pardon," Chief Harper said coldly, and tried not to stare. Phyllis Hurley Applegate's print dress was entirely unbecoming, made her look like Philip Hurley in drag. With her brother sitting right across the table from her, the effect was disconcerting at best. "It's not like I was boring you with trivialities," Harper went on. "This is murder."

"That's what you always say," Phyllis whined. "Then it turns out to be an accident."

"Wrong," Chief Harper said. "It's just the other way around. The first death—Jeff Beasley's—could have been an accident, but turned out to be murder. This time there's no doubt. Annabel Hurley had her throat cut. It's violent, it's personal, and this time it's one of you."

Chief Harper glanced around Arthur Kincaid's law office hoping for a friendly face, but aside from Sherry and Cora and Aaron Grant and Becky Baldwin, all he saw was shock and annoyance. Obviously, none of Annabel Hurley's relatives knew her well. There was considerable grumbling and shuffling of feet.

Chief Harper sighed. "I know you haven't had time for this to sink in. But there's a lot of money at stake here. And there's a killer on the loose. And someone is targeting the Hurley heirs."

"Oh, for goodness sakes," Philip Hurley scoffed.

"You don't buy that?" Chief Harper countered. "Well, think about it. Jeff Beasley starts nosing around the Hurley heirs: he winds up dead in a ditch. Next, Annabel Hurley winds up dead with her throat cut. And you're all involved in some no-holds-barred, winner-take-all extravaganza for millions of dollars. Has it occurred to any of you, with Annabel Hurley out of the running, your chances of winning just went up?"

"She wasn't even playing." It was the first time Daniel Hurley had spoken since the meeting began.

Chief Harper's eyebrows raised. "How do you know that?"

Becky Baldwin, standing next to Daniel Hurley's chair, said, "Daniel, you should be careful what you say."

"Why?" Daniel said. "Facts are facts. And the fact is, she wasn't playing."

"How do you know?"

"She told me."

"When?"

"Here again," Becky said, "I'd like to caution you to think before you answer."

Chief Harper frowned. "Miss Baldwin, are you attempting to act as Mr. Hurley's attorney?"

"Since you ask, yes."

"Fine," Chief Harper said, dryly. "Will you then please advise your client Mr. Hurley that if he declines to answer my questions, I will be forced to arrest him on a charge of obstruction of justice, or perhaps suspicion of murder, and then we will continue this conversation in jail, and, yes, of course, I will read him his rights before I clap him behind bars."

Chief Harper sighed again. "But there's no reason this should come to that. Because I'm sure Daniel didn't kill his aunt." He frowned. "Is that the relationship? I can't keep these Hurleys straight. Would she be your aunt?"

"Can I answer that?" Daniel Hurley asked Becky Baldwin. Then, without waiting for her reply, he proceeded to do so. "She's not my aunt. She's my first cousin, once removed. She was my father's cousin. My grandfather and her mother were brother and sister." He shrugged. "I hope that's not giving away too much."

"And when exactly did she tell you she wasn't playing the game?" Chief Harper asked.

"That would be last night, when she stopped by my bed-and-breakfast shortly after dinner." Daniel smiled at Becky Baldwin. "Which he will find out anyway the minute he questions my landlady, who happened to have let her in."

"She came to call on you?"

"She certainly did."

"Why?"

"Maybe she liked my looks."

Chief Harper scowled. "Young man, this isn't funny."

"I know it isn't." Daniel Hurley glanced around the room, saw that the faces regarding him were decidedly hostile. "You got your work to do, and I'm holding up the game. Why did she call on me? You mean me instead of the other relatives? For one thing, she lived nearby."

"Daniel," Becky Baldwin warned.

"Well, she did. Which he can also find out."

"Yes," Becky said. "But not that you knew it."

"Nonsense," Daniel Hurley said. "She told me she lived a couple of blocks away. Exactly where, I don't know, because I didn't go there and kill her. But somewhere nearby."

"And what did she ask you?"

"About the puzzle."

"What about the puzzle?"

"Exactly. That's what she wanted to know. What I knew about the puzzle. She wasn't playing, she thought it was foolish, and she wanted to know if I had any idea why Emma had done it. As if I'd know—I never met Auntie Emma in my life. But she wanted to know if I'd learned anything from my father—if he knew anything about Emma and crossword puzzles, dating back to when they were kids. Annabel and my father, I mean. The point was, as a kid, she wasn't aware Emma was into crosswords, so where does this forty-year-old puzzle come from?"

"And that was all she wanted to know?"

"That was it. Plus what I thought of my other relatives."

"Which was?"

"Oh, I had nothing but praise," Daniel deadpanned. "Anyway, she left shortly after that."

"Which was?"

"Around nine, nine-thirty at the latest. When did she die?"

"We're still waiting on the medical report. So, any of the rest of you see Annabel Hurley last night?"

None of the heirs spoke up.

"We saw her last night," Cora Felton said sweetly. "She stopped by the Wicker Basket where my niece and I were having dinner. She told me she was suspicious of her relatives, and asked me to make sure Emma Hurley hadn't been murdered."

There was a shocked silence. Chief Harper scowled. Having dismissed the theory in no uncertain terms, he hardly expected Cora to bring it up now.

Still, it was having an effect on the heirs. Philip Hurley looked like he'd been caught trying to sell someone a used car with no engine. "She said what?" he sputtered. "You expect me to believe that?"

"My niece was at the table," Cora reminded him placidly. "You can ask her. As a matter of fact, Annabel singled out you and your sister as being capable of murder. She said you were furious at Emma for throwing you out of the house."

"That's preposterous," Phyllis Hurley Applegate snarled. "Emma threw Philip out, not me."

"And you left of your own accord," Philip said witheringly. "Yes, we've all heard that story. But if there's anybody capable of murder it's you, Sis. How many husbands have you killed?"

For a split second Phyllis Applegate faltered. Then she was back in full snarl. "This is hardly the time for that old joke."

"Joke?" Philip Hurley said. "I doubt if your husbands thought it was funny. They're both dead, aren't they?"

"Of natural causes. I can't believe you could be so low." Phyllis gestured to her husband. "Look at Morty. We've been married seven years, and there he sits."

"What's the matter? Wouldn't he take out insurance?"

"That's it, Philip! The kid gloves are off," Phyllis said. "We all know if anyone killed Emma, it's you."

"Fine. You just investigate that, Officer. I wish you would. You'll find I wasn't even in town when Emma died."

"Would that stop you from sending poison chocolates in the mail?"

"Poison, what a novel idea, Sis. Where'd you get it? Wasn't that how your husband Vinnie died?"

"Vinnie died of food poisoning."

"Vinnie died of someone poisoning his food."

Phyllis Hurley Applegate lunged from her chair.

Philip Hurley leaped from his.

They squared off, jaw to jaw.

Daniel Hurley grinned. "Place your bets, ladies and gentlemen. Which twin would you back? I got ten bucks on Auntie Phyllis. Any takers?"

Chief Harper frowned. He was happy enough to sit back and let the heirs accuse themselves, but he wasn't about to witness a fight. "That will do," he said. "You want to tear each other apart, you wait till I leave. Right now I'm interested in this game. And my interest comes first, because, guess what? If I decide this little contest is interfering with a police investigation, I'm not going to let you play."

"Oh, come on!" Phyllis cried.

Philip looked wounded. "You can't mean that."

"But I do. I'm willing to let the game continue, but under very strict guidelines. So let's answer a few questions I want answered, and then we'll see what's what. First off, you two sit down."

Phyllis and Philip reluctantly sank back into their chairs.

"Now then," Chief Harper said, looking around the room. "I notice Chester Hurley is not here. Is anybody else missing—any of the heirs? I'm not talking about the housekeeper and the yard boy. I mean the ones playing the game."

Arthur Kincaid said, "I think they're all here. Let's see. Philip and Ethel Hurley. Phyllis and Morton Applegate. And Daniel Hurley. Yes, that would be all. There were five playing the game. That is, five individuals or teams. Take away Annabel and Chester leaves three. The two teams and Daniel."

"So only Chester is missing. Has anyone seen him this morning?"

No one had.

"Did you inform him of this meeting?"

"I called him yesterday afternoon," Arthur Kincaid said. "I must say, he didn't seem impressed."

"What do you mean?"

"If he'd cared, you wouldn't have known it. I'm not surprised he isn't here. He made no secret of the fact he thinks the game's stupid."

"Uh huh," Chief Harper said. "But the rest of you—since you're here, can I assume that you've solved the puzzle?"

"I certainly have," Phyllis Applegate said smugly. "And I want the next part."

"Not before me," Philip Hurley said. "I solved it first."

Chief Harper ignored this exchange. He turned to Daniel Hurley. "And how about you, young man? Have you solved it too?"

Daniel tilted his chair back, grinned. "As a matter of fact, I have. Which surprised me. I wasn't even going to work on it. But when it turned out we had all night to do it—and when Annabel made such a fuss about it—I figured, all right, why not take a crack? So, I think I solved it. Anyway, I'm here, and I'm ready for the next lap. So let's have the puzzle."

"Wait a minute, wait a minute," Philip Hurley said. "It's bad enough we gotta wait all night to get the damn puzzle, but there's no way you're giving it to *him* first. I was the first one to call, I should be the first one to get the next set of clues."

"Oh, sure," Daniel said. "Like the extra minute's really gonna help."

"Exactly," Philip Hurley said. "It's totally unfair. I was the first one to solve this, and I'm the one getting dorked." He leveled his finger at Cora Felton. "And it better not happen again. When I solve this piece, I don't wanna hear,

Come in at ten o'clock tomorrow morning to get the next. I wanna know *right now* how it's gonna be."

"Well," Cora said, stepping forward. "Since you ask me so nicely, how can I refuse? So here's your ruling. You take your puzzle piece, go away, work on it to your heart's content. If you solve it, be back here at four o'clock this afternoon and you'll get your next piece to work on. If you solve that, you'll get your next piece tomorrow morning at ten."

"Oh, come on," Philip Hurley protested. "I can work faster than that."

"Then you'll have no problem being done," Cora Felton told him.

"Yeah, but I get no credit for being first," Philip Hurley griped. "This is absurd." Philip was so exasperated he actually stamped his foot. "What is the point of solving the puzzle first, if everyone else is allowed to catch up?"

Cora Felton drew herself up, but before she could retort, Daniel Hurley said, "Where are they?"

"I beg your pardon?" Cora asked.

Daniel smiled. "Where are the puzzle clues? You tell us you're about to hand out the second set of puzzle clues, and everyone accepts that calmly as a matter of course, but yesterday—please correct me if I'm wrong—yesterday *there was only one set of puzzle clues*. The ones we're turning in now. And now you're about to give us a second set. I'd like to know where they came from."

"They come from me," Cora told him. "That's my job. As judge, I was entrusted with the responsibility of getting the clues and giving them out."

"Without telling us where?" Daniel Hurley said. "I must admit, I solved the puzzle too late last night to do anything, but this morning I stopped by the courthouse on my way over here, and you know what, the judge wouldn't let me in. Rather cranky about it too. So I'm just wondering if any of the rest of you might have happened to drop by."

"Well, you can stop wondering," Cora said. "And I'll give you a little hint. Going by the courthouse is not going to help you. Neither is going by any other location disclosed in the puzzle." She shot a glance at Aaron Grant. "And I am counting on no mention of any particular location appearing in the press."

"Let me second that," Chief Harper said. "Aaron, you may have been invited, but you have no legal right to be here. Any irresponsible reporting on anything you should inadvertently learn, and you will not be at the next meeting. Is that clear?"

"As crystal," Aaron said.

"Well, I hope it's as clear to the heirs," Cora said. "But let me spell it out. There is no reason to visit any location suggested by the second part of the puzzle. It will not help you. Don't waste your time."

"Fine, can we have the puzzle now?" Philip Hurley demanded.

"Yeah," Phyllis Applegate pressed forward. "Where's the new clues?"

"I have the new clues," Cora Felton said. She smiled. "And I may or may not give them to you, depending on how well you did on the first set. Because I'm the judge, and what I say goes."

Cora looked around the table to make sure that registered.

"Fine," she said. She reached in her drawstring purse, took out a manila envelope. "Now then. Who wants to show me their grid?"

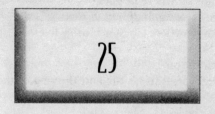

25

AARON GRANT SIDLED UP TO SHERRY AS THE MEETING broke up. "Wanna take a ride?"

She looked at him in surprise. "Where to?"

"Tell you outside."

Sherry looked at the front of the room, where Cora Felton was handing out clue sheets to the heirs. It was not going smoothly: Philip and Phyllis were still squabbling over who went first, much to the amusement of Daniel Hurley, who stood with hands on hips, quietly waiting his turn. Becky Baldwin, Sherry noted, was glued to his side.

"I've got to check with my aunt," Sherry told Aaron. "How long will this take?"

"Not long. I'll drop you off at home. Come on. Slip her the high sign, and let's get out of here."

Sherry caught Cora Felton's eye, waved, pointed to Aaron and herself, waved bye-bye, and mouthed, "See you at home."

From the look on Cora Felton's face, Sherry might have told her there was no room in the last lifeboat. Sherry pretended not to notice, and followed Aaron out the door.

They got downstairs just in time to see Chief Harper drive off.

"Gonna follow him?" Sherry said.

"Depends on where he goes."

"Where are *we* going?"

"You know where Chester Hurley lives?"

"No."

"I do. Come on."

Sherry got in Aaron's car and the two of them pulled out.

"What's the idea?" Sherry said.

"You happen to see this morning's paper?"

"Didn't get a chance."

"That's not good," Aaron said. "Every Bakerhaven resident should start the day with the *Bakerhaven Gazette*."

"Sorry to disappoint you. I've been a little busy, what with finding a corpse."

"That's a pretty poor excuse. There's a copy on the backseat. Take a look."

Sherry undid her seat belt, turned, and retrieved the paper. She resnapped the seat belt, flipped the paper open.

The headline was HURLEY WILL CONTEST.

"Like it?" Aaron asked. "I came up with that. *Will contest*. Neat double meaning, huh? I mean, the heirs often *contest* the will, but this is an actual *contest*. Too bad I don't have the inside dope on the clues."

"Too bad you're not gonna get 'em," Sherry said.

Aaron winced. "Now, that's no attitude. We're having a nice drive here. We're talking this over like two responsible adults."

"Did you take me for a drive just to try to worm the clues out of me?"

Aaron Grant put up both hands. "Absolutely not."

"Will you hold on to the wheel?" Sherry said.

"Sure thing," Aaron said. "Will you hold on to your accusations?"

"Uh oh," Sherry said. "I always know we're in trouble when you start in on the wordplay."

"I'm not starting in on anything. I'm trying to explain to you how it is. That headline is yesterday's news. *Will contest.* It won out over the Beasley murder. For all the reasons I already gave. But not anymore. Tomorrow's headline is HURLEY HEIR MURDERED. But you know what?" He shook his head. "Nobody will care. You know why? Suddenly it's *big* news. It's like the Graveyard Killings all over again. We'll have TV crews in town, it'll be on the evening news. By the time people get the paper tomorrow they'll already know all about it."

"Is there a point to this?" Sherry said.

Aaron slowed down for the covered bridge over the creek to the general store. The rickety wooden bridge was a one-lane affair, with a full stop required before proceeding from either end, which had to be the least-obeyed ordinance in Bakerhaven. The bridge was open-sided, one could see perfectly, and if nothing was coming, no one ever stopped.

"You missed a stop sign."

"No, I saw it," Aaron told her.

Sherry smiled in spite of herself. "You were saying about news crews?"

"They're coming and I hate 'em. Because I can't beat 'em. They're on the air today, I'm in the paper tomorrow. It's a tremendous handicap."

"So?"

"So, I need an angle. Something they haven't got. If it isn't the puzzle clues—and I know it isn't—it's gotta be something else."

"Like Chester Hurley?"

"Why not? As an angle, he's got one major advantage."

"What's that?"

"The TV crews aren't likely to find him."

They had turned off the paved road and were now following a winding dirt road through the meadow and into the woods.

"Mr. Hurley lives up here?"

"That's right."

"He owns this land?"

"No. It's a forest preserve. It's owned by the town."

"Then how can he live here?"

"The town grants him access. Chester has a cabin at the base of the mountain. Lived there since before this land was zoned protected. When the town set up the wildlife sanctuary, they had to leave him the access road."

"How do you know all this?"

Aaron grinned. "Are you kidding? What do you think I write on slow news days? Don't you ever read the *Gazette*?"

As they got closer to the base of the mountain, Sherry noticed the oak and maple trees overhanging the road giving way to fir. The trees stood tall and straight, with the trunks bare, and the branches with pine needles only near the top.

"What do you expect to get out of Chester Hurley?" Sherry asked.

"I have no idea."

"Then what's the point of finding him?"

"Like I said, I need an angle."

"And what's the angle?"

Aaron didn't answer.

Sherry's eyes widened. "I don't like this."

"What do you mean?"

"You figure he hasn't heard. That's your angle, isn't it? You figure he doesn't *know*."

"Sherry."

"You'll tell him Annabel's dead, you'll watch his reactions. You'll write about them."

"That bothers you?"

"It doesn't bother you?"

Aaron pulled off to the side of the road, put the car in park. "Sherry. Of course it bothers me. And, yes, I've done it before, and, yes, it's part of the job, and, no, I don't like it. Usually, it's an accident, and usually, I'm not the first. Usually, I'm following the police. This time it's different. This time it's a murder, and this time I'm not following the police, because they have more important leads. So, yes, I may be telling Chester Hurley something he doesn't know. But that's not what I'm after. I'm after something that will help me figure out why this happened. And who did it. That's my concern with Chester. That's why I'm here." Aaron paused, studying her. "And you know that. Why would you think anything else?"

"I don't know," Sherry said. "It's all fun and games, and then this happens, and two people are dead, and suddenly alliances are formed. I mean, did you see Becky Baldwin defending Daniel Hurley?"

"Is that what this is all about?" Aaron asked quietly.

"Didn't that surprise you?" Sherry insisted.

"Actually, it didn't. She told me he'd consulted her."

"Oh? When was that?"

"She came by the paper last night, trying to get information."

"Oh, is that right? Information about what?"

"Jeff Beasley. He was her client, remember?"

"She wanted information about a dead client?"

"That was my reaction too. Why should she care? That's when she said Daniel Hurley had consulted her."

"Oh? Why had he done that?"

"Because Chief Harper was questioning him about the Beasley death."

"Wait a minute," Sherry said. "Let me be sure I understand this. Becky Baldwin came by the paper to see if you might have some information that would shed some light on whether her present client killed her former client?"

"Technically, he's not her client yet. He just consulted her."

"Better and better," Sherry muttered. "Whether her *potential* client killed her former client. She didn't come to ask you out to dinner?"

"I have dinner sent in."

"Now, there's an evasion worthy of a politician. A less alert person might think you'd answered *no*."

"Sherry—"

Sherry blushed furiously. "I'm sorry. I don't know what came over me. I got caught up in the wordplay. This is absolutely silly. Let's go see Chester."

"Sherry."

"Come on, come on. I can't wait to see where this man lives."

Chester Hurley's cabin was in a little clearing about a mile down the road. It was a small cabin of sturdy pine boards painted chocolate brown. The painting had been some time ago, however, and while it had worn well, the cabin looked decidedly old.

The lawn had been sporadically mowed. The left-side lawn, for instance, was shorter than the front. The right-side lawn was somewhere in between. An ancient hand mower sat in a line between the shortest grass and the longest. Sherry Carter had visions of Chester Hurley mowing his way around the cabin, a few rows each day.

The cabin had a rickety front porch with no roof. A rocking chair sat out on it. There was a red coffee mug on the porch next to the rocking chair.

"I guess he's not here," Sherry said. "His truck's gone."

"Not necessarily. He parks in the back."

"Oh?"

"Yeah. Fooled me too, when I wrote the feature. I came by twice and left, thinking he wasn't here."

"Why does he park in back?"

"So you can't tell if he's here."

"That's a little strange."

"Chester Hurley? Strange? Surely you jest." Aaron grinned. "Come on, let's see if he's home."

The screen door was latched, but the front door behind it was open. They looked through the screen door, but no lights were on, and the cabin was deep in shadows.

"He's home," Sherry said.

"Not necessarily."

"The screen door's latched from the inside."

"Uh huh," Aaron said. "Let's go around the side."

Aaron led Sherry around the right side of the cabin.

"Kitchen door," Aaron told her. "Exit of choice. Chester leaves the screen door latched, then goes out the kitchen door, and you can't tell if he's here or not."

"And why does he do that?" Sherry said.

"So pretty girls will think he's an enigma."

"I can't believe you used that word."

"Enigma?"

"No, girls. Don't you mean pretty women?"

"I often mean pretty women. I seldom get to say it." Aaron knocked on the kitchen door. He waited, but there was no answer. He knocked again.

"Any reason you're knocking on the side door instead of the front?" Sherry asked.

"It's easier knocking on wood than a screen." When Sherry gave him a look, Aaron said, "This is how I got in before. But apparently, he's not here."

Aaron led the way around the back of the cabin. "Yeah, his truck's gone. He's not here."

Sherry pursed her lips. Frowned. "Wait a minute."

"What?"

"His truck's gone doesn't mean he's not here. It means his truck's not here."

Aaron looked confused.

"Let's not take anything for granted, Aaron," Sherry said. "Annabel Hurley was just murdered. After being named in Emma Hurley's will. And Chester Hurley was named in Emma Hurley's will . . ."

"Oh, now look," Aaron protested.

"What's so far-fetched about that?" Sherry argued. "The only evidence to the contrary is the fact his truck isn't here. Well, gee, Aaron, you think a killer might steal a truck? Granted, truck theft's a felony. A serious felony. Might deter most people. But someone who just stooped to murder? I don't know. Can you imagine a murderer thinking, *I'd better not take that truck, I might get in trouble.*"

"Sherry."

"Or the killer doesn't steal the truck, he just runs it off into the woods a little ways, hoping to make it take longer before the body is discovered."

"You've made your point."

Aaron tried the side door. It was locked.

"How about a window?" Sherry said.

The windows in the back were slightly higher than those in the front due to the lay of the land, which fell away to a small, noisy stream before sloping back up the mountain.

"Boost me up," Sherry said.

"You really want to peek in the man's windows?"

"If he's dead he won't mind."

"I can't believe you said that."

"I'm starting to sound like Cora," Sherry said. "Now boost me up."

Aaron laced his fingers together. Sherry stepped in, grabbed the windowsill and pulled up while he boosted.

With Aaron's help she performed a chin-up, managed to peek over the sill.

"What do you see?" Aaron said.

"It's his bedroom. Double bed, unmade. Bureau, night-stand, television. A few clothes on the floor."

"Any dead bodies?"

"I think I would have mentioned that."

"You wanna get down?"

"I kind of like it here."

"I'm glad to hear it. But the elevator's leaving."

Aaron lowered Sherry down to the ground.

"What's the other window?"

"Bathroom, most likely," Aaron said. "Think he's dead in it?"

"No. But I suppose we should check."

Aaron boosted Sherry up again. It was a little harder this time. The sill was narrower, gave less purchase. Sherry had trouble holding on, but with Aaron pushing hard, she managed to pull herself up and peer over.

"Just what do you think you're doing!"

At first Sherry thought the gravelly voice came from the bathroom. Startled, she lost her grip, slid down the wall. Aaron tried to hold her up, but it was no use and she fell to the ground in an ungainly heap. She rolled over and looked up.

Chester Hurley towered over her. His lips were twisted in a scowl, exposing his awful teeth. He was dressed, as before, in plaid shirt and overalls. Standing there in the woods, he looked like a lumberjack.

A furious lumberjack.

Sherry stifled a shudder, managed a smile. "Mr. Hurley. We were looking for you."

"So I see," Chester Hurley said. "You ever heard of doors?"

"We knocked on your door. We got no answer."

"So you decided to spy?"

Aaron Grant helped Sherry to her feet. "Mr. Hurley, you don't understand. We came to tell you about Annabel."

"Annabel? Yes, she's dead. Someone killed her."

"Who told you?"

"Why? Is it supposed to be a secret? A policeman told me. Not the Chief. The other one. Not the kid, either. The other cop."

"Sam Brogan?"

"The one with the mustache."

"That's Sam."

"Well, he told me. Someone killed her. And I come back here and I see someone staking out the place. Spying on me."

"Where's your truck?" Aaron asked. "How come you're on foot?"

"If I drove up, you'd have heard me. I saw your car, left my truck down the road. I don't want trouble, and I don't go looking for it."

"Particularly after someone just murdered your niece," Aaron suggested.

Chester Hurley's pale eyes narrowed. "Particularly any time at all. You live alone, you live cautious. You take nothing for granted. I'm still waiting for your explanation."

"I beg your pardon?"

"Why were you looking in my window?"

"I thought we explained," Aaron said patiently. "Someone killed your niece. And you weren't at the meeting this morning. The meeting at the lawyers. To get the next puzzle piece."

"Oh, that."

"Did you know there was a meeting?" Aaron asked.

"Sure. Lawyer called me yesterday, told me about it."

"Then why didn't you go?"

"What for? It's only if you need more clues."

"And you didn't?"

Chester Hurley snorted. "Stupid game. Don't see the point."

"Then you're not working on the puzzle?"

"I didn't say that. Did I say that?" The ugly light flickered in Chester's eyes again.

"Then you are working on Emma's puzzle?"

"I didn't say that either."

"You know there's another meeting this afternoon?"

"Oh?"

"If you should finish the first set of clues and want some more, just show up at the lawyer's office four o'clock this afternoon and you'll get 'em."

"Is that right?"

"Yes, it is. The other heirs will be there, getting the third set of clues. Assuming they've managed to solve the second. Now, I don't know if there's any way for you to catch up at this point. But maybe there is. Maybe the second set of clues is harder, no one will have solved it by four. But the point is, if you want to get back in the game you should be there."

"And what if I'm not?" Chester Hurley said. "How's this game ever end?"

"Tomorrow morning at ten o'clock there's another meeting. The Puzzle Lady will be handing out the final set of clues. After that, the first person to complete the puzzle and hand it in is the winner."

Chester Hurley shook his head. "Stupid."

"I don't disagree, Mr. Hurley," Aaron Grant said. "I know you felt that way from the start. I'm just wondering if what happened to your unfortunate niece changes anything. If it motivates you in some way. Gives you a reason to want to win. I'm just wondering if you'll be showing up in the lawyer's office this afternoon."

Chester Hurley snorted. "Fat chance."

"Then you're not playing the game?"

Chester Hurley said nothing.

"Can I write in the paper you're not playing the game?"

"You can write in the paper any piece of garbage you want. That don't make it true."

Sherry Carter stepped in front of Aaron Grant. "Mr. Hurley, there's something I need to tell you. Last night I spoke to Annabel. She stopped by the Wicker Basket where my aunt and I were having dinner. She saw us through the window and came in. You know why? Because she was terribly concerned about the game. She believed it was all wrong. She believed it wasn't like Emma Hurley. She wanted my aunt to look into it."

Chester Hurley narrowed his eyes, drew back his lips. The effect was unnerving. "So?" he said.

"Frankly, it's the reason we were concerned about you. Annabel Hurley was skeptical of the puzzle and wasn't playing the game. Someone killed her. You're skeptical of the puzzle and you're not playing the game. You're the only other heir who isn't playing the game. All the rest of them are all gung ho. You strike me as a very intelligent man. Can you see why we'd be concerned for your safety?"

"Sure," Chester Hurley said. "Because you don't know me."

He reached into the pocket of his overalls and drew out the largest handgun Sherry Carter had ever seen. The revolver was ancient, but the blue steel gleamed from having been lovingly cleaned and polished. Sherry had no doubt the weapon was loaded, no doubt it would work.

"You can quit worrying about me, young lady. I can take care of myself. Now, you got any more damn fool questions?"

"Just one," Aaron Grant said bravely. "You have any idea who murdered your niece?"

"Obviously not."

"Why obviously?"

Chester Hurley waggled the gun.

"If I did, they'd be dead."

26

CORA FELTON PACED THE KITCHEN AND FUMED. WHERE were they? That's what she wanted to know. Where had they gone? And why did Sherry have to run out on her now? It was positively infuriating. There they were, with a fresh set of clues to work on, and Sherry chooses to run off. Which wouldn't have been so bad if it hadn't been right after Cora Felton had set the deadline. Four o'clock that afternoon. That was when the heirs would be showing up. That was when the heirs would be demanding these clues. And if Sherry and Cora hadn't solved the puzzle by then—if they hadn't found the closed recycling place, whatever that was, and gotten the next set of clues—then how could she give these out? And wouldn't that be a fine kettle of fish, if she had to go back on that promise so soon after making it. So soon after reassuring the heirs the whole thing would be wrapped up by tomorrow morning. No, that would not do at all.

Cora Felton stalked to the refrigerator, jerked it open, looked inside, and slammed the door. It was not the first time she had done so.

The really infuriating thing was that Cora was being good. Sherry wasn't home, Cora was all alone, Cora was bouncing off the walls, but Cora was not, repeat, *not,* pouring herself a drink. Absolutely not, no way. Cora had had her one wake-up Bloody Mary, and after that she would not drink until dinner. It was a rule that Cora would not violate except under extreme circumstances—though Cora was never quite sure exactly what constituted extreme circumstances—but certainly never on a day when she had been given the responsibility of adjudicating a very important puzzle, not to mention passing Go and collecting fifty thousand dollars. No, Cora would never drink on that day, even with extreme provocation, like Sherry running out on her and leaving her with the puzzle unsolved.

Cora opened the refrigerator again, took out the orange juice, poured herself a glass. Her first husband, Jerry, had made her drink orange juice when he had taken on the formidable task of sobering her up. Cora had loathed orange juice ever since, but drank it religiously in times of crisis, as a deterrent to the other. Cora took a sip, made a face. As usual, the thought *could use a little vodka* crossed her mind.

On the kitchen table, propped up against the sugar jar, was the manila envelope with the clues. Cora set her glass down, opened the envelope, pulled a sheet out, read it over. It was not the first time she had done so. Of course, the clues didn't mean much without the puzzle grid. Cora had the one she'd used at the meeting to compare the heirs' answers, but that grid only had the first quadrant filled in. Since this was the third set of clues, Cora needed the grid with the first and second quadrants, and Cora didn't have that. In fact, she wasn't even sure where Sherry'd put it.

Most likely in the office.

Cora padded down the hall, the clues in one hand, the orange juice in the other. She carried each at arm's length. It was a toss-up which she found more distasteful.

Cora went into the office and looked on Sherry's desk, but the crossword puzzle was not in plain sight. That did not surprise her. Sherry wouldn't leave it lying around. But where would she put it? The desk drawer? The file cabinet? If it was filed, what would it be under?

Glancing around, Cora's eyes lit on the computer. Of course. It didn't matter where Sherry had hidden the grid. Sherry wouldn't have worked on it anyway.

Not in the computer age.

Cora sat at the computer, switched it on. She was greeted by a reassuring whir. But the screen stayed blank. Damn, where's that other switch? Cora found it, clicked it on. Sat and waited while everything booted up. Cora smiled, almost as pleased with herself at having remembered the term *booted up* as at having remembered how to turn on the infernal machine.

Cora absently took a sip of orange juice, then grimaced as she realized what it was.

On the screen, the various startup functions neared completion. Virus Scan completed its search—a process Cora Felton found unnerving, even though no virus was detected—and a series of tiny icons slowly came into focus on the screen. Cora found the one marked Crossword Compiler. She moved the mouse, double-clicked it as she'd seen Sherry do.

Seconds later, a crossword-puzzle grid filled the screen. Only this was a totally empty grid. No numbers. No black squares. No letters. No clues. No nothing. Basically, a blank piece of paper to a crossword-puzzle compiler.

For a non-crossword-puzzle compiler, a slap in the face.

This couldn't be right. She'd seen Sherry working on the screen.

Cora leaned forward, peered at the grid. A quick count showed it to be a fifteen-by-fifteen square, just what Sherry had been working on. Of course, it wasn't. At the top it read Crossword Compiler (untitled). Below there were certain choices. File, Edit, Grid, Words, Clue, Options, Windows, and Help.

Cora needed help, but when she moved the mouse and clicked on it, it offered her Contents, Keyboard, Mouse, Crossword Compiler on the Web, Download updates from the Web, and About. That was definitely more than she wanted to deal with. She moved the mouse back to the beginning, clicked on File. She found New, Open, Save, Save as, Close, Export, Copy to clipboard, Print, Printer setup, Page setup, Headers, Information, Statistics. Who invented these things, she wondered irritably.

And then, down at the bottom, numbered one through five, the last five puzzles Sherry had been working on. They were labeled 1) Will #2-B; 2) Will #2-A; 3) Will #1-B, 4) Will #1-A; and 5) Will Blank.

Cora moved the mouse, clicked on 1) Will #2-B.

And the crossword puzzle filled the screen. Just as Cora had seen it when Sherry had been working on it. The section with *courthouse* was filled in across the top. And the section with *post office* was filled in down the right side. There it was, the most up-to-date version of the puzzle, just as Sherry had left it.

LONGA PRAT PEA
UBOAT HONE SOLD
COURTHOUSE OSLO
YES EONS NATTER
ASSET AMOOSE
TE ENGULF
FRIES FUN
PRECISE
S ACES
IMBEDS
S

Cora Felton held up the new list of clues:

ACROSS

25. Amiable
30. Chinese gelatin
35. Perfect rejoinder
40. Barbie's buddy
41. Do _______ (second chances)
44. Wipe out
48. Unfruitful
52. Me first man
57. Peru city
61. Alda
64. So far

DOWN

23. Attitudes
25. Wolf gathering
26. Monster
27. Close recycling place, so to speak?
31. Worry
36. Golf course features
45. Character in "Wheel of Time" books
48. Stop
49. Spry

Cora Felton looked at the grid and grinned.

Because she had a word. She had an answer. She had a solution to one of the clues. That was why she'd been so eager to find the grid. She'd seen the clue in the kitchen, and she'd wanted to make sure. Because the answer just had to be.

And it was.

The answer to forty across, *Barbie's buddy,* was three letters, just as she'd thought.

Cora Felton triumphantly moved the mouse, and typed in *Ken.*

The doorbell rang.

The smile froze on Cora Felton's face.

Uh, oh. Whoever it was, they mustn't see this. But how did she hide it? A paper she could hide, but a computer?

Cora looked at the screen. Did anything say **Hide**? No. Or **Exit**? No. But she'd seen it. She was sure she'd seen it. Now, what had she opened? **Help** and **File**. It wasn't **Help**, it must be **File**.

Cora clicked on **File**. Scanned down quickly. Eureka! **Exit**. She clicked on **Exit**.

The computer didn't exit the program. Instead, a new screen came up. It read **Puzzle has been modified: do you wish to save Will #2-B?** There were three choices to click on: **Yes, No,** and **Cancel.** Cora wasn't sure what that meant. If she said **Yes**, would that replace Sherry's puzzle with the one she'd just typed? If she said **No**, would it erase Sherry's puzzle?

The doorbell rang again.

Which was it? **Yes**? **No**?

Cora hit **Cancel**.

The puzzle remained on the screen.

Cora jumped up, knocking over her orange juice. It spread on the desk, headed for the mouse.

Cora glanced around for tissues, saw none. She grabbed

the mouse, set it on the keyboard. The orange juice was approaching fast.

The doorbell rang again.

Cora looked around frantically. She grabbed paper out of the printer, slapped it down on the desk in the path of the orange juice, creating a dam.

There. Was that enough to hold it?

Cora grabbed more paper from the printer, slapped it on top.

The doorbell rang again. More insistently this time.

Cora took one last look at the computer screen, then fled from the office, slamming the door behind her.

She hurried to the front door and flung it open to find a rather impatient Chief Harper on her threshold.

"Well, it's about time," the Chief said. "If it weren't for your car in the driveway, I was starting to get the impression you weren't here."

"Oh, yes? Well, I've got news for you. Sherry and I sometimes leave the car here and go out with someone else."

"Well, I'm glad this wasn't one of those times."

"Actually, it is. Sherry's out with Aaron Grant."

"That's all right. I came to see you."

"Why?"

"The new clues. Have you solved them yet?"

"Are you kidding?"

"No, I'm not. Do you have the new clues for me?"

"You have two murders on your hands and you want the new puzzle clues?"

"I have two murders on my hands *connected* to the new puzzle clues. So, what's the solution? Do you have the next part?"

"No, I don't."

Chief Harper scowled. "Well, why not? You're the world-famous puzzle expert. You've had time to work on it."

"I'm sorry," Cora said. "I don't mean to be rude. You want to come in and have some coffee?"

"Coffee wouldn't hurt," Chief Harper said. "But what's with the puzzle? You really don't have it?"

"Actually, I don't," Cora said, leading him into the kitchen.

"And why is that?" Chief Harper asked.

Cora took the coffeepot over to the sink and washed it out, thinking fast. "The problem is, Sherry's not here. While I was giving out the puzzle clues to the heirs, she took off with Aaron Grant."

"So?"

"It's been a full morning, Chief. We went straight from the post office to the crime scene to a powwow with the heirs. We had the puzzle clues with us, of course."

"Don't tell me."

Cora filled the pot with water, brought it back to pour in the automatic drip machine. "I'm sorry, but there you are. Sherry's off with Aaron, and I can't work on the new clues until she gets back. Just one of those unfortunate things. How do you like your coffee, pretty strong?"

"She took *all* the sets of clues?"

"They were all together in an envelope." Cora didn't like lying. So far, every statement she'd made to Chief Harper had been the absolute truth. If he happened to misinterpret those statements, that was hardly her fault.

Cora changed the filter, spooned in coffee, set the machine, and switched it on. "There you go, Chief. We'll have coffee pronto. You want me to see if I've got some sort of pastry to go with it?"

"Coffee will be fine," Chief Harper said.

"So what have you got?" Cora asked him. "Anything new?"

"I really shouldn't discuss it."

"Of course."

Chief Harper sat at the kitchen table, rubbed his head. "But then you helped me before, didn't you? And the long and the short of it is, I got no one to answer to but me." He sighed. "Actually, I gotta answer to the prosecutor, the selectmen, the townspeople. Just about everyone, when you come right down to it. Anyway, here's the scoop. As of right now, everything points to the kid."

"Daniel Hurley?"

"That's the one. The landlady confirms Annabel Hurley called on him last night."

"Well, of course she does. Daniel told you as much. It would only be remarkable if she *didn't* confirm it."

"Yeah, but she also confirms this: right after Annabel Hurley left, Daniel went out."

"Oh?"

"Yes. And he didn't mention that. It is rather interesting, if he was following her home to see where she went."

"And why would he do that?"

"Why would anyone do that? We have no idea what the motive is. At this moment, we're talking opportunity. And here's a great big opportunity, too blatant to ignore."

"Anything else point to him?"

"Indirectly."

"Ugly word. What *indirectly* points to Daniel Hurley?"

"The puzzle. Yesterday, to all accounts, Daniel Hurley had no intention of working on the puzzle. Then this morning he turns it in. That's right, isn't it? Did he give you a solution?"

"Yes, he did."

"Was it correct?"

"It was correct enough to move on."

"What do you mean by that?"

"You gotta understand, Chief, as far as judging this event goes, I'm making it up as I go along. I'm still not sure how I'm gonna judge the final puzzle. As far as the segments go, anyone who's managed to solve the long clue can move on. Even if they don't have everything else."

"And Daniel Hurley didn't have everything else?"

Cora Felton waggled her hand. "There's a gray area on some of the shorter clues. For instance, in what they just solved there's an Italian village intersecting with a Tibetan town. It was possible to get everything else in the puzzle except the one letter that was common to both words. So, if you didn't know either answer, you couldn't fill in that letter, even though you could get everything else."

Cora Felton poured the coffee and explained the crossword-puzzle situation with great assurance. Knowing it would be a bone of contention, Sherry Carter had briefed her very carefully on those points.

Chief Harper accepted the coffee, dumped in milk and sugar. "So you're saying Daniel Hurley didn't get those right?"

"He had one letter wrong. But you were saying. Why does the puzzle point to Daniel Hurley?"

"Because, like I say, he wasn't going to work on it. Everyone confirms that. Even his lawyer. She was surprised he'd done it. Because he told everyone he wasn't. Until Annabel Hurley calls on him. Then he follows her out when she leaves, and the next time someone sees her, she's dead. And she was close to Emma Hurley, has been seen in the places where the puzzle pieces were hidden, and is known to be not playing the game."

"So?"

"So, maybe she knows the solution. Between late last night and early this morning, Daniel Hurley got the solution from somewhere. Why not from her?"

Cora Felton considered. "Then why would he get one letter wrong?"

Chief Harper frowned.

"Anyway," Cora Felton said. "What do you think of my theory?"

"What theory?"

"That Emma Hurley was bumped off."

"I think the less said about that the better," Chief Harper said.

"Really?" Cora said. "Didn't you see what a reaction it provoked? Philip and Phyllis were at each other's throats."

"Philip and Phyllis are always at each other's throats."

"Yes, but not so specifically," Cora said. "You think Phyllis really did in her husbands?"

"Frankly, no. And even if she did, I can't see how it would relate to the current case."

"You can't? Annabel Hurley tells me she's suspicious of her. Annabel tells me to make sure she didn't poison her aunt. Annabel is subsequently killed. And you can't see a possible connection?"

"You're telling me Phyllis Hurley Applegate is a serial killer who bumped off her husbands, her aunt, and her cousin, not to mention the town drunk, by at least three different means—poison, a blunt object, and a knife? Can you imagine me selling that concept to the county prosecutor?"

"Well, when you put it that way," Cora said.

There came the sound of tires in the driveway.

Cora Felton's face lit up. She controlled herself, tried to keep from reacting as if she'd just gotten a death-row reprieve. "There's Sherry now. Relax, drink your coffee, I'll go get those clues."

Cora Felton tore out of the kitchen, sprinted through the foyer, and flung open the front door to find Sherry Carter and Aaron Grant climbing out of Aaron's car.

"Sherry," Cora cried, bounding down the front steps. "Come here, come here. Boy, am I glad to see you. Hi, Aaron, excuse me a minute. Sherry, Chief Harper's here.

You know that, of course, there's his car. He's in the kitchen. And he wants the solution to the puzzle, and I couldn't work on it because of the clues."

"The clues?" Sherry said.

"Yes, yes, the clues," Cora said, grabbing her by the elbow and piloting her toward the house. Cora called over her shoulder, "Aaron, go have coffee with Chief Harper, I've gotta talk to Sherry. Come on, Sherry, in the office."

Cora dragged Sherry through the front door, called, "Be with you in a minute, Chief," and herded Sherry down the hallway. She pushed Sherry into the office, slammed the door. "Thank goodness you're here. What a nightmare. You've gotta help me."

Sherry's eyes widened. "What's *that*!" she said, pointing to the desk.

"Oh, the orange juice! The doorbell rang, and I was so pleased about the Ken doll, and I couldn't find a paper towel."

"What on earth are you talking about? It didn't reach the keyboard, did it?"

"No, it didn't. Sherry, look. I stalled Chief Harper, made him think you had the clues with you so I couldn't work on the puzzle. As far as he's concerned, you're bringing them back to me now. But he's gonna want me to solve them, and what do I do?"

Sherry was still looking at the screen. "You added *Ken*?"

"I'm sorry. I got excited because I knew one."

"It's all right," Sherry said. "Okay, here's what you do. Go out there and stall Chief Harper another five minutes. That should be enough. And get rid of Aaron. You can kill two birds with one stone there, because Chief Harper doesn't want Aaron to have the solution. So go out there, say you're not going to work on the puzzle until Aaron is gone."

"Will he buy that?"

"It doesn't matter if he buys it or not, you're just stalling to give me time. Improvise. There's no time to discuss it. Go out there before he comes in here."

"What do I tell him you're doing?"

"I'm programming the computer for you. You're the crossword-puzzle genius, I'm the computer nerd, remember?"

"Gotcha."

In the kitchen Cora was relieved to find Aaron Grant filling Chief Harper in on Chester Hurley.

"He had a gun?" Chief Harper asked.

"A cannon," Aaron answered. "That pocket in his overalls must go down to his knee."

"But he didn't threaten you with it?"

"No. Just waved it around. He also made a few vague threats at whoever killed his niece."

"He had no idea who that might be?"

"None he wished to share. It's hard to tell what that guy's thinking. So, you got anything I can use for the paper tomorrow? Somehow, VICTIM'S UNCLE PACKING HEAT is going to be a tough headline to sell my editor on."

Chief Harper winced. "I'd appreciate it if you didn't."

"You got anything better?"

"Nothing you can use. Cora's about to give me something, but you can't have it."

"Just the point I was about to make, Chief," Cora said. "Aaron, you're going to have to take off so I can get this puzzle nailed." She gave him a look. "You know how it is."

"I do, and I can't say I appreciate it," Aaron replied. "Look here, Chief. I understand your not wanting me to print the clues. That makes perfect sense. But not knowing them is something else. What's the harm in me knowing the solution if I assure you I'm not going to print it?"

Cora Felton smiled. She knew what Aaron was doing.

Aaron Grant, who knew Cora Felton could no more solve a crossword puzzle than she could fly to the moon, was helping to stall Chief Harper to give Sherry a chance to work on the puzzle.

Not that she needed long. While Aaron and the Chief were still arguing, Sherry appeared in the doorway. She smiled, said, "Okay, Cora, I programmed the computer for you. All you have to do is type in the answers and print it out. Oh, hi, Chief. Aaron fill you in about Chester?"

Cora took advantage of Sherry jumping into the conversation to beat a hasty retreat to the office. She went inside, shut the door, and sat down at the computer.

The solution was there on the screen. Sherry had also laid a hard copy on the keyboard, just to save Cora the anxiety of having to figure out how to print it out.

Cora picked it up, looked at it, compared it to the clues.

¹L	²O	³N	⁴G	⁵A		⁶P	⁷R	⁸A	⁹T		¹⁰P	¹¹E	¹²A
¹³U	B	O	A	T		¹⁴H	O	N	E		¹⁵S	O	L	D
¹⁶C	O	U	R	¹⁷T	H	O	U	S	E		¹⁸O	S	L	O
¹⁹Y	E	S		²⁰E	O	N	S		²¹N	²²A	T	T	E	R
		²³A	S	S	E	T		²⁴A	M	O	O	S	E
²⁵P	²⁶O	²⁷L	I	T	E		²⁸E	²⁹N	G	U	L	F	
³⁰A	G	A	R			³¹F	R	I	E	S		³²F	³³U	³⁴N
³⁵C	R	U	S	³⁶H	³⁷E	R		³⁸P	R	E	³⁹C	I	S	E
⁴⁰K	E	N		⁴¹O	V	E	⁴²R	S		⁴³A	C	E	S
	⁴⁴D	⁴⁵E	L	E	T	E		⁴⁶I	⁴⁷M	B	E	D	S
⁴⁸B	⁴⁹A	R	R	E	N		⁵⁰	⁵¹		S
⁵²E	G	O	I	S	T		⁵³				⁵⁴	⁵⁵	⁵⁶
⁵⁷L	I	M	A		⁵⁸	⁵⁹				⁶⁰
⁶¹A	L	A	N		⁶²				⁶³
⁶⁴Y	E	T		⁶⁵				⁶⁶

ACROSS

25. Amiable
30. Chinese gelatin
35. Perfect rejoinder
40. Barbie's buddy
41. Do _____ (second chances)
44. Wipe out
48. Unfruitful
52. Me first man
57. Peru city
61. Alda
64. So far

DOWN

23. Attitudes
25. Wolf gathering
26. Monster
27. Close recycling place, so to speak?
31. Worry
36. Golf course features
45. Character in "Wheel of Time" books
48. Stop
49. Spry

Cora scanned the grid hastily, noted that the long answer was *laundromat*. She frowned. How did you get *laundromat* from *close recycling place*?

She studied the puzzle. Her eyes widened. Of course. *Close* was a homonym. *Close* equaled *clothes*. That was the *so to speak*. It was a *clothes recycling place*. A terrible, terrible pun. Which was to be expected after *post office*.

Still, Cora wouldn't have gotten it. But Sherry had, and Sherry'd saved the day. Now all Cora had to do was stall a few more minutes to let Chief Harper think she'd had time to solve this new piece of the puzzle, then she could bring him the solution and that would be that.

Cora Felton tipped back in her chair and smiled with a feeling of satisfaction and accomplishment. Now that the peril was past, she felt perfectly pleased with herself.

So what if she hadn't gotten *laundromat*?

She'd gotten *Ken*.

27

"WHAT'S THE ADDRESS AGAIN?" CORA FELTON SAID.

"Nineteen Birch Street," Sherry said.

"Think we can find it?"

"It's a small town."

"Even so."

Cora and Sherry were driving downtown in Cora's car with a large bag of laundry in the backseat.

"We should have brought some soap," Cora said.

"Why? We're not actually going to do the laundry. It's just a prop."

"We brought it to look natural. We're not going to look natural if we don't put soap in the washer."

"You want to waste an hour in the laundromat doing our clothes?"

"Of course not."

"Then we don't need soap. Anyway, I bet they sell little packets out of a machine."

Cora shook her head. "Sherry, you've lived alone too long if you know how to do the laundry."

"Oh? And how did you do laundry?"

"I had a maid. What would be the point of getting married if my husband didn't hire me a maid?"

"You think you could skip that domestic tidbit for the *People* magazine interview?"

"Oh, I'd forgotten about that. When did I say they were coming?"

"Next week. Cora, let's concentrate on getting these clues before Chief Harper decides to pull the plug on this little game."

"Hey, did I talk him out of coming with us?" Cora reminded her.

"Very nicely," Sherry agreed. While Chief Harper had perused the new puzzle solution and speculated on the arrival of news crews in town, Cora had advanced the theory that the TV people would be sure to be monitoring his movements, and if he accompanied Sherry and Cora to the laundromat, the news reporters would certainly want to know why. "You were particularly clever since no one's seen a news crew yet," Sherry pointed out to Cora.

"Even if the TV people aren't here, why should we tip off Aaron Grant? Or any of the heirs, for that matter. I mean, you and I, two local girls out on the town, can stop in and do our laundry without raising an eyebrow. We cannot stop in and do our laundry in the company of the Chief of Police without someone wondering what's going on."

"I didn't say your argument wasn't valid. I'm just surprised he bought it."

"Chief Harper and I have a sort of understanding," Cora said placidly. "I'm not sure what it is, but we do. Ah, here's the street."

"Pinehurst? I thought you said Birch."

"Birch is off Pinehurst."

It was. Three blocks down Pinehurst, Cora took a right

on Birch and pulled up in front of the laundromat, a white two-story building with the dirty sign WASH AND DRY over the door.

"Okay," Sherry said. "I'll take the clothes and go look. You distract the attendant."

"If there is an attendant."

"Of course there's an attendant."

Cora pushed the door open and held it for Sherry, who went inside lugging the bag of clothes.

A long room ran from the front to the back of the house. The dryers were along half of the side wall, with the washers in little clusters on either end, and in little horse-shoe alcoves jutting out from the other wall. There were folding tables in the middle, and, as Sherry had predicted, a machine for dispensing small packets of detergent. The smell of soap and dirty socks was in the air.

Just inside the doorway to the left was a service counter. Behind the counter, a woman in a white apron with short, dark hair and wing-tipped glasses sat reading a movie magazine.

Cora nodded to Sherry and headed for the counter.

"Excuse me."

The woman frowned at the interruption, but when she looked up her eyes widened, and then she smiled. "You're the Puzzle Lady. I've seen you around town, but this is the first time you've ever been in here."

"Well, don't let on," Cora told her. "People will think I never wash my clothes."

The woman giggled as if that were the wittiest remark she'd ever heard. "And I'm so pleased to meet you," she said. "I'm Minnie Wishburn. This is my little establishment. My husband, Ray, and I live upstairs, we take turns running the place. Today it's his turn to go trout fishing with the boys who work the night shift at the old paper mill. And how fair is that? I mean, it's not like *we* had a night shift."

Out of the corner of her eye Cora could see Sherry moving down the row, lifting lids, peering behind washers, and trying not to attract the attention of the half a dozen other customers engaged in doing their laundry.

"Is that right?" Cora said. "The boys really went off fishing today, what with everything that's happening in town?"

"Well, why not?" Minnie said. "It's not as if *we* had any stake in the Hurleys' millions. And you're involved in that, aren't you? It was in the paper. You're the one says who gets it."

"Well, not quite," Cora said modestly. "I don't say who gets it. I just referee."

"Same thing," Minnie said. "Now, what's this I hear about Annabel Hurley?"

"You hear right," Cora said. "Someone broke into her apartment and cut her throat."

Minnie shook her head sadly. "Teenagers. Looking for drug money. Like I was telling Ray. It's not just the city anymore."

Cora Felton didn't think much of that theory, but she wasn't about to argue. "She do her wash here? Annabel Hurley?"

"Oh, yes. Every week. Like clockwork. Every Monday morning, there she'd be."

"Is that the last you saw her, this Monday morning?"

Minnie frowned. "Actually, no."

"No?"

"Seems to me she was in twice this week. Ray even remarked on it. Here she was again, and wasn't that unlike her, unless she was doing her spring cleaning, washing out a whole linen closet of towels and sheets, though it's a little late for spring cleaning, as I pointed out."

"When was this?"

"Why, just yesterday. Which is enough to give you a

turn. There she is, in here yesterday afternoon, large as life, and today—" Minnie shuddered. "I can't even bring myself to say it."

"Washing sheets and towels?" Cora repeated.

"Oh, don't hold me to that. Ray says that's what she must have been doing, but the man wouldn't notice if all of the dryers were on fire. Not that that's ever happened, mind. But Ray, he's just oblivious. If it wasn't unusual seeing her twice a week, he wouldn't have even noticed."

Cora Felton felt a tap on her shoulder, turned to find Sherry Carter standing holding the bulging laundry bag.

"Aunt Cora. Would you believe it? I forgot the shirts. We gotta go back. There's no point without the shirts."

"Oh, Sherry."

"I'm sorry. I just threw it together so quickly. Come on. We'll have to come back later, if we have time."

Sherry grabbed Cora Felton by the arm, practically dragged her out the door.

"You got it?" Cora said as they went down the front steps.

"In the laundry bag."

"Where was it?"

"In a dryer."

"*In* a dryer?"

"No, not *in* a dryer. Underneath."

"Underneath?"

Sherry threw the laundry in the backseat and climbed in. Cora climbed in, started the car, backed out of the space.

"What do you mean, underneath?" Cora demanded.

"There's a filter on the bottom. A lint catcher. You're supposed to open it up to clean out the lint."

"And it was in there?"

"Yes."

"Taped?"

"No. But leaning up. If you were looking for it, you couldn't miss it."

"Did you look at the clues?"

"No, I just shoved them in the bag."

"Wanna look now?"

"Sure. I'll feel real foolish if it's something else, like a warranty for the dryer. But it looks like the other envelopes. Lemme dig it out."

Sherry groped in the laundry bag, came up with the manila envelope. She unclasped the envelope, pulled out a page.

ACROSS	DOWN
50. _____ a hatter	37. Fraught with incident
53. Stove	42. Took off
54. Friend (fr)	46. Thought
58. Fifteen?	47. Style
62. Consumer	51. "Bather by the Sea" artist
63. Observing	54. Dead heat
65. "Luck be a _____"	55. _____ room
66. Shortstop	56. Playwright
	59. "Lady _____ tramp"
	60. Coloring

"It's the clues, all right," she said.

"What's the long one? Or do you know the number?"

"Fifteen."

Cora frowned. "Fifteen? I thought we'd done that section."

"No." Sherry shook her head. "The clue's *fifteen.*"

"What?"

"That's the clue. For number fifty-eight across. *F-i-f-t-e-e-n.* With a question mark. *Fifteen.*"

"What could that be?" Cora said.

"I have no idea."

"Can you solve it from the other clues?"

"I don't have the grid. It would be a little like playing mental chess."

"Could you do it?"

"If I concentrated and— Uh oh."

"What?"

"Looks like we're being followed."

Cora glanced in the rearview mirror. Her eyes widened. The vehicle tailgating them was a Channel 8 News van.

28

"OH, MY GOD, IT'S THE TV PEOPLE," CORA SAID. "THEY'RE right on our tail."

"Maybe they just want to get by."

"Maybe. Think I should pull over?"

"If they're following us, they'll stop too."

"Sure. And I don't wanna talk to 'em," Cora said. "Okay, it's time for the oh-my-God-we-forgot-the-undies routine."

"What?" Sherry said.

"Like you pulled in the laundromat. Only this time I'm pretending we brought our underwear, but we left them *there*."

There was a real estate agency with a circular driveway on the edge of town. Cora veered into the driveway, circled around, and peeled out, heading back the way they came.

"Did we lose 'em?" Cora asked.

"Momentarily," Sherry said. "By not signaling you made them overshoot the driveway. They're turning around now."

"So they *are* after us!" Cora's eyes gleamed. She stamped on the gas. "Okay, start the banjo music!"

"Banjo music?"

"Don't you remember the car-chase music from *Bonnie and Clyde*?" Cora's head started bobbing to it as the Toyota took off. "Or was that before your time?"

"Aunt Cora! We are *not* having a car chase with the TV people."

"Of course not," Cora agreed, flooring the accelerator.

"So you wanna slow down? You just hit eighty."

"That was just to give 'em a thrill." Cora eased up on the gas, glanced in the rearview mirror. "Okay, here they come. Let's lead 'em back to town."

"To the laundromat?"

"Heaven forbid. I was thinking of the police station."

"You'd sic the media on Chief Harper?"

"Better him than us."

Cora drove into town, pulled up in front of the library just opposite the police station. The Channel 8 van pulled in alongside.

Sherry and Cora got out of their car to find Rick Reed, the young, handsome, smooth-talking, ambitious on-camera reporter, climbing out of the van.

Sherry grimaced.

Sherry and Cora's previous encounter with the TV newsman had not been felicitous. Rick Reed had hit on Sherry, and tried to embarrass her aunt. The fact that neither attempt had been successful had not been for lack of trying.

"Well, well, ladies." Rick flashed his best on-screen smile. "This certainly is a happy coincidence."

"Oh, yeah," Cora said. "Major coincidence. Tail us for five miles, then pretend we met by accident."

"I'm pretending nothing of the kind," Rick Reed said.

"The coincidence is that we have another murder involving a crossword puzzle."

"Well, the fact is we don't," Cora Felton said. "And we won't be needing *that*," she added, pointing to the camera the two assistants were unloading from the back of the Channel 8 van. "I'm not giving an interview."

"You don't want free publicity?"

"I don't want free publicity from you. The last time you filmed me you made me look bad."

"No," Rick Reed said. "Actually, the last time I filmed you I made *me* look bad. I figured the Graveyard Killings might be my stepping-stone out of here. Didn't work out that way."

"Too bad," Cora said, sounding suspiciously sincere.

"A lot you care."

"Actually, I do. I'd be thrilled to see you leave."

Rick Reed flushed, turned to Sherry Carter. "What about you? You still angry with me?"

"*Angry* isn't the right word," Sherry said. She pointed to the assistants, who were busy setting up the camera. "Didn't my aunt say she wasn't giving an interview?"

"She's not the only one in town. There's lots of other people to interview. On the other hand, if I want to point the camera at her and have her say 'No comment,' I have that right. She might not want to talk to me, but she can't tell me what to shoot."

"Too bad," Cora said. "Off the record, I was going to give you a hint."

Rick Reed's handsome nose twitched. Sherry could practically hear the wheels whirring in his wee brain. He suspected a trap, but didn't want to pass it up.

"Why would you do that?" he asked suspiciously.

"Don't be dense. To get you off my back, of course."

He frowned. "I'm willing to believe you'd like to point

me in another direction. Why should I believe it's the *right* direction?"

Cora shrugged. "That's up to you. All I'm saying is I'm willing to talk as long as you keep the camera turned off. You want to listen, fine, no obligation. You can sort through and believe what you want. If you'd rather not listen, that's fine too, because then I don't have to bother."

Rick, visions of a major metropolitan news anchor dancing in his head, promptly said, "I want to listen."

"Then keep your camera off."

Rick Reed pointed his finger. "Ernie, don't shoot this. Okay, what you got?"

"I take it you know the background or you wouldn't be here. Annabel Hurley is dead, it's a murder, she was one of several heirs competing for an enormous estate."

"And that's where you come in," Rick Reed said. "There's a puzzle involved, and you're solving it."

"Not quite. There's a puzzle involved, and I'm watching them solve it. But that's not your story."

"What is?"

Cora Felton glanced around, hoping against hope for Chief Harper to come out of the police station, or for medical examiner Barney Nathan to come walking up, or for attorney Arthur Kincaid to drive up in his car. Of course, nothing of the kind happened.

Cora Felton frowned, rubbed her chin, tried to give the impression she was debating whether or not to tell Rick. In reality, she was searching for *anything* to tell him.

"All right," she said. "Annabel Hurley is actually the second murder in Bakerhaven this week. A man by the name of Jeff Beasley was the first."

Rick Reed looked indignant. "Are you stringing me along? That was in the morning paper."

"It was?"

"Don't give me that. It was in the *Bakerhaven Gazette*. Are you trying to tell me you haven't seen it?"

"I've been rather busy."

"So I understand. Would you care to talk about what you've been so busy doing?"

"Not a chance."

"I thought you were going to give me a hint."

"I was. I did. I didn't know you already knew it."

Out of the corner of her eye, Cora saw a pickup truck lumber down the street and turn in the direction of the lawyer's office. Undoubtedly Chester Hurley on his way to call on Arthur Kincaid. A glance at her niece told her Sherry'd seen the truck too. It occurred to Cora that Chester Hurley would be the perfect distraction.

If she didn't want him for herself.

Cora opened her mouth. Closed it again. Tried to think of something to say.

Across the street, a few doors down from the police station, Becky Baldwin came out of Cushman's Bake Shop, sipping coffee from a cardboard container. She turned and headed for the police station.

Cora Felton smiled. "There's your story."

"Huh?" Rick Reed said.

"See the young woman across the street?"

"What about her?"

"She's a lawyer. Her name's Becky Baldwin. She was the attorney for Jeff Beasley before his demise."

"So?"

"It's my understanding she's now representing Daniel Hurley, a young, bearded hippie type, drives around on a motorcycle, believed by the police to be the last person to see Annabel Hurley alive. Looks like Charles Manson. If you want an angle, here's an attractive Bakerhaven High girl goes off to college, gets a law degree, and on her way through town, just stopping by to see her folks en route to interview for a major law firm in Boston, suddenly finds herself smack in the middle of a multimillion-dollar will contest and a double murder. What do you think? Think she might photograph well? And look at that. Heading into the police station. Wonder what business she has there?" Cora mused. She put up her hands. "But, hey, don't take it from me. I wouldn't want you to think I was trying to sell you anything."

Rick Reed seemed torn. He looked at Cora Felton. Looked across the street at the police station. He turned to his cameraman and assistant. "Come on," he said, and the three of them hurried across the street.

"That was close," Cora said.

"I'll say," Sherry said. "I never thought I'd be happy to see Becky Baldwin. Come on, let's get out of here."

Cora and Sherry hopped in the car.

"Was that Chester Hurley who drove by?"

"Sure looked like him."

"And wasn't that the lawyer's street?"

"Hard to tell from this angle, but I think it was."

"Let's check it out."

Cora Felton turned off and drove to Arthur Kincaid's house. Chester Hurley's truck was not there.

"I guess that wasn't where he was going." Cora sounded disappointed.

"Not necessarily," Sherry said. "Arthur Kincaid's car isn't here either. Maybe Chester just didn't find him at home."

"In which case he would have turned around and we'd have run into him. He didn't do that."

"Yes, but Chester's lived here all his life. He probably knows another way out without turning around."

"Well, if he can, we can," Cora said. "Let's see if he did."

"We could also get lost," Sherry objected, but Cora was

already heading out of town on a road that quickly got narrower, and began to twist and turn, and offer various side streets, any of which could have been taken by Chester Hurley in his truck.

"Don't you want to get home and work on the puzzle?" Sherry said. Cora's driving was erratic at best.

"Of course I do. But we're way ahead. These jokers are still working on *post office*. They don't even have the clues to give them *laundromat* yet. But I wish you'd brought the grid with you."

"I thought we were going home."

"So did I. Is that the truck?"

"Where?"

"There."

They were climbing a wooded hill. Sherry looked through the trees and saw Chester Hurley's rusty truck parked next to a little house in a clearing in the woods. There was a car in the carport, but from the angle Sherry couldn't see it well.

"Whose house is that?" Cora asked her.

"I have no idea. Tell me something, why exactly are we following Chester Hurley?"

"Chester isn't playing the game and he's carrying a gun. He made threats against whoever harmed his niece. If he's on to something, I'd sure like to know what it is."

"What makes you think he's on to something? Why couldn't he just be going about his business?"

"With his niece dead, the heirs in town, and the will contest going on? What normal business could possibly concern him?"

Cora pulled into a driveway, turned the car around. She drove slowly back toward the house in the woods.

"What are you doing?" Sherry asked.

"Getting the house number."

"We don't even know the street."

"We can find out."

"Cora, this is silly."

"Maybe, but I'm the judge. And I want to know who he's calling on."

"Oh, phooey."

"I beg your pardon."

"You may want to know who he's calling on, but it's not because you're the judge. It has nothing to do with that. You just want to know."

"And you don't?"

"Aunt Cora—"

"Sherry, look. He's coming out."

Cora Felton braked the Toyota to a noisy stop and stabbed her finger through the trees, where, sure enough, Chester Hurley was coming out the front door of the little house. While they watched, he turned back to speak to someone inside. A few minutes later, the person appeared in the doorway.

"Look at that!" Cora exclaimed. "It's what's-her-name, the housekeeper."

"Mildred Sims," Sherry said.

"Right," Cora said. "Isn't that intriguing? Who would be closer to Emma Hurley than her housekeeper? I can't think of a better person to question about Annabel Hurley's death."

"Then the police have surely done it," Sherry pointed out.

"Of course they have. It's their job. That's not the point. The point is, Chester Hurley's doing it too. And it's *not* his job. Uh oh. Look at that."

Mildred Sims had come out of the house and was climbing into her car.

Chester Hurley's ratty old truck was blocking her. He climbed in, and began to back out of the drive.

Cora Felton shifted into gear.

"Decision time," she muttered. "Do we follow him or her?"

"Why should we follow either?"

"Sherry, for a bright woman you're a bit dense. There's been two homicides. Here's two of our suspects, and—"

"How's the housekeeper a suspect?"

"She was mentioned in the will."

"For a specific amount. Which she has already earned. She has no interest in the outcome of the game."

"She has if she's in league with Chester Hurley."

"Who we know is not playing the game," Sherry said.

Chester Hurley backed out of the driveway and drove past them on up the hill.

Mildred Sims drove out and headed back toward town.

Cora snorted in disgust. "This is where we need two cars. It just doesn't work, us living in the country with only one car."

"It works just fine."

"I think if we get the fifty thousand dollars we get another car."

Cora Felton gunned the motor and took off, her tires kicking up sand and gravel on the dirt road.

"The housekeeper?" Sherry said.

"Uh huh."

"How come?"

"Chester Hurley lit a fire under her. I want to see where she goes."

"If you rear-end her, she won't go anywhere."

"Huh?"

"You want to slow down. This is a narrow, windy road."

They shot around a bend and discovered they'd caught up with the housekeeper's car. Cora Felton dropped back and they tagged along from a safer distance.

"You shouldn't be spending the money on a car," Sherry said.

"What?"

"The fifty thousand. If you earn it, you should keep it. You shouldn't be buying another car."

"But we need one. I suppose I could do another TV ad."

"Don't you dare."

"Or I could get married again."

"Wonderful. You'd get married just for a car?"

"Why not?"

"Can't you be serious?"

"I am being serious. It's annoying to let Chester Hurley go."

Mildred Sims came to the end of the dirt road, turned left.

"We're heading back toward town," Sherry said.

"I wonder if the TV crews are still there."

"I would imagine Rick Reed's interviewing Becky Baldwin. I gotta hand it to you, Cora, that was inspired."

"Sometimes I'm not so dumb," Cora said. "Ah, here we are."

The housekeeper drove down Main Street and pulled up in front of a shop. Aside from the merchandise in the front windows, it was an ordinary Colonial-style building with a hand-lettered sign: ODDS AND ENDS.

"It looks like a general store," Cora said. "I hope it isn't where she's going."

But it was. Mildred Sims got out of the car, went up the steps and in the front door.

"Well, this is boring," Sherry said. "We're tailing a woman who's going shopping."

"We should have followed Chester," Cora said.

"We shouldn't have followed anyone," Sherry said. "We should have gone home and done the puzzle."

Cora Felton pulled a pack of cigarettes out of her pocket, stuck one in her mouth, pulled out a lighter and fired it up.

"I thought you weren't going to smoke in the car," Sherry said.

"Only when I'm tense and nervous."

"Why are you tense and nervous?"

"Because I'm not smoking in the car."

"Well, at least open the window."

Cora Felton pushed the button and rolled down the window. Aaron Grant immediately stuck his head in. "Hi, girls, doing the laundry?"

Cora Felton gasped, dropped the lit cigarette in her lap. "Aaron Grant, you scared me to death, and now I'm going to burn myself up." She snatched up the cigarette. "What on earth do you think you're doing?"

Aaron grinned. "I was about to ask you the same thing. I thought I left you two at home working on a crossword puzzle." He jerked his thumb at the bag of clothes in the backseat. "Now you're downtown doing the wash, and aren't you due at the lawyer's pretty soon? Or is that something else I'm not supposed to know?"

"That's not fair," Sherry said. "We're telling you everything we can. It's Chief Harper who said no."

"Chief Harper doesn't want me to know anything I can't print. Which is one way to play it, but it means I can print anything that I know."

"And just what do you know?"

Aaron shrugged. "How's the headline PUZZLE LADY CLEANS UP grab you?"

Sherry gawked at him.

Aaron grinned. "Not too catchy, huh? But I'll bet you there's something to it. There's a murder investigation, there's a puzzle to be solved, I'll bet you haven't even had lunch yet, and you're running around doing your laundry. I may not be the smartest reporter in the world, but sometimes an idea just hits you over the head. So, is there any chance, even a small one, any chance whatsoever, either the puzzle or the murder investigation has something to do with the laundromat?"

"Aaron."

"I'm just wondering, if I were to pay a call on Minnie Wishburn over at the Wash and Dry, what she might have to say."

"Don't do it."

"That's practically a confirmation."

"Aaron, Chief Harper said to keep out of this."

"No, Chief Harper said he couldn't tell me anything. Anything I find on my own is fair game."

Before Sherry could retort, Cora Felton put up her hands. "Whoa. Kids. It's real nice having you talk back and forth across me like I'm not even here, but if it's all the same with you I'm getting out of the car."

Cora flicked her cigarette ash out the window, backing Aaron Grant up, then pushed the door open and got out. Sherry got out too.

"Aaron, this is absolutely unfair. You know we can't tell you anything, but you think it's all right to tail us around and report on what we do."

"I never said that."

"Then what are you doing now?"

"I'm looking for a lead. Right now I need one bad. There's news crews in town. I just went by the Wicker Basket, and guess who's having lunch."

"Rick Reed and Becky Baldwin." Cora Felton tilted her head back, blew a smoke ring.

Aaron Grant looked at her. "How do you know that?"

"Actually, I made it happen."

"Oh?"

"Rick was trying to interview us," Sherry said. "Cora gave him a better lead."

"Is that right?" Aaron said.

"Yes, it is. Not a bad idea, huh? And I bet Becky photographs well."

Aaron frowned. "I wonder if she'll go on camera."

"Better her than me," Cora said.

"That's very interesting," Aaron said. "So, you girls haven't eaten? What do you say we have lunch?"

29

IT WAS NEARLY THREE-THIRTY AND THE WICKER BASKET wasn't crowded. Rick Reed and Becky Baldwin sat at a table by the window. The camera crew, who had obviously eaten earlier, sat at a table in the back, sipping coffee and looking bored and grumpy, probably due to the fact that the restaurant didn't serve beer.

Aaron escorted Cora and Sherry to a table across the room.

A waitress appeared with menus. "Lunch?" she asked.

"It's too early for dinner, isn't it?" Cora said.

"The dinner menu starts at five."

"Then it's lunch," Cora decided. "Bring me a martini or a cup of coffee."

"I'll have coffee too," Aaron said.

"Decaf," Sherry said.

"One decaf, two regular."

"You always have to be healthy?" Aaron asked, as the waitress retreated.

"I don't want to talk about coffee," Sherry said.

"Oh, why not?"

"I'm just wondering what we're doing here."

"We're having lunch."

"We're not spying on Becky Baldwin?"

"Heaven forbid," Aaron said. "Of course, if there was a story, I'm a little hamstrung not being able to write about *you*."

"Your interest in Becky Baldwin is *professional*?"

"I hate getting scooped by TV in general, and *him* in particular."

"Gee. Maybe we should have sat closer so we could listen in."

"Kids, kids," Cora said. "Quit squabbling and look at the menu."

"I know what I'm having," Sherry said. "A BLT on white toast, hold the mayo."

"You on a diet?" Aaron said.

"Nonsense," Cora said. "If she were on a diet, she'd hold the bacon."

"Oh, and what are you having?" Sherry said.

"Well, the diet plate looks good," Cora said, "if I were a rabbit. I'm thinking of the make-your-own omelet with cheddar cheese, onions, and peppers. What about you, Aaron?"

"I've eaten."

They turned on him.

"So you *are* just spying on Becky Baldwin?" Sherry demanded.

Cora waggled her finger. "If you start bickering, there's no dessert. Ah, thank you," she added to the waitress, who slid coffee in front of them. "I'll be having a cheddar cheese omelet with onions and peppers, and she'll be having a BLT on white toast, hold the mayo. He's just having coffee."

"And an oatmeal cookie," Aaron said.

"So what are we really doing here?" Sherry demanded, as the waitress moved away.

"I would call it damage control," Aaron said. "With all due apologies, Cora, throwing Becky Baldwin to the media may not be the best idea, at least as far as I'm concerned. As Daniel Hurley's attorney, she knows more than I do. At least, more than I'm allowed to know. And if she wants to spill it to the TV people instead of to me, I don't like that. I got a big enough handicap as it is."

"And how are you going to control that?" Cora said.

"I don't know," Aaron replied. "We're sitting here having lunch, not invading anybody's space. We're across the room, not trying to eavesdrop." He jerked his thumb. "But if that crew gets up, that's something else again. The minute they point the camera, Becky and Rick are fair game. It's not a private conversation anymore, it's the news. And I'll step right up next to the camera and listen."

From outside came the growl of a motorcycle. It grew louder, then coughed, sputtered, and died. A minute later Daniel Hurley came banging in the screen door. He stood in the doorway, glanced around the room. Scowled at the sight of Becky Baldwin and Rick Reed. He stomped over to their table, and, in a voice loud enough to be heard across the room, said, "Hi, Becky. Who's he?"

Becky said, "Daniel, this is Rick Reed from Channel 8 News."

Daniel Hurley pursed his lips, cocked his head.

Hesitated.

Sherry Carter smiled. She could practically see his thought process. The media. How did Daniel Hurley want to relate to the media? Clearly, his anti-establishment rebel image, typified by the long hair and the motorcycle, practically demanded that he look down on TV crews with contempt.

But for a young man as arrogant as Sherry Carter judged Daniel Hurley to be, it was hard to pass up a chance to be on television.

"Is that so?" he said to Becky, playing it cool. "Well then, I guess it's a good thing they're talking to you instead of someone who will give them the wrong idea. If you will just excuse me a moment."

Daniel Hurley turned and walked across the room to Sherry, Cora, and Aaron's table. "So," he said. "Everybody's having a late lunch?"

"It's a busy day," Cora said.

"That it is," Daniel Hurley agreed. "And we'll be moseying over to the lawyer's soon, and you'll be giving me another piece of Auntie's puzzle. Or shouldn't I be saying that in front of the newshound?"

"You can say anything you like," Aaron said agreeably.

"Only it'll wind up in print?"

"I *am* hard-pressed for a story."

"Aaron, don't," Sherry said. "No, he's not reporting this, Daniel. Why don't you say what you have in mind?"

Daniel Hurley grinned. "Oh, is that how it is?" he said to Aaron. "She tells you what to do?"

"No," Aaron said. He added, pointedly, "She's not my lawyer."

Daniel Hurley frowned. "What's that supposed to mean?"

"Boys, boys," Cora said. "If you're going to fight, please, wait till they set up the cameras."

In spite of themselves, both Aaron and Daniel looked toward the camera crew. The men were still sipping coffee, but they were definitely watching the exchange. So were Rick Reed and Becky Baldwin. So was the waitress, for that matter.

Daniel Hurley smiled, pushed the hair off his face. "I don't want to start an argument, I just want to talk to the judge."

"Me?" Cora Felton said innocently. "What do you want now?"

"I want a clarification. On the rules. That's your job, isn't it?"

"My job is what I judge it to be," Cora shot back. "You got a problem with the rules, you can bring it up. That doesn't mean you're going to get any satisfaction."

"No, but I should get an answer," Daniel said. "A judge can't simply say I don't know."

"Oh, yeah?" Cora Felton said. "You should talk to Melvin."

"Who's Melvin?"

"My fifth husband. By the end of the marriage, anything he asked me, I said I don't know."

"Yeah, yeah, fine." Daniel Hurley was impatient. "Look, I got a question for you. After what you said this morning, about checking your answers, I went over to the library to look up the Tibetan town. You know the Applegates are practically living there? And they got this kid helping them. Is that allowed?"

"A kid?"

"Yeah. The boy who works there."

"Jimmy Potter?" Cora said. "He's working on the puzzle?"

"Well, he's looking stuff up. Is he allowed to do that?"

"It's his job," Cora said.

Daniel Hurley scowled. "That's no answer."

"I shall withhold a ruling. It's early yet. You've only done half the puzzle." Cora cocked her head. "Can I assume you've completed the second section?"

"You mean have I been down to the post office like everybody else?"

"Post office?" Aaron Grant said.

"Aw, gee," Daniel Hurley said. "Wasn't I supposed to say that? Yeah, I had to mail a letter, I went down to the post office. Wouldn't you know it, Philip and Ethel had already been there. That was a while ago, so I can't speak for the others."

"I thought we agreed you weren't going to do that," Cora said.

"Agreed?" Daniel's smile was haughty. "I don't recall agreeing to anything. I recall certain suggestions. It would appear no one's taking them."

"Is that so?" Cora said. "You realize as the judge I have the right to disqualify anyone who doesn't follow the rules?"

Daniel Hurley grinned. "You're gonna disqualify us all? Who gets the money then?"

"I thought you didn't care about the money," Sherry put in.

"Did I ever say that? I will admit in the beginning I thought the game was dumb, I thought I had no chance to win. But, to tell you the truth, it's not so much I'd like to win the money as I'd like to keep any of *them* from winning it. That's the thing about my family. There's a real pleasure in rubbing it in."

A thought struck him. He smiled in satisfaction. "In fact, that's an excellent idea. It will drive them crazy. I can taunt them on camera. They won't be able to do a thing about it. It will drive them wild."

Much to Sherry Carter's amusement, Daniel Hurley had hit on a way to justify appearing on TV. Sherry couldn't help smiling as Daniel went back over to Rick Reed and Becky Baldwin to reluctantly agree to an interview.

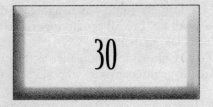

30

"I'M MAKING A RULING," CORA FELTON SAID. SHE STOOD at the front of the table next to Arthur Kincaid, as if to allow the lawyer's authority to lend weight to her pronouncement, and surveyed the assembled heirs. Philip and Ethel Hurley, Phyllis and Morton Applegate, and Daniel Hurley were present. Also on hand were Sherry Carter, Aaron Grant, and Becky Baldwin. Chester Hurley was conspicuous by his absence. So was Chief Harper. Cora was glad. It was a comfort, for once, to begin the meeting without an official police report.

Particularly when she planned to get tough.

Cora drew herself up, tucked in her chin. "It has come to my attention that a number of you showed up at the second location mentioned in the puzzle, in spite of my admonition this morning not to do so. It has been pointed out to me that that was a suggestion, not a ruling." Cora pulled her glasses down on her nose, peered over them. "It is now a ruling. Please take note. In a few moments I will be handing out the third piece of Emma's puzzle. In it is a clue for a ten-letter word. Any of you who show up at any location suggested by that clue are hereby disqualified from playing the game. You will not be given the last piece of the puzzle, and you will be ineligible to receive the bulk of Emma Hurley's estate."

This statement was greeted by howls of protest.

"Oh, now look here," Phyllis Applegate sputtered. "You've got no right to do that."

"Actually, she does," Arthur Kincaid said. "Emma Hurley gave her that right in her will. What she's doing here is reasonable. And it's for your own good. If it will not help you, you shouldn't waste your time doing it. So don't. Is that clear?"

Phyllis set her jaw, sulked in silence.

Cora Felton cast a glance at Daniel Hurley, who was seated in his usual sprawl, with one foot actually up on the table. "On another topic, some of you may have noticed there are news crews in town. On account of the murders. They will undoubtedly be interested in talking with you. If you wish to talk to them, that's your business. However, if you reveal information about the puzzle, that's *mine*. Anyone discussing the inheritance with the media may allude to the fact that there *is* a puzzle. You may even go so far as to state that it is a *crossword* puzzle. But if you reveal any of the *solution* to the puzzle, even one syllable of a clue, then it would be up to me as judge to determine whether or not that revelation constituted a violation of the rules for which action need be taken. Am I making myself clear?"

"I didn't reveal anything," Daniel Hurley said.

The others turned on him.

"You talked to the TV people?" Philip Hurley demanded.

Daniel Hurley shrugged. "Only in generalities."

"We'll be the judge of that." Philip Hurley was red-faced. "What did you tell them?"

"I can't remember," Daniel answered mildly. "Why don't you watch the six o'clock news?"

"You talked to them *on camera?*" Phyllis Applegate shrilled. "Tell me you didn't."

"Okay, I didn't," Daniel said.

Phyllis Applegate's face darkened. "Are you making fun of us, young man?"

Cora Felton held up her hand. "Yes, he is, but so what? I, for one, don't want to hear it. I have a piece of puzzle to hand out. I am going to give it out to anyone who qualifies. And then I am going home. I will be back here tomorrow morning at ten o'clock to give out the last piece of the puzzle. Between now and then, I don't want to hear from you. I don't want to hear *about* you. I don't want it brought to my attention that several of you are violating the rules. I want to go home, have a good night's sleep, come back here tomorrow morning, and find out nothing has happened other than crossword-puzzle solving. Now then, who here among you is ready for the next crossword-puzzle piece?"

The heirs all pushed forward, with the exception of Daniel Hurley, who remained seated at the table, and regarded them with contempt. "That's it, that's it," he said. "Hurry up and get your clues so you can get home in time to see me on TV. Elbow your way right in there as if an extra thirty seconds was going to make the slightest bit of difference. My, my, you're a greedy lot."

The heirs ignored him, continued to crowd around Cora Felton. She held them at bay, managed to accept one puzzle at a time to compare against the computer printout Sherry'd provided her with. The Applegates and Hurleys were letter perfect.

So was Daniel Hurley. When he finally submitted his puzzle Cora found he had corrected *Longa* and *Gar*. Cora handed him the new set of clues. He folded them up, jammed them in the pocket of his leather jacket, and strolled out the door without looking back at Becky Baldwin, who trailed along behind.

"What an insolent boy," Cora Felton said as she gunned the motor and pulled away from the curb, after watching Daniel Hurley take off on his motorcycle with Becky Baldwin clinging to his shoulders.

"I kind of like him," Sherry said.

Cora Felton groaned. "No, no, Sherry. Don't make a big mistake. Like you did with Dennis. You don't *really* like him. You just *think* you like him. Because you see him dumping on Becky what's-her-name. It a tough thing to learn. If a guy treats a woman like dirt, it doesn't make him a nice guy just because the woman he's treating like dirt isn't you."

"Yeah, whatever," Sherry said. "Where's the puzzle? In your purse?"

"Uh huh. Why?"

"I'm a total moron," Sherry said. "I thought I couldn't do the puzzle till we got home because I didn't have the grid. But we *have* the grid. We have the printout you just used to check the heirs' puzzles."

"Yeah, but it's only got the first two quadrants," Cora objected.

"That's all right. I can probably fill in the third from memory. Plus, we got the clues."

Sherry dug in Cora's purse, came out with the grid and the sets of clues. She took out a pen, leaned on the door to brace herself against the swaying of the car, and went to work.

"The long clue is *laundromat,* which dictates the rest," Sherry said, filling in the grid.

Without even looking at the clues, Sherry re-created the lower-left quadrant of the puzzle.

"There. Now for the new clues. The long one's *fifteen*? I won't get that till I get some going down. So, let's see what I got."

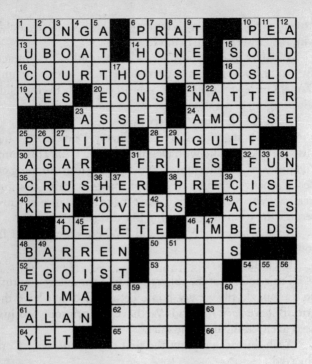

¹L	²O	³N	⁴G	⁵A		⁶P	⁷R	⁸A	⁹T		¹⁰P	¹¹E	¹²A
¹³U	B	O	A	T		¹⁴H	O	N	E		¹⁵S	O	L	D
¹⁶C	O	U	R	¹⁷T	H	O	U	S	E		¹⁸O	S	L	O
¹⁹Y	E	S		²⁰E	O	N	S		²¹N	²²A	T	T	E	R
		²³A	S	S	E	T		²⁴A	M	O	O	S	E
²⁵P	²⁶O	²⁷L	I	T	E		²⁸E	²⁹N	G	U	L	F
³⁰A	G	A	R		³¹F	R	I	E	S		³²F	³³U	³⁴N
³⁵C	R	U	S	³⁶H	³⁷E	R		³⁸P	R	E	C	³⁹I	S	E
⁴⁰K	E	N		⁴¹O	V	E	⁴²R	S		⁴³A	C	E	S
	⁴⁴D	⁴⁵E	L	E	T	E		⁴⁶I	⁴⁷M	B	E	D	S
⁴⁸B	⁴⁹A	R	R	E	N		⁵⁰	⁵¹			S		
⁵²E	G	O	I	S	T		⁵³					⁵⁴	⁵⁵	⁵⁶
⁵⁷L	I	M	A		⁵⁸	⁵⁹				⁶⁰			
⁶¹A	L	A	N		⁶²				⁶³			
⁶⁴Y	E	T		⁶⁵				⁶⁶			

ACROSS

50. _____ a hatter
53. Stove
54. Friend (fr)
58. Fifteen?
62. Consumer
63. Observing
65. "Luck be a _____"
66. Shortstop

DOWN

37. Fraught with incident
42. Took off
46. Thought
47. Style
51. "Bather by the Sea" artist
54. Dead heat
55. _____ room
56. Playwright
59. "Lady _____ tramp"
60. Coloring

Sherry bent over the paper. The pen began flashing in her hand. "Uh oh," she said. "We gotta go back."

"What?" Cora said.

"Stop the car, turn around. We gotta go back to town."

"How come?"

"It's *five-and-ten*."

"What?"

"*Fifteen*. It's *five-and-ten*."

"So? Any six-year-old knows that."

"The solution to fifty-eight across. The clue's *fifteen*? The answer is *five-and-ten*. *F-i-v-e-a-n-d-t-e-n*. We gotta go back to town and see if there's a Woolworth."

"There's no Woolworth in Bakerhaven."

"There's gotta be. The last answer's *five-and-ten*. That's a Woolworth."

"Didn't they go bankrupt?" Cora said, but she turned the car around and headed back toward town. "So what's the solution look like? What about the other clues?"

"What about them?"

"You've now completed the puzzle?"

"Yes I have."

"Every single word is filled in?"

"Of course."

"Let me see."

"You can't read it while you're driving."

"I don't want to read it. I just want to see it."

"What's the point of seeing it if you're not going to read it?"

"Sherry. Humor me. Let me see the grid."

"Then stop the car."

"Control freak," Cora muttered.

Cora pulled off the side of the road, put the car in park, grabbed the paper out of Sherry's hand.

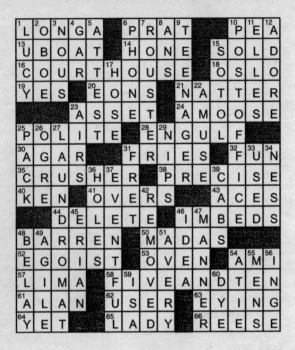

L	O	N	G	A		P	R	A	T			P	E	A
U	B	O	A	T		H	O	N	E		S	O	L	D
C	O	U	R	T	H	O	U	S	E		O	S	L	O
Y	E	S		E	O	N	S		N	A	T	T	E	R
		A	S	S	E	T		A	M	O	O	S	E	
P	O	L	I	T	E		E	N	G	U	L	F		
A	G	A	R		F	R	I	E	S		F	U	N	
C	R	U	S	H	E	R		P	R	E	C	I	S	E
K	E	N		O	V	E	R	S		A	C	E	S	
	D	E	L	E	T	E		I	M	B	E	D	S	
B	A	R	R	E	N		M	A	D	A	S			
E	G	O	I	S	T		O	V	E	N		A	M	I
L	I	M	A		F	I	V	E	A	N	D	T	E	N
A	L	A	N		U	S	E	R		E	Y	I	N	G
Y	E	T		L	A	D	Y		R	E	E	S	E	

ACROSS

50. _____ a hatter
53. Stove
54. Friend (fr)
58. Fifteen?
62. Consumer
63. Observing
65. "Luck be a _____"
66. Shortstop

DOWN

37. Fraught with incident
42. Took off
46. Thought
47. Style
51. "Bather by the Sea" artist
54. Dead heat
55. _____ room
56. Playwright
59. "Lady _____ tramp"
60. Coloring

Cora read the completed puzzle. Frowned. "Is that all there is?"

"Yes, of course," Sherry said.

"It doesn't seem right."

"Oh, you see that, do you?" Sherry said.

"Of course I do. I just figured there'd be some punch line or other. Unless it's at the five-and-ten."

"That's not what I meant," Sherry said.

"Oh? What did you mean?"

"The answer itself. *Five-and-ten*. It's not a pun."

"So?"

"All the others are. This is just a straightforward clue. *Fifteen* does equal *five and ten*."

"Are you saying you think *five-and-ten*'s wrong?"

"No. It has to be right. It's just not a very good answer. But then, this isn't the best of puzzles."

"Maybe not," Cora said. "But if that's all there is—and there is no other hidden meaning that you can detect—then *five-and-ten* is the answer, and what we're looking for must be at the five-and-ten."

"It would seem so," Sherry mused.

"So let's go." Cora slammed the car in gear, peeled out, headed back to Bakerhaven.

A mile down the road she pulled into a gas station.

"What are you doing?" Sherry said.

"If you don't know, ask," Cora said mysteriously. She stopped the car and got out.

The young man at the gas pumps smiled and said, "Can I help you, ladies?"

Cora smiled back. "Well, maybe you could. Would you happen to know if there's a five-and-ten in town?"

"You mean a Woolworth?"

"That's right," Cora said placidly. "Is there one around here? Or did they go out of business?"

He shook his head. "I wouldn't know about that. 'Cause we never had one. It's a rather small town."

"That's for sure," Cora agreed. "So then, tell me this. What's the closest thing Bakerhaven's got to a Woolworth?"

The young man frowned, wiped the sweat off his brow. His hand was greasy, left a smudge on his forehead. "There's a general store over the covered bridge, but that's just a tourist trap. You're talking old-fashioned dime store, right?"

Cora smiled. The attendant didn't seem old enough to have ever *seen* an old-fashioned dime store. "Right," she said. "Anything like that?"

"Not really. There's one shop in town might qualify . . . But it's a stretch."

"What shop is that?"

"Little place on Main Street. Few doors down from the bakery. But it's not really what you want."

"You know the name of this little shop?"

He snuffled and pushed the hair off his forehead, smearing more grease.

"Odds and Ends."

31

THE WOMAN BEHIND THE COUNTER HAD HER HAIR PULLED back in a very severe-looking bun. When Cora and Sherry walked in she arched her eyebrows, said, "I hope you know what you want. We close promptly at five-thirty."

Cora shot Sherry a look, turned to the woman, and beamed. "I must say I approve. There's some of these stores that are open all day long and half the night. And in the long run, they don't sell any more merchandise than the stores that close at six."

"I close at five-thirty."

"Even better," Cora said. "Get you home for dinner."

"Yes, but then people grumble that they can't get here after work. I tell them that's why I'm open Saturday." The proprietor waggled her finger toward the shelves. "You want something, you better look around. I close in nine minutes."

"Sherry's shopping," Cora informed her. "I'm just along for the ride." She frowned, shook her head. "Terrible thing about Annabel Hurley."

The proprietor's face became animated for the first time. "Isn't it now? Murdered. What a shocking thing. Who would want to kill a sweet woman like that?"

"Well," Cora mused, "there is a lot of money at stake."

"You mean the will? I guess so." The proprietor's ugly eyes widened. "Oh, for goodness sakes. It's *you,* isn't it? Well, that's a stupid thing to say, of course it's you. You're the one in charge of the will."

Cora Felton smiled. "Well, actually, the lawyer's in charge of the will. I'm just judging the contest. I'm Cora Felton. Very nice to meet you."

The proprietor shook her hand. "And I'm mighty pleased to meet you. I'm Mable Drake, and this is my little shop. Isn't it terrible about Annabel? I was telling Mildred Sims just this afternoon—she's the housekeeper, you know—I was telling Mildred she's a lucky woman just to get a fixed amount, and not be mixed up in the whole mess. No offense meant, I know you're just doing your job. But isn't that a foolish way to leave one's fortune? Is it any wonder people are getting killed?"

"You think Annabel Hurley was killed because of Emma's will?"

"Don't you?"

"It's certainly possible," Cora said pleasantly. "Do you have any reason to think so? Other than the amount of money involved?"

"Well, Mildred said . . ."

"Yes?"

"I probably shouldn't repeat it."

"Oh, absolutely," Cora agreed. "If you promised you wouldn't."

"Well, I didn't exactly promise . . ."

"Well, if you feel you shouldn't," Cora said.

It was the right tack. Prying would have sealed her lips.

But faced with the suggestion that she not tell, Mable couldn't wait to spill it.

"It's that boy."

"Oh?"

"Mildred Sims doesn't trust the boy. With his beard, his motorcycle, and his nasty ways."

"Nasty ways?"

Mable immediately began to backpedal. "Well, I don't know about his nasty ways. I'm just going by what Mildred said. And she wasn't happy, that's for sure. Never seen her look so glum."

"She was in here this afternoon?"

"That's right."

"Just to talk about the will?"

Mable Drake frowned, and her ugly eyes narrowed. "I beg your pardon?"

"She didn't come shopping, she just came to talk?"

"Don't be silly," Mable said. "What kind of a business would that be, people just come in to talk? She bought a new dish rack. Rack and tray. You know, the rubber tray that goes under. Always a good idea to replace. The mold builds up, no matter how well you think you clean."

"That's certainly true," Cora agreed. "In fact, now that you mention it, ours is a disgrace." She glanced around, saw Sherry ransacking a bin in the back of the store. "Sherry," she called. "We need a dish rack and tray. Now, where would that be, Mable?"

"End of the third aisle."

"Third aisle, down on the end. New dish rack, *and* a rubber tray to go under it." Cora turned back to the proprietor. "Was that all Mildred bought?"

"This time, yes. Of course she's in here all the time."

"And she suspects the young Hurley boy? The one with the motorcycle?"

The proprietor put up her hands. "Now, did I say that? Mildred doesn't like his manner, that's all it is. And she only mentioned it in passing. She came in to buy a dish rack."

"Uh huh," Cora Felton said. "And what about Annabel Hurley? Was she in here all the time too?"

"Well, not like Mildred Sims. But she was certainly in here enough."

"Like yesterday, for instance?"

"Yesterday?"

"Yes. That would be something, wouldn't it, if Annabel had been in here just before she died?"

"I suppose it would if she had."

"You mean she hadn't?"

"That's right. When I heard about what happened to her, it occurred to me I hadn't seen her in weeks."

"Is that right?" Cora seemed more interested in examining a display of nail polish than in the answer to her question.

"Yes, it is." Mabel glanced at her watch. "Now, you got four minutes, and I'm locking the door. Once I lock the door, you can buy what's in your hands, or you can go out. But you can't browse. I don't sit around after hours watching people browse."

"Good operating procedure," Cora said. "I think I'll give my niece a hand."

Cora hurried to the back of the store where Sherry had found the dish racks and was examining the bottoms of the rubber trays. She set down the last one and straightened up.

"Anything?" Cora asked.

"Nothing at all. And there's nothing under the counter and there's nothing on the floor. Are you sure this was where she was?"

"Mildred bought a dish rack."

"Maybe she needed one."

"Hers was moldy. How is ours?"

"We have a dishwasher."

"Oh? So we don't need a dish rack?"

"You don't know we have a dishwasher?"

"At the moment it is not uppermost in my mind. Sherry, *think*. We got two minutes before we're out on our ear. Is there anyplace something could be hidden?"

"There's no way to tell. You'd have to turn the store upside down."

"We're not prepared to do that. Yet."

"So what do we do?"

Out of the corner of her eye, Cora Felton could see the proprietor locking the front door.

She grimaced.

"We buy a dish rack."

32

"THAT'S RIGHT," DANIEL HURLEY SAID. HE DUCKED HIS head, flashed his eyes, and smiled for the camera. "I happen to be engaged in a multimillion-dollar, winner-take-all contest for the Hurley estate. Which would be a real blast—if someone wasn't bumping off the heirs."

Rick Reed's tone was lightly mocking. "Do you feel you're in any danger?"

Daniel Hurley countered with a good-natured grin. "I'm smart enough to look out for myself." He cocked his head. "I can't speak for the other heirs."

Rick Reed's handsome face filled the screen. "Well, there you have it. Once again, more murders in Baker-haven. And, once again, the police have no leads. This is Rick Reed, Channel 8 News."

"Well, that was mercifully short." Cora Felton switched off the TV.

"Yeah," Sherry said dryly. "Rick used up all his time on Becky Baldwin."

"Who had nothing really to say," Cora pointed out. "But she certainly photographs beautifully."

Sherry got up from the sofa, padded into her office, sat at the computer, and stared glumly at the screen.

Cora Felton came up behind her. "What are you doing? The puzzle's solved. It's all over."

"I don't like it," Sherry said.

"Don't like what?"

"There's something wrong."

"What? What do you mean?"

"Take a look."

Cora Felton peered over Sherry's shoulder. There on the screen was the completed grid.

The crossword grid (answers filled in):

1 L	2 O	3 N	4 G	5 A		6 P	7 R	8 A	9 T			10 P	11 E	12 A
13 U	B	O	A	T		14 H	O	N	E		15 S	O	L	D
16 C	O	U	R	T	17 H	O	U	S	E		18 O	S	L	O
19 Y	E	S		20 E	O	N	S		21 N	22 A	T	T	E	R
		23 A	S	S	E	T		24 A	M	O	O	S	E	
25 P	26 O	27 L	I	T	E		28 E	29 N	G	U	L	F		
30 A	G	A	R		31 F	R	I	E	S		32 F	33 U	34 N	
35 C	R	U	S	36 H	37 E	R		38 P	R	39 E	C	I	S	E
40 K	E	N		41 O	V	E	42 R	S		43 A	C	E	S	
	44 D	45 E	L	E	T	E		46 I	47 M	B	E	D	S	
48 B	49 A	R	R	E	N		50 M	51 A	D	A	S			
52 E	G	O	I	S	T		53 O	V	E	N		54 A	55 M	56 I
57 L	I	M	A		58 F	59 I	V	E	A	N	D	60 T	E	N
61 A	L	A	N		62 U	S	E	R			63 E	Y	I	N	G
64 Y	E	T		65 L	A	D	Y		66 R	E	E	S	E	

Cora read the answers over, shrugged. "Looks okay to me."

"Looks okay to me too," Sherry said.

"Then what's the problem?"

"The answer *five-and-ten*."

"What about it?"

"I told you. It's not a pun."

"So it's not a pun, but isn't it a joke?"

"How is it a joke?"

"It's a joke by not being a joke. It's a nonjoke. What's *fifteen*? *Five and ten*. It's kind of funny."

"It's a huge stretch," Sherry said.

"Maybe so, but there you are. Or are you telling me *five-and-ten* isn't the correct answer?"

"No, it has to be. I've checked it and double-checked it. It has to be right."

"So what's bothering you?"

"The fact there's nothing there. We got a bad clue leading to a solution where there's nothing there. The two things taken together would tend to indicate something was wrong." Sherry held up her hand. "I'm not saying there is."

"I'm not thrilled myself," Cora said. "But you can't argue with the facts. There's nothing at Odds and Ends, at least nothing we can find without getting a court order. But I wouldn't expect that there'd be anything there because all we have been finding are crossword-puzzle clues, and what's left to find once the puzzle's complete?"

"I'll grant you that," Sherry said. "But the ten-letter word in the quadrant is *five-and-ten*. And every other ten-letter word in every other quadrant has been a location where something important was hidden. Here's the last one and you're telling me nothing's hidden there?"

Cora grinned. "Role reversal. Here I am, saying a puzzle's just a puzzle, and here you are, making a mystery out of it. But I'll tell you something. If we can't find anything at the five-and-ten—and it would appear that we can't—then whoever solves *this* puzzle is the winner. And that's my ruling. That means tomorrow it's done, and the first person to turn in this completed grid is the heir to the Hurley fortune."

"I think you're being hasty," Sherry said.

"Oh? What would you have me do?"

"We've assumed the five-and-ten is this particular store. Odds and Ends. Because a gas station attendant told us it was."

"And because the housekeeper went there after talking to Chester Hurley," Cora pointed out.

"She needed a dish rack. And there aren't that many stores in town."

"You're saying you think it's the wrong five-and-ten."

"I'm not sure what I'm saying," Sherry said.

The phone rang.

"I hope that's Aaron," Cora said. "You could use some cheering up."

The call was for Cora. "It's my bridge night," she told Sherry as she hung up the phone. "I'd completely forgotten, with everything that's going on."

"You're not going?"

"Of course I'm going. I could use some cheering up myself."

"Cora—"

"It's not like we have anything to do. The puzzle's solved, the stores are closed, we've got to wait till tomorrow morning. There's no reason I shouldn't have a little fun."

Sherry swiveled around in her desk chair. "Aunt Cora," she said. "I don't know how to impress upon you the importance of the meeting tomorrow morning. You have to be in charge, you have to be in control, you have to be *sharp*."

"I'll be terrific. Sharp as a knife."

"It's not a great night to be going out."

"I'm just playing bridge."

"In a bar."

Cora Felton's chin came up. "I don't want to have this conversation. I'm going to change. Then I'm going to play bridge. I'll come home when I'm done, I will not stay out late, I'll be bright-eyed and bushy-tailed in the morning. But I do not appreciate being told to do so, no matter how important it might seem to be."

Cora stormed out of the office. Sherry could hear her

crashing around in her bedroom, trying on clothes. Minutes later she was back, in a simple gray and white dress that buttoned up the front, and a rather outlandish red, green, and yellow scarf, which Sherry figured was probably for her benefit, to spite her for her remarks.

In full array, Cora announced, "Don't wait up," and flounced out the door.

Sherry smiled indulgently, shook her head, and went back to the computer.

The puzzle was bothering her, and it wasn't just *five-and-ten*. The whole thing just didn't seem right. For instance, fifty-four down, the answer to *dead heat,* was *a tie.* Which was wrong, really. The answer to *dead heat* would be *tie,* not *a tie.* Poorly edited, that was the impression Sherry got. Of course, the puzzle was forty years old, and she had no idea what editorial standards might have been back then. Still, she wondered what newspaper it was from. Or if it even came from a newspaper.

It was hot in the office. Sherry got up, went in the kitchen, filled a glass with ice, and poured herself some lemonade. She took a sip, nodded approvingly. She made good lemonade. Tangy. Not too much sugar. Just right.

Sherry went to the front door, opened it, looked out. The driveway was empty. Her aunt was long gone.

Sherry closed the door, went back in the office, sat at her desk. She stared at the computer screen, sipped her lemonade.

Wondered what Aaron was doing.

Actually, she knew what Aaron was doing. Writing his column. That was the problem with being a newspaper reporter. He worked odd hours.

Sherry heard the sound of a motor approaching, and tires in the driveway. Could it be her aunt returning? No, it was a different motor sound.

Very different.

Sherry went to the front door and opened it to find Daniel Hurley climbing down off his big motorcycle. He wore his leather jacket in spite of the heat, and a shiny white motorcycle helmet. He unstrapped his helmet, hung it over the handlebars. Shook the long hair off his face.

"If you're looking for my aunt, you're out of luck," Sherry told him. "She just left."

"Yeah, I thought I passed her on the road," Daniel said. "Where's she heading?"

"It's her bridge night."

"Is that right? Where does she play?"

"At the Country Kitchen. And she won't appreciate you bothering her."

Daniel Hurley grinned. "Yes. She made that pretty clear at the meeting. I assure you I wouldn't dream of it."

"Then why are you here?"

"I came to see you. We didn't really get a chance to talk the other night. After all, I'm an old friend of Dennis's."

"That's hardly a recommendation."

He put up his hand. "I know, I know. Listen, you got anything to drink? It is *so* muggy tonight."

Sherry hesitated. The thought flashed through her mind that the puzzle was still on her computer screen. She immediately told herself she was being silly. He wasn't going to overpower her and storm the office. "I have some lemonade. Come in."

Daniel took the glass of lemonade greedily. Under the kitchen lights the perspiration beaded on his brow. He was sweaty from his ride. He took a huge gulp, grinned, wiped his mouth.

"Not bad. Could use a little sugar."

"You must have a sweet tooth. It's actually just right."

"Well, it hits the spot," Daniel said. "A little tangy, per-haps, but good. So, you see me on TV? Whaddaya think? Will it drive the others wild, or what?"

"Daniel, do you really have time to be doing this? Shouldn't you be solving the puzzle?"

"Maybe I already have."

"Oh?"

"And maybe I haven't. But what's the big deal? The way your aunt's playing it, I've got till ten A.M. tomorrow, and who *couldn't* solve the puzzle in that much time?"

"Particularly with help."

He frowned. "What's that supposed to mean?"

"Isn't your lawyer helping you with it?"

"No, she isn't." He shrugged. "But even if she was, who could object? Anyway, Becky's not helping me, she's too busy chasing after that reporter."

"Rick Reed?"

"No, the other one."

Sherry said nothing.

"Well, you must have noticed she has designs on him. Even that first night in the bar. She's hanging around him every chance she gets. Claims she's doing research. Maybe she even believes it. All I know is it's a good thing I don't really *need* a lawyer."

"Then why do you have one?" The question came out harsher than Sherry had intended.

"I don't really." Daniel's smile was a smirk. Sherry wondered if he was aware he was nettling her. "I consulted Becky about breaking Auntie's will. But that was when I thought I had no chance to win."

"And now you think you do?"

Daniel tossed off the last of the lemonade, set his glass down on the butcher block table, and sized Sherry up. "I didn't come here to talk about the will."

"Then why did you come here?"

"I told you. To see you." He smiled, stroked his beard. "I remember you in college. Little Miss Perfect. So studious all the time. And yet, there was something about you . . . I always thought Dennis was so lucky." He chuckled. "Which he was, wasn't he? More charm than talent, right? Good salesman. Great self-promoter. Still, it amazed me you fell for it."

"I don't want to talk about Dennis."

He nodded. "Of course not. End of subject. Anyway, how you doing now? You're here in this small town, you said you were teaching school. But it's summer. So what are you up to now? Are you just hanging out?"

"I told you. I work with my aunt. On the crossword puzzle thing."

"Yes. That figures. You always were terrific with words. What do you do for fun?"

"Fun?"

"Bakerhaven is not my idea of a hot spot. Young woman like you, I'd think you'd be bored."

"You'd think wrong."

"Uh huh." He jerked his thumb. "Come on. Let's take a ride."

"On your motorcycle?"

"Sure."

"I don't think so."

"Why not?"

"I don't have a helmet."

"Wear mine."

"Then you won't have a helmet."

"Big deal. It's not like this town was crawling with cops."

"I wasn't thinking of a ticket. I was thinking of brain damage."

Daniel grinned. "Hey, I'm not worried. If I rap the bike, I probably kill myself, helmet or no helmet."

"That's encouraging."

"It should be." He took her by the arm and led her

through the living room out the front door. "Here we go. You take my helmet."

"I don't know . . ."

"You ever ride on a bike before? No? Well, no time like the present." Daniel took the helmet off the handlebars. "Here, put that on."

"Daniel."

"Hey, no big deal. It's not like we were going anywhere. Just down the road and back. Come on."

Sherry didn't want to do it. But she didn't want to *not* do it. Which bothered her. Why did she care if Daniel Hurley thought she was an old stick in the mud?

And was that really the motivation?

Or was it what he said about Becky Baldwin and Aaron Grant?

No, not really. She just didn't want to be the type of person who didn't do things. No, not for Daniel Hurley—she couldn't care less what he thought—just for her.

Sherry took the helmet. It was heavier on her head than she expected, and the strap was loose. Daniel reached up, adjusted it. His hand brushed her cheek, briefly, and for a moment Sherry thought he was going to say something. But then he was climbing onto the motorbike and motioning for her to climb up behind. Sherry threw her leg over the bike, scrunched up behind him on the seat.

"Hang on," he said.

Sherry put her hands on his shoulders.

He craned his neck, grinned. "I'd hang on tighter than that."

Daniel wrenched the handlebars, straightened the bike, kicked the kickstand free. He started the bike, revved the engine, eased the clutch, and turned around in the drive. The bike tilted when he did, and Sherry found herself leaning the other way, trying to balance.

"Lean into it," Daniel instructed. "I won't tip over."

He came out of the turn, straightened the bike, gunned the motor down the drive.

At the foot of the driveway he didn't stop, just slowed to see that nothing was coming, and leaned the bike into a slow, lazy turn. Coming out of it, he shifted gears, revved the motor, and popped the clutch.

The motorcycle took off.

Sherry's arms went around Daniel's chest and she hung on for dear life.

The motorcycle rocketed down the winding road, flashing in and out of the tall maple trees. Sherry's heart was pounding. The wind whipped at her face as the fields and trees flashed by. She forced herself to lean in when Daniel did, and then they were out of the turn and hurtling down the road.

Telephone poles flashed by, one after another. It occurred to Sherry she never noticed them in a car. Not like this.

She'd barely had time to have the thought when they were into the S-turn, streaking down the hill toward the turnoff on the way into Bakerhaven. Sherry found herself leaning first one way, then the other, frightened, but thrilled too. And there came a car around the curve, and how did they ever miss it? Though, to be cool and impartial, each vehicle was safely on its own side of the road.

Cool and impartial?

That was a laugh.

At the foot of the hill they reached the main road. For a moment Sherry thought Daniel was going to go back on his word, and keep on going into town. Then, at the last moment, he slowed the motorcycle, and, as no cars were coming, used the intersection to go out around in a semicircle heading back the way they came.

Coming out of the U-turn Daniel gunned the motor

and popped the clutch again, leaving rubber as he took off up the hill.

Sherry wasn't impressed. Or, for that matter, concerned. Whether it seemed safer speeding uphill, or whether she was just used to it, Sherry didn't have the same sense of dizzying exhilaration she'd had coming down. The fear was gone. Sherry was an old hand. Riding a motorcycle was something she had done.

It was worth it just for that.

Or so she told herself.

Daniel Hurley drove his motorcycle up her driveway and stopped. Sherry hopped off, unbuckled the helmet, pulled it off her head. She turned and hung the helmet on the handlebars.

As she turned back, Daniel Hurley took her by the shoulders and kissed her.

Sherry twisted away. "Excuse me?" she said, stepping back.

Daniel Hurley grinned. "In motorcycle circles, when someone gives you your first ride, it's assumed they're entitled to a kiss."

"I don't travel in motorcycle circles," Sherry replied.

"Of course not. That's why it's your first ride."

"Nice try, Daniel."

Daniel Hurley shrugged, made a goofy, aw-shucks gesture. "You could do worse. You know there's a good chance I'm going to be a millionaire."

"And of course I can be bought," Sherry said coldly.

"Sorry. Stupid thing to say."

Daniel smiled. Sherry suddenly realized he was the type of guy who softened everything with a smile. Even that knowledge was not enough to render the trait entirely unendearing.

He asked, "You say your aunt's at the Country Kitchen?"

"You're not going to bother my aunt."

"Absolutely not. But I would like to have a drink. Care to have one with me?"

"Not right now."

"Too bad," Daniel said. "It will be lonely, what with Becky tied up and all. Sure you won't change your mind?"

"I'm sure."

"Suit yourself."

Daniel put on his helmet, climbed on the motorcycle, gunned the motor, and roared off.

Watching him go, Sherry wondered about his last remarks. Wondered how much his calling on her had to do with Becky Baldwin seeing Aaron Grant. Would he do that, chase another woman because she was chasing another man?

Chasing?

Becky Baldwin wasn't chasing Aaron Grant. Any more than Daniel Hurley was chasing *her*.

He kissed her.

Big deal.

Had Becky Baldwin kissed Aaron Grant?

Sherry stopped, put up her hands.

No.

She wasn't doing this.

She'd put it out of her head.

Think of other things.

Sherry felt hot and flushed after the motorcycle ride. She went in the kitchen, poured herself another lemonade. She took a sip and smiled. It was perfect. Not too tangy.

Tangy.

Sherry frowned.

Stop it.

Sherry took another sip of lemonade, eyes on the door of her office. The crossword puzzle was still on the computer screen. She'd left it on while she'd had her debut motorcycle ride. With the front door unlocked, anyone could have come in and seen it. Although no one had. Still . . .

Sherry went in the office, half expecting the puzzle would be no longer there, but, of course, it was. She sat at the computer, studied the screen. There was the puzzle, completely solved, teasing her with its unsatisfying riddle.

What could it possibly mean?

Sherry wondered if she'd ever know.

Even if she didn't, tomorrow the whole game would be over.

Assuming Cora was in any shape to judge the contest.

Sherry sighed.

Wondered how her aunt was doing.

33

CORA FELTON WAS WINNING.

There was nothing particularly unusual in that. A good player, Cora Felton often won at bridge. But not like tonight. Tonight, Cora was winning consistently, rubber after rubber. And it wasn't just that the cards were running hot. But whoever Cora's partner was—for the women switched partners after every rubber—always seemed to play well, and the women who weren't partnered with Cora didn't. As a result, Cora found herself riding an unprecedented winning streak.

The only thing slowing her down was the fact everyone wanted to talk about the Hurleys.

"It's unbelievable," Iris Cooper said. Bakerhaven's first selectwoman as usual wore a dress as conservative as, yet conspicuously more expensive than, that of anyone else at the table. "I've known old Emma Hurley all my life. Annabel too, though not the same way. And Chester, that's another story. Though I understand there was a time before he got weird. Not that I'm old enough to remember *that*."

"Of course not," Lois Greely said. A large, horse-faced, opinionated woman, Lois Greely was the proprietor of the general store, the one just over the covered bridge. Cora wondered if there was any way to tactfully ask her if it had ever been referred to as a five-and-ten. Considering Lois's overbearing manner, there probably was not.

"If you want my opinion," Lois continued, "there's not a good Hurley left, and that's the truth. Annabel was a good woman. Poor, and a little strange, but basically good. Chester's off his rocker, we all know that. And as for the others, they're an ungrateful, greedy lot. I have that from Emma herself. So, if you want my opinion," Lois said again, utterly discounting the possibility someone actually might *not,* "none of them deserves the money, and you should declare them all losers and give it all to charity."

"And give it all to *us,*" Amy Cox piped up. A younger woman who was new in town but who had been welcomed into the inner social circle due to the fact her husband ran a major insurance company in Hartford, Amy Cox laughed unnecessarily loudly at her own joke, as she had a habit of doing.

The women kicked the topic of the inheritance around for a while, then started in on the murders. At which point Cora excused herself and went to get a drink. The table the women used for bridge was in a little room just off the bar, and in the past Cora had often availed herself of the proximity. Tonight she wanted a drink partly to celebrate her winning streak, and partly because Sherry had made such a point about her not having one. Cora needed to show Sherry she was capable of having a drink and still behaving responsibly. She also needed to show Sherry she couldn't be told what to do. She also needed to think about something other than the Hurleys. A drink would be just the ticket.

As Cora came through the door of the bar, however, the first thing she saw was the long black hair of Daniel

Hurley, who was sitting at the end of the bar. And there, not two stools away, sat Arthur Kincaid. Fortunately, the bar was full, and neither of them had seen her. Cora picked a spot about halfway down the bar and squeezed her way in.

"Tall gin and tonic with lime," she called to the bartender.

Miraculously, he heard her. Minutes later, Cora was reaching eagerly for the glass.

"Miss Felton?"

The voice came from behind Cora. But at the moment nothing was going to distract her from her task. She grabbed the gin and tonic, pressed money in the bartender's hand. She raised the glass to her lips and took a huge sip. Then turned to see who had accosted her.

Her face fell.

It was what's-his-name, the constructor, the crossword-puzzle expert. Beerbelly? Beerbaum. That's right. Her worst nightmare. Harvey Beerbaum.

Still, she smiled, said, "How do you do?" and tried to push by him.

But he grabbed her by the arm. "Miss Felton. Miss Felton. I must talk to you."

"Yes, of course," Cora said. "But not now. I'm playing bridge."

"Yes, I know. But it's important."

"I'm sure it is, but so's my bridge game. Do you play bridge?"

"No, I don't. I have to talk to you. It's about the puzzle."

"I'm not talking about crossword puzzles tonight."

"I didn't say crossword puzzles. I said *the* puzzle. The one you're working on. The one you're judging. For the Hurley estate."

"I *particularly* can't talk about that."

"All right, maybe you can't. But in the abstract—can we talk in the abstract?"

Cora's heart was pounding. This was worse than she'd thought. "No, we can't," she said. "I can't discuss the puzzle specifically, I can't discuss it in general, and I cannot, absolutely *will* not, discuss it hypothetically in the abstract. Is that clear? The puzzle doesn't concern you, you shouldn't be discussing it at all, I don't want to hear anything about it."

With that Cora pushed by Harvey Beerbaum and out of the room. She returned to the table, where gossip eventually wound down and the women actually got back to playing bridge.

Cora played, but her mind wasn't on the game anymore. Harvey Beerbaum had distracted her. What could he have possibly wanted? And how did he know anything about the puzzle in the first place? Cora wished she'd been able to ask him. But for her, any discussion of the puzzle at all was entirely too dangerous. Particularly with him. One slip, one tiny slip, and he'd know. And she wouldn't even necessarily know what constituted a slip. No, talking to him was out of the question. She had to put him out of her mind and play bridge.

Cora tried hard. She was aided by the fact that the cards kept running her way. The women played for a penny a point, and Cora wound up winning sixty-seven dollars. She won nearly every rubber, and even made a grand slam.

It didn't help.

Harvey Beerbelly had spoiled her evening.

34

SHERRY COULDN'T HELP WATCHING AARON GRANT. SHE stood in the back of Arthur Kincaid's office next to Aaron, and tried to read Aaron's body language. Was he relating to Becky Baldwin? If so, she certainly couldn't tell. He'd given no indication whatsoever. No sign that he'd dated her the night before.

On the other hand, Daniel Hurley wasn't relating to Sherry either. He'd strode in with Becky Baldwin, arrogant as ever, taunting his relatives with his TV performance, and sprawled out in his usual chair. He hadn't even acknowledged Sherry's existence.

Sherry reminded herself that she didn't care.

She frowned as Arthur Kincaid called the meeting to order and turned the floor over to Cora Felton.

"All right, this is it," Cora said. "This is the final piece of Emma's puzzle. Once I hand it out, the race will begin. The first person to bring back the completed grid will be the winner." She raised her finger. "Provided the grid is correctly filled in. If there is an error, you lose. So check your work. Don't come complaining to me if you blow it."

Cora Felton raised her chin, looked around the room. Philip and Phyllis didn't look pleased, but as far as Cora could tell, the only one who out-and-out disagreed with what she'd just said was Sherry Carter. Sherry and Cora had been outside Odds and Ends when the cranky Mable Drake had opened up at eight-thirty that morning, and an exhaustive but surreptitious search of the store under the guise of shopping for a set of dish towels and a magazine rack had turned up absolutely nothing. Whereupon Cora had decided completing the grid would mean winning the game.

Much to Sherry's disapproval.

"One more thing," Cora said. "As I said, this time it's a race. And I will be staying right here in this room until there's a winner. No checking in. No calling on the phone. No leaving messages on my answering machine. You must be here in this room, personally hand me the grid. If it's right, you win. If it's wrong, you don't. First correct grid wins. Now, if there are no questions, I will begin validating the grids."

The heirs gathered around while Cora made the comparisons, as usual using the printout Sherry had provided.

Cora checked Phyllis Applegate's first. Her grid was still perfect.

So was Philip Hurley's.

Daniel Hurley handed his in with an insolent flourish, and didn't even wait for Cora to look at it before slumping back into his seat. She said, "Yes, this seems to be correct," and then stood there holding the grid, waiting him out until he had to get up and come around the table to take it back from her. He looked slightly pained as he did so. Still, he managed a strut, and an arrogant wink in the direction of Becky Baldwin, who looked on with what Cora would have characterized as fascinated disapproval of his behavior.

"All right," Cora said, holding up the manila envelope.

"Here is the final set of clues. If you'd all care to form a line in front of the door. Not a single-file line, but a line straight across. Would the three principals—that is, Philip Hurley, Phyllis Applegate, and Daniel Hurley—if the three of you would line up next to each other. Then with the help of my niece, Sherry, I will be able to hand out the last set of clues to all of you simultaneously."

Cora Felton slid the final set of clues from the manila envelope. She gave a copy to Sherry, took two for herself. They went around the table to the door, where Philip and Phyllis were elbowing, jostling, and shoving each other, and doing everything except standing in an orderly line.

Cora Felon smiled. "This is the part that makes it all worthwhile. You will keep quiet and hold still. Until you do so, no one gets a clue. I will wait."

After what seemed like forever, but couldn't have been more than twenty seconds of grumbling accusations, blame shifting, and off-color language, Philip and Phyllis were quiet. Cora nodded to Sherry, and the two of them held out the clues. Philip and Phyllis grabbed theirs from Cora and bolted out the door.

Daniel Hurley took his from Sherry. As he took the page his hand brushed hers, and for an instant their eyes met. He smiled briefly, then he was ushering Becky Baldwin out the door.

Outside in the street, car doors slammed, engines revved, and tires squealed, as the heirs took off on the final leg of the puzzle.

"Where do you think they're going?" Aaron asked.

Cora Felton frowned. "What do you mean?"

"Well, we know the Applegates are going to the library, but the rest of them? I mean, it's a crossword puzzle. And it's a race. If I were one of them, I'd sit down and do it right *here*."

"Maybe," Sherry said thoughtfully. "But then you'd

have us all looking on. Which might inhibit you. You gotta remember, this is their fourth time around. So they got their little routines established, how they're comfortable working. And it's a small town. Nothing's more than a few blocks away."

"That's well thought out," Aaron said. "You have a real insight into how people solve crossword puzzles."

Sherry blushed, and averted her eyes. She had a guilty thought, both for what she suspected, and for what she hadn't told him.

Aaron turned to Cora. "Now that it's over, you gonna let me see the grid?"

"It's not over yet," Cora reminded him.

"No, but it soon will be. We're only talking one quarter of a puzzle left. Odds are you'll have a winner before lunch. When you do, I want it. So, can I publish the grid?"

Cora Felton looked at Arthur Kincaid. "What do you think?"

The lawyer shrugged. "When it's final, I don't see why not. But it's not final yet, and Aaron probably shouldn't see it till then."

"Well, let me ask you something," Aaron said. "Have you been solving the grid? Have you been working the puzzle? Has Cora Felton been giving you the clues?"

The lawyer shook his head. "No, she has not. She's kept me apprised of the situation. But she has kept the clues entirely in her possession, given them only to the heirs. There's no possibility whatsoever of any clues falling into the wrong hands."

"And why is that?"

Kincaid smiled. "Because I'm an attorney. And because there's a great deal of money involved. Because in a case like this, the first person I want to protect is *me*."

"So," Aaron said. "The only people who could possibly have the clues are the three sets of heirs who just left?"

"That's correct."

"And the next person to walk through that door will most likely inherit Emma Hurley's fortune?"

"If they have a perfect grid."

"Who would you bet on?" Aaron persisted. "If you had to pick right now, who would you bet on?"

Cora Felton frowned. "Hard to say. The way I've been playing it there's no way to tell. Now, the first set of clues, Philip Hurley was first. Then Phyllis Applegate."

"But that was before Daniel decided to play," Sherry pointed out.

From out in the street came the sound of a vehicle approaching fast. Brakes squealed. Tires shrieked to a stop. An engine roared and died. A car door slammed.

Moments later, footsteps pounded up the stairs.

"Sounds like we have a winner," Aaron commented. "Could they have finished it this fast?"

"I wouldn't think so, but it could be," Cora said.

But it wasn't.

Instead, Chester Hurley slammed into the room. He was a sight, which was saying something, as Chester Hurley was always a sight. But even to Sherry Carter, who had seen him up close and holding a gun, the man looked particularly out of sorts. His eyes were wilder and brighter than usual, his scraggly hair more unkempt, his two-day growth bordered on three. His rotten teeth could scarcely look worse, but they did. Saliva welled up among them and drool dribbled down his chin.

"I'm through," he snarled.

He shoved past them, stomped to the head of the table.

"I'm through with this stupid game."

Chester Hurley raised up his right hand. In it was a piece of paper. He clenched his fist, shook it over his head.

"I don't want this stupid puzzle. I didn't want it then,

and I don't want it now. I took it because Emma wanted me to. But I don't have to like it. And I'm turning it in."

Chester Hurley slapped the paper down on the table, looked up, glared, and stabbed his finger at Cora.

"I'm serving notice on *you*. As of now, I am done. Over. Finished. Through with this wretched game. I didn't understand it to begin with, and I don't understand it now. I don't know why Emma did this to me, and I'm angry, but there's nothing I can do about it. All I know is it got Annabel killed, and if I can figure out why, I aim to do something about that.

"But as for this other thing." Chester Hurley's eyes flashed. "This puzzle that's poison, that makes men kill. Or women, for that matter. I'm through with it, I give it back, there it lies. Do with it as you will."

Chester Hurley glared at them all in turn, especially Cora, then shook his head.

"Stupid, stupid game," he snarled, then banged past them out the door, and thundered down the steps.

Cora, Sherry, Aaron, and Arthur Kincaid heard the front door slam, then his old truck starting up. Even so, his performance had been so captivating it was moments before anyone could speak.

Finally, Sherry broke the silence. She turned to Aaron, and grinned. "Well," she said. "You gonna write that up?"

"Somehow I doubt it," he replied. "It's an amusing sidelight, but that's all. And I suspect this won't be a slow news day."

"Well, we knew Chester wasn't playing the game," Cora said, "but this makes it official. Rather over the top, turning in his grid. But right in character. Just what you'd expect from him."

"At least he didn't pull his gun," Sherry said.

"Yeah," Cora said. "Thank goodness for small favors."

Chester Hurley's grid was lying facedown on the table. Cora absently picked it up and turned it over. Her eyes widened.

"Sherry."

Sherry was talking with Aaron and didn't hear her.

"Sherry!"

Sherry heard her that time. "What?"

"Come here."

"What is it?"

"Come. *Here!*"

Sherry joined her aunt at the head of the table. Cora was holding Chester Hurley's grid.

The grid had been filled in in pencil.

Sherry gawked at the grid.

"Is it right?" Cora murmured.

"I think so."

"What's going on?" said Arthur Kincaid.

"What is it?" Aaron Grant asked.

Before Sherry or Cora could answer, there came a sickening screech of brakes from outside. A car door banged, and then the front door, and footsteps slammed up the stairs.

Sherry and Cora looked at each other. Reading each other's thoughts, they shared the same unspoken question.

Which of the three heirs was about to come racing through the door with a completed puzzle, having left the others in the dust, and never dreaming he or she could possibly lose?

Once again, it was none of them.

Dan Finley burst into the room. The eager young Bakerhaven police officer was out of breath from pelting up the stairs, but his face was animated, and his eyes were wide.

"There's been another one!"

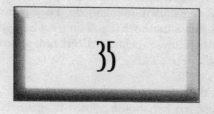

35

CHIEF HARPER WAS GRIM. "YOU WERE AT THE COUNTRY Kitchen last night?"

"That's right," Cora Felton said.

"That's where you saw the puzzle maker?"

"Constructor."

"Huh?"

"They call themselves constructors."

"And you do too."

"I beg your pardon?"

"You said *they*. But you're one of them, aren't you?"

Cora squirmed in her chair. "Hey, Chief, it's me, Cora. What's with the third degree? You drag me into your office, you won't even let Sherry come in with me, you interrogate me, and then you pick on everything I say. Yes, I saw what's-his-face at the Country Kitchen last night. How was I to know he was going to be assaulted?"

"He's lucky he isn't dead," Chief Harper said. "Barney Nathan says an inch more to the left, and he wouldn't be waking up."

"He was hit with a pipe?" Cora perked up.

"He was hit with a blunt object. Just like Jeff Beasley. After leaving the Country Kitchen. After talking to *you*."

"Are you making an inference?"

"No, I'm not. You're not a suspect, you're a witness. So try to be a cooperative one and do not play word games with me. I know that's what you do for a living, but please do not do that now. So, Harvey Beerbaum approached you in the bar?"

"That's right."

"What time was this?"

Cora opened her mouth, closed it again. "Chief," she said. "We don't have time for this. Chester Hurley has completed his grid. The other heirs are working on theirs. They'll be arriving at the lawyer's any minute, wondering what's going on. You've got me in here, you've got Sherry and Arthur Kincaid cooling their heels in the outer office, and what's gonna happen when the next heir shows up and goes ballistic when he finds no one's there?"

"Oh, I think we can handle it," Chief Harper said. "I know this whole will contest is very important to you, Cora, but, frankly, a murder investigation is far more important. Now, it's just taken a bit of a turn, which is good in a way, because it gives us a lead. And it's even better, in that this time nobody died. Granted, it's touch-and-go, but Barney thinks the guy will pull through."

"You got a guard on his room?"

Chief Harper frowned. "Why?"

"Well, someone wanted him dead. I doubt if anything's very much changed."

"Oh, no? I thought you have a completed grid."

"Yes, I do, but . . ."

"But what?"

"That was Chester Hurley's."

"Right. Not what you expected, but still a winner. My point is, if Beerbaum was assaulted because of the game, the game is over." Chief Harper put up his hand. "Granted, that is an unfounded assumption. And, yes, I have a guard on his room. Now, could we get back to the questions that are important to me? You saw what's-his-name—now you've got me doing it—you saw Harvey Beerbaum at the Country Kitchen last night. At approximately what time?"

"I would say around eight-thirty to nine o'clock."

"You saw him in the bar?"

"That's right."

"Could you describe that meeting?"

"The bar was crowded. I had squeezed in to order a drink. What's-his-name tapped me on the shoulder. Wanted to talk about the crossword puzzle."

"The one the heirs were solving?"

"So he said."

"And what did he know about that?"

"I don't know, because I refused to discuss it with him."

"Why?

"It was none of his business. He was an outsider, he had no right to ask me about it."

"But if he knew about it . . . ?"

"That wasn't my fault."

"I'm not saying it was your fault. But if he knew about it, wouldn't you want to know how he knew?"

"Not at all. Everyone in town knew about the puzzle game. It's no secret. I don't know *how much* he knew about it. And I didn't want to know. I was at the Country Kitchen playing bridge. I just wanted to get my drink and get back to the game."

"You remember exactly what he said?"

"Not word for word."

"But it was about the puzzle? And he said it was impor-tant?"

"That's my impression."

"And were any of the heirs present at the time?"

"The bar was crowded. There could have been any number of them there. They all could have been there, for that matter."

"But did you see any of them?"

"I saw Daniel Hurley."

"And where was he?"

"Sitting at the bar."

"Where you were standing?"

"Not where I was standing. A few stools down."

"But close enough to have heard?"

"I don't think so. In a crowded bar with all that noise."

"But you don't know?"

"How could I know? I wasn't paying attention."

"Aha. And did you see any of the other heirs in the bar last night?"

"No, I didn't."

"Just Daniel Hurley?"

"Yes, just him. But the lawyer was there."

"Arthur Kincaid?"

"Yes. He was in the bar."

"With Daniel Hurley?"

"No. A few stools away."

"So Daniel Hurley wasn't with him?"

"No, he wasn't."

"Was he with his lawyer? Was Becky Baldwin there?"

"No."

"He was alone?"

"That's right."

"He was alone drinking in the bar when Harvey Beerbaum talked to you about the puzzle. Just as he was alone drinking in the bar the night Jeff Beasley was assaulted."

"Are you making a connection, Chief?"

"No, just an observation."

"Well, you'll forgive me, Chief, but I think you're off on

the wrong track. I'd like to point out it was Chester Hurley who solved the puzzle. Without even having the clues."

Chief Harper didn't seem impressed. "He had the first set, didn't he?"

"Yes. So?"

"Chester always was a strange cuss, went his own way. If he was one step ahead of you, I'm not surprised. I don't suppose *he* was in the Country Kitchen last night too?"

"Not as far as I know."

"No, and if he had been, I think you would. Chester Hurley's hard to miss." Chief Harper nodded. "Okay, that's all for now. You wanna send in the lawyer?"

"You don't want to talk to Sherry next?"

"Was she at the Country Kitchen last night?"

"No, she wasn't."

"And Arthur Kincaid was? Then I gotta talk to Arthur. Send him in."

Cora Felton went back to the outer office of the police station where Sherry Carter and Arthur Kincaid were seated by one of the desks. They were alone in the office, as both Sam Brogan and Dan Finley were out investigating the assault.

"Okay, you're next," Cora told Kincaid. "I should warn you, he's not in a great mood."

Arthur Kincaid went into the office, closed the door.

"So, what's up?" Sherry demanded. "Is he going after Chester?"

"No. He seems to want Danny Hurley."

"How come?"

Cora Felton gave Sherry Carter a rundown of her interrogation.

"That's awful," Sherry said. "He's missing the whole point."

"Yes and no," Cora said.

Sherry frowned.

"Someone knocked this guy out," Cora explained. "It could be Daniel Hurley as well as anybody else."

"Yeah, but I don't think so," Sherry said.

Cora snorted in exasperation. "There again, you're going on nothing but the fact he's young and good-looking. Which, trust me, doesn't mean a thing. I'm not saying he did it, I'm just saying there's no reason to cross him off the list."

"Is that what you told Chief Harper?"

"No, I told Chief Harper it's ridiculous, I don't suspect him for a minute. And I don't. But that's no reason why you shouldn't."

"Aunt Cora, you're making no sense."

"Maybe not. Where's Aaron?"

"He went back to the paper."

"You tell him about your joyride with laughing boy?"

"It didn't come up."

"You ask him about his rendezvous with golden girl?"

"It didn't come up."

"A lot of things between the two of you don't seem to be coming up."

"Aunt Cora."

"What do you think Chief Harper's gonna say when he finds out Aaron left?"

Sherry shrugged. "He may not be pleased, but the fact is, he didn't ask Aaron to stay. He's got a story to write, there's news crews right outside, and he doesn't want to be left behind. So, Harper's not looking for Chester Hurley?"

"Not that I know of. Why?"

"Well, how about the fact Harvey Beerbaum's a constructor, and Chester Hurley had to get the answers from somebody?"

Cora shook her head. "Doesn't fly. At least, not for

Chief Harper. He's not that surprised Chester cracked the puzzle."

"Without the clues?"

"Chief Harper points out Chester had the first set of clues. He could have beat us to the rest."

"Which he must have done," Sherry mused. "But surely someone would have seen him. If he'd been in the post office and the laundromat . . ."

Cora Felton just smiled.

Sherry grimaced. "Of course. Annabel Hurley." She shook her head. "That tears it. I've been so caught up in my personal life I'm not thinking clearly. But that's why Annabel wasn't playing the game. She was working for Chester."

"Exactly," Cora said. "You got Annabel Hurley doing Chester Hurley's legwork, then everything fits. She was in the post office and the laundromat, and she must have been in the courthouse too. She wasn't hiding the clues for Emma Hurley, she was fetching the clues for Chester."

"Then why wasn't she at Odds and Ends?"

"Huh?"

"If she was everywhere else, then why wasn't she there?"

"Because she got her throat sliced before she could get there."

Sherry winced.

"Say Chester Hurley solves the last set of clues and gets *five-and-ten*," Cora continued, in her Miss Marple mode. "So what happens then? Either he can't figure out what that means, or he does but it's too late and Odds and Ends is closed—we know that woman closes like clockwork—or he does, but to him *five-and-ten* means a different place. Which is what I've been afraid of all along, that we have the wrong store."

Sherry shook her head. "We've been through the phone book. There *is* no other store."

"I agree. It's gotta be Odds and Ends. Mildred Sims went there. After talking to Chester Hurley. Which makes sense. With Annabel dead, he'd send another woman."

"Yeah, but why?" Sherry objected. "What's at Odds and Ends?"

"I don't know. But the puzzle leads there."

"Right," Sherry said. "Which really bothers me. There's something about the puzzle I don't understand."

"There's a lot about the puzzle I don't understand," Cora retorted. She patted her drawstring purse. "Anyway, I got it right here. Whaddaya say we take a look?"

"I don't see what good that will do. It is what it is."

"Maybe," Cora agreed. "But what's-his-face, the puzzle guy, thought something was wrong. I'd like to know what he knew."

There were a number of manila envelopes in Cora Felton's bag. One had computer printouts of grids in various stages of completion. The others held the remaining copies of the clues that had been handed out. Cora pulled a paper from each envelope.

"Okay," she said. "Here's the first set, here's the second set, here's the third, and here's the last. Let's look them over, and see if there's any— Well, will you look at that."

"What is it?" Sherry said.

"We don't have to go any further. It jumps out at you."

"What? What jumps out?"

"Look." Cora Felton held up the third and fourth sets of clues, side by side. "Look at the typing. It's entirely different. It's not even the same size."

"You're kidding."

"Not at all. Look. The first three sets of clues all look alike. They were probably done on the same machine. They could even be computer printouts. But the last set, the type is smaller—I think they call it elite. And, look, it's dirtier, was obviously done on a typewriter. It's a photocopy, but you can still tell."

"Good lord," Sherry said. "We've gotta show this to Chief Harper."

But Cora Felton stopped her. "He's awful busy right now, and he won't wanna hear it. I say we find Chester."

Sherry looked at her in surprise. "We can't leave."

"Why not?" Cora said. "The Chief's done with me, and he doesn't want you."

"He doesn't want me?"

"No, I asked him. You weren't in the Country Kitchen last night." Cora tugged at Sherry's arm. "Let's go."

Sherry wasn't convinced. "Shouldn't we tell him we're going?"

"I wouldn't bother him right now," Cora Felton said decisively. She went to the door, flung it open. "Come on, come on," she said.

As they went out the front door, Cora murmured, "I'm pretty sure he doesn't mind if we go, but why take a chance?"

36

As they drove up to the cabin, Chester Hurley's truck was nowhere to be seen.

"Just our luck," Cora groused. "He's not home."

"Don't be too sure," Sherry told her. "He hides his truck down the road so people will think he's not here. He could be inside, with his gun trained on us right now."

"Why would he do that?" Cora objected. "We're obviously not here to hurt him."

"Oh, sure," Sherry said. "We suspect him of assaulting Harvey Beerbaum and rigging the game, but we're really no threat."

"I don't suspect him of assaulting Harvey Beerbaum. 'Cause the odds are the same person who attacked Harvey also killed Annabel Hurley, and I can't see Chester doing that. Can you?"

"I don't know what he's capable of," Sherry said. "I'm just saying be careful."

"I'm always careful," Cora said mendaciously.

She was already out of the car and up on the porch. She

banged on the door, tried the knob. "Locked," she declared. "I bet a stiff kick would open it . . ."

"Aunt Cora."

"Just making an observation. Is there another door?"

"Around the side."

The side door was fastened with a hook.

"Hmm, latched from inside," Cora said. "But not that well. You'll notice there's a crack between the door and the jamb."

"So what? The point is, Chester's not here."

"I thought you said his truck could be hidden."

"And he's hiding inside and not answering the door?"

"It's a thought." Cora slipped the bulging drawstring purse off her shoulder, rummaged in it, came out with a pocketknife.

"What are you doing?" Sherry asked in horror.

Cora flicked the knife blade open. "Making a little experiment."

Cora slipped the knife blade between the door and the jamb.

"Aunt Cora, I don't think that's a good idea."

"Then get back in the car."

"Aunt Cora—"

"Oops," Cora said, as the knife blade popped the hook out of the eye. She turned to her niece. "Well, the door seems to be open, so I'm going in. Why don't you sit in the car and honk the horn if someone comes?"

"Phooey on that," Sherry said, and decided she sounded just like Cora. "If the door's open, let's go."

Cora and Sherry slipped inside. They found themselves in an exceptionally dingy kitchen. The sink was piled with dirty dishes. The electric range was missing two of its four burners. The refrigerator was of the kind with the exposed motor on top, which made it look just one small step up the evolutionary scale from an icebox.

On the table was a large brown paper bag. Cora peered inside it, then whistled. "Take a look at this," she said, and pulled its contents out of the bag.

It was a dish rack with a rubber tray.

"How about that," Sherry said. "Isn't that the same one we just bought?"

"It sure is. And Mildred Sims too."

"What's going on here? Everyone's buying a dish rack."

"It means we're on the right track." Cora rubbed her hands together, eyes sparkling. "Okay, let's toss the place. Open the cabinets and look under the sink. In particular, look for a large tin of sugar. Sugar canisters are a prime male hiding spot. An old coot like Chester will figure it's the last place anyone would look."

Sherry found the sugar canister, but, disappointingly, it was empty except for a dead cockroach. A quick search of the kitchen turned up canned and powdered foods, mostly of the cheaper brands, and some boxes of stale crackers.

"Living room next?" Sherry suggested.

Cora shook her head. "Only if it's in plain sight. A man's ten times more likely to hide something in his bedroom."

"You're an expert on what a man's likely to do?"

"Well, I married enough of 'em."

Chester's living room was stark, with a couple of chairs, a table, and a dilapidated couch. The only bright spot, a working fireplace, might have been cheery in winter, but didn't help in July.

The women pushed on into the bedroom. Though also poorly furnished, it was far more comfy. There was a double bed with sagging box springs and a brass frame, a rickety bureau piled high with clothes that wouldn't fit in the drawers, a bookcase made of cinder blocks and planks filled two rows deep with well-thumbed paperbacks, and a straight-backed chair practically buried in dirty clothes.

"Typical," Cora said. "The man could use a laundry hamper."

"When he inherits the Hurley fortune, maybe he can buy one," Sherry said. "Uh oh. Look at that."

Sherry stepped gingerly between the possessions strewn on the floor. In a corner of the room, resting on a stack of faded newspapers, was a small, portable Smith-Corona typewriter.

"You think this could have typed the last clue list?" Sherry asked.

"There's one way to find out," Cora said.

There were sheets of paper on the floor next to the typewriter. Cora ratcheted one into the machine, typed *The quick brown fox jumps over the lazy dog.* She ripped the paper out of the roller, said, "We can compare this later. Right now we search the room. Okay, I'm Chester Hurley and I've got something to hide. So, it's either under the mattress or taped to the bottom of a bureau drawer."

Cora marched to the bed, flipped the quilt down, reached her hand between the mattress and the box spring.

"Aha," she said, eyes sparkling. "I certainly hope this isn't a men's magazine."

What she pulled out from under the mattress was a manila envelope.

"Don't tell me," Sherry said.

"What do you mean, don't tell you. It's what we were looking for." Cora unsnapped the envelope, pulled out the sheet of paper. "Well, well," Cora said. "Fifty across, _____ *Ababa (Ethiopian city);* fifty-three across, *Idiot;* fifty-four across, *Tax man.*"

"Let me see," Sherry said. She took the paper, looked it over. "It's the missing clues all right. How does the typing look?"

"It looks okay. What do you say we get out of here before Chester comes back and blows us away?"

"Best idea you've had all day."

Sherry and Cora hurried out of the bedroom to the kitchen. Sherry half expected to find Chester Hurley waiting at the screen door with a scowl on his face and a huge pistol in his hand. Of course, there was no one there. They slipped out, hopped in the car, and took off. Sherry's heart didn't really stop racing until they reached the main road.

"Okay, let's go home, put this up on the grid," she said.

"You think it's from the original puzzle?"

"I don't see what else it could be."

"What's the long clue?"

"*Bakery, so to speak?*"

"*Bakery?* How is that a pun?"

"I have no idea until I solve the puzzle."

"Can't you solve it in the car?"

"If I had a Dramamine."

"Oh?" Cora said. "Am I driving too fast?"

"Well, I didn't see a speed limit posted, but I bet it isn't eighty-five."

"This is practically an emergency," Cora said, spinning the wheel. "There's a killer on the loose, and we hold the key to his identity."

"That might be a legitimate excuse if we were heading for the police station."

"We can't go to the police until you solve the puzzle," Cora objected. "If I drive in there now, he'll expect me to solve it."

"Yes, I know," Sherry said.

"So hang on and let me get you home."

It took less than five minutes. Cora sped up the driveway, screeched to a halt. The car was still rocking as they hopped out.

"Okay," Sherry said. "Let me boot up the computer."

"Can't you do it by hand?"

"Actually, it's faster this way. Much faster, since I left the computer on again."

Sherry clicked on Crossword Compiler, pulled up a blank grid. "Let's see, I need the third quadrant. What did I save that as?"

Sherry clicked on it. A grid filled the screen.

¹L	²O	³N	⁴G	⁵A		⁶P	⁷R	⁸A	⁹T		¹⁰P	¹¹E	¹²A
¹³U	B	O	A	T		¹⁴H	O	N	E		¹⁵S	O	L	D
¹⁶C	O	U	R	¹⁷T	H	O	U	S	E		¹⁸O	S	L	O
¹⁹Y	E	S		²⁰E	O	N	S		²¹N	²²A	T	T	E	R
		²³A	S	S	E	T		²⁴A	M	O	O	S	E
²⁵P	²⁶O	²⁷L	I	T	E		²⁸E	²⁹N	G	U	L	F
³⁰A	G	A	R		³¹F	R	I	E	S		³²F	³³U	³⁴N
³⁵C	R	U	S	³⁶H	³⁷E	R		³⁸P	R	E	C	I	S	E
⁴⁰K	E	N		⁴¹O	V	E	⁴²R	S		⁴³A	C	E	S
	⁴⁴D	⁴⁵E	L	E	T	E		⁴⁶I	⁴⁷M	B	E	D	S
⁴⁸B	⁴⁹A	R	R	E	N		⁵⁰	⁵¹			S
⁵²E	G	O	I	S	T		⁵³				⁵⁴	⁵⁵	⁵⁶
⁵⁷L	I	M	A		⁵⁸	⁵⁹				⁶⁰
⁶¹A	L	A	N		⁶²				⁶³		
⁶⁴Y	E	T		⁶⁵				⁶⁶		

"Now the new clues," Sherry said.
She propped them up beside it.

ACROSS

50. _____ Ababa
    (Ethiopian city)
53. Idiot
54. Tax man
58. Bakery, so to speak?
62. Mail delivery org.
63. Rub out
65. Medieval instrument
66. Drugged

DOWN

37. Fraught with incident
42. Take on again
46. Out of work
47. Beveled
51. Extinguish
54. Fellow
55. Say cheese
56. Mimicked
59. College
60. Sold out

She looked up from the computer. "Care to have a crack at it, Cora?"

"No, I'd like to have you do it. Before someone shows up and you can't."

"There's a thought," Sherry said. "Okay, what have we got here?"

The phone rang.

Sherry and Cora looked at it, then looked at each other.

"I can't think of anyone I wanna talk to," Sherry said.

"Me neither," Cora said. "Why don't we let the answering machine pick up?"

"Good idea. Why don't you monitor it, see who it is."

"Gotcha," Cora said. But when she reached the kitchen, the answering machine had already picked up.

"Hey!" snarled the irate voice of Phyllis Applegate. "What's going on? I solved the puzzle, I went to the lawyer's, and there's no one there. That's a fine kettle of fish, no one there. You said you'd be there, and you aren't. The lawyer's not there either. And the office is locked. I'm calling from a pay phone, and I'm serving you notice. If I lose this inheritance, you'd better have insurance, 'cause I'm suing you for every dime."

Phyllis Applegate banged the phone down, and the answering machine reset. When that happened, Cora noticed it was blinking many times.

"Uh oh," Cora said.

She pressed the button.

Beep.

The first caller was Philip Hurley in an absolute tizzy.

"This is Philip Hurley! Something's happening, you've gotta stop the game! There's been another assault! Another attack by the killer! The police are investigating and asking questions, and how can I possibly play with that going on? You gotta call a time-out, you gotta call a do-over. You gotta stop this, right here, while there's still time, before anybody else gets hurt."

There was a sound like, "Huh?" then low mumbling, then Philip Hurley came back on the line.

"Not that I'm not doing great. Not that I'm not in position to win. I just don't want to win like *this*. Just shut it down right now, I'll pick it up again as soon as the police clear up these attacks."

Beep.

"It's Aaron Grant. I got nowhere at the hospital. The puzzle guy's still in a coma. I could use a jump on the TV people, save me something if you can."

Beep.

"This is Chief Harper. I don't recall telling you to go anywhere. When you get this message, get back in here. And I mean *now*."

Beep.

"Miss Felton, Arthur Kincaid here. Chief Harper is most unhappy. I don't know where you went, but it wasn't my office, because Chief Harper just drove me back here to find you, and wasn't pleased when he didn't. He just called you from my phone. I'm not sure he mentioned where he was. He probably didn't, he was rather upset. He just left, and I'm all alone here waiting for the heirs, who aren't going to be too happy either. Call me as soon as you can. Please."

Beep.

"Hey!" the Phyllis Applegate message began again. "What's going on? I solved the puzzle, I went to the lawyer's, and there's no one there—"

Cora clicked the answering machine off.

Sherry burst into the kitchen with a paper in her hand. "Okay, I got it," she said. "Here, take a look."

Cora grabbed the paper.

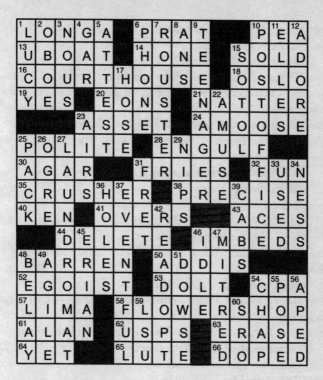

L	O	N	G	A		P	R	A	T			P	E	A
U	B	O	A	T		H	O	N	E		S	O	L	D
C	O	U	R	T	H	O	U	S	E		O	S	L	O
Y	E	S		E	O	N	S		N	A	T	T	E	R
		A	S	S	E	T		A	M	O	O	S	E	
P	O	L	I	T	E		E	N	G	U	L	F		
A	G	A	R			F	R	I	E	S		F	U	N
C	R	U	S	H	E	R		P	R	E	C	I	S	E
K	E	N		O	V	E	R	S			A	C	E	S
	D	E	L	E	T	E			I	M	B	E	D	S
B	A	R	R	E	N		A	D	D	I	S			
E	G	O	I	S	T		D	O	L	T		C	P	A
L	I	M	A		F	L	O	W	E	R	S	H	O	P
A	L	A	N		U	S	P	S		E	R	A	S	E
Y	E	T		L	U	T	E			D	O	P	E	D

ACROSS

50. _____ Ababa
    (Ethiopian city)
53. Idiot
54. Tax man
58. Bakery, so to speak?
62. Mail delivery org.
63. Rub out
65. Medieval instrument
66. Drugged

DOWN

37. Fraught with incident
42. Take on again
46. Out of work
47. Beveled
51. Extinguish
54. Fellow
55. Say cheese
56. Mimicked
59. College
60. Sold out

"*Flower shop?*" Cora said.

"That's right."

"How does that work?"

"Perfect," Sherry said. "It's a bad pun, just what we expected. A bakery is a flower shop. *Flour* shop. *F-l-o-u-r* shop. Get it?"

"So what's the point? What does *flower shop* mean? And why did Chester Hurley go to such trouble to send us to a five-and-ten instead?"

"Obviously, to keep us away from the flower shop."

"What flower shop?"

"I don't know. Where's the phone book?"

The Yellow Pages of the Bakerhaven phone directory had no listing for flower shops.

"Of course not," Sherry told Cora. "It's not *flower shops*. It's *florists*."

There were no florists either.

Sherry looked at the Yellow Pages in disbelief. "In the whole town?"

Cora Felton shrugged. "Well, it's not that big a town."

"Even so, they must have flowers."

"Maybe it's listed as something else."

"What could it possibly be?"

"I have no idea." Cora Felton's eyes widened. "Oh!"

"What?"

"*People* magazine."

"I thought that was next week."

"It is."

Sherry looked at her aunt in exasperation. "Aunt Cora."

Cora Felton put up her hand. "Sherry. Sweetheart. What was I doing for *People* magazine?"

Sherry frowned. Then her eyes widened. She smiled. "Planting flowers."

37

THE CEDAR GROVE GREENHOUSE WAS NORTH OF TOWN IN a secluded meadow about half a mile off the main drag. The proprietor, Vince, a middle-aged man with horn-rimmed glasses and dirty hands, smiled when he saw Cora Felton.

"Well, well, if it isn't the Puzzle Lady. How did the interview go?"

"Haven't had it yet," Cora told him. "This is something else. Is that Chester Hurley's truck outside?"

"You bet. He's been here all day." Vince waggled his hand. "Off and on. And yesterday too. Out in the greenhouse, pawing through the pots."

"He tell you what he's doing?" Cora asked.

"Of course not. Tight-lipped old coot. Off his rocker. I mean, here's his niece newly dead, and he's spending all day here."

"Did you ask him why?"

Vince shook his head. "No use. Never get a word out of him. I did tell him he couldn't browse all day. This isn't a library. You want something, you buy it. You don't come in just to look."

"What did he say to that?"

"Took a zinnia, bought it, put it in his truck. Came back in to look some more. And what am I supposed to do then? The worst he is, is a slow shopper."

"Where is he?" Sherry asked.

"Last I looked he was in the coleus house. That's straight through marigolds, straight through geraniums, left through pansies and petunias. It's the third wing on the left."

"How big is this place?" Sherry said.

"Plenty big. And he's pawed through most of it."

Sherry and Cora pushed though the double doors into the greenhouse, which consisted of a series of long, narrow, glass-enclosed rooms. Each was climate-controlled, with subtle variations for the different varieties of plants. There were fewer than half a dozen customers, which made the sprawling greenhouse seem practically empty.

Sherry and Cora made their way through the brightly hued flowers following the proprietor's directions. Chester Hurley was in the coleus house, as Vince had said. Chester was alone, which was not surprising—no customer would have wanted to go near him. Aside from his appearance, he was acting like a man obsessed. As they watched, he moved down a row of pots, snatching one up, peering at its bottom, looking at its top, poking his finger into the dirt, squinting at the spot where the pot had been, putting it back, grabbing the next. His concentration was such they were sure he had no idea they were there.

"Well, what do you think?" Sherry asked her aunt. "We gotta call Harper?"

"I suppose we have to. I don't like it. The Chief's not going to be thrilled."

He wasn't. When Chief Harper drove up to the greenhouse in response to their phone call, he looked like he was on his way to a lynching. By the time Sherry and Cora had filled him in on the situation, he looked like they were the ones he intended to hang.

"Let me be sure I have this straight," he told them. "Chester Hurley got ahold of the crossword puzzle. Stole the last set of clues. And put a whole new set in their place?"

"So it seems," Cora Felton said.

"And the reason he did this?"

"Is obvious," Cora said complacently. "Chester thinks the puzzle means something, the last answer is *flower shop,* this greenhouse is the only game in town, and he wants it for himself."

"Uh huh," Chief Harper said. It occurred to Sherry he didn't look particularly sold on the proposition. "And what do you expect me to do about this?"

Cora Felton frowned. "Why, arrest him, of course."

"On what charge?"

"Are you kidding?" Cora said. "We've had three murders connected to the Hurley estate. Well, two murders and an assault. All tied into this will contest. And here's Chester Hurley, tearing the greenhouse apart, proving conclusively he's totally obsessed with either winning the game or finding out what it means. Clearly, he would stop at nothing to do so. He's even gone so far as to rig the game. And who was the last person assaulted? A crossword-puzzle constructor! A man who was desperately trying to tell me, the judge, that there was something wrong with the puzzle. I rest my case."

"I'm sorry, but I'm not sold," Chief Harper said. "How could Harvey Beerbaum know there's something wrong with the puzzle?"

"Clearly he's seen it."

"Say he has. Who showed it to him? Chester?"

"Well, wouldn't that fit?" Cora argued. "Someone rewrote the last quarter of the puzzle. Suppose it was Harvey what's-his-face—Beerbaum? Suppose Chester was in league with Beerbaum all along? Harvey was solving the puzzle for him, and Harvey rewrote the clues."

"In return for which Chester hits him over the head?"

"For getting cold feet," Cora said. "Beerbaum gets cold feet, starts to chicken out. He tries to tell me, but I won't listen. So, before he can tell anyone else, Chester makes sure he doesn't."

"I'm not saying it couldn't happen," Chief Harper said. "I'm just saying there's no proof that it did."

"So you're not going to look into it?"

"Did I say that? Of course I'm going to look into it. I suppose I have to talk to Chester."

"Have to talk to him? You mean you're not going to bust him?"

"Not at the present time. I can bring him in for questioning."

"Yes, but—"

Sherry Carter groaned. "Time out! You're starting to give me a headache. Chief Harper, stop equivocating. There's clearly something you're *not* telling us. Why don't you think Chester is guilty, and why are you so reluctant to arrest him?"

Chief Harper nodded to Cora Felton. "Smart girl, your niece. Gets right to it every time."

"Gets right to what?" Cora demanded. "What's the point here? How come you don't think old Chester bashed the crossword-puzzle guy?"

Chief Harper sighed.

"Because I just arrested Daniel Hurley for it."

38

CHESTER HURLEY, IGNORING THE BARRAGE OF SHOUTED questions, stomped out of the police station, pushed his way through the crowd of reporters, heirs, and onlookers, hopped in his truck, backed up, gunned the motor, and peeled out, leaving rubber just like a rebellious teenager.

The news crews filmed his exit gleefully. They hadn't a clue what it meant, but it was great footage. And they could get comments on it from the other heirs, who were already speculating on the arrest of Daniel Hurley, which was widely rumored, but as yet unconfirmed, as the police had still not issued a statement.

In the station, Chief Harper, who had just released Chester Hurley, let Cora Felton and Sherry Carter into his inner office.

"Well," Cora demanded, "what did he say? I assume it was pretty good, since you let him go."

"I all but had to." Chief Harper was glum. "I can't have two suspects arrested for the same crime."

"You really arrested Daniel Hurley?" Sherry said.

Chief Harper jerked his thumb. "He's in the back

room. His lawyer's over at the courthouse trying to get Judge Hobbs to release him now."

"What did you arrest him for?" Sherry asked.

Chief Harper hesitated.

That was more than Cora could take. "Never mind that," she said. "You can figure out how much you want to tell us later. Right now I want to know what Chester Hurley *said*. Did he mess with the puzzle?"

"So he says. According to him he's always been a whiz at puzzles. Ever since he was a kid. Ripped right through them. Only one in his family who did. Didn't know Emma had the knack. Was absolutely flabbergasted to find out what she'd done. But once he had his piece of the puzzle, he solved it like that. He drove Annabel Hurley to the courthouse, where they found the next set of clues. He took one copy, left the rest for the others. He solved that, drove Annabel to the post office, where she fetched the next set of clues. Solved that, drove her to the laundromat. Solved that, then went to the greenhouse."

Chief Harper leaned back in his desk chair, spread his arms. "Where, as you know, he found nothing. Which was very frustrating to him. He was determined to solve the puzzle. Not because he wanted the inheritance. But because he wanted to know what Emma was up to. That was very important to him. He said the wording of her will made him think there was something behind her game. That it was really important in some way. Not so much who won, but in reaching the right solution."

Chief Harper drummed his fingers on the desk. "I must say that makes no sense to me. I'm not saying I don't believe Chester—I do—I'm just not sure what he's getting at. Anyway, if the solution of the puzzle was at the greenhouse, he didn't want anyone else to find it first. So, when he couldn't find it, he rewrote the puzzle to throw the heirs off the track. He took the puzzle as far as it went, three-quarters finished, then wrote a different solution. How he did it is beyond me, but he says it was easy. He just needed another store besides a flower shop. He chose a five-and-ten because it had ten letters. Filled it in, filled in the rest of the words, and made up a set of clues. He typed them up, Xeroxed them, and had Annabel Hurley swap them for the real set of clues hidden in the laundromat. He says if we check, we'll find out Annabel was in there twice that day."

"The woman who runs the place only remembered her once," Cora said.

"Yeah, but Minnie's husband's on duty half the time," Harper pointed out. "And Ray Wishburn's got a brain like a sieve. Anyway, Chester claims that's what he did. So when you found that phony set of clues, and declared that solving them would mean winning the game, Chester Hurley couldn't have that. It wasn't that he wanted to win. He just didn't want anyone *else* to win. Which is why he showed up and turned in his puzzle. Yes, it's a solution from bogus clues, and should mean nothing. But him being first eliminates the nuisance of some other heir claiming to win, if you get what I mean."

"It makes sense in a very convoluted way," Sherry said carefully.

"And what about Mildred Sims?" Cora said. "What's the story there?"

Chief Harper smiled. "I must say, that one I kind of like. According to Chester, he was having no luck at the greenhouse. He tried to get Mildred to admit she was the one Emma Hurley had sent around with the puzzle clues. He says Mildred denied it, and he believes her. Apparently, they'd always had a decent enough relationship."

"And just *why* do you kind of like this?" Cora said.

"Amateur detectives," Chief Harper said. "Far be it for me to say anything against amateur detectives."

"Come again?"

"Chester Hurley's rather sharp. Has to be, living alone in the woods like that. Has keen senses. Animal instincts, you might say."

"So?"

"So, he comes out the door of Mildred Sims's house, and what does he see? Two women in a Toyota watching him from the road. And darned if it isn't the car belonging to the contest judge. Chester Hurley takes one look, and knows he's being tailed by amateurs. So, what's he gonna do? He's not gonna let you follow him to the greenhouse, that's for sure. Not that he couldn't ditch you if he wanted to, but why should he bother? Plus, he's got his own bill of goods to sell.

"So, he ducks back inside to Mildred Sims, who has just gone through this whole routine saying she's sorry she couldn't help him, but if there was ever anything she could do, and Chester says, As a matter of fact, you can, Mildred. Could you rush on down to Odds and Ends before it closes and buy me a dish rack? I'd go myself, but I don't have time because of the puzzle. If you could do that for me now, I'll pick it up later tonight. Only, don't tell anyone it's for me, because I don't want them to know what I'm doing.

"And Mildred figures it's a pretty weird request, but she can't really say no, because she just offered to help. So, off she goes and gets in her car, and, just like Chester Hurley intended, you follow her to Odds and Ends. Which does two things. It helps sell the five-and-ten in the puzzle he altered, and it keeps you away from the greenhouse."

"And what about the puzzle?" Cora Felton demanded. "Do you buy the fact he did it all himself? I mean, what about the theory the puzzle expert did it for him, and that's why he brained him?"

"I don't much like it. I could see Beerbaum helping Chester solve the puzzle—nothing really wrong with that—but altering it is something else. Beerbaum's gonna help

Chester rig a contest with millions of bucks involved? I don't think so. He'd be risking his whole reputation. I just can't see him doing it."

"Because you have Daniel Hurley in jail?" Sherry said.

"For one thing."

"You gonna tell us why?"

"For starters, he's the one with the big opportunity. You'll recall he was in the parking lot with Beasley just before Beasley got killed. Annabel Hurley came to call on him the night she got killed. And he was in the Country Kitchen last night with Harvey Beerbaum."

"Not *with* Harvey Beerbaum," Cora objected. "They were both there, big deal."

"But close enough to have overheard you, isn't that right?"

"He—"

"Oh, please," Sherry interrupted. "Let's not quibble. Daniel had opportunity. So had lots of people. What about motive? *Why* is he doing this?"

"How's fifteen million dollars sound? Say Daniel Hurley wants the money. He came here to get it by fair means or foul. Jeff Beasley knew that—how, I don't know yet—but he did. Beasley said so in the bar. Called Daniel prodigal son. Let Daniel Hurley know he was on to him."

"On to *what*?" Sherry said. "Give me a break."

Chief Harper's face darkened. "You want this or not?"

"We want it, we want it," Cora said. "Sherry, shut up, let the man make his case. Go on, Chief, what else have you got?"

"Well, that's Beasley. He's in the Country Kitchen that night with Daniel Hurley and Harvey Beerbaum. So say Daniel Hurley came here specifically to win the contest. Only he's no good at crossword puzzles. And his way of cracking the puzzle happens to involve Harvey Beerbaum."

"Wait a minute," Sherry objected. "I'm not going to be quiet and let something like that go by. This is the night *before* the will is read. Nobody even *knows* there's a puzzle. How could Harvey Beerbaum be part of Daniel Hurley's plan *then*?"

Chief Harper shrugged. "You say nobody knows there's a puzzle because the will hasn't been read. But who wrote the will? Emma Hurley. *Emma* knew there was a puzzle. She could have *told* someone there was a puzzle. Like the housekeeper, Mildred Sims, for instance. Or like Annabel Hurley. Or anyone else, for that matter. So, say someone knows there's a puzzle. And say that information reaches the ears of Daniel Hurley. And say that night at the Country Kitchen he has a reason to be meeting with the puzzle constructor."

"You arrested him on speculation like that?" Sherry said, incredulously.

"I did *not*," Chief Harper said. "I'm *indulging* in speculation like that to counter some of the objections I've been hearing. But it's not why I arrested him at all."

"You said this was his motive."

"It's tied into his motive. But go back to the original premise. Daniel Hurley's trying to outfox the other heirs and get the millions. Jeff Beasley's on to him. Daniel does Jeff in. Annabel is Daniel's confidant and co-conspirator. Not in the murder, but in trying to solve the puzzle. She's shocked and terrified by Beasley's murder. She goes to Daniel, to find out if he's involved. He denies it, of course, but she's suspicious. She becomes expendable."

Chief Harper raised his hand to override any possible objections. "But I don't wanna argue that now. I'm just trying to give you an idea of where I'm coming from so you won't be so shocked when you see the news tonight."

"When we see *what* on the news tonight?" Cora Felton asked.

"My statement on the arrest of Daniel Hurley. I'm going to have to make one sooner or later. When I do, I can assure you none of this will be in it."

"What will be?" Cora said.

Chief Harper grimaced. "Well, now, that's the thing. At the moment I'm waiting for confirmation. I kind of hate to say anything until I get it."

"Confirmation of what? No one's quoting you here, Chief. Just spit it out."

"Okay, but this doesn't leave this room." Chief Harper ran his hand through his hair. "I got witnesses."

Sherry Carter and Cora Felton stared at him.

"Witnesses?" Cora said. "You care to elaborate on that, Chief?"

"Not particularly. It's a little tricky. The problem is, they're kids."

"Kids?"

"Yeah. The Goldfarb kids. Jesse and Abby Goldfarb. They had a sleepover last night at the Olsen house. This morning they're coming back through the meadow behind the old paper mill, you know where I mean?"

"Not at all," Cora Felton said.

"Right, you wouldn't," Chief Harper said. "Well, the mill's by the creek, of course. And there's a culvert, where the stream goes under the road. The road's barely used anymore, now that the mill's shut down. Well, except if you were going up to the ranger station, only no one ever does, it's not like it was a public park."

"Chief."

"Sorry," Harper said. "Well, like I say, the Goldfarb kids are coming home across the meadow. And they see a motorcycle coming up the road. Which is a rare enough occurrence that they pay attention. Particularly when it stops just where the stream goes under the road. So they're there watching while Daniel Hurley in all his long-haired glory gets off his motorcycle, unbuckles his saddlebag, takes something out, climbs down the bank beside the road, and throws whatever it is into the culvert. Then he climbs back up, gets on his motorcycle, and drives off.

"Well, the Goldfarb kids are falling all over themselves to see what it is, and they scurry down the bank, and Abby winds up knocking Jesse into the creek, and Jesse gets up and pushes Abby down, and they're both wet and muddy and hopping mad by the time they find it. Plus they're kids, which is why they just pick it up without stopping to think."

"Pick what up?" Cora was raging with impatience.

Chief Harper shrugged. "I won't know for sure till the lab's done with it. Which is why I'm holding up my statement. But it's a big carving knife with blood on it, and five will get you ten it's our murder weapon."

39

"IT DOESN'T ADD UP," SHERRY SAID.

"Eat your pasta," Cora told her.

Sherry, who'd been too agitated to cook, had still managed to whip up a pasta salad with the pesto she'd made the day before. Cora was digging in ravenously, but Sherry had barely touched hers. "I'm not hungry," she muttered.

"You *are* hungry," Cora told her. "You just *think* you're not hungry, because you're upset. *I'm* upset, but I don't let that affect my appetite. It's a good lesson to learn. You can't accomplish anything if you don't take care of yourself."

"What are you babbling about?"

"Well, I like that." Cora was indignant. "Look, I'm not telling you not to think. I'm just saying think *while* you eat. You put the fork in the pasta, you put the pasta in your mouth. You chew it around and the mind keeps going. Your mind doesn't short-circuit just because some young man gets accused of a murder."

"That's not it."

"Or because some other young man's too busy to see you because he's writing the crime up."

"That's not it either."

"Well, that should be. This murder, quite frankly, is none of your business. Your personal life is more important."

"Is that how you feel?"

"No. But I've been married several times. A relationship right now is not my number one priority."

"Aunt Cora—"

"You, on the other hand, have had one disastrous marriage. You now have a shot at something better. You would be wise not to blow it."

"Aunt Cora. Not now."

"And the way to blow it would be getting hung up on a young man just because he was unfortunate enough to get charged with murder."

"I am not hung up on Daniel Hurley."

"Then what are you obsessing about?"

"Something's not right."

"Granted," Cora agreed placidly. "In fact, there are a lot of things that aren't right. But I assume you are referring to the arrest of Daniel Hurley."

"Of course I am. It simply makes no sense."

"I'm not saying I don't agree, but you want to tell me why you think so?"

"Come on," Sherry protested. "He kills Annabel Hurley, holds on to the murder weapon, carries it around with him for a day and a half, and then—and only then—decides to get rid of it? I mean, what is his thought process supposed to be here, assuming he's a clever murderer?"

"That's your argument?"

"What's wrong with it?"

"Nothing, expect for one thing."

"What's that?"

"Becky Baldwin should be making it."

Sherry glared at her sharply.

Cora Felton put up her hand. "Sorry. But that's the case. And that's what's hanging you up here. Daniel Hurley's been busted, and who's helping him? Becky Baldwin. Not you. And it's not so much that you want to do it, it's that you don't want her to."

"That's not fair."

"Maybe not. But you wouldn't be normal if you didn't feel that way. Hey, *I* feel that way, and I'm old enough to be her mother." Cora fed a forkful of pasta salad into her mouth. "Now, eat, and let's discuss this like normal people."

Sherry absently speared a piece of rotelli. "The premise is all wrong . . ."

"Which premise?"

"The whole thing. The idea Daniel Hurley is the killer."

"That's a given. Besides *that*."

"The idea he was in league with Harvey Beerbaum."

"What's wrong with that?"

"It doesn't fly. Oh, I heard what Chief Harper said. Maybe old Emma Hurley let something slip, maybe Daniel Hurley knew all about the puzzle before her will was read, and that's why Beerbaum was there the first night. But, granted all that, why does Harvey Beerbaum freak out last night and try to talk to you?"

"Okay, why?"

"Chief Harper's theory is Harvey Beerbaum got nervous because he knew the puzzle we were all working on was bogus. Well, that works if Beerbaum was in league with Chester Hurley. Beerbaum would know it was bogus because he'd be the one who helped Chester rig it. But if he was helping Daniel Hurley, it just doesn't fly. Because Daniel Hurley wouldn't have had the fourth quadrant of the puzzle."

"How do you know?"

"Because you hadn't given it out yet."

"Sure, but I hadn't given it out to Chester, and he got it easy enough."

"What are you saying?"

"Suppose Daniel was as fast as Chester. Suppose he beat us to the puzzle pieces too."

"Yeah, but he didn't," Sherry said. "You remember where he went when he got the first piece of the puzzle? Well, you probably don't, you were in no great shape. But that's when he hooked up with Becky Baldwin. And if he was hanging out with her, he *wasn't* solving the puzzle with Harvey Beerbaum."

"Then how do you account for Harvey Beerbaum?"

"I can't. And that's the whole problem. By all rights, Harvey Beerbaum only saw the first three quadrants of the puzzle. So how could he know the puzzle was a fake?"

"He couldn't."

"Then what was bothering him?"

"I don't know. Maybe he *did* know the puzzle was a fake."

"How could he know? He'd only seen the first three quadrants. The first three quadrants are genuine."

"How do you know?"

"How do I know anything?" Sherry shot back. "The first three quadrants are consistent with each other. They're consistent with the missing quadrant Chester Hurley stole. The clues were typed on the same machine and are absolutely genuine."

"Well, they can't be, by your premise. Have you looked them over?"

"Of course I looked them over."

"Well, maybe *I* should," Cora said. "You got a grid?"

"You gonna do the puzzle?"

"Don't be silly. I can't do puzzles, but I can read. Give

me a grid three-quarters filled in, and the first three sets of clues."

Sherry got up, went into the office, came back with the pages. "Here's your grid," she said, "and here's your clue sets."

"Which is the third set?"

"The higher numbers, of course. Why, aren't you starting with the first one?"

Cora shook her head. "Harvey Beerbaum was panicked last night. *After* the third set of clues was handed out. If something was bothering him, it has to be in those clues."

Cora shoved aside her plate and bent over the pages. "Okay," she muttered. "Here's the three-quarters grid."

LONGA PRAT PEA
UBOAT HONE SOLD
COURTHOUSE OSLO
YES EONS NATTER
ASSET AMOOSE
POLITE ENGULF
AGAR FRIES FUN
CRUSHER PRECISE
KEN OVERS ACES
DELETE IMBEDS
BARREN S
EGOIST
LIMA
ALAN
YET

"And here's the clues for the third quadrant."

ACROSS

25. Amiable
30. Chinese gelatin
35. Perfect rejoinder
40. Barbie's buddy
41. Do ______ (second chances)
44. Wipe out
48. Unfruitful
52. Me first man
57. Peru city
61. Alda
64. So far

DOWN

23. Attitudes
25. Wolf gathering
26. Monster
27. Close recycling place, so to speak?
31. Worry
36. Golf course features
45. Character in "Wheel of Time" books
48. Stop
49. Spry

"Okay," Cora said. "Let's see. First the across. *Amiable* is *polite. Chinese gelatin* is *agar,* whatever that is. A *perfect rejoinder* is a *crusher. Barbie's buddy*—that's the one I got—is *Ken. Do* blank *(second chances)* is *do overs.*" She looked up. "That's not very good."

"Cora."

"*Wipe out* is *delete. Unfruitful* is *barren.* A *me first man* is an *egoist. Peru city* is *Lima. Alda* is *Alan.* And *So far* is *yet.*"

"That's all the across. Then we have the downs." Cora Felton's eyes widened. "Oh!"

"What?" Sherry said, leaning forward.

"Alan Alda."

"What about him?"

"You know who Alan Alda is?"

"He's an actor."

"Yes. He became famous for the TV show *M*A*S*H.*"

"Yeah. So?"

"*M*A*S*H* was one of the most popular TV shows ever. The final episode got huge ratings. It was the most-watched single episode of all time. In fact, I think it still is. Unless the Seinfeld finale beat it."

"So?"

"*M*A*S*H* began in the nineteen seventies. Early seventies, maybe, but no earlier than that, because the movie came first, and the movie was nineteen seventy."

"How do you know that?"

"Because I went with Randy, and I always regretted not marrying him." Cora waved this away. "It's not important. But the fact is, I know."

"Aunt Cora—?"

"*You* miss it because you're young. But Harvey Beerbaum's old like me, so he gets it right away. This puzzle is supposed to be forty years old. Well, it can't be, with Alan Alda in it. He may have been acting forty years ago, but he wasn't famous then. He became famous for *M*A*S*H,* which is thirty years old, tops. You could have a puzzle twenty-five years old, maybe thirty, with Alan Alda's name in it. But forty years old, never. I know it, and Harvey Beerbaum would have known it too."

"Let me see that." Sherry snatched the clues and grid away from Cora and studied them.

Looking over her shoulder, Cora said, "What's forty-five down, *Character in "Wheel of Time" books*? Do you know what that is?"

"No, I don't. I filled it in from the words going across."

"You didn't look it up?"

"No, but I will now," Sherry said. She hurried down the hallway into the office, with Cora at her heels. Sherry sat at the computer and logged on to the Internet.

"And what's this here in the second quadrant?" Cora asked. "*I shot a moose*? You know what that is? The clue's *I shot* blank, parenthesis, *Stand-up Comic*. And *Stand-up Comic* is capitalized and in quotes. You know why? It's not just any stand-up comic. It's Woody Allen, and *Stand-up Comic* is the name of the album. I used to have it. It's old, but I bet it isn't forty years old." Cora's eyes widened. "And you know what? I'm not sure the Ken doll's even forty."

"Never mind that," Sherry said. "Look at this. The *Wheel of Time* books are from the nineteen nineties."

Sherry and Cora looked at each other.

"Nineteen *nineties*?" Cora said. "Well, that explains why good old Harvey was so upset."

"The whole puzzle is a fake?" Sherry said. "That makes no sense."

"It's not necessarily bogus, but it doesn't agree with what Emma Hurley said in her will. She said specifically the puzzle was forty years old. *This* puzzle isn't. So, it's either not Emma's puzzle, or Emma Hurley was deliberately trying to mislead us."

"And why would she do that?" Sherry demanded.

Cora frowned. "I really wouldn't put anything past her. I never met the woman, but I feel like I know her. And I get the impression she's laughing in her grave."

"You mean this whole thing was just a joke? An elaborate trick played on all the heirs? That it all means nothing?"

"Well, wouldn't that be ironic? Particularly, with them killing each other over it?"

"How is that possible?" Sherry said. "The money exists. There *is* an inheritance. Fifteen million dollars. It has to go to someone. And you're in charge of saying who that someone is."

"No, I'm in charge of judging the puzzle. And my current assessment is there is no puzzle to judge."

"Then who does the money go to?"

"That's not my problem. I'm not a lawyer, just a referee. But I'm going to have to make a ruling. The question now is, forty years old or not, did Emma Hurley set up this puzzle?"

"Misplaced modifier."

"What?"

"Emma Hurley was not forty years old."

"Sherry. Stick with me here. We gotta work this out. We got two possibilities. One, this is the puzzle Emma Hurley mentioned in her will. The one she wants her heirs to solve. The one she asked me to judge. And she was merely mistaken about it being forty years old.

"Or, two: this is not the forty-year-old puzzle Emma Hurley asked me to judge at all."

"How can that be?" Sherry asked. "The will was very specific. The first clue will be found in the writing desk in the master bedroom. We looked and there it was, exactly where she said it would be. We were all there, we all saw it."

"Yes," Cora said. "Just as we were supposed to."

"What do you mean by that?"

Cora Felton was animated. "Sherry, all along, my problem with this puzzle has been it's too easy. Well, not for me, but you know what I mean. You split it up and hide the clues around, big deal. It's still a simple, dumb crossword puzzle. But if it's an elaborate trick, I like that. I like the idea of the heirs running around solving it, and all the time it's meaningless."

"But if it's meaningless, what did Emma Hurley mean in her will?"

"Just what she said." Cora ticked the points off. "There's a forty-year-old puzzle to solve. Her dough will go to the first heir to crack it. The first clue is in the writing desk in the master bedroom."

Cora pointed to the crossword puzzle.

"And this isn't it," she said triumphantly.

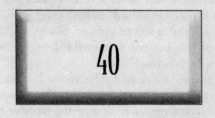

40

SHERRY CARTER PUT THE CROWBAR DOWN, AND HELPED her aunt move the heavy sheet of plywood away from the window. "Are you happy now?" Sherry said. "You got your wish. We're breaking into the Hurley house."

"Like we should have done two nights ago," Cora Felton retorted, shining her flashlight. "Well, better late than never." Cora stuck her hand through the broken glass, unsnapped the lock, and raised the window. "Come on, give me a boost."

"It's easier from inside," Sherry said. "I'll go first."

Sherry climbed over the windowsill, then turned around to help her aunt.

In her eagerness, Cora lost her balance climbing over the sill. Sherry grabbed her, and the two of them crashed to the floor. Cora's flashlight flew out of her hand and skittered across the rug.

"Aunt Cora!" Sherry exclaimed. "Take it easy!"

"It's all right. No harm done," Cora said. "And the nice thing about a flashlight is it's easy to find, as long as it doesn't go out."

Cora pushed herself up on her hands and knees, crawled over, and picked up the flashlight. "There we go. Now, where are we?"

Cora heaved herself to her feet, and shone her flashlight around the foyer. "Good lord! What's that?"

"Relax. It's just a suit of armor," Sherry said. "I would have warned you, but you've seen it before. Of course, you don't remember, do you?"

"Don't snipe," Cora said. She shone her flashlight on the battle-ax, nodded approvingly. "Is there anything else you'd like to warn me about despite the fact I've seen it before?"

"Not in the foyer. But Evan Hurley's portrait takes a little getting used to."

"Oh? And where is that?"

"At the top of the stairs. The painting is rather unfortunate. It wasn't really meant to be viewed close up."

"And how was it meant to be viewed?" Cora asked, starting up the circular staircase.

"I would recommend pitch dark," Sherry said.

"It can't be that bad."

"No? Evan Hurley makes Philip and Phyllis look good."

Cora climbed the stairs, shone the light on the painting. "Oh, yes," she said. "The old Hurley bulldog jaw. You suppose Daniel has one under that beard?"

Sherry shuddered. "That's a frightening thought."

"Well, it's something to consider. So, where's the bedroom?"

"First doorway on the right," Sherry said.

They shone their lights, opened the door, slipped inside the shadows of the huge bedroom. Cora Felton ran her beam over the canopied bed, the bureau, the chair, the vanity table, and stopped on the writing desk. The rolltop was down and the key was in the lock.

"Is it locked?" she asked.

Sherry pushed the top; it rose easily. "Nope. That's just the way it was." She raised the top all the way up, shone her light. "And here's where the clues were. Under the blotter. And before we found them, we checked out the drawers."

"*All* of the drawers?"

"No. Or the cubbyholes, either. But we will now."

An exhaustive search of the cubbyholes of the desk turned up nothing more interesting than Emma Hurley's phone bill, and a deck of pinochle cards.

The desk drawers were no more productive. One was crammed with receipts. Another held bank statements from the Bakerhaven Savings & Loan.

Cora Felton pulled a statement out of an envelope, shone her light on it, and whistled. "Wow. The woman had forty-six thousand dollars in her checking account, and over half a million in savings."

"Is that all?" Sherry said.

"*All?*" Cora said. "Did you really apply the word *all* to half a million?"

"She was worth a lot more than that. So where's the rest of the money?"

"In a secret drawer, perhaps? Is that how you're thinking? Come on, Sherry. You're the logical, rational one. *I'm* the wide-eyed romantic."

"You certainly are," Sherry said. "I don't recall mentioning any secret drawer."

"Well, that doesn't mean there isn't one," Cora said. "And, like you say, the money's got to be somewhere. Come on, let's check it out."

"Check what out?"

"The desk. How deep are these drawers?"

"What do you mean?"

"Is there room for anything behind them?"

"I don't think so."

"Well, let's make sure. Come on. Pull one out."

Sherry pulled the top drawer all the way out and Cora shone the light where it had been.

"Nothing in this one," Cora reported. "Here. Let's measure. Hold it up to the side of the desk."

Sherry held the drawer along the side of the desk. It went almost to the back. "It's a full drawer. No room for anything behind it."

"Uh huh. Hold it up, let me check the bottom."

Sherry held the drawer up. Cora bent down, shone the light, banged on the bottom.

"Okay, nothing there, just a simple wooden drawer. Put it back and let's check the next."

"I bet they're all the same."

"I bet they are too. That's no reason not to look."

There were seven desk drawers, three on each side, and one thin pencil drawer across the middle. Sherry and Cora pulled each one out, checked each side and bottom.

It was on the bottom of the middle drawer on the right side of the desk. Cora's flashlight lit up a large circled inscription in black Magic Marker:

#1.

Underneath, also in black Magic Marker, was a rhymed couplet:

The kitchen will do
For your next clue

Cora Felton grinned. "Well, this is more like it," she said.

"More like it?" Sherry exclaimed. "Are you kidding me? This is utterly fantastic! Are you telling me there's a whole different puzzle?"

"Why not? It's what we were looking for."

"Even so. I don't see how you can be so calm about it."

"Calm? Who's calm? I'm jumping out of my skin." Cora struck a pose. "Come on, let's go! The kitchen will do for our next clue!"

They replaced the drawer and hurried off to find the kitchen.

"Keep your flashlight down," Cora counseled as they descended the stairs. "In case anyone's driving by."

"We'd see the headlights," Sherry told her.

"Even so," Cora said.

Downstairs, they went through a living room that was a medley of styles, including a marble fireplace, a modern convertible couch, a love seat, an ottoman, and Queen Anne chairs. Next, a formal dining room where a massive oak table seated twelve, and the walls were lined with antique breakfronts and serving stands. Sherry and Cora detoured around the table and pushed through a pair of swinging doors into the kitchen.

The Hurley kitchen was extensive for a private house. On one wall were two stoves, one with six burners, the other topped by metal grills. Another wall held a floor-to-ceiling refrigerator and a walk-in freezer. Still another held sinks and an industrial dishwasher, the type racks of dishes were fed through on a conveyor belt. On the fourth wall were shelves of pots and pans, and a door to a separate pantry lined with provisions.

The center of the kitchen was dominated by a huge butcherblock table, nearly as large as the table in the dining room. Knives and kitchen utensils hung neatly around the perimeter from racks.

"Well," Sherry said. "Where do we begin?"

Cora shone her light around, considered. "Under the table," she decided. "I would expect writing on the bottom of the table, just like on the bottom of the drawer."

Examining the bottom of the table was slightly complicated by the fact that it had a lower shelf, which was crammed with pots and pans. Still, Sherry and Cora managed to squeeze in and shine their lights enough to see that there was nothing written there.

"Next theory?" Sherry said, disappointed.

"Same theory, different location," Cora told her. "I'd still look for writing underneath. How about that counter leading from the sink to the dishwasher?"

There was nothing there. But there was underneath the counter leading out of the dishwasher. The message, once again, was in Magic Marker:

#2.

**How low can you go
To find your clues?
Here's an offer
You can't re-fuse**

"How low can you go," Sherry muttered. "Would that mean the basement?"

"Sure sounds like it," Cora replied. "But what's this offer you can't refuse?"

"It's hyphenated," Sherry said.

"What?"

"*Refuse* is hyphenated. *Re* hyphen *fuse*. That's got to be significant."

"Fuse box!" Cora exclaimed. "I bet there's a fuse box in the basement."

"I bet you're right," Sherry said. "You think we can find it in the dark?"

"We will if we have to," Cora answered. "If there's no basement windows, we can turn on the lights. So where's the basement door?"

It was in the back hallway off the pantry. Sherry nudged the door open, exposing the stairway leading down. There was a light switch on the wall near the top.

"Shall we risk it?" Sherry asked.

"You stay here," Cora said decisively. "I'll go down, see if there's windows. If not, we'll switch the light on."

Cora crept down the stairs while Sherry waited by the light switch. Cora reached the bottom and moved off, leaving the stairs dark. Sherry aimed her flashlight down the stairwell. The beam didn't reach the bottom. She played the light around the stairs, fingered the switch. The shadows in the basement were impenetrable.

Sherry waited impatiently as the seconds ticked by. Told herself she was stupid for being nervous. Even so, it was taking too long. A few more seconds and she'd either switch the lights on, or go downstairs and—

"Sherry!" Cora hissed from the shadows below. "It's okay. Turn 'em on."

Sherry threw the light switch. Nothing happened.

"It's all right, turn 'em on," Cora said.

"I did," Sherry said.

"Then they're not working," Cora told her. "I guess we'd better find the fuse box. Come on."

Sherry joined Cora at the bottom of the stairs.

"There's no windows that I can see," Cora reported. "It's hard to tell, because there's lots of partitions. There's a stairs up to the back lawn—you know the kind I mean—concrete steps up to a flat door that would pull up from the outside—but that's not going to let any light out, besides it's in the back. I found the furnace and the water tank. I haven't found the fuse box, but it can't be far."

"Okay. Then we can trace the electricity from it."

"That's what I like about you. Always thinking. Come on."

Cora led the way through the dingy basement, keeping

the flashlight down to illuminate the debris scattered on the concrete floor.

Sherry followed with her flashlight up, trying to spot the spiderwebs, which seemed to be everywhere. Most of them were old, but many were new and occupied, and some of the spiders seemed aggressively large. Sherry's flesh began to crawl. She shuddered, hurried along after her aunt.

"Watch out for that rake," Cora warned.

Sherry stopped, shone her light down, saw that she had nearly tripped over a pile of garden tools. She detoured around it, checking carefully for overhanging webs, then followed Cora's bobbing flashlight to the other side of the cellar.

"Okay, here we are," Cora announced. "Here's the water heater." She played her flashlight over it. "There. Isn't that an electric cable coming out of the top?"

"There's two of them," Sherry said, shining her light. "One in each direction. Either could lead to the fuse box."

"Wanna split up?"

"Not particularly. But it would be faster."

"All right. You go right, I'll go left."

Sherry shone the light, followed the shiny silver electrical conduit along the wall. It was difficult, because every now and then she'd hit a partition she'd have to go out around, and pick up the conduit on the other side. Fortunately, it ran fairly straight, only occasionally detouring around a column, beam, girder, or whatever they called structural supports in an old house—Sherry had majored in linguistics, not architecture.

At one point the cable swooped upward, ran along the ceiling, which made tracking it harder. Running it must have been harder too, and Sherry couldn't help wondering why the electrician had bothered. Still, she followed it diligently, while keeping an anxious eye out for arachnids.

She lost it in the corner. The corner was particularly dark and inaccessible, with two partitions thrown up, in Sherry's estimation, solely for the purpose of frustrating her. She couldn't really get in between them without squeezing into a rather uninviting space, with rubble on the floor, cobwebs on the ceiling, and a stack of old lumber piled upward against the wall. Her only real hope was to pick it up on the other side. Only the conduit didn't come out of the other side. On the far side of the second partition there were no cables at all. No electrical work of any kind.

Sherry shone the light, sized up the situation. Decided either the conduit had taken a turn in the corner and was now running away from the wall along the ceiling, or else this corner was where the power ran upstairs to the rest of the house.

She took a step backward, played the light along the ceiling.

Heard a noise.

She snapped off the light, stood very still.

"Got it!" Cora Felton muttered triumphantly.

Sherry felt silly. She and Cora had circled the whole basement, and wound up right next to each other.

"Where are you?" Sherry called.

"Right here. Can't you see me?"

"Can you see me?"

"No."

"Then how do you expect me to see you?"

"There must be another wall here. Come out around."

"You found the fuse box?"

"Yeah, but I can't reach it."

"Why not?"

"It's near the ceiling."

"The fuse box is near the ceiling?"

Cora didn't reply.

Sherry picked her way toward the center of the cellar,

detoured around a storage area of some sort, and immediately saw Cora Felton's flashlight. It was trained on a fuse box on the wall near the ceiling just out of reach.

"Wonderful," Sherry said. "There's no box or step stool?"

"Not that I can see."

"Then how do they change the fuses?"

"I would imagine they're circuit breakers."

"That's not the point. How do they get up there?"

"They stand on something. Emma Hurley probably removed it after she left the clue."

"Assuming she left it here."

"Or assuming someone left it here for her. I bet whoever left the clue took the step stool away just to make it harder for us."

"As if it wasn't hard enough," Sherry said. "Okay, I'll find something."

Sherry went back to what had appeared to be a partitioned-off storage area. Investigating, she found it to be exactly that. A makeshift Sheetrock door was unlocked, and swung back on squeaky hinges to reveal boxes, trunks, and suitcases. Sherry chose a trunk that was sturdy but empty and light enough for her to carry. She hefted it by the handle, lugged it back to her aunt.

"I hope this is high enough," Sherry said.

"We could stand it on end."

"I don't think so. I wouldn't get on it, and I wouldn't advise you to."

"All right. Let's try it flat."

Standing on the trunk on tiptoe, Sherry was just able to reach the cover of the fuse box. She reached up, pushed it open to reveal a panel of circuit breakers.

"There we go," Cora said.

On the back of the fuse box was:

#3.

My, oh my
The attic's high
Where the light comes
From the sky

"Skylight," Sherry said. "Would an attic have a sky-light?"

"Don't be so literal," Cora scolded. "I don't know what the attic has, but that's where we want to go."

"Just a moment . . ." Sherry said.

She shone her flashlight over the fuse box. One of the circuit breakers was tripped. Sherry reached up, stretched her finger, pushed it over.

The cellar lights came on, and proved to be bare bulbs screwed into ceiling sockets with dangling pull cords. Several of them were on, though not the one where Sherry and Cora were standing. Cora reached up, pulled the cord, turned theirs on, lighting up the alcove.

"Well, that certainly would have helped," Cora said. "Too bad the breaker was tripped."

"Yeah," Sherry said dryly. "I suppose we can thank Emma Hurley for that."

"Oh, doubtless," Cora agreed happily. "Any other breakers tripped? It would be a shame to run into the same thing in the attic."

"We probably can't risk the lights there," Sherry said.

"Even so."

"No, the circuit breakers are all okay. Come on, let's go."

With the lights on they had no trouble negotiating the basement floor, and in a minute they were climbing the stairs. At the top Cora threw the switch, plunging the basement into darkness.

"Okay, let's find the stairs to the attic."

"I don't get it," Sherry said, as they went up the circular front stairs.

"Don't get what?"

"If the heirs were doing this, it would be a stampede. They'd all be finding the clues at the same time."

"That's the purpose of the crossword puzzle," Cora said. "It sends them off on a false scent. Only the smartest ones figure it out and come back."

"That's your theory?"

"What's wrong with it?"

"A lot of things." Sherry stopped in the second-floor hallway, shone her light. "Okay, the staircase does not continue, and the stairs to the third floor are not readily apparent, so they must be down here."

Sherry set off down the hallway, with Cora trailing behind.

"What's wrong with my idea?" Cora persisted.

"Ah, here we are," Sherry said. Her light illuminated a narrow staircase at the end of the hall. "The problem with your idea is if the crossword puzzle was just to throw the heirs off the scent, why four sections? One section is enough. If all she wants to do is send 'em away so the smart ones come back, why send 'em all over creation? Why go to the trouble of planting the other three quadrants, which couldn't have been easy for a woman in her condition?"

"Someone did it for her."

"Even so, why do it at all? Okay," Sherry said, shining the light around the hallway. "This is not the attic, this is the third floor. Probably for servants. Now, unless the attic is an adjunct on one end, we're looking for another set of stairs."

"Or a ladder," Cora said.

"True," Sherry said. "Though this is not the type of house where you'd expect to find a pull-down ladder."

Sherry shone the light down the hallway, began pulling open doors. "You see my point," she said. "If all she wants to do is get 'em out of here, why bother to plant the other puzzle pieces?"

"Because Alan Alda's in the third one."

"What?"

"Alan Alda doesn't show up until the third quadrant, and that's the one that tells you it's a fake."

"Oh, yeah? What about the Woody Allen quote in the second quadrant? That tells you it's a fake too."

Cora shook her head. "No, it doesn't. You only know it's Woody Allen because I told you. His name's not in the clue or the answer. You can solve the puzzle just fine without knowing that. The tipoff is Alan Alda. That's what sends 'em back."

"Big deal. If there's no second quadrant, they'll come back anyway."

"Yeah," Cora said, "but they'll come back *grousing*. Telling 'em the puzzle's wrong makes 'em come back *looking*."

"It's a theory. I'm not sure I like it." Sherry pulled open a door. "Ah, here we go."

A narrow staircase led up into more darkness.

"Light switch on the wall," Cora told her. "You wanna risk it?"

"Let me check it out first."

"I'll do it," Cora said.

"You did the cellar. This one's mine."

Sherry went up the narrow stairs, darting her light ahead of her. At the top she emerged through a rectangular hole in the attic floor. Before stepping off the stairs, Sherry shone the light and discovered the floor was unfinished. Some of it was covered with planks and sheets of plywood, but at least half of it was just two-by-four studs holding the insulation and Sheetrock from the ceiling below.

Negotiating the attic would be even trickier than the basement.

Sherry waved the light around the walls, which were sharply pitched from the slant of the roof. The attic was very long, apparently running the length of the house, and relatively wide. Sherry's flashlight couldn't begin to reach into the recesses of it without her stepping on the boards, which she was reluctant to do. She scanned the walls for windows, saw none.

The musty odor Sherry had noticed on entering the attic seemed stronger on not finding a window. Sherry shuddered. Told herself she was being foolish.

She turned, called down to Cora, "It looks okay. Try the light."

Cora threw the switch.

The lights blazed. Half a dozen naked bulbs hanging on cords running the length of the attic.

The lights lit up what the flashlight had not revealed. The attic was clearly a storage area. Off to the sides, on planks and plywood sheets, were piles of boxes covered with drop cloths. An occasional item poked out or stood off to one side. A baby carriage. A croquet set. A gramophone.

"Well, look at that," Cora said, pointing. "An old Victrola. I bet there's a fortune here in antiques."

"You wanna stop and look?" Sherry said sarcastically.

"Another time. Right now I wanna see where the light comes from the sky."

"You can't see it from here. I think we're going to have to negotiate walking on these boards."

"No problem," Cora said.

"Oh?"

"Whoever planted the clues did it just fine."

Cora stepped out on the boards near the stairs. They

creaked a little, but were steady underfoot. Cora set off down the attic.

Sherry looked where her aunt had just walked. The boards were covered with dust, and Cora's footprints left a trail across the attic. There was clearly nothing else that fresh. But was that a faint trail next to Cora's prints? Sherry couldn't tell. She grimaced, hurried after her aunt.

Cora went by a pile of boxes, said, "Aha!"

Sherry crept up beside her and looked.

There was a gable in the wall of the attic with a window in it. Planks nailed across the two-by-fours formed a three-foot-wide path to the window.

"Careful, don't push me off," Cora said as they made their way across.

"As if I could even keep up," Sherry grumbled.

They reached the window. It was a small wood-framed, sliding window, with two panes on the bottom and two on the top.

"Okay," Cora said. "This has to be where the light meets the sky or whatever that was, so where's the clue?"

On top of the window was a small roller blind. Sherry reached up, jerked it down.

There written on the blind was:

#4.

Where, oh, where
Is the secret stair?
You might
Ask the knight

Cora Felton grabbed Sherry's arm.

"Sherry! Look!"

"I see."

"Secret *stair*!"

"You're squeezing my arm."

"Oh. Sorry. But we might ask the knight. That's gotta be the guy in the foyer, doesn't it?"

"Guy?"

"Sherry, don't be a nudge. It's the armor! The suit of armor! Come on! Come on! *Secret stair*!"

Cora Felton practically dragged Sherry back down to the foyer.

"Okay," Cora said, breathing hard. "So where's the stair? I might ask the knight, but he's not talking, is he?"

Cora went up to the suit of armor. The helmet had a visor. Cora reached up, and lifted the visor.

Nothing happened.

Cora refused to believe this, waited several seconds for a result.

"What's supporting the battle-ax?" Sherry asked.

Cora looked. The knight's right arm was bent, the chain mail glove holding up the frightening ax.

Sherry pointed. "I mean, it's not like the ax had a long handle resting on the floor. That arm's holding it up. If the armor's hollow, how can that be?"

"Let's find out," Cora said. She reached up, pulled down on the hand with the ax.

The right arm of the suit of armor swung slowly down.

There came the metallic clang of a bolt releasing.

A wood panel in the wall next to the knight swung open.

"*Sherry!*"

"I see it. I see it."

"Come on! Come on!"

Cora Felton had already pushed through the opening. Sherry followed, found herself in a narrow passageway running along the wall toward the back of the house.

"Slow down, you'll miss something," Sherry said.

"Slow, hell!" Cora said. "Where's the stair?"

Cora forged ahead, reached a wall where the passage-way turned left. Cora squeezed around the turn, plunged ahead.

Sherry followed at a more conservative pace. There were spiderwebs overhead, and there was dust on the floor. Shining the light, Sherry could see Cora's footprints in the dust. As in the attic, theirs were the only recent footprints.

Sherry tried to let that thought calm her.

"Look!"

Cora Felton had reached a small spiral staircase. The metal treads twisted around up into the dark.

"Okay," Sherry said. "You found your secret stair. Now, is there anything at the bottom?"

There wasn't. Not that Cora was willing to search long, but a swift perusal with the flashlights showed there was nothing there.

"Let's go," Cora said, and flung herself onto the spiral staircase.

The metal swayed under her weight, but the stairs held. Cora grabbed the center pole, and clomped on up.

"Could you make a little more noise?" Sherry said.

"Hey, give me a break. There's no one here, and we're in the wall. Come on."

Cora spiraled around to the second floor, stepped off the stairs, and found herself in a room not much bigger than a phone booth. She scrunched her shoulders, shone the flashlight.

Her eyes widened.

"Sherry! Look!"

Sherry Carter came up the stairs and squeezed in next to her aunt.

Cora's flashlight lit up an eight-by-ten photograph taped to the wall. It was a head shot of an emaciated old lady with stringy white hair, dressed in a nightgown and propped up in bed. She looked like a creature from hell. Her eyes were sunk in their sockets, and yet they seemed to glow. And her smile was positively wicked. It was a devilish smile, crinkling the wizened remains of what had undoubtedly been at one time a solid, bulldog jaw.

It was also a knowing smile.

The smile of someone enjoying a private joke.

"Emma Hurley," Sherry murmured.

"Gotta be," Cora agreed. "But what's she laughing at?"

"And what's she looking at?" Sherry countered.

"What do you mean?"

Sherry turned, shone her light at the opposite wall. There, directly in line with Emma Hurley's photo, was written:

#5.

See your buddy
In the study

"Who's our buddy?" Sherry asked.

"Who cares?" Cora replied. "Let's get out of here."

Cora shone her light, found a metal lever in the wall. She pulled it, and the wall swung out. Immediately ahead was another door. Cora pushed, and it swung open.

Cora and Sherry came out into the upstairs hallway.

"Where are we?" Cora said. "No, more to the point, where *were* we?"

Cora looked back, saw that they had just emerged from a linen closet. She reached in, pushed the wall with the shelves of sheets and towels until it clicked back into place.

Cora closed the closet door, then flashed her light on the door across the hall. "Is that the master bedroom?"

"I think so. I'm a little disoriented from being in the wall. Come on, let's find the study."

"Wouldn't that be on the ground floor?"

"I should think so."

"Wanna go down the secret stair?"

"Not on your life."

They located the study just off the dining room. Their flashlights lit up a massive oak desk, a leather chair, and bookcases built into the walls.

"This must be the study," Cora said.

"Unless it's the library," Sherry pointed out.

"Maybe it is," Cora said. "But it's really the same thing."

"Then why call it the study?"

"She probably couldn't rhyme library," Cora said promptly. "Okay, that's the front window, so we don't dare risk a light. Gimme a hand. Let's check out the desk drawers."

"You really think she used the drawers again? I mean, there's a lot of places to hide something here."

"I think she'll stick to the tried and true. Give me a hand, and—" Cora stopped, put her finger to her lips.

"What is it?" Sherry whispered.

"Kill the light."

Sherry clicked the flashlight off. Her aunt had already extinguished hers.

Cora grabbed her by the arm, squeezed. Hard.

Sherry tensed, cocked her head, listened.

A board creaked.

Then another.

Sherry grabbed her aunt's arm, squeezed back. As she did, she realized Cora was fumbling in her purse. In the dim moonlight filtering through the window Sherry could see Cora's hand clear the purse with something in it.

A gun.

Her aunt had a gun.

Sherry felt a sudden pang of guilt.

Because she was glad.

Because the footsteps in the hallway were either an heir, or a killer, or both.

Probably both.

Sherry held her breath, stayed still, flattened against the wall, heart thumping wildly.

The footsteps drew nearer to the study door, which they had left ajar.

The door creaked open.

A flashlight beam played around the room.

A figure stepped through the doorway.

"Hold it right there!" Cora thundered.

With a cry, the intruder dropped the light. It fell to the floor and went out, plunging the room into darkness.

"Oh, no you don't!" Cora Felton bellowed.

Sherry Carter clicked on her flashlight . . . to find her aunt jamming her gun into the intruder's stomach.

Becky Baldwin.

41

SHERRY WAS INSTANTLY ANGRY. ANGRY WITH BECKY FOR scaring her unnecessarily. Angry with herself for being scared. Angry because it was Becky. Angry that it made a difference because it was Becky. Angry with herself for letting it make her angry.

"What are you doing here?" Sherry said it as calmly as possible. Still, it came out hard as nails.

"You mind moving that gun?" Becky said. "It makes me a little nervous, being poked with a gun."

"Then you might lay off the criminal trespass," Cora said. "Or don't the laws apply to you lawyers?"

"They apply to me as much as they do to you," Becky Baldwin replied. "Look, I'd like to pretend to be very brave, but I've never had a gun pointed at me before. Could you please put it down?"

"Once I'm sure you're not armed," Cora told her. "You dropped your flashlight. Where's your purse?"

"In the car."

"No one drove up. Where's your car?"

"Down the road. I walked up."

"So as not to be seen?"

"What do you think? I didn't see your car outside either. Look, will you put away the gun?"

"I won't put it away, but I'll stop aiming it at you. If you start talking. What are you doing here?"

"You know what I'm doing here. I'm Daniel Hurley's attorney."

"And?"

"And Daniel didn't kill anyone. I know it looks bad, but he didn't. Someone planted the knife on him. He found it, he tried to get rid of it. It was a stupid thing to do. He should have come to me. If he had, I could have handled it. I can handle it still, but, frankly, I'm a little desperate. I need help. I have to find a clue."

"Why look here?"

"Because this is where it all began. It all comes back to Emma Hurley somehow. And now this puzzle constructor's in a coma. And word is out there's something wrong with the crossword puzzle. At least, that's what they're saying on the news."

"You mean Rick Reed?" Sherry said.

"Why do you say it like that?"

"Never mind. The point is, he's saying it on the air?"

"Sure he is. And why not?" Becky gestured to Cora. "I understand you suspended the game. And not just because Daniel's in jail. And not just because of the assault. Because there's some question as to the puzzle's authenticity. Which throws doubts on the will, which leads us back here."

"You been upstairs yet?" Cora Felton asked.

"No, I just got here. Why?"

"The will says the first clue's in the master bedroom. If you questioned the will, you'd start there."

"Then why are you down here?"

Cora frowned. "That's on a need-to-know basis, and you don't need to know, sweetie. Tell you what. Show of good faith. Wait outside this door a few minutes while Sherry and I decide what to do."

"Wait outside the door?" Becky sounded appalled.

"Yeah. You stay there, you don't run off, you don't come in. You show us you're cooperating. Convince us we *shouldn't* turn you in for B&E."

"Oh, yeah, like that's really going to happen," Becky Baldwin said. "When you're breaking and entering yourselves."

"I don't really want to argue," Cora said with commendable patience. "You gonna wait outside or not?"

"If I do, what happens then?"

"We shall see." Cora gestured with the gun. "For one thing, I won't shoot you."

"That's not funny."

"No, it isn't. You wanna wait outside?"

"I'm not sure I understand."

"I'm sure you don't. Let me put it another way. You're trying to get your client off. If he's really innocent, the truth will help him, so helping us helps you."

"You expect me to buy that?"

"I don't care if you do. Just so you give us a few minutes alone so we can move this along."

Becky Baldwin glared at her, then stalked out, and slammed the door.

Cora cocked her head and listened. Then she turned to Sherry and whispered, "Okay, she's right there, so keep it quiet, but let's hurry. We'll try the desk first. I wish we could lock the door . . ."

"You don't trust her?"

"Do you?"

"Of course not. Let's get those drawers out."

Quietly, they pulled the desk drawers out, shone their lights underneath.

This time it was the top drawer on the left. Cora's

flashlight lit up a white business-size envelope. The envelope was taped to the bottom of the drawer. On the face of the envelope was:

#6.

The flap of the envelope was open.

Cora reached her hand in, felt a piece of paper. But it was not the size of a letter. It was smaller, and of irregular shape.

Cora's eyes narrowed at a sound from the hall.

The door clicked open.

Cora yanked the paper from the envelope, slammed the drawer, and struggled to her feet, thrusting the paper deep within her purse. She was suddenly impaled by the beam of a powerful flashlight.

Becky Baldwin walked into the room. But it was not she who held the flashlight.

"Aw, gee," a voice said. "Aw, gee whiz."

A man walked in, reached up, and flicked the switch.

The lights came on.

The man with the flashlight was Dan Finley. The young Bakerhaven police officer looked from Cora to Sherry and back to Cora again, then shook his head, disapprovingly.

"Miss Felton," he said. "I'm sorry about this. I can't tell you how sorry. I just hate this."

He frowned, looked down, shook his head, then looked up at Cora like a child who knows he has to take his medicine, even though he knows it's going to taste bad.

"You're under arrest."

42

"DON'T TALK TO THEM," BECKY BALDWIN SAID.

"Oh, for goodness sakes," Sherry said. "Can't you see how silly this is?"

"I really don't see why I can't talk," Daniel Hurley said.

"You don't have to see," Becky retorted. "That's my job."

"Well, I'm the one charged with murder."

"Exactly."

Sherry Carter, Cora Felton, Becky Baldwin, and Daniel Hurley were in holding cells in the back of the Bakerhaven police station. Daniel Hurley was in one, and the three women were in the other. As the cells were adjoining, there was every opportunity for them to talk, had Becky Baldwin allowed it. So far, all she would allow was a discussion as to whether they should.

Cora Felton sat on a bench in the back of the cell and kept an eye on the room outside. In particular, she kept an eye on her purse. Cora Felton's purse had not been searched and itemized, as would have been standard procedure for someone under arrest. However, Dan Finley was the only officer on duty, and at the moment Finley had his hands full. He was not used to arresting three people at one time—the paperwork alone was overwhelming—and he hadn't even started fingerprints and mug shots yet, so itemizing the prisoners' property was a very low priority. As a result, Cora Felton's purse was hanging in plain sight on a hook next to a wanted poster.

In the bottom of Cora Felton's purse was a gun. While that might have surprised Dan Finley, Cora Felton was not particularly concerned with his finding it. The paper from the envelope on the bottom of the desk drawer was another matter, however. And it wasn't just that she didn't want Dan Finley to see it.

Cora Felton was dying to know what the paper was.

Cora Felton held her tongue, watched the purse, let the others bicker.

The discussion as to whether or not they should talk was interrupted by the arrival of Chief Harper, who came stomping in, put his hands on his hips, and said, "Well, well, well. What have we here?"

Dan Finley, at his heels, said, "As I told you, Chief—"

"Yes, you did," Harper interrupted. "And now I'd like to hear it from them. Miss Felton, what were you doing in the Hurley house?"

Before Cora Felton could answer, Becky Baldwin stepped in front of her. "Excuse me, Chief, but are you suspecting Ms. Felton of a crime?"

"I'm suspecting her of being stupid and doing something she shouldn't."

"I'll take that as a yes," Becky Baldwin said. "Under the circumstances, as an attorney, I would have to advise Ms. Felton not to answer your question."

"You're not her attorney."

"No, I'm not. But she doesn't have one, do you, Ms. Felton?"

"I don't need an attorney."

"See, Chief?" Becky Baldwin said. "She doesn't have an attorney, and she doesn't think she needs one. That's exactly the type of person the law was designed to protect. Ms. Felton is in jail. If you want to talk to her, and you suspect her of any crime, you have to advise her of her rights. And you *must* suspect her of a crime, or she wouldn't be in jail. And if you *don't* suspect her of a crime, you have to let her go. Those are her rights, and she should know them, whether she has an attorney or not."

"Well, thank you for making that clear," Chief Harper said dryly. He took out a set of keys, unlocked the cell door. "Miss Felton, Miss Carter, come with me."

Cora Felton got up, followed Sherry Carter out of the cell. Becky Baldwin tried to follow too, but Chief Harper closed the cell door and locked it again. "I'm sorry, Miss Baldwin, but at the moment I just need to talk to them. But I assure you, when I come back to talk to you, I will read you your rights."

Chief Harper ushered Sherry Carter and Cora Felton into his office. "Sit down," he told them. "Let's try to make this as painless as possible. Do I need to point out to you two why you can't go breaking into the Hurley house?"

"I don't think so," Cora Felton said.

"What were you doing there?"

"Looking for clues."

"Did you find any?"

Cora Felton smiled. "I refuse to answer until you read me my rights."

Chief Harper gawked at her. "Are you kidding me?"

"Yes, I am," Cora Felton replied. "But there's no reason to tell little Miss F. Lee Bailey that. As far as she's concerned, I'd be happy if you gave her the impression we clammed up."

"Done," Chief Harper said. "So what exactly did you find?"

Cora Felton gave him a rundown of the thought process by which she and Sherry Carter had discovered the new clues.

Chief Harper was disbelieving. "You mean the whole crossword-puzzle game was a hoax?"

"That's the way it looks right now."

"Any reason you couldn't let me in on this, instead of breaking the law?"

"Chief," Sherry said, "you'd made an arrest. How would you have felt if we'd come in and said, You wanna help us find something to undermine your case?"

"I might not have been pleased, but it's what you should have done."

"You wanna release Daniel Hurley?" Cora Felton said.

"I can't release Daniel Hurley," Chief Harper said. "There's too much evidence against him. He's gotta go before the judge."

"Even in light of what we found?" Cora Felton said.

"What you found doesn't prove he didn't do these killings. For all we know, the one thing has nothing to do with the other." Chief Harper sounded grim. "But that's not the point. The point is this is a murder case. *My* murder case. If you have any leads that would shed some light on that murder case, you bring 'em to *me*."

"We're bringing them to you now," Cora Felton pointed out helpfully.

"Yes," Chief Harper replied. "And entirely of your own volition. I'm sure being dragged in in handcuffs had nothing to do with it."

"You want to gripe about it, or you wanna try to figure out what it means?"

"As I understand it now, Emma Hurley has little jingly rhymes leading you all over her house?"

"That's the gist of it."

"And you think this was the real game, not the cross-word puzzles?"

"We were trying to find that out when we were dragged in here."

"And you got as far as the study?"

"Yes, we did," Cora Felton said. "Which would have been pay dirt."

Chief Harper frowned. "What do you mean?"

"I'm not entirely sure," Cora Felton answered. "But since we're all cooperating here, would you mind if I got my purse?"

"Your purse?"

"Yes. Your officer took it away from me. Which was probably wise on his part, since there's a weapon in it."

"A weapon?"

"Relax," Cora said. "I have a permit for it. But the point is, there is a gun in my purse. Among other things."

"What other things?"

"The last clue—the one in the study—was in an envelope. Just before the officer burst in on us, I shoved it in my purse."

"Wait here," Chief Harper ordered brusquely. He strode to the door, jerked it open, and went out. He was back moments later carrying the floppy drawstring purse. He pulled the gun out of it, scowled. "I'm going to take your word that you have a permit for this. I'm also going to hold on to it for the moment so it doesn't go off accidentally while you rummage through your purse. Now," he said, handing the purse to her, "you wanna show me that clue?"

"I sure do," Cora Felton said. "Because it's the payoff. All the other clues are written in place in Magic Marker.

The first clue was on the bottom of a drawer. This clue was also on the bottom of a drawer, but it wasn't written, it was in an envelope. So it's not apt to be directions to somewhere else."

"So where is it?" Chief Harper said.

"I'm looking, I'm looking," Cora Felton mumbled, fumbling through her purse. She kept pulling out handfuls of junk, heaping them on Chief Harper's desk. Combs, lipsticks, eyeliners. Tissues, playing cards, double-A batteries, a wallet, a key chain. Pens, pencils, film cases, stamps, coins. A paperback murder mystery. A video game cartridge. A diaphragm case. A pack of cigarettes. A silver flask. An ancient 45 Everly Brothers record. A rubber cow.

Chief Harper looked at the growing pile in disbelief. "Good lord, how will you even know what it is you found?"

"When I come to something I don't recognize," Cora Felton said. "Ah, what's this?"

Cora Felton held up a crumpled piece of bright red construction paper. She unfolded it, smoothed it out. It was a piece of paper about six inches long, three inches wide, cut in the shape of a fish.

Chief Harper and Sherry Carter crowded around to look.

It was quite clearly a fish. An eye, gills, and scales were drawn on it in pen.

"What's on the other side?" Chief Harper said.

The other side had been drawn on exactly the same.

Chief Harper snorted. "A fish. So, is that it? Is that the clue?"

"It's the clue, all right," Cora Felton said. "And we have to go back."

"Back? Back where?"

"To the Hurley house."

"Why?"

"Because I know what kind of fish this is."

Chief Harper looked at her in exasperation. "Oh? And what kind of fish is that?"

"A red herring."

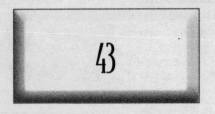

43

CHIEF HARPER, CORA FELTON, AND SHERRY CARTER
stood in Emma Hurley's master bedroom.

"Okay," Cora Felton said. "This is where it all began,
and this is where it has to end. I'm the judge, it is up to me
to figure it out, and this time I have to be right. And this
time I think I can."

"You wanna tell me why?" Chief Harper said.

"Because of the fish," Cora Felton answered. "The fish
tells me a lot. It tells me what Emma Hurley planned."
Cora paused, looked around the room. "And what she
didn't plan."

Chief Harper snorted in disgust. "I got two people
dead, and a third in critical condition. You're still technically under arrest for breaking and entering, so give it to
me straight."

"I assure you I will," Cora Felton said with great dignity. "We started out with the assumption Emma Hurley
left the crossword-puzzle clues. Then the crossword puzzle
turned out to be a phony. Then the question became: Why

would Emma Hurley leave bogus clues? The second puzzle gave an answer. Look."

Cora Felton strode over to the desk, pulled out a drawer, and held it up. "See. Clue #1 is written on the bottom of this drawer. Without the crossword-puzzle clues, the heirs would all find this clue at the exact same time. Which would send them en masse to look for the second. Emma Hurley didn't want that. She wanted *one* person to figure out her game. *One* winner. The crossword-puzzle clues made sure that happened. They were a red herring to send the heirs off on a false scent. Only the smartest of them would come back and find the real puzzle."

"That's obvious," Chief Harper said. "What's your revelation?"

"This." Cora Felton set down the drawer and held up the paper fish. "This is a red herring. And if this is a red herring, then that clue written on the bottom of that desk drawer is a false scent. *It* is what was intended to send the heirs off in the wrong direction. But if this is a false scent, then there is no longer any reason for the crossword-puzzle clues. Which means Emma Hurley didn't leave them."

"Then who did?"

"Someone who didn't want the other clues found."

"Why not?"

"Because that someone was trying to win the game."

"Then why would he or she be playing?" Chief Harper pointed out. "If they knew the crossword-puzzle clues were fake because *they* left them, why weren't they looking for this *other* set of clues?"

"I don't know yet," Cora Felton replied. "But it's a good point, Chief. Whoever planted the crossword-puzzle clues was not necessarily trying to win the game."

"Jeff Beasley," Sherry Carter said.

"What?" Chief Harper said.

"He was arrested for breaking and entering. He was found in that bed. But he didn't steal anything. So what if he was *planting* the clues?"

"And the heir he was working for killed him," Cora Felton said.

"What heir? I hate to be a broken record, but if an heir's behind this who knows the clues are fake"—the Chief pointed at the desk drawer—"why isn't he looking for *this*?"

"Like I say, we're working it out," Cora Felton said placidly. "But go back to the premise. If someone else planted the crossword-puzzle clues, it had to be someone who didn't want this drawer found. Maybe because they wanted to win the game, or maybe for another reason entirely. But whatever the reason, they didn't want it found. Why? Because they didn't *know* it was a red herring. They thought it was real. And if it was real, they didn't want it found.

"Now set that aside for a moment. And think about what Emma Hurley did. Emma Hurley doesn't know anything about the crossword-puzzle clues, naturally, because she had nothing to do with them. Emma Hurley set up this. These were her clues, and they led straight to a red herring. Her clues were designed to send the heirs off in the wrong direction. We know that because of the paper fish. So what's the real puzzle? We don't know. So we come back here, and we start over. As Emma Hurley wanted us to do. So we go back to our original instructions. There's a forty-year-old puzzle to solve. And the first clue is in that desk."

Cora Felton rubbed her hands together. "So, let's find it."

Cora Felton, Sherry Carter, and Chief Harper descended on the desk. Chief Harper pushed the rolltop open and began searching the cubbyholes. Cora Felton began pulling out the drawers. Sherry Carter picked up the blotter and began taking it out of its frame. They attacked their jobs with relish.

Fifteen minutes later found them considerably dispirited. An exhaustive search of the desk had turned up absolutely nothing.

"Well, that's it," Chief Harper said. "We've been over every inch of this desk. There's nothing to find."

"There must be," Cora insisted.

"Maybe not," Chief Harper said. "If someone planted the puzzles, how do you know they didn't take the real clue?"

"Because they couldn't find it," Cora Felton said.

"How do you know that?"

"Because they didn't find the writing on the drawer, and the writing on the drawer would be easier to find."

"How do you know they didn't find the writing on the drawer?"

"Because if they had, they wouldn't have left the puzzle clues. Because the writing on the drawer makes the puzzle clues unnecessary. Worse than that, it brands them as false."

Cora exhaled noisily, shook her head. "We're missing something. It's a puzzle but the obvious clues lead nowhere. So the clue we want is *not* obvious. It's a clue that doesn't appear to be a clue."

Cora paused, considered.

She said, *"It's a clue in plain sight."*

Cora nodded in agreement with herself. "Yes. That would be perfect. That would be what Emma Hurley would want."

"Oh, come on," Chief Harper said. "If it's a clue in plain sight, where is it?"

"I don't know. Maybe someone took it."

Chief Harper scowled. "You just got through telling me no one could find it."

"Yes. But if they didn't *know* it was a clue . . ." Cora's eyes gleamed. "Sherry. Refresh my memory. The first time we were up here. When the heirs were all in the room. I'm a little hazy on the details. Remind me what happened."

"Of course," Sherry said, fully aware her aunt couldn't remember a thing about that incident. "You'll recall we came in last. The heirs were already in the room. And the lawyer and the banker. And Chief Harper. And Becky Baldwin and Aaron Grant."

"And did any of them go near the desk?"

"They were all gathered around it."

"Was it open or shut?"

"Shut. I remember the lawyer mentioned that the roll-top was down but was unlocked, and he raised the top."

Cora's eyes widened. She snapped her fingers, pointed to the desk.

"Lock it."

"Huh?" Chief Harper said.

"Lock the rolltop. Every time we've opened the desk, it's been unlocked. We've never unlocked it. Or locked it. Lock it now."

Chief Harper, looking baffled, closed the rolltop, turned the key.

The key wouldn't turn.

"Well," Cora Felton said. "Go ahead and lock it."

"I can't," Chief Harper said. "The key doesn't work." He pulled it out of the lock, looked at it. "Of course it doesn't. Look. It's entirely the wrong kind of key."

Cora Felton smiled.

"Exactly," she said.

44

JUDY GELMAN WAS CURIOUS. A NOSY WOMAN UNDER normal circumstances, the banker's wife could hardly contain herself at the sight of two women and the Bakerhaven Chief of Police on her front porch at one A.M. She scrunched her nightgown modestly around her neck, and said, "What's this all about, Chief?"

"I'm sorry to bother you, Mrs. Gelman," Chief Harper told her. "I need to talk to your husband."

"Marcus is asleep. What do you want?"

"I'm sorry. It's a police matter, and it's urgent. Would you wake him up, please?"

"A police matter?" Mrs. Gelman's eyes traveled over Sherry Carter and Cora Felton. From her look, they might have been the women who'd led her husband astray.

"That's right," Chief Harper said. "I'm looking into the death of Annabel Hurley. Among other things. These two women are helping me out. You know Cora Felton and Sherry Carter, of course. We urgently need to talk to Marcus. Would you wake him, please?"

Mrs. Gelman frowned. "I thought you'd already made an arrest."

"I'm sorry, but my business is with Marcus," Chief Harper answered firmly. "Now, with all due respect, Mrs. Gelman, the sooner I talk to him, the sooner you can go back to bed."

Mrs. Gelman looked at him for a moment. Her expression did not change, but she clearly was not happy. "All right, come in."

She ushered them inside. They entered, found themselves in an unlit foyer. Mrs. Gelman retreated into the darkness, and moments later a light came on. It proved to be a single bulb from a wooden floor lamp in the living room.

"Wait here," Mrs. Gelman said, and trudged up the stairs.

Chief Harper, Cora Felton, and Sherry Carter stood in the living room and looked around. The floor lamp stood next to an overstuffed chair and footstool, obviously a favorite reading spot. The room also boasted a couch and coffee table, a breakfront, a sideboard, and several end tables, all period pieces.

Cora Felton nodded approvingly. "Some of those are worth money," she said.

"Oh?" Chief Harper said.

"Yes. My fifth husband, Melvin, collected antiques." She frowned at the remembrance. "That's why I don't."

Chief Harper was about to comment when the stairs squeaked. He turned to the door as the plump form of Marcus Gelman entered the room. The banker was barefoot. He wore a blue bathrobe and bright orange pajamas. He had stopped to put on his glasses, but not to comb his hair, which stuck out from either side of his bald head.

His wife was not with him, which, in itself, spoke volumes. Chief Harper could imagine the whispered argument, and was sure, though not present, Judy was in earshot.

Cora Felton sized Marcus Gelman up with interest. The only other time she'd met him, at the Hurley mansion, she'd been somewhat indisposed. He was clearly nervous, yet he seemed eager too. He peered at the faces of his unexpected guests intently, as if looking for a sign.

"Yes?" Marcus said. His voice broke slightly, and it came out as a croak.

Chief Harper said, "Mr. Gelman, I don't mean to alarm you. I just have a few questions to ask you, and these women do too. You remember Cora Felton and Sherry Carter. They were there the other day when you unlocked the Hurley house. As you know, Miss Felton is the woman designated as the judge in Emma Hurley's will. As such, she has something to say to you. I do too, but I'm going to let her go first. Miss Felton?"

"Thank you," Cora said. "Mr. Gelman, you're a banker, you have certain responsibilities. And you are a man of discretion. You are privy to information that is confidential. You do not discuss your depositors' accounts. However, it is my contention that Emma Hurley had business with your bank that *no one* knew about, no one except you. And I am asking for information about that business now."

"One moment," Chief Harper interjected. "Let me add something to that. Marcus, you know I wouldn't want you to do anything you shouldn't. But I have to tell you, this has become a murder investigation, and I have reason to believe that you have information pertinent to a crime. I'll get a warrant if I have to. I'll wake up Judge Hobbs right now if I need to. Because I would like an answer to a question I have a feeling you would normally not want to answer. I'm giving you the background to show you why you should answer. Now I'm just going to come right out and ask."

Chief Harper reached in his pocket, took out the key. "Miss Felton, would you do the honors?"

"Yes, I will. Mr. Gelman, I hand you a key. I'm going to ask you now in my official capacity as Emma Hurley's representative, would you tell me please, as president of the bank, if this is a key to Emma Hurley's safe deposit box?"

Marcus Gelman took the key, held it up, and inspected it. He was sweating, and his fingers trembled as he turned it over in his hands. Then his plump body heaved, and a gusty sigh rattled his flabby cheeks. He seemed to cling to the little silver key as to a life preserver.

"Thank God," Marcus Gelman murmured.

45

THE COURTHOUSE WAS JAMMED. EVERY AVAILABLE SEAT was taken and every inch of floor space was filled. From her vantage point in the back of the courtroom, Sherry Carter stood and surveyed the scene.

Judge Hobbs sat at his bench, calmly awaiting the time to begin. He seemed impassive, as befitted a judge. From his manner this was nothing special, just another courtroom session.

But it clearly was not. For one thing, there was no defendant. Clustered around the defense table sat Chief Harper, Cora Felton, county prosecutor Henry Firth, Dr. Barney Nathan, and bank president Marcus Gelman, who were conferring with one another, thick as thieves.

Nor were there any jurors. The jury box was nearly empty, having been set aside for the heirs. The Applegates and the Hurleys were in the front row, sitting as far apart from each other as possible. Whether by accident or design, Philip and Phyllis sat at the extreme ends, with their spouses in between, as buffers.

Mildred Sims and the young yard boy whose name

Sherry could not recall were also in the jury box, sitting second row center. The housekeeper sat stiff as a ramrod, her chin elevated, looking neither left nor right. The yard boy, by contrast, was looking everywhere. He seemed thrilled by the proceedings, and was constantly shifting in his seat, which was, Sherry noted, the one under which they had found the second set of clues.

Daniel Hurley sat with Becky Baldwin in the first row behind the defense table. In spite of his recent incarceration, he looked none the worse for wear. He had showered and shaved and put on clean clothes, and he had clearly washed his hair, which was glossy, flowing down the back of his head. To Sherry, who had been married to a rock musician, the image grated.

Next to him, Becky Baldwin looked chic, modern, attractive, and coolly efficient, in a smart, no-nonsense ivory pants suit. Her image was a triumph of understated elegance and calculated simplicity. The overall effect was to make her look good without trying, which was almost unfair.

Particularly since Daniel and Becky were sitting with Aaron Grant. Which was not Aaron's fault—this was the press row, it was where he was supposed to sit. They were the interlopers. They were the ones who had been offered seats in the jury box and had not taken them. The fact they were sitting together was in no way Aaron Grant's fault. Sherry knew that. It didn't stop her from blaming him for it.

Chester Hurley stood in the back of the courtroom on the side opposite Sherry. If he had dressed for court, she would not have known it. He wore a faded yellow T-shirt with a frayed collar, and a pair of ancient overalls, only one shoulder strap of which he had bothered to button. He was unshaven. A baseball cap of dubious vintage was on his head. Though she was way too young to tell, Sherry suspected the *B* on the cap was not for the Red Sox, but either the Boston Braves or the Brooklyn Dodgers.

Arthur Kincaid was there. Sherry saw him moving through the courtroom, conferring with various groups. As she watched, the lawyer leaned over the jury box rail to talk to Mildred Sims.

Glancing around, Sherry could pick out people she knew in the crowd. Minnie Wishburn from the Wash and Dry had a seat next to a tiny man with a big nose and thick glasses who Sherry figured must be Ray. If so, he was not at all what she expected. From Minnie's description, Sherry had pictured some hulking fisherman.

Also in the crowd were Jimmy and Edith Potter from the library, Mable Drake from Odds and Ends, Betty Roston from the post office, the young waitress from the Wicker Basket, and the bartender from the Country Kitchen.

Conspicuous by his absence was crossword-puzzle constructor Harvey Beerbaum.

The news crews had squeezed in too. The TV cameras were set up along the sides of the room, where the on-camera reporters had carved out niches for themselves from which to shoot their lead-ins. Rick Reed was shooting one now, though what he was saying, Sherry couldn't begin to guess. Other cameras were focused around the court, picking up shots of the principals in the case. Several of the cameras, Sherry noted, seemed to be focused exclusively on Becky Baldwin. At least, that was Sherry's impression. Though, to be fair, she had to admit Becky was sitting next to Daniel Hurley, the chief suspect in the case. Even so, the coverage seemed excessive.

Judge Hobbs banged the gavel, trying to quiet the crowd. With so many people in the courtroom that took quite a while. When the rumbling had subsided somewhat, he pulled the microphone to him and said, "Thank you, ladies and gentlemen. If I may have silence, please, I would like to start out by making something clear. Court is not in session. This is not a courtroom proceeding. At the request of the Bakerhaven Chief of Police I am allowing my courtroom to be used at this time. The media are in town. We wish to welcome them, not turn them away. The courtroom has the facilities to allow them to film, although I cannot recall the last time we have ever done so. But through the coverage generated by this case, it would appear there is a need.

"Now, before I turn the floor over to Chief Harper, I have some housekeeping to take care of. The charges against Daniel Hurley have been dismissed. They have been dismissed without prejudice. I would like to explain what that means. All it means is Daniel Hurley is not a defendant at this time. There are no charges against him, and he is not under arrest. This does not mean he is not a suspect, this does not mean he has been cleared of suspicion. And no jeopardy has been attached. This dismissal is in no way a bar to a future prosecution, should evidence be uncovered linking him to the crime. All it means is he is not under arrest at the present time.

"You are now going to hear from various parties in this case. They will speak from the witness stand. That is because there is a microphone there. But they are *not* witnesses, they are *not* testifying under oath. They are speaking from the witness stand merely as a matter of convenience.

"With that, I will turn the floor over to Chief Harper."

Chief Harper walked over to the witness stand, sat down, pulled the microphone over. "I must admit, this feels rather strange," he began in a rather strained voice. "But then this whole case has been bizarre. There have been several recent developments, and I have called this meeting to bring you all up to speed. I have been in consultation with prosecutor Henry Firth, and Dr. Barney Nathan, and here is what we know.

"First off, prosecutor Firth is not only in accord with, but it is on his recommendation that the murder and assault charges against Daniel Hurley have been dropped. As a show of good faith, and on advice of counsel, Daniel Hurley has signed a waiver of false arrest. But none of that, as Judge Hobbs has pointed out, would be a bar to future prosecution.

"And from Dr. Barney Nathan I have the following news." Chief Harper's manner made it clear that no matter how much the prosecutor and doctor were cooperating, he was not about to let either speak. "The condition of Harvey Beerbaum, the man brutally attacked two nights ago, has been upgraded from critical to stable. He would appear to be out of danger. He has not yet regained consciousness. However, when he does we are hoping he can shed some light on the attack.

"The blood on the knife Daniel Hurley attempted to dispose of has been typed to the blood of the decedent Annabel Hurley. DNA testing is yet to be done, but there is every indication we will get a match, and the knife will prove to be the murder weapon."

Chief Harper winced at the excited buzz that statement produced. Judge Hobbs assisted him by banging the gavel.

"I know," Chief Harper continued. "This new evidence would not seem consistent with letting Daniel Hurley go. However, further evidence has come to light. I know you are all aware of the contents of Emma Hurley's will. She left a puzzle for her heirs to solve, and appointed the Puzzle Lady, Cora Felton, as the judge and referee. Emma Hurley charged Miss Felton with solving the puzzle first. I might even say, she *challenged* Miss Felton to do so.

"Well, I am happy to announce that, this morning, Miss Felton solved the puzzle. And in so doing, uncovered a key piece of evidence. She is going to present that evidence to you now. Miss Felton?"

Cora Felton got up from her seat at the defense table, walked to the witness stand and sat down. Her eyes were bright, her manner dignified.

"Thank you very much, Chief Harper."

She opened her drawstring purse, took out a manila envelope, pulled the microphone to her.

"I discovered this envelope early this morning. It is the final piece of the puzzle. Written on the envelope are the words, *Last Clue*. Underneath, just in case there was any doubt, are the words, *Yes, this is it*. In the envelope is Emma Hurley's final communication to her heirs. I shall read it to you now."

Cora Felton pulled the pages from the envelope and began to read.

> "*Congratulations. You have won the game. Are you familiar with the term* Pyrrhic victory? *If you've gotten this far, I would imagine you probably are. But in case you aren't, another way to put it is: you've won the battle but lost the war.*
>
> "*Unless you're Chester.*
>
> "*Is it you, Chester? Somehow I doubt it. I can't see you caring enough, at least about the money. But you might just want to know. And maybe that would be enough. So maybe it's you. If so, you will probably understand what I've said. Though in your case it will not apply.*
>
> "*But if it's one of the other heirs. Particularly Philip or Phyllis. I almost hope it is. It pleases me no end, the thought of one of you reading this now. You, whose sibling rivalry is unparalleled. I can imagine the lengths you must have gone to to get here. Clawing and sniping at*

each other. Using every underhanded, dirty trick in the book. Lying. Cheating. Making up stories. Hurling false accusations. I wouldn't even rule out accusing each other of murdering me. Though I can't imagine anyone foolish enough to believe such a stupid premise."

Cora Felton cleared her throat.

"But down to business. I presented you with a forty-year-old puzzle. I now present you with its solution. You have earned the solution by ignoring the elaborate trappings I laid out. The mysterious treasure hunt that led nowhere. The contest that wasn't a contest, but was made to look so by the dramatic and extravagant gesture of hiring a judge. Extravagant in one sense, though if you are reading this, she has undoubtedly earned her fee.

"And what, you ask, is she rambling about? Why can't the old crone be direct? She tells us we've won, but we haven't won. What can she possibly mean?

"It was just over forty years ago that my father, Evan Hurley, died. He had been sick for some time with cancer, though not as long as he would have lasted nowadays. As the disease ate him up, he surveyed his life.

"And made his will.

"You are familiar with the terms of that will. Evan cut his other heirs off with fixed sums, and left the bulk of his estate to me. I'm sure you know why.

"My brother Randolph predeceased him, and while there were children, Father never entertained a thought of skipping generations.

"Of my sister, Alicia, the less said the better. Suffice it to say Father was rather straitlaced, and Alicia's actions did not meet with his approval.

"Then there was Chester. Dear brother Chester. Dear

odd brother Chester. What we would call nowadays a nerd or a geek. Did we have those expressions then? I'm getting old, and I can't recall.

"But I'm rambling again. If I were alive, you could get mad at me. As it is, you'll just have to take it. At any rate, dear Chester, Father's will bypassed you. And for those reasons. For giving the impression of being not all there.

"It is plausible. It was possible. It was accepted without question by the other heirs.

"But it wasn't true.

"It was a lie.

"It was a falsehood.

"It was a forgery.

"Yes, Chester. I can't imagine you were really fooled. You, who were so smart to begin with. And yet you were never keen at social situations. Not particularly adept at reading social cues. But did you really think Father disapproved? When he was such a prim, proper, prudish man himself? Did you really think he'd see you as odd? A chip off the old block, is what you were. The logical successor, most likely heir.

"Then how did I inherit and not you?

"Well, that's another story. Yes, you may groan while I digress. But I have a tale to tell. A tale of unrequited love. And isn't love an awful thing, the things that love will make one do?

"Like altering a will.

"You see now why you have not really won the game? Why you may hold an empty prize?

"The lawyer does.

"The lawyer who prepared the will.

"Prepared it twice. As written, and then with the substituted page.

"For love, unrequited.

"*Ironic, isn't it, that I should never marry, live my life alone? Supported by the wealth supplied me by the man I rejected.*

"*But more ironic, I think, for the fact I did not know it.*

"*No, my dear relatives, whatever else you might think of me, I was not that. Scheming, lying, deceitful, covetous. None of those adjectives applied. I was as shocked as any by my vast inheritance.*

"*It was a most pleasant surprise.*

"*But having inherited so much, it was no surprise when suitors arrived at my door. Indeed, in that respect Father's money was a curse. It drew suitors like flies. And I turned them away, knowing why each had come.*

"*One was persistent, however. He would not give up, and could not go away, acting, as he was, as my solicitor.*"

Out of the corner of her eye, Sherry Carter saw Arthur Kincaid, who from the beginning of this speech had been working his way toward the back of the room, slip out the door.

"*I staved him off,*" Cora continued. "*Deflected his advances. Dismissed them with a joke.*

"*I should have been direct.*

"*I should have just said no.*

"*Because, years later when I finally did, he told me what he'd done. How out of his regard for me he'd altered my father's will, transferring the bulk of the estate from my brother to me.*"

One other person had observed the lawyer's departure. While Sherry watched, on the far side of the room a baseball cap with the letter *B* could be seen weaving among the spectators, heading for the back door.

"I was devastated by this confession," Cora read. "And I wanted to make things right.

"And yet . . .

"It came so late. Years had gone by. I was used to a certain lifestyle. As was my brother. A reversal of fortunes could have destroyed me, and would not have benefited Chester. Or so I told myself. And it would not have affected the other heirs, whose bequests would not change. So why speak out?

"Yes, I was weak.

"Yes, I went along.

"And it has eaten away at me all these years like a cancer.

"Which is why I devised my game.

"Did you figure it out? Before you got this letter, I mean? There were so many clues. The fact I placed the banker, not the lawyer, in charge of my house. Because, of course, the lawyer might realize what I'd done if he were to peek at my will.

"Did you do that, Arthur? Frightened by a sealed will, and my instructions to summon the heirs, did you steam the envelope open to see why I had barred you from my home? Did you panic? Did you do something foolish?

"Or is it you who is reading this now?

"You see, in my game even you had a chance, Arthur.

"Even you might have gotten away.

"Did you get away?

"If not, let me state here and now, lest there be any doubt, that it was Arthur Kincaid, forty years ago, who altered my father's will, transferring our father's fortune from my brother Chester to me. Chester was and is my father's rightful heir. And the money conveyed by my last will and testament is rightfully his."

In the jury box, Philip Hurley shot to his feet. "No!" he cried. "It can't be! That money is rightfully mine!"

"The hell it is!" thundered Phyllis Applegate. She lunged to her feet, brushing her husband aside. "It's mine and you know it!"

Brother and sister charged forward. They met in the middle of the jury box, clawing and scratching at each other in savage fury.

The gunshot stopped them. They froze with their hands on each other's throats. Looked toward the sound.

The shot came from outside the courthouse.

There was a moment's stunned silence, then everyone began shoving toward the exit. A crush of heirs and by-standers and media tried to push out the doors.

Chester Hurley fooled them. Wily as ever, he avoided them all, slipping in the side door while they were rushing out the back. He made his way calmly around the jury box, down the press row, and through the gate. He walked up to Chief Harper, pulled the enormous gun from his overalls, and laid it on the defense table.

"I'm turning myself in," he said. "I just killed Arthur Kincaid."

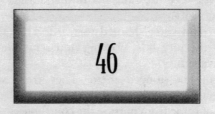

46

"DON'T YOU WANT TO TAKE MY PICTURE WITH THE FLOW-ERS?" Cora Felton said. Cora was all decked out in her gardening togs and holding a trowel.

"Oh, absolutely," the interviewer from *People* magazine said. A thin woman with angular features, she gestured toward the young man with a light meter and three cameras slung around his neck. "Roger will be shooting while we talk. Pay no attention to him, pretend he's not there. We'll just have a little chat."

"Would you like to see the marigolds? I'm very proud of my marigolds."

"I'm sure you are. I have a few questions first. It's not every day you see someone gunned down in the street."

"I didn't actually see it," Cora Felton said meekly.

"No, but you made it happen, didn't you? I mean, you were in the courthouse, reading the will."

"It wasn't the will. It was more of a confession, really. Can I get you some tea? I make the most wonderful iced tea. My niece, Sherry—that's her over there with the young reporter—would be delighted to get you some."

"Not just now." The interviewer checked the volume on the microcassette recorder she was holding. "Now, the woodsman shot the lawyer for cheating him out of fifteen million dollars?"

"No," Cora Felton said. "Chester couldn't have cared less about the money. He shot him for killing his niece. Annabel Hurley. Chester couldn't forgive him for that."

"It was Chester Hurley who shot the lawyer?"

"That's right."

"And the lawyer's name was . . . ?"

"Arthur Kincaid. The lawyer who, four decades ago, altered Evan Hurley's will, leaving his money to Emma instead of Chester. Did you see the geraniums? I've had good luck with the geraniums."

"Yes, I'm sure you have. And where did the banker come into all this?"

Cora Felton sighed. "Okay, let me give you a rundown of what happened, so we can get on with the interview. Emma Hurley was dying, she had a lot of money to leave. But she was haunted by the fact the money was not really hers. She had inherited it unjustly due to the connivance of a lawyer. That lawyer, Arthur Kincaid, was still her attorney. I think she enjoyed toying with him, that that was her way of punishing him for what he had done.

"With her death, however, she meant to set things right. So she concocted this incredible scheme. She would summon her heirs, all of them, including Chester, the one she had wronged, and invite them to play a game. The game purported to be a contest to see who would inherit her fortune. Actually, the game was designed to lead to a revelation of what she had done.

"And what the attorney had done. I think that was the real purpose. To make Kincaid suffer.

"To carry this out, she placed a letter in a safe deposit box in her name. She instructed her banker, Marcus

Gelman, to open that box for anyone named in her will who presented him with the key, on the condition that the box be opened *only* in the presence of the person she had appointed judge and referee."

Cora smiled, and did a mock curtsy.

"That, of course, was to prevent Arthur Kincaid from opening the box and destroying her letter.

"So was locking up the house. Which was the other instruction she gave Marcus Gelman. Upon her death, Gelman was to seal up Emma's mansion, and not unlock it for anyone, including the lawyer, until after the reading of her will. That was because she was afraid Arthur Kincaid would peek at the will, learn of the contest, and try to destroy the clues.

"Which he would have done, and which he attempted to do. He had already read the will, and was in the process of searching the bedroom when the banker showed up to throw him out. After that, the house was locked up and Kincaid couldn't get in without breaking in, which he was reluctant to do, as he couldn't afford to be caught at it. He had also spent enough time searching for the clue to realize finding it wouldn't be easy.

"Which gave him an idea. He didn't know how to get rid of the clue, but all he had to do was leave another clue that was easier to find, and the real clue would go undiscovered.

"In her will Emma Hurley referred to her game as a *puzzle.* She didn't mean a crossword puzzle, but Arthur Kincaid didn't know that. Or care. If Emma Hurley said *puzzle,* then *puzzle* it would be. He took a crossword puzzle from a newspaper, printed the grid, and divided up the clues in four groups, one for each quadrant of the puzzle. He typed the quadrants up and Xeroxed them, and planted the first set of clues under the blotter in the rolltop desk, just where Emma Hurley's will said they would be.

"Except he couldn't plant the clues himself, because he couldn't get in. And, as I say, he didn't dare risk breaking in.

"But he knew someone who could. For years he'd been acting as attorney for Jeff Beasley, the town drunk. Who'd been arrested for breaking and entering many times. Jeff Beasley owed him, and Jeff Beasley would be happy to pay. Happy to get the lawyer in his debt, actually. Jeff Beasley took the first set of clues, broke into the Hurley mansion, and planted them in the desk.

"Unfortunately for Arthur Kincaid, Jeff Beasley was so polluted—er, intoxicated—when he did that he passed out in Emma Hurley's bed and got arrested.

"And that's when everything began to come apart. Kincaid couldn't very well represent Beasley when he was representing the Hurley estate. A bit of a coincidence he was not too happy to have to reveal in court. Plus it necessitated assigning Beasley another lawyer. Becky Baldwin seemed perfect— Do you know her? Young and inexperienced, she would do what he said, and the matter could be quickly disposed of.

"Bad luck for Arthur Kincaid, Becky Baldwin was no pushover. Neither was Jeff Beasley, who didn't take kindly to being plea-bargained into jail. As a result, instead of being quickly disposed of, the matter was set for trial. Jeff Beasley, bailed out by Becky Baldwin, wound up at the Country Kitchen that night, hitting the heirs up for drinks, and making enigmatic comments in a most insinuating manner. Which everyone passed off as the ravings of a drunk.

"Except Arthur Kincaid, who knew exactly what Beasley was getting at. Particularly when he threw around phrases like *prodigal son*. Which Beasley could only have picked up by hearing his lawyer discussing the heirs. Listening to Beasley at the Country Kitchen that night, Arthur

Kincaid realized he'd made a terrible mistake. Jeff Beasley was a conniving drunk who could not be trusted. A serious liability and a real threat.

"Jeff Beasley had to be eliminated."

"So the lawyer killed him?" the photographer asked, enthralled.

Cora Felton raised an eyebrow. "Are you taking pictures, or what? Yes, of course he killed him. Snuck up behind him and clobbered him on the head. Left him in a ditch. A drunk like Beasley, who would be surprised? And that might have been the end of it, if that was the only one he had to kill."

"Annabel Hurley," the interviewer said.

"Yes." Cora Felton nodded. "I think Arthur truly regretted that one, but he really had no choice. She was on to him. Annabel Hurley had been helping Chester Hurley collect the clues. She was with Chester when he solved the puzzle. Learned that it led nowhere. That's when Annabel started poking around, questioning people. She spoke to Daniel Hurley; she even spoke to me. She must have also questioned Arthur Kincaid, which wasn't wise. Only she had no way of knowing that. Her questions were just shots in the dark.

"But not to him. Arthur Kincaid hears Annabel zooming in with leading questions, and he figures she's after him. He's terrified, and he acts. He's flustered, but not so flustered that he doesn't take the knife away, afterward. And plant it where it will do the most good. When he learns Annabel called on Daniel just before she died, he puts the knife in the saddlebag of the boy's motorcycle. Daniel finds it, panics, and throws it away."

"And the clues," the interviewer said. "The puzzle clues you say the lawyer planted. How did that work?"

"That was actually rather clever," Cora said. "He found a puzzle where the four long answers were all types of buildings—a courthouse, a post office, a laundromat, and a flower shop—and he turned that into a treasure hunt for finding the clues."

"And Chester Hurley solved it first?"

"That he did." Cora Felton made a self-deprecating gesture with the trowel. "And well ahead of me. Chester was a whiz with words, had no problem zipping though a simple puzzle like that. He solved the first part, then drove Annabel Hurley around and had her pick up the rest of the clues."

"And then he forged part of the puzzle?"

"Yes." Cora Felton smiled. "Just as Arthur Kincaid forged part of Evan Hurley's will. Chester Hurley completed the puzzle, and the last answer was *flower shop*. That sent him to the greenhouse, where he couldn't find a thing. And if something was hidden there, he didn't want the other heirs to get there until he found it. So he stole the last set of puzzle clues, and made up a new set to lead the heirs somewhere else. Then he sent Annabel Hurley back to the laundromat to substitute his false set of clues for the real ones. That worked, because Chester was so far ahead of the game no one else had gotten there yet." She made the self-deprecating gesture again. "Even me."

"And he was able to do that?" the photographer asked. "Create a whole new piece of the puzzle?"

"Actually, it wasn't that hard. He just had to come up with a ten-letter word for a building—he chose *five-and-ten*—and fill in words around it and write up clues. The job he did was good enough to buy him time to search the greenhouse. The only reason it didn't work was there was nothing at the greenhouse for him to find."

The interviewer frowned. "That's the part I don't understand. If the lawyer devised this whole thing to send the heirs to the greenhouse and there was nothing in the greenhouse, how did he expect to get away with his deception?"

"Actually, he almost did. And it would have been my fault. You gotta remember, he was the attorney for the estate. He was there at my elbow all the time, advising me, pushing me in the direction he wanted to go. And, I must admit, he had me on the verge of ruling whoever completed the puzzle would be the winner. Regardless of the fact the clues actually led nowhere." Cora Felton smiled. "Plus, you have to remember at that point I had never been to the greenhouse. Following Chester Hurley's false clues, I had just reached the conclusion there was nothing hidden at the five-and-ten." She cocked her head. "You sure you wouldn't like some iced tea?"

"Not just now," the interviewer said. "And the expert—this crossword-puzzle guy who got assaulted. Beerbaum. What was the deal with that?"

Cora Felton frowned. "You're not going to write this?"

"Absolutely not." The interviewer smiled. "Why do you ask?"

"For one thing, I would not want to embarrass a colleague. Or myself, for that matter. Well, the story is this. Some of the heirs were no good at crossword puzzles." Cora Felton shrugged modestly. "Some people aren't. Anyway, with so much money at stake, the heirs were leaving nothing to chance. The ones who weren't good at crossword puzzles got outside help. Phyllis Applegate went to the library. Philip Hurley went to Harvey Beerbaum. Philip had met him at the Country Kitchen the night before and knew he was an expert. He asked him to help."

"And he did?"

Cora Felton waggled a finger. "This is what you're not going to write. Yes, he did. And there was nothing wrong with that. And he had every right to do it."

"Yes, but why would he? A respected expert like him."

"Again, this is not for publication. Crossword-puzzle construction is not nearly as lucrative as you might think.

Most constructors have other sources of income. I was being well paid for refereeing the contest. No reason why Harvey Beerbaum shouldn't pick up a few bucks."

"Why was he attacked? As I understand it, he found something wrong with the puzzle."

"The puzzle was supposed to be forty years old. But it was full of modern references. Harvey Beerbaum found them in the puzzle. He knew something was wrong, and tried to warn me. Only I wouldn't listen. As judge, I wasn't about to discuss the puzzle with anyone, as I'm sure you can understand. But Arthur Kincaid overheard him asking, and realized he'd become a threat."

"And tried to murder him. But he's out of danger now?"

"Last I heard." Cora Felton pointed toward the edge of the house. "You know, I got a box of violets I was going to put in over there. If you wouldn't mind walking around."

"Just one more thing," the interviewer said. "Who gets the fifteen million now? I mean, that's up to you, isn't it? Who really won Emma Hurley's game?"

"No one did." Cora Felton shrugged her shoulders, smiled ruefully. "No one even played. Due to Arthur Kincaid's interference, no one found the real clues." She shook her head. "But it doesn't matter. The money wasn't hers to leave. By rights, it was Chester's all along."

"And what's going to happen to him?"

Cora Felton frowned. "That's not exactly a secret. It's been on every news channel."

"I know. Forgive me. Force of habit. Interviewers often ask questions to which we know the answers, just to see what someone will say."

"I thought you weren't writing this."

"Like I say, force of habit. And, of course, we have to *allude* to your extracurricular activities. As an aside."

"Uh huh," Cora Felton said, dryly. "Well then, as you

know, Chester Hurley's been arrested for Kincaid's murder. He's hired Becky Baldwin as his attorney. As he has no money to pay her retainer, she'll have to petition the Hurley estate for her fee. Which should be fun to watch. She'll probably have to work harder to collect his inheritance than to save him from the murder rap. Much harder. In this town it won't be easy to find twelve jurors eager to convict Chester Hurley." She put up her hand. "I'm no advocate for vigilante justice, but if there ever was a popular shooting, this is it."

"And the other heirs—what's happening with them?"

"Chester's declared he'll honor his sister's bequests. So, even if they can't touch the money legally, the other heirs all stand to pick up ten grand each.

"What the boy will do with his, I can't say. But if the twins run true to form, Philip will invest in some shady scheme, and Phyllis will take out an insurance policy on her husband. If so, they'll bear watching, but that's really not up to me."

Cora Felton cocked her head. "Now, if there's nothing else, I'd like to go to my daughter's wedding."

The interviewer frowned. "What?"

"Marlon Brando in *The Godfather* after solving all the problems of the world." Cora Felton gestured to the flower box near the corner of the house. "Could I show you my petunias?"

"Be my guest," the interviewer said.

On the front lawn Aaron Grant grinned at Sherry Carter. "You think they'll use any of these pictures?"

"Only if they can't get shots of Chester," Sherry said. "I'm afraid this human interest piece has taken a little turn."

"Yeah. I hope Cora's not too disappointed."

"Don't be silly. If the truth be known, she's more proud of her detective skills than anything else."

"Yeah, I know," Aaron Grant said. He raised his hand. "Come here, will you?"

"What is it?" Sherry said.

"I'd like to get away from the media for a minute. Come on out back."

Aaron Grant led her around the garage to the backyard. The prefab had no porch, but there was a picnic table, a clothesline, and a barbecue grill.

"Here, sit down," Aaron said.

He escorted Sherry to the picnic table, sat her on the top with her feet on the bench.

"Okay," he said. "I'm sorry to be theatrical, but I've got something to say to you."

"What's that?"

"I know who you are, Puzzle Lady."

"What's that?"

Aaron Grant ducked his head, grinned. He spread his arms, looked up at her, still grinning. "I feel like I'm Lois Lane and you're Superman. Except Lois only suspected. I *know* your secret identity. And don't blame Cora. She didn't tell me. I figured it out myself. I'm a reporter, and the clues were all there. Cora can't do crosswords to save her life. But you're a natural. I just wanted to tell you I know, and your secret is safe with me."

"Is it?" Sherry said.

"Yeah, it is." Aaron frowned, looked at the ground. "Then there's the other thing . . ."

"What other thing?"

He looked up again. "Becky. Yes, we used to have a relationship. But that was a long time ago. And now she's here, and it looks like she's going to stay. She's got Chester's case to handle. And there's an opening for a lawyer in town, now that Arthur Kincaid's dead."

"Aaron."

"Let me finish. Becky's news, and I will have to write

about her because she's news. And I cover the courthouse, it's one of my beats."

"I know."

"She was interested in Daniel Hurley. Maybe just as a client, or maybe there was something else. It's hard to imagine, an uncouth guy like that, what a woman could see in him."

"You *are* rather young, aren't you?" Sherry said.

"I'm younger than you or Becky. By a little."

"I didn't mean chronologically," Sherry told him. "Go on. I'm sorry I interrupted. You were telling me you couldn't see Becky Baldwin being interested in Daniel Hurley."

"Is that what I was saying? I can't recall. I think I was saying it couldn't matter to me if she is. Besides, I think she's much more interested in that TV guy. Not that that matters to me either, except I don't like him at all."

"Do I have to stay up on this picnic table?" Sherry asked.

"You, as usual, can do anything you like." Aaron took her hands. "I'm trying to say whatever you choose to do, I'd like to do with you."

"Oh, is that what you're trying to say?"

"Sort of. I'm not good with words."

"Oh?" Sherry said, sliding down from the tabletop. "You're usually fine."

"I know," he said. "Older women fluster me."

Sherry let go of his hands. His arms went around her.

Sherry smiled. "Older women?"

"Your designation, not mine."

"I was talking about emotional maturity."

"I was talking about *you*."

"You talk too much," Sherry said.

"So do you," Aaron Grant said.

And kissed her before she could reply.

About the Author

PARNELL HALL is the author of the critically acclaimed Stanley Hastings mystery novels and the Steve Winslow courtroom dramas, as well as seven Puzzle Lady mysteries, *A Clue for the Puzzle Lady; Last Puzzle and Testament; Puzzled to Death; A Puzzle in a Pear Tree; With This Puzzle, I Thee Kill; And a Puzzle to Die On;* and *Stalking the Puzzle Lady*. Nominated for the Edgar, the Shamus, and the Lefty awards, he lives in New York City, where he is working on his eighth Puzzle Lady mystery, *You Have the Right to Remain Puzzled*.

If you enjoyed Parnell Hall's *Last Puzzle & Testament,* you won't want to miss any of the tantalizing Puzzle Lady mysteries!

Look for the next, *A Puzzle in a Pear Tree,* available at your favorite bookstore.

And turn the page for an enticing preview

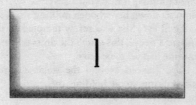

1

"No, no, no," Rupert Winston cried, silencing the piano, and vaulting up onto the stage with all the spry grace of a much younger man. Rupert tugged at his turtleneck, a habit he had when not particularly pleased. Which, in Cora Felton's humble opinion, was almost all the time. In the few rehearsals she'd had, Cora had come to detest the *"innovative and gifted"* director, as the *Bakerhaven Gazette* had termed him, who had left the *"stifling constraints of the Broadway stage"* in order to *"ply his craft in the liberating atmosphere of an enlightened village."*

Although no linguist, Cora Felton didn't have to be hit over the head with a condescending remark to recognize one. Rupert Winston had Cora's back up before she'd even met him. Being tapped to appear in Rupert's Christmas pageant was the last thing in the world Cora Felton wanted. Had she been able to think of any polite way to get out of it, Cora would have done so.

Had she known what rehearsals would be like, an impolite way would have sufficed.

"*Miss* Felton." Rupert Winston extracted his hand from his black turtleneck, entwined his long, slender fingers together, and rolled his steel gray eyes to the heavens, as if invoking the deities to witness his tribulations in dealing with mere mortals, and inferior ones at that. "You are a *milkmaid*. A hearty, robust milkmaid, fresh from the fields, sunny and bright and imbued with a lust for life. If you are to sing the solo line, I have to *hear* the solo line. You cannot mumble it into your sleeve."

Cora Felton set down her wooden milking stool, fixed the director with an evil eye. She was sorely tempted to remind him that she hadn't *got* a sleeve, this *wasn't* the dress rehearsal, and her milkmaid costume had *yet* to be sewn.

Instead, Cora glanced around the stage, where the seven other maids-a-milking stood holding their stools. "You're absolutely right, Rupert," she said sweetly. "I'm totally wrong for this part. I'm sure any of the other milkmaids could do better. I understand *completely* why you'd wish to replace me."

Rupert Winston looked shocked. "Miss Felton. Did I say any such thing? Of course not. You're perfect for the part. It's just a question of pulling a performance out of you."

Cora bit back a groan. Were there any way to agree with this fool and get on with it, Cora would have done so, but she knew from experience Rupert loved to pontificate. Under the guise of giving direction, he could run through his entire Broadway résumé at the drop of a hat. Already, she could see the other actors emerging from the wings to listen. They soon filled the stage. The piece was *The Twelve Days of Christmas,* complete with pipers piping, drummers drumming, and so on. Cora could barely calculate how many actors were in the show, let alone the odds of all of them ever doing it right.

"I'm *not* perfect for the part," she protested. "I'm dead wrong for the part. I'm way too old. Just like the rest of your milkmaids—no offense, ladies—but your maids-a-milking should be rosy-cheeked country girls, in fetching peasant blouses."

"You're saying you can't work without your costume?"

"No, I'm saying someone else should be wearing it. It's just bad casting." Cora pointed stage left, where her niece, Sherry Carter, stood in a cluster of nine attractive young women. "Look at your ladies dancing. They're all young and pretty. *They* should be the lusty milkmaids, and we old biddies should be the refined ladies dancing."

Rupert didn't get mad. The director never got mad. Instead,

he exhibited, as he always did, a tolerant amusement at the misguided views of the unenlightened.

"Yes, Miss Felton," he replied. "That is how it is usually cast. Which is precisely why I have *not* done so here. This skit is deliberately 'miscast,' as you would characterize it, for, one would hope, humorous effect. Which, as you might have gathered, is the same reason for so many entrances and exits. Which is also why rehearsal time is so crucial. I hope I don't have to spend too much of it reassuring you that you are ideal for your part."

"I thought you were the one telling me I *wasn't* doing it right," Cora countered.

Rupert Winston chuckled. "Well, there is a huge difference between not doing it right and not being right for it. Trust me, you're right for it."

Harvey Beerbaum stuck his oar in, as the annoying, pedantic cruciverbalist was wont to do. "Come on, Cora," he chided. "If I can be a lord-a-leaping, surely you can be a maid-a-milking."

That was hard to argue with. The sight of bald, portly Harvey leaping about the stage was so ridiculous, if he was willing to make a fool of himself, how could anyone else object?

"Can we get on with it?" Becky Baldwin griped. "I'm meeting a client in half an hour."

"Did you hear that?" Rupert Winston said. "Becky has only half an hour. So this is hardly time to be worried about *our* motivation."

Cora Felton bit her lip. She hadn't said a damn thing about her motivation, but she couldn't point that out to Rupert without starting another argument, which would seem boorishly insensitive and inconsiderate, since Becky had to go.

Cora resented that too. Becky Baldwin—young, attractive, and as fashionable as ever in a scoop-neck sweater and pale blue skirt and vest—might have actually had a client, but as far as Cora was concerned, Becky's pointing it out served only to remind everyone that she was a lawyer on the one hand, and a Star on the other.

Which, in the pageant, she was. Becky had been cast as the young woman in the song, the one who receives all the season's bounty. In Rupert Winston's version of the piece, Becky started each verse alone onstage, singing *"On the whatever day of Christmas, my true love gave to me,"* and then reacting to the stampede of gifts that surrounded her. A plum role, one that Cora felt should by rights have gone to her niece. But, as always happened between Sherry and Cora, Cora was the one pushed out front.

Rupert turned to the piano, where Mr. Hodges, the high school music teacher, was dutifully waiting to play. *"You* don't have to go anywhere, do you?"

"I have a chorus rehearsal at four-thirty."

"Oh, for goodness' sakes!"

Mr. Hodges, a thin-faced, sallow man with a hawk nose, did not take kindly to the suggestion that *he* would be responsible for breaking up rehearsal. *"The Twelve Days of Christmas* is *not* the only piece in the pageant, you know," he retorted huffily. "The bulk of the show still happens to be the school choir."

"Yes," Rupert snorted. "Standing and singing. They don't *move.* What's to rehearse?"

Mr. Hodges had no desire to get into *that* argument. "We lose the gym at four-fifteen anyway for varsity practice," he pointed out acidly.

The Christmas pageant was being performed on the stage in the Bakerhaven High gymnasium, where it shared the space with the basketball team. It also shared the stage with the upcoming high school production of Anton Chekhov's *The Seagull,* so the English village square Becky Baldwin was performing in looked suspiciously like a Russian country manor. In a corner of the gym, the Bakerhaven High tech director, a wiry young man in splattered overalls and work shirt, was diligently if somewhat messily painting scenery flats to transform one into the other.

"Then we can't be wasting time now," Rupert declared virtuously, as if he hadn't been the one prolonging the squabble. "Let's take it from the twelfth day, get a look at everyone. Aaron Grant? Where's Aaron Grant?"

The young *Bakerhaven Gazette* reporter, who was standing onstage beside Sherry Carter, put up his hand, and said, "Here, Rupert."

"Aaron, we're going to take it from your line, the twelve drummers drumming. Do you have your drummers ready?"

"I've got nine of them."

"Only nine?"

"That's the trouble with afternoon rehearsals," Aaron said. "People have to work."

"Well then," Rupert said with heavy irony, "are your *nine* drummers drumming ready?"

"Yes, except we haven't got the drums yet."

"I *know* you haven't got the drums yet. This is for choreography." Having made that pronouncement, Rupert instantly contradicted it by demanding, "What props *do* we have? I know we don't have the swans and the geese, but at least we have the pear tree."

Rupert looked around and spotted Jimmy Potter, the librarian's son, sitting on the apron of the stage, listening attentively. Jimmy, a tall, gawky boy of college age, who had always been a little slow, was just thrilled to death to be part of the pageant, and he had, as usual, a goofy grin on his face. However, he had nothing in his hands.

"Jimmy!" Rupert cried. "Where's your pear tree? How can you play your part without your pear tree?"

Edith Potter, the librarian, and one of the maids-a-milking, pushed out of the pack to defend her boy, but Jimmy wasn't upset.

"It's offstage, Mr. Rupert." Jimmy pointed stage left. "You want me to get it?"

"No, Jimmy. I just want you to have your tree for the runthrough. I want you to come on carrying it, so you get used to carrying it. Okay, places please, people. Let's take it from the top of the last verse, starting with Becky's line."

The actors took their positions in the wings.

Rupert called. "And, Miss Felton. Project, project, *project!*"

Cora, in the wings, raised her prop and muttered to Sherry, "I'd like to *pro-ject* this milking stool. Can you guess where?"

"Cora! Think of your image."

"I'm thinking of *his* image. And how I could change it with this damn stool."

"Are we ready?" Rupert Winston yelled from out front. "And . . . begin!"

The pianist played a note.

Becky Baldwin, alone onstage, rolled her eyes toward the piano. Becky was, Sherry had to admit, quite good. The expression on her face in response to that lone note was priceless. This being the twelfth day of gifts, one could scarcely wonder what her lunatic lover had sent her now. In a voice tinged with resignation and dread, Becky sang, *"On the twelfth day of Christmas, my true love gave to me,"* then with hands upraised, shrank back from the onslaught.

Aaron and eight other men entered from stage left, pantomiming drums.

"Twelve drummers drumming," sang Aaron.

The drummers marched on Becky Baldwin as if she were Richmond, then turned and sang in chorus, *"Eleven pipers piping."*

The pipers, eight strong without pipes, marched on from stage right, singing along with the drummers.

Ten lords-a-leaping—actually eight, not leaping very high—emerged from all sides of the stage. Had it been the tenth day of Christmas, the solo would have been sung by Harvey Beerbaum. As it was, the lords sang in chorus along with the pipers and drummers.

Nine ladies dancing, led by Sherry Carter, waltzed on from stage left.

Eight maids-a-milking swooped in from stage right, sat on their stools, and had just begun to pantomime milking when the seven swans-a-swimming (six men who would be carrying cardboard cutout swans, which had not yet been made), followed directly by the six geese-a-laying (five in number, not laying, and without geese), sent the milkmaids diving for cover.

As always, everyone got a breather during the retarded line *"Five golden rings."* The rings, presented on velvet pillows borne by liveried servants (pillows, rings, and livery yet to come), were paraded in a circle around Becky Baldwin. She broke free just in time to be confronted with four calling birds, three French hens, and two turtledoves (birds, hens, and doves to be made later).

The chorus reached a crescendo. All turned toward stage left.

"AND A PARTRIDGE IN A PEAR TREE!" everyone sang lushly.

Jimmy Potter, pleased as punch, marched onstage, carrying the pear tree. It was actually a small, artificial fir tree with papier-mâché pears, but Jimmy couldn't have been prouder. He strode up to Becky Baldwin and presented her with it.

He certainly wasn't prepared for what happened next.

"Jimmy!" Rupert Winston shrieked. "Where's the partridge? Don't tell me you've lost the partridge! It's the only bird we've got!"

Jimmy, completely taken aback, gawked at the pear tree. "Gee, Mr. Winston. It was right here."

Rupert Winston leaped onto the stage. "All right!" he cried. "Who's been screwing around with our props?"

"I . . . I . . . I . . ." Jimmy Potter stuttered.

Rupert ignored him. "Jesse!" he bellowed. "Where the hell is my tech crew!"

Jesse Virdon, the paint-smeared tech director who had been working on the flats, put down his brush. "Whaddya want?" he said, sauntering up.

"What do I want?" Rupert stormed. "You're my stage manager. Where the hell's my prop?"

Jesse shrugged. "Dunno. Been out here painting. Never went backstage."

"Well, who did?"

Alfred, a gawky teenager with black-rimmed glasses and an unfortunate nose, emerged from the wings, protesting as he came, practically stuttering in his desire to distance himself from the theft. "I didn't see anything, Mr. Winston. I was in the light booth. I never saw the tree."

Cora Felton pushed forward. "Wait a minute. What's *that*?"

There was something red among the green pine needles.

Jimmy turned the tree.

Hidden among the branches was a red envelope. It was greeting-card size. The back was facing out, and the flap had been tucked in.

Jimmy Potter blinked at it in amazement.

"What the hell is that?" Rupert scoffed. "A ransom note for the partridge?"

Cora lifted the red envelope off the branch. She opened the flap, reached inside.

Frowned.

Sherry, at her elbow, said, "What's the matter?"

Cora pulled the contents from the envelope.

It was not a card. Just a folded piece of paper.

Cora unfolded it.

Scowled.

"Well, what is it?" Rupert demanded.

Cora turned the paper around for them to see.

1 J	2	R 3	B	4	R 5	E 6	G	7	O 8	F 9	10 H	11 C	12 U		13 W	14	X 15 N
16 Q	17 L	18 S		19 S	20 P	21 D	22 V	23 H	24 N	25 W	26 G		27 P	28 X	29 J	30 E	31 P
32 S	33 H		34 J	35 N	36 C	37 P	38 A		39 L	40 X		41 W	42 S		43 K	44 O	45 G
46 K	47 P	48 G		49 P	50 L	51 C	52 G	53 V	54 M	55 O	56 A	57 X	58 T	59 N	60 H		61 W
62 G	63 X	64 U		65 O		66 P	67 A	68 M	69 G	70 S		71 I	72 N		73 H	74 B		75 J
76 X		77 D	78 W	79 W		80 J	81 T	82 B	83 U	84 G		85 F	86 V	87 E		88 W	89 Q	90 U
91 S	92 L	93 J		94 B	95 Q	96 M	97 J	98 C	99 I	100 S	101 X	102 X	103 G		104 L	105 P	106 R
107 F	108 U	109 K	110 N	111 G	112 L		113 I	114 W	115 F	116 Q		117 I	118 O	119 C	120 D	121 S	122 W
123 C	124 G	125 H	126 J	127 K		128 K	129 H	130 T		131 C	132 D	133 B		134 X	135 E	136 D	137 M	138 H
139 V		140 M	141 A	142 F	143 X		144 T	145 N	146 X	147 U		148 C	149 T	150 I		151 A	152 H	153 T
154 C		155 T	156 V		157 T	158 A	159 B	160 M	161 E	162 C	163 P	164 I		165 V	166 R	167 F	168 T

A. Christmas stealer
$\overline{38}\ \overline{158}\ \overline{67}\ \overline{56}\ \overline{151}\ \overline{141}$

B. Pressing
$\overline{159}\ \overline{82}\ \overline{94}\ \overline{133}\ \overline{3}\ \overline{74}$

C. Don't cry for her, Argentina (2 wds.)
$\overline{154}\ \overline{98}\ \overline{36}\ \overline{131}\ \overline{148}\ \overline{51}\ \overline{119}\ \overline{11}\ \overline{162}\ \overline{123}$

D. Bright
$\overline{21}\ \overline{132}\ \overline{136}\ \overline{120}\ \overline{77}$

E. Fire a gun
$\overline{161}\ \overline{135}\ \overline{5}\ \overline{87}\ \overline{30}$

F. Evil
$\overline{85}\ \overline{8}\ \overline{107}\ \overline{115}\ \overline{142}\ \overline{167}$

G. "The Fall of the ___" (3 wds.)
$\overline{62}\ \overline{111}\ \overline{6}\ \overline{84}\ \overline{45}\ \overline{78}\ \overline{26}\ \overline{48}\ \overline{103}\ \overline{69}$
$\overline{124}\ \overline{52}$

H. "___ a home" (3 wds.)
$\overline{152}\ \overline{23}\ \overline{138}\ \overline{73}\ \overline{125}\ \overline{60}\ \overline{33}\ \overline{129}$

I. Broken
$\overline{71}\ \overline{117}\ \overline{113}\ \overline{99}\ \overline{9}\ \overline{164}\ \overline{150}$

J. Carton of sorts (2 wds.)

$\overline{97}\ \overline{80}\ \overline{34}\ \overline{1}\ \overline{93}\ \overline{29}\ \overline{75}\ \overline{126}$

K. Mad

$\overline{43}\ \overline{109}\ \overline{128}\ \overline{127}\ \overline{46}$

L. Tails counterpart (2 wds.)

$\overline{112}\ \overline{92}\ \overline{50}\ \overline{17}\ \overline{104}\ \overline{39}$

M. Warming

$\overline{54}\ \overline{160}\ \overline{114}\ \overline{140}\ \overline{96}\ \overline{137}\ \overline{68}$

N. Applause

$\overline{72}\ \overline{59}\ \overline{145}\ \overline{15}\ \overline{24}\ \overline{35}\ \overline{110}$

O. "The ___" (Grisham novel)

$\overline{7}\ \overline{65}\ \overline{44}\ \overline{118}$

P. Bullets

$\overline{49}\ \overline{66}\ \overline{163}\ \overline{10}\ \overline{105}\ \overline{20}\ \overline{27}\ \overline{31}\ \overline{47}\ \overline{37}$

Q. More shipshape

$\overline{100}\ \overline{116}\ \overline{89}\ \overline{16}\ \overline{55}\ \overline{95}$

R. Rooney or Griffith

$\overline{2}\ \overline{166}\ \overline{106}\ \overline{4}$

S. Fought

$\overline{101}\ \overline{42}\ \overline{19}\ \overline{91}\ \overline{32}\ \overline{134}\ \overline{70}\ \overline{18}\ \overline{121}$

T. Dancing like Chubby Checker

$\overline{130}\ \overline{144}\ \overline{81}\ \overline{168}\ \overline{155}\ \overline{58}\ \overline{149}\ \overline{157}$

U. "Shake, ___, and roll"

$\overline{90}\ \overline{108}\ \overline{147}\ \overline{64}\ \overline{83}\ \overline{12}$

V. Repeats exactly

$\overline{53}\ \overline{22}\ \overline{86}\ \overline{156}\ \overline{165}\ \overline{139}$

W. Yelled

$\overline{122}\ \overline{88}\ \overline{13}\ \overline{79}\ \overline{61}\ \overline{25}\ \overline{41}$

X. Naughty, naughty! (3 wds.)

$\overline{57}\ \overline{28}\ \overline{63}\ \overline{153}\ \overline{102}\ \overline{76}\ \overline{146}\ \overline{143}\ \overline{40}\ \overline{14}$